A LITTLE
CHRISTMAS MAGIC

BY
ALISON ROBERTS

MILLS
BOON

Published in Great Britain 2014
by Mills & Boon, an imprint of Harlequin (UK) Limited,
Eton House, 18-24 Paradise Road, Richmond, Surrey, TW9 1SR

© 2014 Alison Roberts

ISBN: 978-0-263-90803-9

Harlequin (UK) Limited's policy is to use papers that are natural,
renewable and recyclable products and made from wood grown in
sustainable forests. The logging and manufacturing processes conform
to the legal environmental regulations of the country of origin.

Printed and bound in Spain
by Blackprint CPI, Barcelona

Dear Reader

Many years ago, I lived in Scotland for two years. I loved getting out of Glasgow and into the country villages.

The gorgeous countryside is not unlike my home of New Zealand, but we don't have the magic of the cobbled streets and ancient cottages.

Christmas here is in summer, of course, but I remember the winters in Scotland very well—when the cold and dark days made the lights brighter and the warmth of home so alluring.

What better setting for a Christmas story? Romance has a magic of its own, and so does Christmas. Mixing them together is a recipe for something special. I do hope you enjoy Adam and Emma's story as much as I loved writing it.

Merry Christmas!

With love

Alison xxx

Dedication

For Becky—who will always be with me for Christmas,
no matter where she is.
With all my love.

Praise for
Alison Roberts:

'Readers will be moved by this incredibly sweet story about
a family that is created in the most unexpected way.'
—*RT Book Reviews* on
THE HONOURABLE MAVERICK

Recent titles by Alison Roberts:

200 HARLEY STREET: THE PROUD ITALIAN◊
FROM VENICE WITH LOVE‡
ALWAYS THE HERO††
NYC ANGELS: AN EXPLOSIVE REUNION~
ST PIRAN'S: THE WEDDING!†
MAYBE THIS CHRISTMAS…?
THE LEGENDARY PLAYBOY SURGEON**
FALLING FOR HER IMPOSSIBLE BOSS**
SYDNEY HARBOUR HOSPITAL: ZOE'S BABY*
THE HONOURABLE MAVERICK

◊*200 Harley Street*
‡*The Christmas Express!*
*Sydney Harbour Hospital
†*St Piran's Hospital*
**Heartbreakers of St Patrick's Hospital
~*NYC Angels*
††*Earthquake!*

**These books are also available in eBook format
from www.millsandboon.co.uk**

Did you know that THE HONOURABLE MAVERICK
won a 2011 RT Reviewers' Choice Award?
It's still available in eBook format
from www.millsandboon.co.uk

CHAPTER ONE

WHAT EMMA SINCLAIR needed right now was a magic wand.

One that she could wave over the calendar on her wall and simply make the month of December vanish.

Turn it into January and the start of a new year. A new life.

Or not.

Maybe she could use the wand not to wish time away but to freeze it. To make it always early December, with her feeling so well she could imagine the last few years had been nothing more than a very bad dream.

It was getting a little stuffy in her tiny London apartment. Emma moved to crack open the window to let some fresh air in for a moment. Very fresh air. The sky was a dark slate and that cloud cover clearly swollen with moisture but it wasn't likely to start falling as pretty snowflakes. A bit of stinging sleet, maybe. Or freezing fog.

London could be so grey at this time of year.

So bleak. It was only mid-afternoon but already there were lights on everywhere. In the street below and in the windows of the apartment buildings she looked out onto. Not just ordinary lights either. Some people already had their Christmas trees up and the row of shops at street level had them in their front windows with multi-coloured lights flashing and twinkling. Somebody was dressed as

Father Christmas on the street, too, handing out flyers to passers-by, probably offering a discount on some seasonal service or product.

There were lots of people hurrying about their business, wrapped up in coats and scarfs. Umbrellas were opening as the clouds decided to let go of some of the moisture. Mothers made sure their prams were well covered and tried to juggle parcels and small children to keep them sheltered.

So many people.

Families.

Funny how a crowd could make you feel so much more alone.

The phone ringing was a welcome distraction.

'Sharon… What's the weather like in sunny California?'

'Gorgeous. Doesn't feel right when it's December. And how did that happen? It feels like yesterday that I was having my summer wedding in good ol' Blighty. Is it all grey and freezing?'

'Sure is.' She would need to remember to close the window as soon as she'd finished talking to her closest friend. She stepped closer to the friendly glow of her small, gas fire.

'What are you doing?'

'Right at this minute? I'm looking at one of your wedding photos on my mantelpiece. You were the world's most beautiful bride. You look *so* happy.'

'Aww…I had the best bridesmaid. That helped.'

Emma laughed. 'You were marrying the love of your life—that's what helped. How's Andy?'

'Gorgeous. We were talking about you last night and he told me to ring. We want you to come and have Christmas with us.'

'Ohhh…' The sound was a mix of frustration and regret. 'I can't. I have to be here for when they call me in.

The three-month mark will be late December and they'll have to squeeze me in when they get a space. Jack told me I'd better not go too far away.'

'I feel awful I can't be with you for that. It's such a horrible procedure to have to go through on your own.'

'I'll cope.'

'I want to be with you. To drive you home afterwards and make sure you take your painkillers.'

'I know. It'll be okay, Sharn.'

'You could put it off until the new year...I'm sure that adorable Dr Jack of yours would be happy to oblige.'

Emma had closed her eyes as she took a deep breath. 'The waiting's hard enough without making it longer. I... don't think I could handle that.'

'I understand... It's rotten timing but the sooner it happens, the better. You'll let me know, won't you? The instant you have news?'

'Of course. You'll be the first to know.'

'It'll be good news. I'm totally sure of that.'

'No. It won't be good.' Emma had to swallow hard now. 'It'll either be the best news ever or the worst. No middle ground this time. If it hasn't worked it's the end of the road. Nothing more they can do. Just a matter of time...'

Her words went all wobbly and Emma kicked herself mentally for giving in to voicing her deepest fear. Maybe the uncharacteristic weakness had sneaked up on her because her gaze was resting on other photographs on her mantelpiece. The father she'd lost long ago. Her beloved mother who'd died just over a year ago now.

'You need distraction,' Sharon told her. 'Being cooped up all by yourself isn't helping.'

'You're right. I'm thinking of getting a job.'

'Really? Are you feeling that good?'

'I am. And there are plenty of temporary jobs that come

up at this time of year. Do you remember the year that I was an elf?'

'One of Santa's helpers.' Sharon was laughing. 'I'm sure I've got a photo of you in that outfit somewhere. I'd better not show it to Andy or he might think he married the wrong girl.'

'Yeah, right…' But Emma was grinning. 'Or I could busk…' She shifted her gaze to a far corner of the room. 'My poor guitar's just gathering dust at the moment.'

'Sounds cold. Being an elf would be more fun.'

'Yeah…' It was getting cold in the apartment now. Definitely time to close the window. To get moving properly, even. 'You know what? I'm going to go down to the corner shop and get some papers. See what's being advertised under the situations vacant.'

'Go, you! Keep me posted.'

'I will.'

'Love you. Miss you heaps.'

'Same.'

When the call ended, all Emma could hear was the soft hiss of her fire and the patter of rain on the window. After the joy of conversation it was an unpleasant quietness.

A very lonely one.

Threatening. If she stayed in here it would pull her back into her pity party so allowing it to continue wasn't an option. Latching the window, Emma shrugged into her warmest coat and wrapped a scarf around her neck. She slung her bag over her shoulder and picked up her umbrella as she let herself out the door. She wouldn't get the papers at the corner store. She'd walk all the way to the high street and get the bonus of a decent bit of exercise on her mission.

'Ouch… That *hurts*, Daddy.'

'Sorry, pet.'

Adam McAllister suppressed a growl of frustration. Fine blonde hair was refusing to co-operate. How could his fingers be so deft when it came to removing a foreign object or stitching up a wound so that it barely left a scar but be seemingly incapable of braiding a small girl's hair?

'How about a wee ponytail instead?'

'No.' The headshake pulled the almost finished braid from his fingers and what had already been accomplished unravelled at the speed of light. 'Jeannie always has plaits and I want to look the *same*.'

'Dad? Where's my shoe?'

'Where you left it, I expect, Ollie.' Adam picked up the hairbrush again and the movement made him notice the face of his watch. 'It'll have to be a ponytail, Poppy, otherwise you're going to be late for school and I'll be in trouble with Mrs Stewart at the clinic. The waiting room will be full of cross people asking where their doctor's got to.'

Poppy burst into tears.

A crashing sound came from the living room, accompanied by a wail from her twin, Oliver. 'It wasn't my fault. It just falled over and now it's *broken*…'

The wind must have caught the front door to make it slam so loudly. 'I'm sorry I'm so late. The roads are so icy and old Jock was blocking the road with his tractor, helping someone whose wheels were in the ditch. I…' She stopped talking, taking in the scene of chaos in the kitchen.

'I take it she's gone, then?'

'Aye…' Gratefully, Adam pushed the hairbrush into his mother's hand. 'I've almost got the bags ready. I'd better go and see what Ollie's broken.'

'Little minx. I can't believe she's run off like that. With no notice.'

'She's nineteen. In love. Getting pregnant probably made the decision a wee bit urgent.'

'What's pregnant?' Poppy had stopped crying and was standing very still while her grandmother rapidly braided her hair.

'It means that you're going to have a baby.'

'Auntie Marion's going to have a baby.'

'Aye…she is. So's Kylie.'

'But Kylie looks after us. She's coming back, isn't she?'

'No. She's going to Australia—where her boyfriend comes from.'

'What's Australia?'

'It's a country a long way away.' Adam had gone as far as the door to see that the standard lamp had fallen in the living room, sweeping a photograph from the corner of the mantelpiece onto the hearth. Nothing life-threatening. He could sort it out later when he had a minute to spare. Stooping, he picked up an abandoned shoe.

'Ollie? Where are you? It's time for school.'

A small, tousled head with wide eyes appeared slowly from behind the sofa.

'Come and see your gran. You need your hair brushed too.'

'It's even further away than Canada.' By some miracle, his mother had found ribbons to tie on the ends of Poppy's plaits. 'Where Aunty Marion lives.'

She looked up as Adam came back with Oliver in tow but then her gaze shifted to take in the pile of books and papers on one end of the kitchen table. A milky spoon from a bowl of cereal was sitting on top of a school book. Turning her head to look at the dishes piled up on the kitchen bench, she clicked her tongue.

'I can't do it,' Catherine McAllister said. 'I'm no' going

to take off for Canada and leave you to cope with this lot alone.'

'You have to. Marion needs you. The bairn's due next week.'

'She'll understand.'

'This is my sister we're talking about.' Adam's smile was wry. 'She'd never talk to me again. She'd say I've had years of your help and she only needs you for a few weeks. It's not her fault my nanny's run off to Australia.'

Catherine raised her gaze to the old clock on the wall. 'You'd better go, son. Or you'll be getting the evil eye from Eileen Stewart. She's bad enough when an emergency comes in and puts out all the waiting times. I'll get these wee lambs off to school.'

'Thanks, Mum.' Adam pushed his arms into the sleeves of a coat that hadn't made it off the back of a kitchen chair last night. 'And you're not to even think of cancelling your trip. I've got ads in papers everywhere for a temporary nanny. I'll find help for while you're away at least, and then we can worry about something more permanent.'

'We'll see about that.' Catherine sounded unconvinced. 'My flight's not till Tuesday. If you haven't found help by then, I'm staying and that's an end to the matter.'

The train from London to Edinburgh arrived on time. The connecting train Emma needed to get out into the middle of a Scottish nowhere was clearly less reliable. The wicked draught coming into the waiting room was chilling her to the bone and Emma huddled between the backpack full of clothes and her guitar case.

How crazy was this?

But that Dr McAllister had sounded so enthusiastic on the phone yesterday. Said he'd pay for her travel if she could come up for an interview and he was sure she'd be suitable so she might as well bring what she needed for the next few weeks and that way, if she was happy to take the position, she wouldn't need to go all the way back to London again.

And it all sounded so perfect. She already had the image of a pretty, old Scottish village with the stone buildings softened by a layer of fluffy snow and the sound of Christmas carols being sung by rosy-cheeked village children. What better place to spend these few weeks of the unbearable waiting? It wasn't as if she would have the responsibility of caring for a tiny baby or something. Looking after six-year-old twins—how hard could *that* be?

A piercing whistle and then a squeal of brakes announced the arrival of her new train. Emma picked up the straps of her backpack with one hand and the handle of the guitar case with the other. Then she put it down again to fish in her coat pocket. To make sure she had the appointment details for the meeting later this afternoon.

Yes. Four p.m. at the medical centre in the village of Braeburn. Only a short walk from the station, apparently. Across the square at the end of the high street and down the street. She couldn't miss it but if she got as far as the village hall she needed to turn around. She'd be able to meet not only the nice-sounding doctor but the children *and* their grandmother.

Gathering her courage, Emma got herself and her belongings stowed into an eerily empty train carriage. Braeburn didn't appear to be a very popular destination. With no one to distract her with conversation, there was plenty of time to think about what lay ahead in her immediate future.

That last addition of the grandmother to the interview panel was the one that made her a little uneasy. Her imagination could conjure up a fierce, elderly Scot with no trouble at all. Short and wiry, with a hairnet keeping the corrugated-iron waves of her hair in place and a disapproving glare that would miss nothing remotely unsuitable about an applicant.

She'd be the one to convince.

Emma rested her head back on the faded seat and watched green hills and paddocks and the occasional river drift past. Beautiful country. A long, long way from London and big hospitals and fear of what the new year might bring.

She couldn't go back.

She *had* to get this job. It would be a reprieve from the fear. Time out. A family to spend Christmas with even, and wouldn't that be magic?

A touch to her hair reassured her that the unruly curls were suitably restrained. How good was it that her hair had grown back so enthusiastically after all the chemo? It would have been better to have had the time to buy some new clothes, though. She didn't have a skirt or dress to her name and, having lost so much weight, she was swimming in her jeans and pullover. Hardly the outfit to make much of an impression with but it was personality that mattered, wasn't it?

And this Dr McAllister sounded perfectly nice, with his deep voice and broad Scottish accent. A bit brusque maybe. Possibly a little terse after she'd replayed the conversation in her head a few times but he'd definitely sounded keen.

Almost…desperate?

Maybe the children were little monsters that ate nannies for breakfast and the granny would be glaring at her from a corner and constantly criticising her every move. And the doctor would take one look at her and ask what on earth she was thinking—that she could look after his precious children when it was obvious how sick she was herself?

No. Emma slammed a mental door shut on her unfortunately vivid imagination.

Fate was bringing her here. It had been the first advertisement she'd seen and, when she'd rung, the phone had been answered virtually on the first ring. She hadn't even had to queue for a train ticket. It felt like it was meant to happen.

She needed a bit of faith, that was all. Hardly surprising that that particular mental resource was somewhat depleted at the moment but it felt good to scrape a bit up and hang onto it.

Very good indeed.

It felt remarkably like hope.

The village was every bit as pretty as she had imagined with stone buildings and cobbled streets. Not that Emma had time to admire more than a passing impression because the train had been a bit late and now she had to hurry. That it was much darker for the time of day and probably a lot colder than London didn't seem to matter when the brightly lit shop windows revealed colourful decorations already in place.

She found herself smiling when she hurried past a pub called simply The Inn, which had sprigs of holly on the door framing a handwritten sign that said, 'There's plenty of room.' Maybe the innkeeper with the sense of humour was one of the group of people under the streetlamps, installing a massive Christmas tree in the village square that needed men with ropes and a lot of shouting in a brogue so thick it sounded like a foreign language.

Her heart sank, however, when she entered the medical centre and the grandmother of her imagination fixed her with a look that could probably strip paint.

'D'ye have an appointment? The doctor's no' got time for extras unless it's an emergency. Clinic hours are over.'

The bell on the door behind Emma clanged again before the grandmother had finished speaking and her attempt to decipher more than half the words she had just heard was interrupted by a woman's voice.

'I'll take care o' this, Eileen. We're expecting Emma.'

Her jaw dropping, Emma turned to face an elegantly dressed and very beautiful older woman, who was smiling warmly. 'I take it you *are* Emma?'

'Um…yes. And you're…?'

'Catherine McAllister. Adam's mother.' She looked past Emma's shoulder. 'Is Adam in, Eileen?'

'Aye. The wee bairns as well.' The sniff was disapproving. 'I've told the doctor it's no' a good idea, having bairns in there. They'll break something. Or—'

'Why don't you head off early, Eileen?' Catherine was still smiling. 'I know how busy you must be at the moment. Isn't there a choir practice this evening?'

'Aye…well, if you're sure, Mrs McAllister.'

'I'm just sorry I won't be here to hear all the Christmas carols.'

'It's tomorrow you leave, aye?'

'Mmm. I hope so.' She turned back to Emma. 'Adam's sister is having her first baby. In Canada.'

'Oh…how exciting.' Emma couldn't miss the play of emotion on the older woman's face. 'She'll be so happy to have you there. I…I lost my mum last year and I miss her all the time but *that's* when I'll miss her the most, I think.'

When she had a baby? *If* she ever had a baby would be more truthful. But she'd said too much already, hadn't she? Maybe revealed too much as well, judging by the searching look she was getting. Emma bit her lip but Catherine was smiling. Her eyes were full of sympathy and the touch on Emma's arm was more like a reassuring squeeze.

'Come with me, Emma. We'll go and find that son of mine.'

Could she leave her backpack and guitar in the waiting room? About to step away, Emma caught another glare from Eileen that was punctuated by another eloquent sniff. Hastily, she picked up her luggage and followed Catherine across the waiting room and through another door. She was still trying to readjust her mental image of the children's grandmother and, because she wasn't watching, the guitar was at enough of a sideways angle to catch on the door in front of her so she almost fell into what was obviously a consulting room.

The man, who had one hip perched on the edge of a large wooden desk, jerked his head in her direction. The two children, who were on the floor in the middle of a game that involved a stethoscope and bandages, looked up and froze.

There was an awkward silence and Emma could feel herself blushing furiously as she manoeuvred herself into the room. What had possessed her to bring such an unwieldy extra piece of luggage, anyway? Did she think she might go busking in Braeburn's village square if she didn't land this gig of being a nanny?

What made it so much worse was that the doctor who'd sounded nice but brusque on the phone was just as different from what she'd imagined as the grandmother had been. The fuzzy image of a plump and fatherly country GP had just been bombed. Adam McAllister was tall and fit. More than fit. With his jet-black hair, olive skin and sharply defined angles of his face, he was probably one of the best-looking men Emma had ever seen.

Except that he was scowling. While his mother had surprised her by being so unexpectedly nice, the pendulum had swung in the opposite direction now. Adam McAllister looked uncompromising. Fierce. Angry even?

At *her*?

'I'm sorry I'm late,' she said, the words rushing out. 'The train was…it was…' Oh, help. He was looking at her as if he *knew*. Had he somehow managed to access her medical records or something?

'The train's always late.' Catherine was pulling out a chair. She smiled down at the children. 'What's happened here? Has Poppy broken her leg *again*, Ollie?'

'Aye. I'm fixing her.' But the small boy's attention was diverted now. 'Who are *you*?' he asked Emma. 'And what's *that*?'

'I'm Emma. And this is my guitar case.'

'I want to see.'

'Maybe later.' Adam McAllister's offer did not sound promising. 'Your gran's going to take you to see the tree going up in a minute. And then you're going home for your supper.'

'After some proper introductions,' Catherine said firmly. 'Emma—this is Oliver and this is Poppy. Ollie and Poppy—this is Emma…Sinclair?'

'*Miss* Sinclair,' Adam corrected.

'Emma's fine,' said Emma. 'Hello, Poppy and Ollie. You're twins, aren't you?'

They stared at her. They had brown eyes like their father but their hair was much lighter. Poppy still had golden streaks in her long braids. She also had something clutched in her hand.

'Is that Barbie?'

Poppy nodded. 'She's got a pony,' she offered. 'At home.'

'Lucky Barbie. I love ponies.'

'I've got a pony, too.'

'Jemima's not a *pony*,' Oliver said. 'She's a *donkey*.'

Emma blinked. Catherine laughed. 'Adam probably didn't say much on the phone,' she said, 'but there are a few pets at home. Do you like animals?'

'Yes. I had a job in a pet shop once. We had lots of puppies and kittens and rabbits. Oh, and hamsters and mice and rats, too.'

Poppy's eyes were round. 'I *love* puppies. And kittens.'

'I love *rats*,' Oliver said. 'Can I have a rat, Daddy?'

'We've probably got some out in the barn.'

'I want one for a pet. Inside.'

'No.' The word was almost a sigh. 'You can't have a rat, Ollie.'

'But why *not*?' With a bandage unfurling in his hand to roll across the floor, Oliver scrambled to his feet. 'You said I could tell you what I wanted most for Christmas. And I want a *rat*.'

'They smell bad.' Emma had been the cause of what was becoming a family disagreement. She needed to do something. 'And they've got long tails that are all bald and pink and…icky.'

'Icky?' Adam was looking at her as if she was suddenly speaking Swahili.

'Icky,' Poppy repeated. She giggled. 'Icky, icky, icky.'

'You're icky,' Oliver told her.

'No. *You* are.'

'Time to go,' Catherine decreed. 'You've met Emma and she's met you. Now it's time for her to talk to Daddy.'

In the flurry of putting on coats and hats and gathering schoolbags, Catherine found time to squeeze Emma's hand.

'I do hope you'll still be here when I get back,' she said softly. 'I'd like the chance to get to know you better.'

She managed to say something to Adam as well, just

before she ushered the children out of the room. Emma couldn't hear what she said but, as she sank into the chair as the door closed behind Catherine, he was still scowling at her.

Strength. That was what he needed.

This was his one shot at finding the help he needed so that his mother would not cancel her trip to Canada and this young woman was clearly... He closed his eyes for as long as it took to draw in a new breath. A complete flake?

She looked like a refugee from the sixties or something, carrying a guitar and a backpack. So pale he could almost count the freckles scattered over her nose and she was thin enough to have a waif-like air that probably made her look a lot younger than she was. And what was it with those oversized clothes? It reminded him of when Poppy clopped around the house with her feet in a pair of her grandmother's high-heeled shoes and a dress that was trailing around her ankles.

She was so obviously unsuitable that it was deeply disappointing. He'd have to go through the motions of an interview, though—if only to have ammunition for the argument he'd have to have with his mother later. Her whispered impression had been very succinct.

She's lovely. Give her the job, Adam.

How had this musically inclined waif managed to impress Catherine so much in such a short time?

'So...' He did his best to summon a smile. 'You're fond of animals, then?'

'Mmm.' She was smiling back at him. She had blue eyes, he noted. And brown curls that had a reddish glint where the light caught them. 'I am.'

'And children?'

She nodded enthusiastically. 'I like children, too.'

'Do you have any experience with them?'

'I've taught music classes. And…and I had a job working with children over a Christmas period a while back. I loved it.'

Because she'd never quite grown up herself? How many adults would use a word like 'icky' with such relish?

'But you've never been a nanny?'

'No.'

'Do you have any younger brothers or sisters? Friends who have small children?'

'N-no.' The smile was fading now.

'Do you have a full driver's licence?'

'Yes. I've got a motorbike licence, too.'

The image of this child-woman astride a powerful two-wheeled machine was disconcerting.

'I've even got a heavy-vehicle licence. I had a job driving a bus once.'

Maybe that image was even more of a worry. How had she had the strength to even turn such a large wheel? Or was it the overlarge sleeves on her pullover that made her arms look so frail?

'Can you cook?'

'Well…I did have a job in a restaurant once. I—'

But Adam was shaking his head. 'How old are you, Emma?'

'Twenty-eight.'

Really? Only a few years younger than he was? Hard to believe but the surprise wasn't enough to disturb his train of thought. 'Just how many jobs have you had?'

'I don't know,' Emma admitted. 'Quite a lot. I tend to like part-time or temporary work. That's why this job appealed so much. It's only for a few weeks, isn't it?'

'Aye.' But just because he only needed help on a temporary basis it didn't mean that he wanted to employ someone who was incapable of commitment or even reliability, did it?

Perhaps he should have tried to find something permanent instead of a stop-gap, but who went looking to move and start a new position in the weeks right before Christmas? How many people wanted to move to an isolated Scottish village anyway?

His mother was due to drive to Edinburgh tonight, ready for an early departure tomorrow. If he didn't take a chance on Emma, she would cancel her trip and she'd miss the birth of her new grandchild. She'd be miserable and Adam would feel guilty and the children would pick up on the tension and it could quite likely spoil Christmas for all of them. Not that Adam had found much joy in the season in recent years but the children were his priority now, weren't they?

And Emma had made Poppy giggle with that ridiculous word.

That delicious sound of his daughter's merriment echoed somewhere in the back of his head and it was enough to soften the disappointment that Emma was so unsuitable.

'It *is* only for a few weeks,' he heard himself saying aloud. 'But…ach…' The sound encompassed both defeat and frustration. How bad could it be? He really only needed a babysitter for the hours he had to be at work. 'Fine. The job's yours if you want it, Emma.'

'Oh…' Her eyes widened with surprise. 'Yes. Please. But…don't you have other people to interview?'

'You were the last.' She didn't need to know that she had also been the first, did she? 'I'll lock up here and then we'll head off.' He looked at the unusual luggage on the floor beside Emma's chair. 'Is that all you'll need?'

She nodded.

'And you don't mind being here over the Christmas period? You don't have family who will be missing you?'

'No.' She shook her head this time and dipped her chin so that her gaze was hidden, as if she didn't want him to see how she felt about that.

Maybe it stirred too many memories that were too painful—like it did for him? An emotional cocktail of grief and anger that the season of goodwill and family togetherness only served to exacerbate? The thought gave him an odd moment of feeling potentially connected to this pale stranger in her oversized clothes. Or maybe it was the poignant tilt of her head as she looked down.

He shook off the unwelcome sensation. He had more than enough people to worry about, without adding someone else. Emma's job was to make life easier for him for a little while, not to complicate it any further.

'Right, then.' His movements were brisk as he logged out of his computer and flicked off the desk lamp. 'It's getting late. I suppose I'd better take you home.'

CHAPTER TWO

THE DARKNESS OF a winter's night engulfed the vehicle as it left the outskirts of Braeburn village behind.

Emma eyed the dashboard radio controls longingly. Driving anywhere without music was an alien experience for her but Dr McAllister clearly wasn't going to allow distractions while he was driving. Fair enough. It was raining hard now and the lights were catching a mist of white speckles that suggested it was trying to turn into sleet.

Would conversation also be deemed a distraction? She risked a sideways glance and had to tilt her chin upwards. Even sitting down, Adam McAllister was tall. Well over six feet. Walking beside him into the clinic's car park had made Emma feel very small. He hadn't said anything then either, apart from an offer to carry her bag, which had sounded more like a command than an invitation.

Clearly she hadn't really made a good impression on her new employer but at least he was prepared to give her a chance. Any optimism that she could change his mind was fading now, however, as she took in a profile that was stern enough to suggest an inability to suffer fools gladly.

Imagine running the gauntlet of that snappy little terrier of a receptionist in order to see such an unapproachable GP? You'd have to be really sick, Emma decided. And I'll bet his patients never forget to take their pills.

'What?'

The terse query was enough to make Emma jump. Coupled with the effect of Adam taking his eyes off the road to glare at her for a second, it actually made her heart skip a beat, but the fear that she might have spoken aloud was forgotten as fast as it had appeared.

In the dim reflected light of the dashboard controls, Adam's eyes looked black under equally dark brows. His hair was long enough to be a little unruly and a single lock had detached itself from the rest to flop across his forehead. The crazy desire to reach out and put that curl back where it belonged was so inappropriate that Emma caught her breath in an audible gasp.

She must have sounded as if she'd suddenly decided she might be in the company of an axe murderer, given the way those dark brows lifted. With his gaze safely back on the road, Adam sounded vaguely uncomfortable with the effect he'd had.

'I thought I heard you say something,' he muttered. 'About the hills.'

'Oh...' Emma turned to stare ahead through the windscreen but her gaze caught Adam's hand on the steering-wheel as she did so. He had long fingers and neatly cut nails and...dear Lord...a wedding ring? Why hadn't he mentioned his wife? Why hadn't she been at the interview instead of his mother? Confused, Emma struggled to find a response to his comment. 'It *is* hilly, isn't it? Do you live far from the village?'

'Only another mile or so. Don't worry, you'll have a car to use.'

'Wow...that's great.' Personal transport was an unexpected bonus. 'Thank you.'

The soft snort sounded exasperated. 'You'll need it. There's a lot of driving involved in getting the children to where they need to be. Poppy has a Highland dance class once a week and Oliver is starting drumming lessons in addition to his bagpipes class. On top of that, the school does a nativity play and there'll be rehearsals almost every day after school. You'll also be responsible for grocery shopping and other chores, like going to the vet. One of the dogs is having treatment at the moment for a foot injury.'

Emma was trying to listen carefully to her job description but she was still thinking about the mysteriously absent wife. And then it was too easy to get distracted by the cadence of Adam's deep voice and the gorgeous accent. She only realised she was smiling when she caught the movement of his head as it turned in her direction again. Hastily, she rearranged her face.

'I'm so sorry to hear that. I hope it's nothing serious.'

'A torn pad, that's all. But I didn't notice in time and it got infected.'

Although it looked like they were in the middle of nowhere, Adam put the indicator on and slowed the vehicle, turning through a gap in a tall stone wall. The headlights shone on what looked like a scene from a gothic movie, with the bare branches of massive old trees twisting out to meet each other and create a tunnel—the smaller branches like claws reaching out towards Emma. She shivered.

'It'll be warm inside.'

Startled, Emma looked sideways but Adam was concentrating on driving around the biggest lumps the tree roots were making in the driveway. He couldn't possibly have seen her shiver unless he had exceptionally acute peripheral vision. She hadn't forgotten the way he'd looked at her in his clinic either…as if he knew something she'd rather he didn't know.

A prickle of sensation ran down her spine. She really needed to curb her overactive imagination. Any minute now and she'd have Mrs McAllister buried somewhere down that spooky driveway and she'd be going into the rather forbidding-looking two-storeyed stone farmhouse to find it devoid of a friendly grandmother or any children. There would just be a dark hallway and a ticking grandfather clock and Dr McAllister would shut the door behind her and turn the lock and say—

'So…here we are, then.'

She made an odd squeaking sound as Adam took on his role in her wild train of thought with such perfect timing but then the absurdity of it all surfaced and she had to stop herself laughing aloud.

And then—unexpectedly—she got a rush of pure relief. She'd come here in the hope of finding a distraction from the fear of waiting for news that would have her imagining only her own funeral. Well…she'd already succeeded, hadn't she? She hadn't given her upcoming tests a moment's thought since she'd arrived in Braeburn.

She found herself beaming at her new employer. 'I'm excited,' she confessed. 'I do love starting a new job.'

'So it would seem,' Adam said drily. 'Let's go inside, shall we?'

He led Emma in to the vaulted hallway of the house his family had owned for generations, making a mental note not to forget to wind the grandfather clock this week, heading straight for the door from which the most light was spilling, along with the sound of voices and laughter.

The kitchen. The heart of his home.

Halfway there they were mobbed by the dogs, who gave their master only a perfunctory welcome before investigating the interesting new arrival. Adam paused to watch the effect, knowing that if Emma had been less than honest about liking animals, it would show up in a matter of seconds. And if she didn't like dogs, she probably didn't like children either and he'd know if he'd made a huge mistake in bringing her into his home.

Almost knocked off her feet by fluffy paws being planted on her stomach, Emma gave a startled exclamation but then her voice was stern.

'Paws on the floor, please,' she commanded. 'And then I can pat you.'

Amazingly, the dogs sat promptly, gazing adoringly up at the newcomer. Emma dropped to her haunches, abandoning her guitar case in favour of cuddling the animals. Getting her face washed enthusiastically, she was laughing as she looked up at Adam.

'They're gorgeous. And so...*hairy*.'

'That's Benji. He's a beardie. And Bob's the Border collie.' Part of him wanted to smile back at Emma but another part was fighting a sense of...disappointment? His new employee had passed this test with flying colours, hadn't she?

It looked like he was stuck with her for the foreseeable future.

The children weren't far behind the dogs.

'Emma—Emma! Gran says you're going to be looking after us now.' With practised ease, Poppy squeezed past the dogs to grab Emma's hand. 'Come with me. I want to show you Barbie's pony. And her caravan. And her swimming pool.'

Oliver eyed the guitar case and then his father. 'It's "later" now, isn't it, Dad?'

'Ach...' Catherine came out of the kitchen door, wiping her hands on her apron. 'Let's give Emma a wee bit o' time to get settled, shall we? Come on. All of you. Supper's almost ready.'

Adam left the backpack he'd been carrying beside the

clock. Poppy kept hold of Emma's hand to show her where to go, with Benji following as closely as possible. Oliver picked up the guitar case, which was as big as he was, and struggled in their wake. Bob stayed sitting and held up a bandaged paw.

'I know.' Adam stooped to scratch the hopefully pricked ears. 'I need to take care of that paw but it'll have to be later. It's a bit of a circus for now.'

Like his life. A juggling act. One that entailed keeping far too many balls in the air without dropping them. There was no applause for keeping them going either—just the prospect of disaster if they got dropped.

After the spooky driveway and the austere outlines of the huge, old stone farmhouse, walking into the kitchen was so far towards the other end of a welcoming spectrum that it was almost overwhelming.

A crackling open fire at one end of the room made it so warm Emma knew she'd have to take her pullover off very soon. The lights gave the oak cabinetry a golden glow and there was an amazing smell of something hot and meaty that made her mouth water. Good grief…she couldn't remember the last time she'd actually felt *hungry.*

'Look…' Poppy pointed to a fridge that was covered with pieces of paper and photographs held in place by small magnets. 'I drawed that. It's my mummy. She's got wings because she's an angel.'

'Oh?' The statement had been completely matter-of-fact but Emma wasn't sure how to take it. Was Mummy exceptionally kind or was she dead? Catherine was busy putting oven gloves on and didn't seem to have overheard the comment and she didn't like to ask Poppy. No doubt she would find out in good time.

'I drawed this one, too. It's Daddy and Bob and Benji.'

'It's very good. They all look very happy.'

Not that Emma could imagine Adam actually having such a wide grin on his face. Glancing back, she saw him standing in the doorway, all but glowering at the scene in front of him. She also saw Oliver bumping the guitar case on the flagstone floor.

'That's a bit heavy for you.' Easing out of Poppy's firm grip on her hand, Emma went to rescue the guitar. 'I'll put it over here for now, yes?'

'No,' Oliver said. 'I want to see.' With his eyebrows fiercely frowning like that, he looked remarkably similar to his father.

'It's time to eat,' Catherine told him. 'Poor Emma's been travelling all day and she must be famished. And then I'm going to show her to her room and drive all the way to Edinburgh to the airport.'

Poppy's face fell dramatically. 'But I don't want you to go, Granny. You'll miss *Christmas*.'

'No, I won't.' Catherine was opening a door on the stove that was set into an old chimney lined with blue and white tiles. She took out a cast-iron pot that looked as old as the kitchen and carried it to the table. 'They have Christmas in Canada too, you know. I'll be calling you and telling you all about your new wee cousin.'

'We can video chat.' Adam moved to the table and picked up a bread knife. He began slicing the crusty loaf on a thick wooden board. 'You'll be able to see the bairn as well.'

Poppy sniffed loudly. Emma took hold of her hand again and bent to whisper in her ear. 'Can you show me where to sit? It's such a *big* table.'

'You can sit beside me.'

In a short space of time Emma was installed on one of the old, oak chairs beside Poppy, with Oliver and Catherine on the other side of the table. Adam was at the top. Past him, she could see the dogs stretched out in front of the fire, with her guitar case propped against the wall nearby, looking as out of place as she was.

Except, oddly, she didn't *feel* out of place at all. She looked up at the whitewashed ceiling with its dramatic dark beams, across at the pretty tiles around the stove and the cluster of antique kettles and pots on the floor beside it. The room could have been part of a museum, except that it was so alive with the feeling of family.

It wasn't just the fridge that was covered with works of art and photographs. There was a huge corkboard on the wall and a bookshelf that had framed photographs amongst the books and a shelf clearly devoted to things the children had made, like an odd-looking robot constructed out of cardboard boxes and tubes and a chunky effort in clay that could possibly represent Benji. Or maybe Daddy.

'It's only stew, I'm sorry,' Catherine said, as she ladled an aromatic mix of meat and vegetables onto Emma's plate. 'I forgot that we might be welcoming a visitor today.'

A visitor? The feeling of family was so strong Emma had forgotten that that was what she was. How could anyone not feel completely at home in here? And the food was delicious.

'This is perfect,' Emma assured Catherine. A lot better than anything she'd be able to produce in the kitchen. Oh… help… Had she really made Adam believe she could cook in that interview? Her job in the restaurant had been limited to clearing tables and washing dishes. And had Catherine made that bread herself, too? Possibly even churned the butter, she thought as she accepted the blue and white dish being passed her way by Adam.

She didn't need to cross that bridge quite yet, though. And maybe it was Catherine that Adam had inherited that fey ability to see things from. She was smiling at Emma as they all tucked into their dinners.

'I've left lots of meals in the freezer and there's a modern oven as well as the big stove, if you need it. The children get a hot lunch at school so you'll only have to cope with breakfast for most of the time.'

'Did the turkey for Christmas arrive?' Adam asked.

'Aye. It's in the freezer as well. Don't forget to take it out at least a couple of days early. Leave it in the big tub out in the dairy to thaw.'

'I don't like stew,' Oliver announced a few minutes later. 'It's got carrots in it.'

'Carrots are good for you,' Emma offered. 'They help you see in the dark.'

'I don't need to see in the dark,' Oliver said with exaggerated patience. 'I'm *asleep*.'

'If you don't eat your carrots,' Adam said calmly, 'there'll be no ice cream.'

'I don't like ice cream.'

'I do,' Poppy sighed. 'I *love* ice cream.'

'Me, too,' Emma said. She beamed at Poppy. Impossible not to fall in love with a child who was so prepared to love everything life had to offer. Poppy beamed back. Shifting her gaze back to her plate, Emma caught Adam staring at her but he quickly shifted his attention back to his son.

'No television before bed, then,' he said. 'Vegetables are important.'

Catherine stood up to start clearing plates. 'Can I leave you to do the children's pudding?' she asked Adam. 'I'll need to head away soon and I'd like to give Emma a tour of the house and show her where her room is.'

'But Emma loves ice cream, too.' The horrified look on Poppy's face at the prospect of such an unwarranted punishment for someone stole another piece of Emma's heart.

Oliver might prove to be more of a challenge but she knew that she was going to love her time with Poppy.

'I'll come back,' Emma promised. 'Save me some, okay?' She looked at Oliver, who was scowling down at his plate—the only one still on the table. He was pushing slices of carrot around with his fork. 'And by then,' she added casually, 'you'll have scoffed those carrots, Ollie, and I'll be able to show you my guitar.'

A lightning-fast glance back as she left the kitchen revealed a fork laden with carrot slices making its way towards Oliver's mouth and Emma hid a smile. Maybe the little boy wouldn't be too much of a challenge after all.

The tour of the house was a whirlwind and it wasn't just the speed of viewing the more formal rooms, like the lounge and library downstairs or the rapid climb to the upper level that had taken Emma's breath away.

'How old is the house?'

'The main part dates back to the seventeenth century but there's been a lot of additions and renovations, and thank goodness for that. I'd hate to be offering you a room that didn't have an en suite bathroom.' Down the end of a wide hallway that had dozens of framed photographs displayed, Catherine opened one of the dark oak doors. 'And here it is.'

'It's gorgeous.' Emma looked around the space that would be hers for the next few weeks. The brass bed had a pretty patchwork quilt. The fireplace was tiled in blue and white, which seemed to be a theme throughout the house, and any draught from the windows was kept at bay by the thick velvet curtains that Catherine whisked shut.

'Poppy and Ollie's rooms are next door and they have their own bathroom between them. There's a playroom on this side and down the other hallway there are a couple of guest rooms and Adam's room is at the end. Have a good explore tomorrow, when you've got some daylight.' Catherine glanced at her watch. 'I'm so sorry, but I'm going to have to dash. I need to get home and collect my suitcase.'

'Home? Don't you live here?'

'Not any more. I moved out when Adam and Tania got married. It's been a family tradition for generations that the eldest son raises his family here. I have a cottage in the village.'

So it had been a family home for generations? That would explain the astonishingly homely feel of the house. And the enormous collection of photographs. Emma followed Catherine back into the hallway. She bit her lip but her curiosity refused to subside.

'Would it be awfully rude if I asked about...Tania?'

'Of course not, pet.' Catherine stopped in her tracks, turned her head to scrutinise the gallery of photographs and then pointed. 'That's her. I think that picture was taken on their honeymoon in the Maldives.'

A stunning beach scene. An even more stunning young woman with long, blonde hair and a model's body frolicking in the surf. Laughing. The joy was unmistakeable and Emma could imagine Adam standing there with the camera, capturing such a happy moment with his new wife.

'She's beautiful.'

'Aye...' The word was a sigh. 'Poppy has the look of her, I think. Ollie's more like his dad.'

There were more photographs, of course. Emma spotted a wedding portrait, with Adam gazing adoringly at his bride. A lovely black and white image of Tania and the newborn twins and more with the babies as toddlers.

'The bairns were only three when it happened,' Catherine said softly. 'They barely remember their mother so it's good to have so many pictures for them.'

Emma swallowed hard. 'What did happen?'

'A terrible tragedy. Tania liked to do her Christmas shopping in Edinburgh and she'd stay in a B&B so she could get it all done in a couple of days. There was a fire that year and she was trapped. She didn't get burned but they said she died of smoke inhalation.'

'Right before *Christmas*? That's so sad.'

'Aye.' Catherine caught her gaze for a long moment. There was a hint of warning in her gaze. And a plea. 'You might need to be patient with Adam. It's no' an easy time of year for him.'

'I can imagine.' No wonder he seemed so terse and grumpy, Emma thought. Or that she had yet to see him smile. How hard would it be to have the whole world joyously celebrating family and times of togetherness when it marked the anniversary of losing a beautiful and beloved young wife? The mother of his children?

'But Christmas is for the bairns, isn't it?' Catherine added. 'And they're old enough to see that their Christmas is no' like all the other bairns in the village and that's no' really fair, is it?'

Emma held the older woman's gaze. 'I'll do my best to make it a special Christmas for them,' she promised.

'Aye...' Catherine patted her arm. 'I've a feeling you might do just that. Thank you.' Her smile was poignant. 'The bairns think their mother is an angel who's still looking after them. Maybe that was why you got sent to us.'

When his mother drove away from the house on the first leg of her journey to Canada, Adam was left standing on the front steps.

Stunned.

What had just happened here?

He'd been dreading this moment for months. Ever since he had learned of his sister's due date and realised that—

for the first time since Tania's death—he might have to
face this Christmas without the emotional support of the
most important woman in his life. And worse, that the
twins would be without their beloved grandmother, who
was the one who insisted on making the day as special as
possible for them.

He'd expected tears. Possibly tantrums, especially from
Poppy, who simply adored her gran. Oliver was just as
attached, of course, but he didn't wear his heart on his
sleeve like Poppy. He was more like himself, in guarding
his heart and not letting others see any private misery. His
children were his life—both of them—but he did worry
more about Ollie. Because he knew just how much misery
it was possible to hide?

But the moment had come. They'd all been out there
to say goodbye to Catherine. Even the unknown quantity
that was the new arrival of the temporary nanny because
his mother wouldn't let her hang back from the family
farewell. She'd been standing there beside the children—
looking remarkably like a wayward, teenage sister—getting one of those warm hugs that Catherine was so good
at. And then she'd whispered something in Ollie's ear and
his little boy had given a solemn nod and turned to lead
the way back inside. Poppy had jumped up and down and
tugged on Emma's hand and she was bursting with excitement as she dragged Emma back up the steps.

'We're going to see the *kit-ar*,' she informed Adam as
they went past. 'I *love* kit-ars.'

Benji had bounded in their wake, of course. It was Bob
who was sitting by Adam's feet and he saw the dog shiver.
How long had he been standing here, wondering how on
earth something he'd been dreading had turned out to be
so easy?

Long enough for his dog to shiver noticeably.

'Come on, then, old boy.'

Back in the warmth of the house, he pushed the heavy door closed and then he heard it.

The sound of music coming from the kitchen.

Expertly plucked guitar strings. A song being sung in a clear, sweet voice that filled the air and made it somehow more of a pleasure to breathe.

A childish song, he realised as he stepped closer to the bright glow of the kitchen door. A nonsense song with tongue-twister words about a copper coffee-pot.

And it wasn't just Emma singing. Poppy was getting the words wrong and giggling but Oliver must have learned the song at school because he was joining in part of the chorus.

Not very loudly but he knew his son's voice.

He stopped again. Puzzled.

What *was* it about this girl?

His mother had seen it instantly. Poppy was prepared to love everybody. But Ollie…?

How on earth had she put her hands on a key to that little heart so quickly?

Adam shook his head and Bob lay down and put his nose on his paws to wait.

He knew when something big was changing. And he knew that it took longer for his master to recognise any joyful possibilities that something new could offer. His job was simply to keep him company while he had a little think about it all.

CHAPTER THREE

'So Mrs McAllister's likin' Canada, then?'

'Aye.' Adam glanced over his shoulder, reaching for the file on the end of Eileen's desk, as his next patient joined him for the short walk to his consulting room. The waiting area was still full, and while the women amongst the group seemed busy with their knitting or magazines, he knew perfectly well that they'd all been discussing his business while he'd been taking Shona Legg's blood tests.

Or, to be more accurate, they'd been comparing notes on the new arrival in the village. Emma had been here for a few days now and there was nothing like a bit of new blood to stimulate opinions.

Eileen had overheard the comment by way of greeting from the elderly woman who was moving slowly beside him. She sniffed audibly.

'Don't hold wi' havin' Christmas in foreign parts,' he heard her mutter. 'It's no' natural to be away from your home.'

Adam suppressed a sigh as Miss McClintock's progress slowed even more as she turned her head. 'Canada's no' so foreign,' she informed Eileen. 'And Christmas is about people, no' places. Dr McAllister's sister's there and she's having a bairn. It's where the first Mrs McAllister *should* be.'

'Come in, Joan.' Adam closed the door firmly behind them. 'And tell me what's brought you here today.'

'I'm a bit peaky is all.'

'Oh?' Adam smiled encouragingly but his heart was sinking. It had been, ever since that reference to the first Mrs McAllister. The title had come from the need to distinguish Catherine from the new woman with the same name—Tania. This was really what that overfull waiting room was about, wasn't it? It had happened all those years ago, too, when he'd brought his new wife home from the bright lights of Edinburgh. Who knew what interesting piece of information he might let slip when faced with the relentless curiosity of people who'd known him all his life?

They loved him. He knew that. They'd been prepared to accept and admire Tania, too, despite her being a foreigner from the bright lights of Edinburgh, and the excitement that her pregnancy and the birth of the twins had generated had kept the older biddies happy for months. So had the tragedy of her death. They'd closed ranks around him now and anyone who might pose even the smallest threat was going to be regarded with deep suspicion.

How on earth was Emma coping with that side of village life?

'What sort of peaky?'

Joan McClintock removed her hat. Adam obediently took it and placed it on his desk as she began unwinding her hand-knitted scarf from around her neck.

'I don't feel quite right,' his patient said vaguely. 'A wee bit giddy in my head when I stand up sometimes.'

Adam's nod was brisk. Blood pressure first, then. Possibly an ECG to check for an arrhythmia. At the very least a review of the medications Joan was taking. It was unlikely he'd be finished within the fifteen-minute slot that

Eileen would have allocated in her appointment schedule but he would have to try.

'I saw the bairns in the square yesterday,' Joan told him as he helped her off with her thick coat. 'Watching the decorations go up on the tree. It's such a blessing they don't remember, isn't it?'

'Aye.' The agreement was as terse as Adam could make it without causing offence. A warning that discussing his private life was not an option. 'No, you don't need to take off your cardigan, Joan. We can just roll up your sleeve for me to do your blood pressure.'

It *was* a blessing that his children couldn't remember the dreadful Christmas of three years ago. Had Emma been given the story in lurid detail, as she'd done her chores in the village over the last few days? December wasn't just about a season of goodwill in Braeburn. It marked the season of remembrance for Tania McAllister.

His mother was lucky she was in Canada. She was getting a reprieve from being the unspoken centre of attention when family was being celebrated. Away from a village where Christmas had a distinct flavour of being a shrine to someone who had been elevated to the status of a saint.

Dear Lord…if they only *knew* the truth…

But he hadn't known so why should they? Oh, they'd all seen how she'd escaped the village more and more often but, while eyebrows had been raised about her time away from the children, it had been accepted as part of a glamorous woman's life and it had been forgiven and forgotten after her tragic death.

What none of them knew was that she probably hadn't been alone on any of those trips away.

He'd only found out because fate had stepped in and provided the evidence and Adam had made sure that the scandalous information had gone no further.

Maybe that was the real blessing here. That the village—and therefore his children—would never know.

It was his burden and that was only fair, wasn't it? If he'd been a better husband, Tania wouldn't have needed anyone else. And it was a burden he was getting used to carrying. In many ways it was getting easier and he could hope that some time in the future he'd be able to cope with this particular time of year. Enjoying it was too much to ever hope for but another few weeks and things could get back to normal. A normality he would never have chosen, of course, but he could live with it.

He had no choice.

'That English lassie was wi' them.' Joan only just managed to wait until Adam was removing the stethoscope from his ears. 'I hear she's made friends with Caitlin McMurray at the school?'

His grunt was intended to express a lack of interest in his temporary nanny's social life. Why did some people assume that a monosyllabic response simply needed more effort on their part?

'I hear she's been *singing*.'

'Aye.' Adam was still having difficulty getting used to the sound of Emma singing. She did it *all* the time. When she was busy with some mundane task, like doing the dishes or sorting laundry, and a session of songs with the children was already a favourite part of their evening routine. She probably thought the nursery wing was far enough away from the rest of the house for him not to notice but she was wrong. He'd heard her late last night, too, well after the children were sound asleep. Alone in her room, playing her guitar and singing softly.

It wasn't that he didn't *like* the sound. It was just... different. Nothing like normal.

'She's no' a teacher.' Joan clicked her tongue. 'What's she doing at the school *every* day?'

It was the tone that did it. Adam was jolted out of his automatic defence mechanisms by the unexpected urge to defend his new employee. 'She *has* been a music teacher and she plays the guitar. The school's piano is apparently broken and the children want to learn carols. Now…stand up, please, Joan. I'm going to take your blood pressure again to see if position makes any difference.'

Joan levered her ample frame out of the chair. 'We knew about the piano. The committee's talking about whether to use the hall fund to replace it, but if we don't fix the hall it's going to get condemned and what would we do without the village hall? Where would the children put on their Christmas play?'

Adam resorted to his customary grunt and put the earpieces of his stethoscope into place to signal an end to the conversation. As he held the disc over Joan's elbow and pumped up the cuff, he took a quick glance at the clock on his wall and remembered the number of people in the waiting room.

It was going to be a long day.

The conversation stopped as soon as Emma entered the general store that was between the greengrocer and the bakery. She lifted her chin and put on her brightest smile.

'Good morning. I'm looking for some coloured paper. Do you have the kind that's sticky on the back?'

The blank stare made Emma reconsider her decision to shop in the village instead of driving for half an hour to get to the nearest larger town. It wasn't easy to keep the smile on her face.

'I want to make paper chains,' she explained. 'For Christmas decorations.'

The women exchanged heavily significant glances.

'*Christmas* decorations?' one of them murmured. 'In Dr McAllister's hoose?'

The subtext was in capital letters. You couldn't really celebrate Christmas in the McAllister house. Not without being duly reluctant anyway. Even the children were all too aware of that and it wasn't fair. She'd taken them to watch the big tree in the square being decorated yesterday and Poppy's eyes had been huge.

'I *love* Christmas trees,' she'd whispered. 'They're so *pretty*.'

'We'll make your Christmas tree just as pretty at home, you'll see.'

'We don't have a tree at home,' Oliver had said. 'Gran says it's because it makes Dad sad.'

'It makes me sad,' Poppy had said, '*not* having a tree.'

Emma had lain awake last night, mulling this over. She was here for the children, wasn't she? And she was here for Christmas.

And Christmas was for children.

It was a no-brainer, really. Surely she could find a way to persuade the taciturn Dr McAllister to put up with a few decorations? When Catherine had called from Canada early that morning to talk to the children before they went off to school, Emma had gathered her courage and asked quietly if it would be such a terrible thing to do.

'It would be the best thing to do,' Catherine had assured her. 'It's no guid for anyone, being stuck in the past. I've tried but...' The sigh said it all. 'Maybe *you'll* succeed, pet. He can't afford to chase you away, can he? Not before Christmas, anyway.'

The tone that suggested it wouldn't be an easy task was being heavily underlined by the shocked look these women were now sharing.

'It's for Poppy and Oliver,' Emma said firmly. 'They've been making decorations at school and they want to make some at home, too. Paper chains are what I always made when I was their age.'

The mention of the children made one of the women nod. 'Aye,' she sighed. 'It should be all about the bairns, shouldn't it?'

'The paper's over yon,' the shopkeeper told Emma. 'Beside the magazines.'

The conversation didn't stop this time as she returned to the counter.

'Poor man,' one was saying. 'To lose the love of his life so young.'

'Like a princess, she was,' another agreed. 'Always so well dressed.'

Emma felt the collective scrutiny of her jeans and over-sized jumper beneath her puffy anorak and she was per-versely delighted that she was wearing her Tibetan knitted hat with its rainbow stripes and ear covers that trailed into long tails she hadn't bothered tying. That would really give them something to disapprove of at length as soon as she went out the door.

Her bravado faded as she picked up the guitar case she'd left by the umbrella stand at the shop door and went out into the chilly, grey afternoon, however. If making a paper chain or two was such a big deal, maybe she was only going to make things worse? How happy would the children be if their father was even more upset by some-one who wasn't prepared to spend Christmas in a kind of muted mourning?

The Christmas tree in the square had taken days to decorate but it was looking magnificent now, with big, coloured lights and enormous red and silver baubles. Despite the cold, Emma perched on a bench near the church.

She had half an hour before she was due at school. Checking her watch, she made a quick calculation. They were about eight hours behind Californian time and that meant that Sharon was probably at home. She hit the speed dial.

'Emma…I was just thinking about you. Is it snowing in Scotland?'

'Feels like it could be any second. I'm in the village square and it's absolutely *freezing*.'

'Ohh…I'm homesick. It's too warm to be Christmastime here. It's just *wrong*. But…you shouldn't be sitting out in the cold. Go and find somewhere warm, for heaven's sake. You have to take care of yourself.'

'I'm fine. It's too cold for bugs to survive here and my immune system is pretty much back to full power. I'm just killing some time before I go to the school for carol practice.'

Sharon laughed. 'I got your email. I can't believe you've got involved with village life that fast. No…on second thoughts, it doesn't surprise me at all. You'll be starring in the Christmas pantomime by next week.'

'No. That's Ollie and Poppy. They've been chosen to be Joseph and Mary for the school nativity play. They're so excited. I'm going to have to make costumes for them.'

'Uh-oh… Do they know you can't sew?'

Emma laughed. 'No. They don't even know I can't cook yet. Their gran left so much food in the freezer I've been able to keep my lack of talent well hidden.'

'Imagine if you gave the only doctor in town food poisoning?'

'Hey…that only happened once. I give chicken a wide berth now.'

'Good thinking. He wouldn't be happy.'

'He's not happy anyway. Do you know I haven't seen him smile once yet?'

'He's Scottish. He's supposed to be dour.'

'He still wears his wedding ring and it's three years since his wife died.'

'Hmm. He must have loved her.'

'Who wouldn't? From what I've heard, she was either a princess, an angel or some kind of saint.'

'Nobody's that perfect. People just forget the bad stuff when they're dead.'

Emma smiled but couldn't help wondering if Sharon would forget about the food poisoning incident if...

'Oh, my God...what *is* that horrendous noise?'

Laughter chased away the dark thought. 'There's an old guy in a kilt near the Christmas tree. He's warming up his bagpipes.'

'What? Sounds like a tribe of donkeys braying.'

'No. That's even worse. You should hear Jemima waking us all up in the mornings. She's very cute but remind me that I never want a donkey as a pet in the future, will you?'

'What was that? I can hardly hear you.'

'I'd better go, Sharon. I'm due at school. Talk soon. Love you.'

The piper was playing a real tune by the time Emma tucked her phone into her pocket and, instead of the brisk walk she had intended to get her circulation moving again, she sat there and listened for a minute.

It was such an evocative sound with a haunting edge that was a song of what...courage? Loneliness?

Maybe it was just the quintessential Scottishness of it but it made her think of Adam McAllister.

Did he ever wear a kilt?

The notion gave her an odd curl somewhere deep in her belly.

What *was* it about men in kilts that could be such a sexy image?

Or was it the image of Adam in the attire that was making her feel a little odd?

It was easy to dismiss such a ridiculous idea because something else was happening in her head.

Or maybe her heart.

Perhaps it was the Christmas tree she was looking at in combination with the haunting music. Or maybe it had something to do with that moment in her phone call to Sharon when she'd wondered if her friend would only remember the good things.

Whatever it was, Emma was facing the realisation that this could possibly be the last Christmas she would ever have.

And she was going to be sharing it with children who had no memory of what a happy, family Christmas should be all about.

With a man who couldn't see how precious life was and how you had to catch joy—not shut it out or allow it to be dimmed by shadows.

The fey notion that fate had sent her here for a reason suddenly made sense. If this was going to be her last Christmas, how lucky was she that she could share it with Poppy and Oliver?

She was going to make this the *best* Christmas ever.

Starting with paper chains.

CHAPTER FOUR

FLIGHTS OF FANCY first thing in the morning were a bit much but Emma seemed to have no control over this one.

Here she was, standing by the kitchen bench, break-ing eggs, and a single glance over her shoulder to where the man of the house was having his breakfast had been enough to trigger it.

She could see Adam McAllister wearing a kilt. With his hair even longer than the current shaggy style so that dark, tangled waves kissed his shoulders. Standing in soli-tary splendour on the top of a hill, with a set of bagpipes tucked under his arm, offering a mournful lament to the universe. It was almost enough to bring a tear to her eyes. She certainly had to stifle a sigh.

In fact, Adam was wearing a dark jumper over his shirt and tie, buttering his toast and adding marmalade, just like any normal mortal. There was no excuse for the words that popped out of Emma's mouth.

'Is there a McAllister tartan?'

'What?' Adam's hand stopped halfway towards his mug of tea. He sounded both impatient and bewildered.

Emma made herself walk to the fridge to get some milk for the eggs but she couldn't look at Adam. She'd woken up a little nervous that this was the start of the weekend and she'd be seeing a lot more of the children's father. She'd been hoping to impress him by how well she'd settled into this new job but she'd obviously annoyed him by asking a stupid question.

'It's just that I saw a man playing the bagpipes in the village yesterday and he was wearing a kilt. I know that the colours and patterns vary according to clan and I just wondered…' Oh, help. Now she was prattling on. 'If, you know, you had one for your family.'

'Of course we do.'

'Oh…' Emma waited but that seemed to be the end to the conversation. 'That's nice.' She poured milk into the bowl of eggs and started whisking them. The silence stretched on.

'We're a branch of Clan Donald,' Adam said, with an air of having realised he might have been rude in giving such a terse response. 'The tartan's red and green with white stripes and a little bit of royal blue.'

'Sounds lovely.' Emma pressed her lips together but the question refused to stay unspoken. 'Do you ever wear a kilt?'

'Only for weddings.' She could feel Adam glaring at her back. 'And funerals.'

Oh…*man*. She took a deep breath. This was going to be a long weekend. 'Would you like some scrambled eggs? I'm making them for Poppy and Ollie.'

'No.' Adam's chair scraped as he pushed it back. 'I'm due at the medical centre. We have a Saturday morning clinic until eleven and then I've got my house calls to make.' Reaching for the crust of toast he'd left on his plate, Adam divided it and gave a piece to each of the dogs, who were flanking his chair. The action was as automatic as picking up his napkin to wipe his mouth and it made Emma feel better.

There *was* kindness lurking under that gruff exterior, wasn't there?

She almost changed her mind as he went to the kitchen door and raised his voice.

'Poppy—are you out of those pyjamas yet? Oliver—hurry up and find your chanter and don't forget your music book this time.'

He turned back to pick up the coat draped over the arm of the old couch near the fire. 'Do you know where you're taking them?'

'Yes.' Emma's nod was confident. 'I drop Ollie at Mr McTavish's house at nine o'clock, take Poppy to her dance class at the hall for nine-thirty, go back to get Ollie at ten and we pick up Poppy at ten-thirty.'

Adam gave a single nod. 'Good.'

'I thought we'd go into the village after that. We can see if they've finished decorating the big tree and get some fresh bread to go with our soup for lunch. Will you be back by then?'

'I don't know.' In his coat now, Adam reached for the leather doctor's bag that had probably been his father's before him. 'If I am, you can have the afternoon off. And tomorrow, of course, being Sunday.'

'But what would you do with the children if you got a call?'

'They come in the car with me. They're used to it.'

'I don't need a day off,' Emma told him. 'I'm loving being with the children.'

Adam paused en route to the door and the look Emma received was one of surprise. Had she sounded too enthusiastic perhaps?

Needy even?

Or maybe he thought it was some sort of rebuke directed at how little time he seemed to spend with his children.

Whatever was going on behind that dark, unreadable gaze, the eye contact made Emma's heart skip a beat. How could just a look feel like a physical touch?

It went on for long enough to make her start feeling a little peculiar and maybe he would have held her gaze even longer because Emma found herself unable to look away, but then the children burst into the room. Ollie had an instrument that looked like a recorder in one hand and a very dog-eared book in the other.

'I found them, Dad. They were under my bed.'

Poppy was right behind him. 'And I'm all dressed now. I just need Emma to do my hair.' Her face fell when she saw the bag in her father's hand. 'Are you going out now?'

'You know I have to work on Saturday mornings, love.'

Emma's gaze had been drawn straight back to Adam's face so she could see the softening as he looked down at his children. There was even a curl to his mouth that most would probably label as a smile but it wasn't a *real* smile. Had his children ever seen his eyes crinkle with happiness or basked in the joy of hearing him laugh aloud?

'I'll be back this afternoon,' he said. 'We can take the dogs for a walk if it stops raining and see if there's enough ice on the pond to go skating.'

His son's hair got ruffled and Poppy got a kiss on the top of her head and then he was gone. The children—and the dogs—were left staring forlornly after him.

'Who wants eggs?' Emma asked brightly.

'Me. I *love* eggs.' Poppy climbed up onto a chair.

'I don't.' Oliver kicked his chair leg before sitting down. 'I think they're *icky*.'

'Icky eggs.' Poppy giggled but then cast a doubtful look towards the pan Emma was stirring.

'That's only because you haven't tried my special scrambled eggs,' Emma said firmly. 'They're from your very own hens and they look yummy. I'm going to have some too and then we're going to get our skates on and get you to your classes on time.'

Poppy frowned. 'I don't think I can dance with my skates on.'

Emma laughed. 'It means that we need to be quick.' She put a plate of scrambled eggs in front of Poppy. 'To go fast, like we're pretending to be on skates.'

'I love skating.' Poppy picked up her fork. 'I hope the pond is all frozen up. Will you come and have a look on our walk, too, Emma?'

The wide-eyed, hopeful look that accompanied the invitation was irresistible but Emma rapidly replayed Adam's words in her head. He'd offered to take the children for a walk. He'd told her she could have the afternoon off. That added up to him wanting time alone with his children, didn't it?

'I might have some things I need to do,' she told Poppy. 'But you can tell me all about it later.'

Adam wasn't home by the time the soup was hot and the crusty loaf of bread had been sliced and buttered.

'I don't think we'll wait,' Emma decided. 'I can leave some soup on the stove to stay hot for Daddy and we'll save him lots of bread.'

'And a chocolate?'

'Does Daddy like chocolate?'

'Mmm.' Poppy nodded her head enthusiastically but then frowned. 'Not as much as me.'

Emma eyed the small bowl on the table. 'You didn't open too many doors on your calendar, did you?'

Poppy shook her head. 'That's Ollie's chocolates too. Is there really one behind every door until it gets to Christmas?'

'Sure is. Have you guys never had an Advent calendar before?'

Poppy shook her head again. 'Jeannie told me about them at school but I didn't believe her.'

A momentary doubt surfaced as Emma looked at the two Advent calendars now pinned to the bottom of the big corkboard, within easy reach of the children. Surely Adam wouldn't object to them having the excitement of opening the doors to find the treat and the tiny Christmassy picture every morning?

'Ollie? You can stop practising now. Come and have lunch.'

'I'm going to wait for Dad.'

'But we don't know how long he'll be. You must be hungry.'

Sitting on the sofa, Oliver shook his head and kept blowing on his chanter, laboriously changing his finger positions over the holes. The noise was terrible. No wonder the dogs were looking unhappy.

'Tell you what…' Emma had to raise her voice to be heard over the shrill notes. 'Why don't you have a little bit now and then some more when Dad gets home?'

Oliver appeared not to have heard the suggestion but when the telephone rang he dropped his chanter and ran to answer it. He came back scowling. 'Dad says Mrs Jessop is having her baby and it's coming too early so he has to stay and look after her until the ambulance comes and he might have to go into the hospital with her, too. He might not be home till teatime.'

'Oh…' Emma's heart gave a squeeze at the small boy's obvious disappointment. 'We'll just have to find something fun to do until then, won't we?'

Oliver's scowl deepened.

Emma tried hard to keep the children amused and cheer

Oliver up. They all put wellies and coats on and took some carrots out for Jemima the donkey, who was very happy to have visitors. Emma scratched her woolly head and stroked the extraordinary ears.

'She has beautiful eyes.'

'She's really clever,' Oliver said. 'She can undo knots. Dad says it's no use ever tying her up.'

Poppy was being nuzzled gently.

'She's kissing me, Emma. See? She loves me. She 'specially loves it when I ride her.'

'Really? Does she have a saddle?'

'You don't need one,' Oliver told her. 'There's lots of fluff to hang onto and she never goes fast.'

'How does she know where to go?'

'She follows *me*,' Oliver said. He stood a little taller. 'That's why she's so good at undoing knots. She doesn't like being tied up because she wants to follow me. Jemima loves me, too.'

'She's quiet now,' Emma observed. 'She's pretty loud in the mornings, isn't she?'

'That's because she's lonely,' Poppy said sadly. 'Donkeys need to have a friend.'

'Can we go and look at the pond now?'

'Do you know where it is, Ollie?'

'Up there.' His arm waved vaguely towards the wooded hill behind the house that separated the garden from surrounding farmland. 'Somewhere.'

'Hmm.' It was tempting to take the children and dogs off for a walk but Emma had a sudden vision of them all getting lost in the Scottish highlands. She could imagine the activation of the local search and rescue team as the snow started falling thickly and what Adam's face would be like if she put his children into such danger.

Maybe it was fortunate that the leaden sky overhead decided to release the first fat raindrops on top of them.

'Let's get Jemima tucked up into her nice warm stable. I've got something special we can do inside.'

'What?'

'It's a surprise.'

It was certainly Oliver that the donkey was willing to follow. He didn't even need to hang onto her halter as he led her into the straw-covered stable. They closed the bottom half of the door so she could see out but the mournful braying started even before they got back to the house.

'She's lonely again,' Poppy said. Her bottom lip quivered.

'Oh…look.' Emma wanted to distract Poppy. 'That's a holly hedge. Let's pick some.'

'Why?'

'Because it's what you do at Christmas. We need branches that have lots of lovely red berries. Let's see how quickly we can find some and get inside before it really starts raining.'

The rain was pouring down by the time they reached the warmth of the kitchen again. The dogs left muddy paw prints over the flagstone floor and curled up close to the fire that Emma stoked. She cleared the table and produced the packets of coloured paper she had purchased in the village the day before and showed them how to cut strips and make interlocking loops by sticking the ends together.

'Do lots of different colours,' she said. 'And make them really long. I'll find something to stick them up with and we'll make the kitchen so pretty it will be a lovely surprise for when Daddy gets home.'

The task was a novelty that the children loved. The strips were a bit wobbly and the loops a variety of sizes but it didn't detract from the overall effect as the simple decorations grew. Emma cleaned up the lunch dishes and found a big bowl to arrange the holly branches in. She sang the Christmas carol the children had never heard about the little donkey and Poppy made her sing it again and again as she tried to learn the words.

Then she searched cluttered drawers until she found some drawing pins and tape that she could use to hang the paper chains. This required some effort, moving the table and then standing on a chair on top of it but by the time daylight had faded completely they were able to stand back and admire the team effort.

Rainbow chains linked all four corners of the room, dipping between the beams to give graceful curves to the lines. The whitewashed ceiling made the colours seem even brighter and the transformation from ordinary to festive was very gratifying. Who wouldn't love it?

The sound of singing was the last thing Adam needed when he stepped into his home after a long and difficult afternoon. The happy sound was totally inappropriate when he'd just left people who were suffering—like poor Aimee Jessop, who looked like she might lose yet another bairn.

The clock had stopped, he noted. Because he'd forgotten to wind it.

At least Bob wasn't limping as much but it had been Emma who had decided to take him to the vet to have his dressing changed and receive instructions on how to care for the dog. Had Jim, the vet, made some comment about how it was just as well it wasn't going to be left entirely in Adam's hands?

And it had been Emma who'd made him feel like he wasn't doing enough for his children, too. The way she'd said how much she loved being with them this morning.

He loved being with them, too, but how many others would realise that?

He'd promised to spend the afternoon with them today and look what had happened.

A premature labour at only twenty-seven weeks for poor Aimee. Four weeks longer than the previous two pregnancies and she'd really begun to hope that this time she would get to take her baby home. He'd tried to keep her calm until the ambulance arrived and he couldn't have let her go to the hospital alone. Not when her husband was out on the oil rig for another two weeks.

Not even noticing the muddy streak Benji's paw left on his trousers, Adam kept moving. Maybe a wee dram of whisky before his tea would help. And some time with the children. He could read them a story before bed.

The words of the song were audible now. "'Little donkey, little donkey, on the dusty road…'"

Maybe the children would prefer to hear songs than a story.

Adam stepped into the kitchen. He was expecting warmth and the smell of hot food. The loving greeting his children always gave him and the prospect of winding down in the comfort of his favourite part of his house. He wasn't expecting to be hit in the face with a blinding kaleidoscope of colours.

'What in heaven's name is *going on* in here?'

'Daddy…' Poppy flung her arms around his legs. 'We've made decorations. Aren't they bee-*yoot*-i-ful?'

Adam took another upward glance at the desecration of the ancient, oak beams.

'And we've learned a song all about Jemima.'

'It's not about Jemima.' Oliver was right beside his sister now. 'It's about another donkey. The one that Mary was riding to get to Bethlehem.'

Christmas again. How did it manage to accentuate the worst of life in so many ways? Impossible not to think about a donkey carrying the pregnant Mary. With a full-term pregnancy that everybody knew ended up with a healthy baby, despite less than adequate birthing facilities. Unlike poor Aimee who had access to the best of modern care but now had a scrap of a bairn who was on life support in a neonatal intensive care unit in Edinburgh.

Adam tried to push the concern away. To focus on his own healthy children. Tried to centre himself by a glance around the room below ceiling level. At least that looked relatively normal. Or did it?

'What…' he actually had to swallow before he could find any more words '…are *those*?'

The children had fallen strangely silent. Even Poppy, who could never be called a quiet child. It was Emma who answered.

'They're Advent calendars. You get to open a little door every day until Christmas Eve and there's a new picture and a little chocolate. Very little and the children haven't eaten them all from the doors that already needed to be opened. They saved them. For *you*.'

She sounded nervous, Adam realised. He looked over the twins' heads and looked at her properly for the first time since he'd come into the room. He still hadn't got used to the way she looked, with that air of being a stray gypsy waif, but he was certainly letting go of the idea that she could be unreliable or unable to commit to anything. She'd thrown herself into being his children's nanny with her heart and soul, hadn't she? They loved her.

And she loved them. The way she'd said how much she loved being with them this morning had touched his heart in the way that only total honesty could.

And now she was looking at him with eyes that looked

too large for her thin face. With a glow that was telling him that she was doing this to make his children happy.

Because she already loved them.

And because it was Christmastime.

There was a hopeful expression in those eyes, too, that was a plea that he wouldn't spoil it all by being cross.

He found himself unable to look away. Adam got a sudden vision of what it would be like to be seeing himself through her eyes and he didn't like what he saw. He forced a smile to his lips as he managed to break the eye contact with Emma.

'As long as you don't eat too much chocolate before dinner.' He looked up again. 'I don't think I've ever seen such long paper chains. You must have been busy all day.'

'I did my practice, too. D'you want to hear what I learned today, Dad?'

'Aye. Let me get my coat off, son. And I need a wee something to drink.'

He glanced across at Emma, feeling like he should apologise, although he wasn't quite sure why. 'D'you drink whisky, Emma?'

She shook her head but smiled. 'Let me find one for you while you listen to Ollie's new tune. You've had a long day. Dinner will ready in no time.'

There was no recrimination in her tone that she'd been left with the children all afternoon and that they'd been left without their promised walk or time with their father. No… Both the tone and the way she was looking at him gave him the odd feeling that she knew exactly how hard his day had been. He didn't have to say anything about what had happened but she was still willing to try and make it better.

Even more oddly, it *was* starting to feel better. He could almost dismiss the edge of panic at seeing how Christmas was invading his house again. Maybe that was because the decorations were so obviously made by children with their wobbly shapes and sizes. Tania might have gone overboard with decorations but she would never have tolerated something so far less than perfect. Even the bunch of holly on the table was real instead of a perfect, plastic replica.

This was different. This was Emma, not Tania. Couldn't be more different, in fact. Maybe it would even be okay.

'Thank you.' It felt like the first time Adam had ever smiled at Emma but surely that wasn't the case?

Maybe it was because he'd never seen *her* smile quite like that. A slow, delighted curl to her mouth that lit up her face and gave her a faint flush of colour on those pale cheeks.

She was pretty, he realised. Not flaky looking at all. Too young for her years, still, and too thin, but…yes…pretty.

Beautiful even.

CHAPTER FIVE

EMMA HAD A lot of time to herself on Sunday because Adam didn't get called out, although he seemed to spend a lot of time on the phone and she overheard a snatch of conversation about a sick baby who was in Intensive Care. The children—and the dogs—got their long walk to see whether the pond was frozen and Emma was glad of the time on her own.

She sat in her room, with her laptop and her guitar, working on her Christmas gift for Sharon. She was writing a song about friendship and the strength it could give someone to get through hard times, and she intended to record it as a background to a slide show of all the best photos she and Sharon had taken over the last few years. She might even use the very private ones—like the one in her hospital bed where she'd been so swollen by the steroids she'd been taking and completely bald from the chemo. Sharon had insisted she needed a photo so that Emma would be able to look back and see how far she'd come and then she'd said something about eggheads and made Emma laugh, and that was the moment she'd captured.

She'd been so right. It was hard to believe how far she'd come. And maybe—Emma squeezed her eyes tightly shut for a heartbeat—she would be able to look back from the distance of many more years. But if she couldn't, Sharon would have this gift from her heart for ever.

Back in the routine of the school week again, Emma was delighted to feel so at home with the routine of her new job. She was loving her time at the school, helping with the music classes, and the new friendship with the junior-school teacher, Caitlin, promised to be something special.

It was a bonus that Oliver took so long to find everything he needed to take home after school because it gave the young women a few minutes extra to chat.

'I was telling Moira Findlay that you have one of the most amazing voices I've ever heard,' Caitlin confessed on Monday afternoon. 'She said they might consider offering you an invitation to join the village choir.'

Emma grinned. 'I take it that's a huge honour?'

'You'd better believe it. Normally you have to be second-generation Braeburn, at the very least.'

'Did you tell her I'm only here till Adam's mother gets back?'

'No.' Caitlin's face fell. 'I'm kind of hoping you'll fall in love with the place and decide to stay. He's still going to need a nanny, isn't he, and the last few have been disasters—especially that Kylie, who was far more interested in her boyfriend than the children.'

Emma backed away from the conversation fast. 'My plans are totally up in the air for next year. I couldn't commit to anything and Adam hasn't mentioned the possibility, either. I…'

The urge to say something more was strong but this wasn't the time or place. Caitlin must have sensed something big but her curious glance lasted only a moment. Poppy was tugging on Emma's hand.

'Sing Miss McMurray the new song, Emma. The Christmas one.'

'We've got lots of carols we're learning already, Poppy,' Caitlin said.

'But this is Jemima's song. About Mary.'

'"Little Donkey",' Emma supplied.

'Oh…' Caitlin's eyes shone. 'That's one of my all-time *favourite* Christmas songs. How could I have forgotten it?' She began to hum but then stopped. 'That's the chorus. How does it start again?'

Emma could see that Oliver had been totally distracted from finding his reading book by watching the goldfish in their bowl on the science table so she sang the first few lines about the little donkey on the dusty road, plodding on with its precious load.

Poppy beamed and Caitlin sighed happily. 'Imagine our play with our Mary coming in on a donkey with Joseph leading her, and all the children singing that.'

'I'm Mary,' Poppy reminded her.

'I know, pet.' Caitlin patted her head.

'And I've *got* a donkey.'

'I know that, too. But Jemima's a *real* donkey. We can't use her in our play.'

'Why not?' Emma was caught by the image. Adam would be there in the audience, wouldn't he? How amazing would that be, to see his two children and their pet creating Christmas magic for the whole village? She could take photos and give them a new memory that would always remind them of a joyous moment.

Caitlin was staring at her as if she had lost her mind.

'She's a very good donkey,' Emma continued. 'And Poppy's used to riding her.' From the corner of her eye she noted that Oliver had stopped watching the fish and was now watching them. 'Would she still follow you in a strange place, Ollie? Would you be able to lead her?'

Oliver scowled at her. ''Course I would.'

'They could just come down the centre aisle and then the children could take their place on the stage and someone could take Jemima out the side door.'

'Ohh…' Caitlin was clearly completely captured. 'How would we get her to the hall, though?'

That was a problem. 'It *is* too far to walk,' Emma agreed.

'My brother's girlfriend's aunt runs a donkey sanctuary not far from here,' Caitlin said thoughtfully. 'I wonder if we could borrow a float?'

Poppy was bouncing up and down on her toes. 'Hooray…Jemima's going to be in our play.'

'Hang on,' her teacher warned. 'Don't get too excited. And don't tell anybody else about it. We'll have to get all sorts of permission, like from the hall committee and from your daddy.'

The bright glow of the idea dimmed for Emma. Neither authority was likely to be too enthusiastic about this inspiration but she suspected Adam would be the hardest to convince.

But he was okay with the paper chains now, wasn't he? And the Advent calendars and the holly? Maybe another small push forward would help get him into feeling the goodwill of the season more. When they passed a man selling Christmas trees off the back of a lorry on their way home, Emma stamped on the brakes.

'I think we need a tree,' she said aloud. 'What do you think, kidlets?'

The twins were silent.

'We could put it in the big living room,' Emma suggested. 'And we could make decorations for it. And then your presents can go underneath it on Christmas Eve. Is that what you usually do?'

'We don't have a tree.' Poppy's voice was very small. 'We only go and see the tree by the church and the one in Gran's house.'

A glance in the rear-view mirror revealed an expression on Oliver's face rather like the one that had been on Caitlin's when Emma had suggested adding Jemima to the junior school's play. As if she was completely crazy.

'Maybe that's because Daddy gets too busy at Christmastime. Would you like to have a tree, Poppy?'

Poppy thought about this for a long moment. 'Jeannie has her very own tree.'

'So does Jamie,' Oliver said. 'And Ben and…and *everybody*.'

Emma channelled Catherine McAllister. It was up to her to make Christmas happen for these children, even if the thought of the repercussions of this step were more than a little scary.

'Right, then.' She reached for her wallet. 'Come on. You can help me choose the *best* one.'

'No.'

'But, Daddy…I *want* Jemima to be in our play. *Please*…'

'*No*.' Adam's fork clattered against his plate in the silence that followed the resoundingly negative response.

It was just as well that Emma had waited until dinner was almost finished before broaching the subject of including the largest family pet in the nativity play. Her appetite evaporated in the face of the atmosphere that instantly filled the McAllister kitchen—her favourite room in this grand old house. That single word had somehow created an impenetrable barrier and Adam was clearly angry. Was he even tasting the casserole he was forking into his mouth?

The last of the wonderful meals Catherine had left in the freezer, Emma had noted with some alarm. She would have to cook the evening meals herself from now on.

The children began simply pushing pieces of food around their plates with as little enthusiasm as Emma.

'Eat your dinner,' Adam ordered, 'or there'll be no ice cream.'

'I don't *want* ice cream.' Poppy's voice wobbled. 'I *want...*'

No, Emma begged silently. Don't say it.

'I want Jemima to be in our play.'

Adam dropped his cutlery and his chair scraped back with a screech that made Emma flinch.

'It's the most ridiculous idea I've ever heard,' he snapped. 'And it's *not* going to happen. I don't want to hear another word about it.' The stern glare Poppy was being subjected to was transferred to Oliver. 'From *either* of you.'

Then it was Emma's turn to get the look. 'I expect this was *your* idea in the first place?'

For a heartbeat she felt frightened. It wasn't just about potentially getting fired from a job she was coming to love far more than she'd expected. It was more about the glimpse into what Adam McAllister would be like if he lost control. She was sensing the depth of emotion hidden away in this man for the first time and who knew what might happen if it broke through those rigid, self-imposed constraints?

But then Emma was aware of something she rarely felt. Anger.

She could see that the children really *were* frightened. Sitting there, like small statues, with pale faces and probably holding their breath. Scared that their daddy didn't love them any more because they'd done something bad.

Was it so bad to dream of doing something a bit out of the ordinary? Okay…a lot out of the ordinary, but this was about *Christmas*, wasn't it? About making a little bit of magic?

So she held Adam's angry glare and lifted her chin.

'Yes,' she said clearly. 'It *was* my idea. And Caitlin McMurray loved it. She said she'd talk to the hall committee about getting permission and that she could probably arrange transport to get Jemima into the village for the evening.'

Adam was on his feet now. He crumpled his serviette into a ball and threw it down beside his unfinished plate of food.

'Have you seen the state of the village hall? It's crumbling inside. The floorboards all need replacing. Quite apart from the public-health issues of an animal needing to relieve itself indoors, there would be the danger of the floor giving way. Imagine the panic that would create? Not only could Jemima get injured but so could anybody who was unfortunate enough to be sitting anywhere nearby. Like my *children*. You're suggesting that I allow you to put them in danger for the sake of a school *play*?'

'It's a *Christmas* play.' Emma was not going to let her voice wobble like Poppy's had but it was a close call. 'It's special.'

'*Ach*…' Adam turned and strode towards the door. 'I'm going to find somewhere I can get away from this nonsense. And I don't want to hear anything more about it. From *any* of you.'

Bob followed his master from the kitchen but his head was hanging low. Benji started to follow Bob but then stopped and slowly slunk back beneath the kitchen table.

Emma swallowed a gulp. She reached out with one hand to squeeze Poppy's hand. She would have squeezed

Oliver's too, but he promptly put both his hands in his lap to avoid her touch.

'It's okay,' she told them with as much confidence as she could muster. 'Daddy just needs time to get used to the idea. He's a little bit cross but he'll get over it, you'll see.' She found a smile. 'Why don't we all have some ice cream?'

'We're not allowed,' Oliver informed her. 'We haven't eaten all our vegetables.'

'I'll bet Benji would eat them if we put them in *his* dish.'

The children looked astonished. Was an adult actually suggesting something naughty?

It wasn't the first time that Emma had been struck by how like his father Oliver was. He was deep, this little boy, and there was a sadness in him that shouldn't be there. It made her heart ache.

'Sometimes,' she said softly, 'we all need a cuddle. And having a treat like ice cream—it kind of gives us a cuddle from the inside and makes us feel better. A tummy cuddle.'

Poppy climbed off her chair and onto Emma's lap. She wound her skinny arms around Emma's neck and buried her face on her shoulder. Emma happily gathered the little girl closer and rocked her a little as she cuddled her. She held out her other arm in an invitation for Oliver to join them but he stayed where he was with his head bent as if he was staring at his hands.

They heard the roar from Adam all the way from the living room. Oh...dear Lord...Emma had forgotten the tree they'd installed in there as soon as they'd got home, thanks to the clever stand the Christmas-tree man had sold her along with the spruce the children had declared the best.

They could hear the furious footfalls as he came storming back into the kitchen.

'Whose idea was *that*, as if I couldn't guess?'

It was Emma receiving the full force of the glare this time.

'It has to stop, do you hear me? I won't have it.' Adam didn't have to reach far above his head to grab hold of one of the paper chains. And it didn't take much of a tug to have it break and drift down in pieces.

'We don't do Christmas.' He wasn't shouting but the quiet words were chillingly final. 'Not in this house.'

Poppy burst into tears. Oliver was staring at the falling paper chains and Emma just knew she was going to see this staunch little boy cry for the first time, too. But the sound that came out of his mouth was more like a cry of fear.

'*Daddy…*' His pointing was urgent and Emma turned her head automatically, in time to see the flames from the paper chain that had landed on top of the stove.

With a vehement curse Adam flung himself towards that side of the kitchen. He grabbed a tea towel, put it under the cold tap and then covered the pile of burning paper. It was all over in seconds.

Except that it wasn't over. Both the children were sobbing and this time Oliver had no objection when Emma gathered him under her free arm and took both children out of the kitchen and away from their father.

They were still sobbing by the time she'd got them bathed and into bed. Poppy fell asleep almost instantly, totally worn out by her misery. When Emma went back to check on Oliver again, she found he was also asleep—a tight ball of child entirely covered by bedding, with only his nose poking out. She bent and kissed the cold little nose.

'It'll be okay,' she whispered, just in case he wasn't really asleep. 'I promise.'

She would just have to make it okay, she decided as

she forced herself to go back downstairs instead of going to hide in her room, which was what she would have preferred.

Somehow she would have to put things right.

Adam didn't hear Emma coming down the stairs but he knew she was on her way by the subtle change in the dogs. The way they pricked their ears and Benji's tail made an almost apologetic sweep of the tiles that he couldn't suppress.

He didn't look up, however, so he was still sitting there at the table with his forehead resting on one hand and a whisky glass encircled by the other as she came into the kitchen. He hadn't cleaned up the mess of charred paper yet and all he'd done with the plates of half-eaten food had been to push them to one side to make room for the whisky decanter and two glasses.

Two glasses?

Well…he had to start somewhere, didn't he?

'I'm sorry.' It was harder than he'd expected to get the words out. A shame it made it sound like he didn't really mean it but he did. He was absolutely appalled at how he'd behaved. And in front of the *children*…

He shoved the empty glass towards the closest chair at his end of the table. 'Help yourself.'

She probably didn't even drink whisky, he thought, as he remembered her refusal the other night. The night when he'd had the impression that she understood exactly how he was feeling.

Could he make her understand *this*?

The fact that she sat down in the chair and then reached to pull the stopper out of the decanter gave him a glimmer of hope. At least she was prepared to listen. He waited until he'd heard her pour herself a dram and then the clink of the stopper going back. He still couldn't look up to meet her gaze, however.

'It was the tree,' he said. 'It was in the same place. *Exactly the* same place.'

There. He'd said it. Only maybe it wasn't enough because all he got back was an expectant silence. He risked a glance up from the amber liquid he was swirling in the bottom of his glass.

Blue eyes, she had. With a hint of grey, like the sea when there was a storm on the horizon. Right now they looked as big as oceans, too. She looked as though she could already see all she needed to know but she wanted to hear the words as well.

Adam took a sip of the warmed whisky and felt the fire trickle down his gullet.

'The tree was right there beside the fire,' he said finally. 'When I got back home on Christmas Eve. It was covered with all its decorations and the lights were still flashing as though nothing had happened. All the presents were underneath, waiting for the bairns in the morning.'

Still Emma said nothing.

'I'd had to go all the way to Edinburgh,' Adam continued. 'To identify Tania's body. I'd been thinking all the way that she would be terribly burned and it would be the worst thing I'd ever seen but there wasn't a mark on her, apart from the soot in her hair and around her nose and mouth.'

It had still been the worst thing he'd ever had to deal with, though. The shock of seeing his dead wife had been terrible enough. To be told she hadn't been alone in her bed had been an additional blow he hadn't been able to handle.

The police had been so understanding. Apologetic, really, at having to deliver the extra blow. Sympathetic. It could be kept quiet, if that's what he would prefer.

Of course he would. Nobody would ever know. Emma

certainly didn't need to know, even though it was tempting to tell her, thanks to the look of appalled empathy in her eyes. Did he want her to really understand? To feel… sorry for him?

No.

He cleared his throat. 'She'd died from the smoke inhalation, not the flames.'

Flames. How shocking had it been to see that paper chain erupt? The children must have been terrified and it was all because he hadn't known what to do with that dreadful surge of feelings that had been unbearable.

'It was very late by the time I got back. My mother was asleep upstairs with the children and it was the early hours of Christmas Day. The day I would have to tell my bairns that their mummy wasn't coming home.'

'I'm so sorry, Adam.' The words were a whisper and when he looked up again there were tears rolling down the side of Emma's nose.

'It's not your fault.' He wanted to reach out and catch one of those tears with his thumb and wipe it away. He wanted to go upstairs and kiss his children and tell them he was sorry and that they would never see him like that again. He would do that. Soon. Even if they were asleep. And then he'd do it again tomorrow.

'None of this is your fault,' he told Emma. 'It's me.'

'It's me who's tried to force you to bring Christmas into the house. I'm so sorry. For your loss and for the hurt I've caused. I was thinking about the children and *their* Christmas and I lost sight of how much it might hurt you.'

Emma was clearly not a practised whisky drinker. She took a gulp that made her cough and splutter and Adam had to resist the urge to pat her on the back.

To smile even.

'I'll get rid of everything,' she offered. 'I'll explain to

the children that you're not ready to celebrate Christmas yet. That we can go and see the tree in the village and we don't need to have one in the house. We can take the paper chains to school and I'm sure Caitlin will let us put them up in the classroom. And I'll—'

Adam reached out and put his hand over hers. Only because she wasn't looking at him and he wanted her to stop talking.

It worked. Emma went very still but Adam didn't take his hand away from hers. It felt tiny and soft and warm under his and he liked it.

'No,' he said softly. 'What you can do is show me how to make a paper chain. I want to fix this one so it's right for when the children come down in the morning. And to-morrow I'll go up into the attic and find the box of decorations for the tree.'

'Oh…' There was a sparkle in those blue-grey eyes that looked like more than the remnants of tears. And her hand moved under his. Turned and twisted so that her fingers were grasping his palm. *Squeezing* it. 'Really? You'll let us have a real Christmas? In the *house*?'

'Aye.' It was impossible not to catch a little bit of that childlike enthusiasm. The sheer joy that was breaking through. 'Three years of grief is enough, I'm thinking. We'll do this for the children.'

'Oh…' Emma jumped to her feet and Adam found himself standing up, too. Had he guessed that she would stand on tiptoe and throw her arms around him?

'*Thank* you, Adam. Thank you *so* much…'

'I'll talk to the hall committee too, about Jemima being in the play. I still think it's a bit daft but if they know it's for the children—for the first real Christmas they're going to celebrate since their mother died—they might just come on board.'

She was beaming up at him. Impossible not to smile back. She was so loving, this gypsy waif of a woman. So full of joy.

It was he who should be thanking her. He knew that but somehow the words wouldn't form themselves. Instead, he felt his arms go around her. How long had it been since he'd felt the soft curves of a woman like this?

Three years—that's how long. He'd actually forgotten how *good* it could feel.

He smiled back at her and she stretched up even more and kissed him on the cheek. Except that he moved his head somehow and it was the corner of his mouth that her lips brushed.

And, heaven help him, for a heartbeat he wanted her to do it again. To kiss him.

And not on his cheek.

Maybe Emma had sensed the longing. She sprang away from him. 'I'll get the sticky paper,' she said. 'There's plenty left.'

Oh...*help*...

She hadn't intended to kiss Adam at all and she *certainly* hadn't been aiming anywhere near his mouth, but he'd moved somehow and her lips had been aware of exactly where they'd landed, albeit so briefly.

She'd dismissed the tingle that had run right through her body as embarrassment but it wasn't going away as they sat cutting strips of coloured paper. It was more than embarrassment at being so inappropriate, wasn't it? And hadn't the lines between employer and employee been blurred beyond recognition by Adam talking about something so personal?

So incredibly *sad*...

Emma could understand completely how Adam felt

about celebrating Christmas now and yet he was prepared to put his own feelings aside for the sake of the children.

How brave was that?

She stole a glance at the man sitting at the table with her. Such a serious face. And skilful hands that could probably do all sorts of incredibly intricate medical procedures but were currently being used with intense concentration to manipulate strips of rainbow-coloured paper. It was ridiculous but she actually felt…*proud* of Adam? For putting his children first. For being staunch.

And that seemed to intensify the lingering tingle. Emma needed to distract herself before she said or did something else that might overstep a boundary that was becoming more difficult to identify. She looked at what Adam was doing. He had made two loops. Separate loops.

'Once you've made one loop, you need to thread the next strip through before you stick it into a loop. That's how they join up. Like this…see?'

'Oh…aye…' Adam made a face. 'I was distracted by the taste. I might need another wee dram to wash it away soon.'

He looked happier when he had three and then four loops joined together. 'I can see why the children enjoyed doing this. It's quite satisfying, isn't it?'

Emma nodded, smiling as she remembered how much the twins had loved the activity. 'Poppy and Ollie are easy to entertain,' she told him. 'They're gorgeous children.'

'You manage them very well. For someone who's never been a nanny, you're doing a good job, Emma.'

It felt like high praise. Especially when it came with a smile and a softening of those dark eyes. Yes…the lines of those boundaries had definitely been blurred. Where exactly did they stop now?

Inexplicably, that silent query kicked the tingle up by

several notches. In a kind of backwards trickle that went through her limbs and pooled somewhere deep inside.

'How do you know how to get on so well with kids? You said you didn't have any younger brothers or sisters, didn't you?'

She nodded again. 'I did have a kind of older brother, though. Jack.'

'A kind of brother?'

'He was the son of my parents' best friends. A lot older than me but we got on really well. Still do. He's...important in my life.'

That was an understatement but Adam had obviously picked up on the vibe.

'Your boyfriend?'

'Heavens, no...' Emma almost smiled at the question but there was something in Adam's tone that she couldn't place. Did he *want* her to have a boyfriend? So that those boundaries were clearly flagged? What would happen when he knew the truth?

'I love Jack dearly,' she said quietly, 'but definitely in the brother category. And he's happily married now with his first baby on the way. No...he's even more special now because he became a doctor and then a specialist in oncology. He kept Mum going for a lot longer than she might have had otherwise and she had a good quality of life until...the end.'

And he'd been her primary physician ever since her own diagnosis. How many people were lucky enough to get a doctor who cared so much? Who was so determined to succeed?

'How long ago did you lose your mother?'

'Just last year.' Emma met his sympathetic gaze. The boundary lines were totally invisible now. It felt like she was sitting here talking to a friend, not her employer. 'And

I miss her terribly. You're very lucky to have your mum as part of your life.'

'I know. But she does too much. It's not fair…' For a heartbeat, as Adam held her gaze, it seemed like he was going to say something else. About his mother? About *her*?

Something that might reveal he was feeling the extraordinary connection that had Emma slightly stunned?

No. Emma couldn't tell if it was relief or disappointment that coursed through her as Adam frowned and looked away. Normal service was being resumed. Maybe a breathing space was a good idea. For both of them. Or maybe she'd just been imagining that connection.

He held up his paper chain.

'Will this be long enough, do you think? When it's joined to yours?'

By the time breakfast was ready the next day, the paper chains were back in place as though nothing had happened last night.

Poppy and Oliver had bounced back to normal in the delightful way children could. Not only was Adam apparently forgiven for his outburst, the twins were impressed that he had fixed the paper chain himself.

'All by yourself?' Poppy asked.

'Emma showed me what to do.'

Emma looked up from where she was spooning porridge into bowls and grinned at him. 'I expect you could have worked it out all by yourself,' she said generously. 'Coffee?'

'Please.' It made him feel good to remember their time together last night. Talking about things he would never normally share. Feeling as if he was in the company of someone he could talk to about anything at all. Adam began to smile back at her but he was aware of the intense scrutiny of the children so he smiled at them instead.

'It makes your mouth taste funny after a while, doesn't it? Licking the sticky paper?'

'Aye…' Oliver nodded solemnly as he climbed onto his chair. 'It does at that.'

Adam's mouth twitched into a wider smile at the adult turn of phrase from his small son but then it faded as he caught the glance slanted in his direction as Oliver reached for his glass of milk. There was a hint of wariness in those brown eyes that were so like his own. Ollie was on his best behaviour, wasn't he? Just in case…

And that hurt. How often had his children tiptoed around him? he wondered. To stop him being cross.

Or sad.

The resolution to put the years of mourning behind this family and move forward had seemed more of a mountain to climb when he'd woken this morning after a somewhat disturbing dream that had included the new nanny but Adam had gathered it back and shored it up.

Things *were* going to change around here.

And Christmas was the perfect time to start.

'Tonight,' he told his children, 'when I get home from work, we're going to have an expedition.'

'What's an exposition?' Poppy looked at the bowl Emma put in front of her. 'I don't like porridge.' She frowned. 'It's *icky.*'

'Not when you put a little bit of cream and some brown sugar on it. Here, I'll help you.'

'An expedition is an adventure,' Adam told his daughter. 'And when I get home, we'll get the ladder out and go up into the attic.'

Oliver stopped making roads through his porridge with his spoon. 'The *attic*? Where the ghost is?'

'There's no such thing as ghosts,' Adam said firmly. 'It's where the box of Christmas decorations is. We're going to find it and then decorate your tree.'

Poppy's gasp was one of pure excitement. She had to climb off her chair, onto her father's lap, throw her arms around his neck and plant a kiss—sticky with brown sugar—in the middle of his cheek.

The dogs caught the excitement. Benji barked and chased his tail over by the fire and staid old Bob's tail was waving like a flag. Even studious little Oliver was grinning widely.

Adam could almost taste the sweetness of the sugary kiss Poppy had bestowed but when she returned to her own chair he looked across to where Emma was sitting with her own bowl of porridge. He might have expected to see her beaming at him with that infectious joy she had but, instead, her smile was poignant and there was a sparkle in her eyes that reminded him of when they had been full of tears.

She knew how much of an effort he was making here. That things were going to change and that this was going to be the best Christmas he could manage for the twins.

The memory of that butterfly's-wing touch of Emma's lips on the corner of his mouth came flooding back. And that peculiar moment when he'd caught her gaze after she talked about her mother and he'd had the disconcerting notion that he was actually falling into those blue pools. And that merged into a remnant of his dream that he couldn't quite catch and probably didn't want to anyway, but *something* was hanging in the air between him and Emma.

Yes. Things were changing. Had he thrown a pebble into a still pond and the ripples were only just beginning?

That was disturbing. Adam fed his crust to the dogs and drained the last of his coffee.

'Time for me to go to work,' he announced gruffly, careful to avoid any more eye contact with Emma that might add to the alarming impression that he might have started something that could get completely out of control.

'You won't forget, will you, Dad?'

'What's that, Ollie?'

'About the adventure. In the attic.'

'No, son.' He ruffled Oliver's hair. 'I won't forget. I promise.'

He kissed Poppy and nodded farewell to Emma. And it only took that microsecond of a look to realise that there were other things he wasn't about to forget either.

However much he wished he could.

CHAPTER SIX

HE'D BEEN WRONG about the ghost in the attic.

Adam realised that the instant he stepped through the hole in the ceiling, even before he turned to help first Oliver and then Poppy to climb off the steep set of stairs cleverly concealed behind a door that had been locked for years.

The light switch he flicked made several bulbs glow but the light was inadequate for the huge space. Despite the shadows, however, his gaze went straight towards that long rack of dresses in the far corner where the roofline sloped sharply towards the small latticed windows. And the stacks of boxes beside it, full of other clothing and shoes and handbags. He could even make out the jewellery case sitting on top.

They represented what had attracted him to Tania in the first place. The beauty. The glamour. In retrospect he was ashamed of how shallow it was to judge people on their outward appearance like that. Look at how he'd judged Emma in her oversized clothes with her musical accessory as a refugee from the sixties. If fate hadn't stepped in and made it imperative that he give her a chance, he might never have discovered what an astonishing person lay beneath that appearance.

And fate had been responsible for discovering the real

reason for more and more of those 'shopping' trips that Tania had needed to keep her happy. Had she even worn half those clothes or had they only ever been a mask for her infidelity?

The presence of Tania's ghost was all he was aware of by the time Emma's head appeared through the hole.

'Oof... I feel like I'm climbing a mountain.'

The steps were certainly steep but shouldn't have been enough to make a young woman like Emma seem out of breath. Adam could feel his frown deepening as he automatically held out his hand to assist her. For a moment he thought she might refuse the offer but then he felt his hand grasped firmly as she climbed the last of the steps.

Like the children, Emma's eyes widened as she looked around. 'Oh, *wow*... This is a *real* attic. Full of *treasure*.'

She was grinning at Adam now and she still hadn't let go of his hand. He could feel the connection and it was warm and as alive as the sparkle in her eyes.

She'd never be able to cover up a lie, would she? Not with the way her emotions played over her face like this. The idea that she might need to lie felt ridiculous. The conviction that Emma would never be unfaithful to a man she loved came from nowhere.

So did the unexpected pang of something that felt like envy. Letting go of her hand didn't entirely dispel the disturbing sensation. Whoever it was, he would be a very lucky man.

'Ohh...' The gasp from Poppy was full of wonder. 'Look, Emma... It's a *pram*.'

She ran towards the part of the attic on the opposite side from where Tania's effects had been stored. Alongside an antique pram that had probably carried his grandmother and the double model that had been for the twins much more recently, was a smaller cane one. The one that had caught Poppy's eye had been made for small girls to carry dolls in. Adam had completely forgotten it was up here.

'Can I play with it, Daddy? *Please*?'

'Of course you can, chicken. We'll take it downstairs and clean all the dust off. I think it might have been Gran's when she was a little girl like you.'

Maybe it was the delight on Poppy's face or the warmth he could still feel from Emma's hand but the presence of Tania's ghost was receding. Being pushed into the past where it belonged by not only being in the present but thinking about the immediate future when they would all be safely downstairs and he could lock the old door again.

Poppy was squeaking with pleasure as she manoeuvred the cane pram out from behind the bigger wheels of the others. Oliver was not far away from her, peering into a tin trunk in front of a pile of old leather suitcases. His quietness wasn't unusual but the intent body language was unmistakeable.

'What have you found, Ollie?'

'I think it's a…*train*.'

It had been some time since he'd let go of Emma's hand. Odd that he still could feel the absence of it so strongly. Maybe moving further away from her would help. Adam walked towards his son.

'It *is* a train. An old wind-up one.' He lifted the heavy, metal engine from the trunk to hand to Oliver and then reached to pick up something else. 'These are the tracks that you can clip together. I used to play with it when I was your age, Ollie. And my father played with it when *he* was a little boy. I'm pretty sure he got it for a Christmas present one year.'

Oliver's face was solemn. 'That's what I'd like for *my* Christmas present.'

'You can't buy these now.' Emma had come over to

look as well. 'They're very old and very special. Antiques. Adam, this is extraordinary. Is that a *harp* over there?'

'Aye.' There was a dusty, old cello keeping it company. Music had been in his family for generations. When had it stopped so completely? When his desire to make it had died along with the trauma of Tania's death?

Oliver was crouching beside the tin trunk with the train engine cradled in his arms.

Adam crouched down beside him. 'You don't have to wait till Christmas, Ollie. We'll take this downstairs, too, and you can play with it whenever you want.'

Oliver looked as though he couldn't believe his luck. As if something truly magic had just happened, and something squeezed inside Adam's chest. How easy it was to make children happy but he had never given a thought to the abandoned toys up here. He would never have thought of even unlocking that door if he hadn't remembered the Christmas decorations.

And he wouldn't have considered retrieving those if it hadn't been for Emma pushing him towards celebrating Christmas again.

Right now Emma was plucking the strings of the old harp, sending dust motes flying into the dim light in the attic. And she was singing...just softly. More of a hum really—as though she was in her own world and making music came as naturally as breathing.

Poppy had left the cane pram. She had a sad old teddy bear with an almost severed arm dangling from one hand and she was skipping through the gaps towards *that* corner.

Adam got to his feet hurriedly. 'Let's find those decorations,' he said. 'And get downstairs. I can hear Benji crying in the kitchen.'

But it was too late. Poppy had found the rack of dresses and her cry of delight made Emma stop playing with the harp and look up. Adam tried to distract them. He'd had an idea of where the boxes of decorations were and he flipped one open and held up a handful of tinsel and then a huge silver star.

'Here we are. Look at this star. Shall we put it on top of our tree?'

'Daddy…are these *Mummy's* dresses?'

The shocked look on Emma's face said it all. The ghost was here again. The tug of nostalgia and the pleasure in finding unexpected gifts for his children vanished. Now he could feel the pain of loss yet again. The *guilt*. The burden of the lie that kept the mother of his children as a perfect memory.

'It's a *blue* dress. Emma, look. You're going to make me a blue dress for when I'm Mary in the play, aren't you?'

'Um…yeah…' Emma had started to go towards Poppy but she'd stopped right beside Adam and she gave him an uncertain glance. 'Come on, sweetheart. We need to go downstairs. It's nearly teatime.'

But Poppy wouldn't let go of the folds of the shimmery, blue dress. 'Why are Mummy's clothes here, Daddy?'

Adam had to clear his throat. 'I…' What could he say? He'd had to get them out of sight and this had seemed the quickest and easiest solution? 'Maybe I thought you'd want them one day, Poppy.'

He hoped she wouldn't, he realised suddenly. He didn't want his daughter growing up to be consumed with keeping up appearances. Better that she didn't care. That she was happy to wear baggy jumpers and peculiar, bright hats and could shine with an inner joy instead. Like Emma.

'I want this one *now*, Daddy. For the play.'

'It wouldn't fit you.'

'Emma could make it fit.'

'Could you?' Adam caught Emma's gaze again.

She still looked uncertain but nodded. 'I guess so... but...'

'That's settled, then.' Adam wanted to get out of there. As quickly as possible. 'You and Ollie go downstairs with Emma and I'll bring the dress down with the other things.'

Emma helped the children down the steps but then her head appeared again.

'You don't have to do this,' she said quietly. 'I can explain to Poppy. We can find some fabric to make her dress.'

'They're only clothes,' Adam growled. He shoved the rolled-up dress towards her. 'This one was never even worn—it's still got its label on it. They're only *clothes*,' he repeated, turning away to pick up a box. 'I should never have kept them.'

But Emma was still there when he went to put the box down close to the steps. 'You can still change your mind later.'

'I won't.'

'You might.' There was a curve to Emma's lips that suggested sympathy but she wasn't looking at his face. She was staring at the hand he had curled around the corner of the box of decorations. His left hand.

The one that still carried his wedding ring.

And then Emma was gone and he heard Poppy's excited voice fading as she went along the hallway, telling Emma that she wanted the dress to be really long so that it floated on the ground.

It took time to get the treasures down the steps, especially when he had to unpack half the tin trunk because it was so heavy. Even in the inadequate light every movement seemed to create a glint on that gold band around his finger—an accessory he never normally noticed at all.

Why *was* he still wearing his wedding ring? Because

everybody assumed that he kept it on as a tribute to a perfect marriage and they would have noticed the moment he'd removed it? A perfect marriage? Good grief… In the short time Emma had been here, it felt like she'd been more of a mother to his children than Tania had been. Guilt nipped on the heels of that admission. It wasn't something he'd ever needed to acknowledge—not when his mother had always been there to fill in the gaps that his nannies couldn't.

Or did he still wear the ring because he wanted to punish himself? To keep a permanent reminder of his failure as a husband in clear view?

It was, after all, *his* fault that his children were growing up without their mother, wasn't it? Had he been too absorbed in his work or too besotted with his babies to give Tania what she needed?

The ring had served its purpose even if he'd never articulated what that was. There had been times when the truth had been like acid, eating away at him, and he'd been desperate to tell someone. His mother or his sister perhaps. And then he'd touch the back of the ring with his thumb and would know that he couldn't.

Even the remote possibility that his children could learn the truth about their mother and be hurt by it was enough. This was a burden he had to carry alone. For ever.

He might have been wrong about there being no ghost in the attic but he'd been right when he'd worried about the ripple effect of things changing.

Unusually, he could actually *feel* that ring on his finger, without touching it with his thumb, late that night as he climbed the stairs to go to bed. They hadn't ended up decorating the tree after dinner because he'd spent the time before the children went to bed setting up the clockwork train set for Oliver, and Emma had been busy helping Poppy clean the cane pram. And when they'd looked into the box the children had been a little disappointed by the ornaments.

'They're all the same colour,' Poppy had pointed out. 'They're all *silver*.'

Of course they were. Everything Tania had done could have been photographed for a home and garden magazine, including the silver perfection of the family Christmas tree.

'I could get some special paint,' Emma had offered. 'And we could make them all sorts of colours…if that's all right with Daddy.'

Of course it was all right. How did she always seem to find an answer to everything that would make things better?

Would she have an answer to what he should do about the ring that seemed to be strangling his finger?

He could hear the soft sound of her singing again and, as had become a habit, he stopped before turning towards the other hallway and listened for a minute. The song was becoming hauntingly familiar, even though he was sure he'd never heard it before Emma had come into the house.

Was she sitting on her bed, with her guitar cradled on her lap and her head bent as she sang quietly? Did she have the fire going perhaps, with the light of the flames bringing out the flecks of red-gold he'd noticed in her hair sometimes?

The urge to find out was powerful. He could find an excuse to tap on her door, couldn't he? To reassure her that the blue dress meant nothing perhaps, and that she was more than welcome to cut it up to make Poppy's costume?

Any excuse would do, if it meant he could be close to her for an extra minute or two.

Because he was starting to feel lonely when he wasn't?

With a mental shake Adam stepped firmly towards his own room. She wasn't the first nanny his children had had and she probably wouldn't be the last. It was just as well this was a temporary position, though, because he'd never felt this way about any of the women who'd come to live here and look after his children before.

About any women he'd met in the last few years, come to that.

Maybe it was part of the ripple effect. The step forward. Something had been unlocked when he'd agreed that three years of grief was more than enough. Perhaps his body was following his heart and finally waking up again.

Three years of being celibate wasn't natural for anyone. It didn't mean that he had to fall for someone who happened to be in the near vicinity. It didn't mean he had to fall for anyone.

No. The last time that had happened had ended up almost ruining his life. He wasn't going to let it happen again.

Ever.

The solution, Adam decided over the next few days, was to focus on his work.

His priority in life was his children, of course, but work came a close second. It had been his father, the first Dr McAllister, who'd built up this small general practice. Without it, the villagers would have to travel fifteen miles or so to the nearest town and a lot of them would find that difficult enough to make their health care precarious, especially in the middle of a harsh Scottish winter.

People like old Mrs Robertson, who needed dressings changed on her diabetic ulcers every couple of days and was on the list for this afternoon's house calls. And Joan McClintock, who had a phobia about getting into any vehicles smaller than a bus and was only happy when things were within walking distance. She was in the waiting room again this morning, as his somewhat disconcerting working week drew to a close.

At least here Adam could stop thinking about the Christmas tree in his living room sporting a rainbow of brightly painted balls that had only been the starting point for the hand-made decorations that Emma seemed to have unlimited inspiration about. Like the gingerbread stars she had baked last night and the children had helped to decorate with brightly coloured sweets.

It was probably just as well that the gingerbread was destined to be only decorative if Emma's baking skills were on a par with her cooking. The meals this week had been a fair step down from what his mother had left in the freezer. Not that the children had complained about the rather burnt sausages and that peculiar shepherd's pie. Everything Emma did was wonderful in Poppy's eyes and Oliver wasn't allowed to go and play with the clockwork train until he'd finished his dinner so even the carrots were disappearing in record time these days.

Adam found himself smiling as he walked through the waiting room. Miss McClintock looked surprised but nodded back at him. Old Jock, who was sitting in the corner, disappeared further under the brim of his cap. The smile faded. Old Jock—the farmer who owned the land behind his where the skating pond was located—was as tough as old boots. What was he doing in here, waiting to see the doctor?

And had he really thought that work was the solution to forgetting about the ripples disrupting his personal life?

It didn't help that Caitlin McMurray, the schoolteacher, came rushing in with a wailing small child even before he could call Joan McClintock into the consulting room.

'It's Ben,' she said. 'He jammed his finger in the art cupboard.'

'Come straight in,' Adam told her. 'Eileen, could you call Ben's mother, please, and get her to come in?'

'I can stay with him for a bit.' Caitlin had to raise her voice over the crying. 'Emma's practising carols with the children and the senior teacher's keeping an eye on everything.'

Adam eyed the handkerchief tied around Ben's finger. There was blood seeping through the makeshift dressing.

'Let's have a look at this finger, young man.'

'No-o-o... It's going to hurt.'

Distraction was needed. 'Did our Oliver tell you about the train he found in our attic?'

'Aye...but we didn't believe him.' Ben sniffed loudly. 'He said it's got a tunnel and a bridge even.'

'Well, it's true. It's a bonny wee train. I played with it when I was a wee boy, too.' Adam had the finger exposed now. A bit squashed but there were no bones broken. The pain was coming from the blood accumulating under the nail and that could be swiftly fixed with a heated needle.

'And he says he's bringing a donkey to the Christmas play.'

Adam raised his gaze to Caitlin's. 'Did the committee agree, then?'

'Aye. And that's not all. Have you heard about the recording?'

'What recording?'

'Moira Findlay heard about the children singing the carols and she came to listen. She says that Emma's got the voice of an angel and she's ne'er heard small children singing sae well. That's when we got the *idea*.'

'Oh?' Adam struck a match to get the end of a sterile needle hot enough. Ben was watching suspiciously.

'We're going to make a CD of the carols. To sell and raise funds to help fix the village hall. Or get a new piano for the school. Maybe both. She's amazing, isn't she, Dr McAllister?'

'It does sound like a grand idea. Moira's a clever woman.'

'Not Moira…' Caitlin laughed. 'I mean Emma. How lucky are we that she came to be the twins' nanny?'

'Look at that, Ben… Out the window… Was that a… *reindeer*?'

The split second it took for Ben to realise he'd been duped was enough to get near his nail with the needle and release the pressure. A single, outraged wail and then Ben stared at his finger and blinked in surprise.

'Not so sore now?' Adam swabbed it gently with some disinfectant. 'We'll put a nice big bandage on it and you can get back to singing your carols.'

With Emma.

'I hear she sings like an angel,' Joan McClintock informed him minutes later. 'Eileen says she might be joining the choir.'

'I don't know that she'll have time for that,' Adam said. 'And she's only here until my mother gets back from Canada.'

'Och, well…we'll see about that, then, won't we?' The nod was knowing.

'Aye. We will.' Adam reached for the blood-pressure cuff. 'Now, let's see if that blood pressure's come down a wee bit. Are you still getting the giddy spells?'

Even Old Jock had something to say about Emma when it came to his turn.

'I'm losing my puff,' he told Adam. 'And it's no' helping with the pipes. Yon lassie o' yours saw me sittin' down after I was playin' in by the tree, like I always do at Christmastime. She tol' me to come and see you.'

'I'll have a listen to your chest,' Adam said. 'Your dad

had problems with his heart, didn't he? We might do a test on that, too.'

'Aye.' Jock took his cap off. 'You do what you need to, lad. That lassie said you'd find out what was ailin' me.'

How could a complete stranger weave herself into the lives of other people so quickly? It seemed like the whole village was being touched by Emma's arrival in Braeburn. Maybe she didn't have a gypsy streak after all, because the sort of magic she was creating was more like that of a fairy.

A Christmas fairy.

And magic wasn't the only thing she was weaving. On Saturday afternoon, when it had stopped raining, they had taken Jemima down into the orchard so that Oliver could practise leading her, with Poppy riding. Not only had their little donkey proved herself very co-operative, Emma had spotted the greenery amongst the bare branches of an old apple tree.

'Is that mistletoe? *Real* mistletoe?'

'Aye. Looks like it.'

'Can we pick it?' Emma had asked. 'For Christmas?'

'It's poisonous,' Adam had told her. 'Causes gastrointestinal and cardiovascular problems.'

'We won't *eat* it, silly.' Emma had laughed. 'I'm going to make a wreath.'

So here she was, sitting at the kitchen table under all the paper chains, after the children were in bed, cutting sprigs of the mistletoe and weaving them around a circle she'd made with some wire she'd unearthed out in the barn. Adam had poured himself a wee dram to finish the day with and he paused to watch what she was doing.

'Where did it come from?' she asked. 'Do you know? The tradition of kissing under the mistletoe, that is.'

Kissing…

Adam stared down at Emma's deft hands weaving the sprigs into place. And at the back of her head, where the light was creating those copper glints in her curls. He took a mouthful of his whisky.

'It's very old,' he said. 'I've heard that it got hung somewhere and the young men had the privilege of kissing the girls underneath it, but every time they did they had to pick one of the berries, and when the berries had all been picked, the privilege ceased.'

Emma held up the half-finished wreath with its clusters of waxy white berries. 'It's got a lot of them,' she said, tilting her head to smile up at Adam.

That did it. The magic was too strong to resist. Adam put his glass down and then reached out and plucked one of the tiny berries from the wreath.

Emma's eyes widened. 'You can't do that,' she objected. 'You haven't kissed a girl.'

Adam didn't say anything. He just leaned down until there was no mistaking his intention.

And Emma didn't turn her face away. If anything, she tilted her chin so that her lips parted, and for a heartbeat—and then two—she held his gaze.

There was surprise in those blue eyes. She hadn't expected this but, then, neither had Adam. And she could feel the magic, too—he was sure of that, because there was a kind of wonder in her eyes as well.

Joy was always lurking there, he suspected, but this was an invitation to share it. An invitation no man could resist.

The moment his lips touched Emma's, the tiny white berry fell from his fingers and rolled somewhere under the table. Adam wasn't aware of dropping it. He was aware of nothing but the softness of Emma's lips and the silky feel of her curls as he cupped her head in his hand. And then he was aware of a desire for more than this kiss. A fierce shaft of desire that came from nowhere and with more force than he'd ever felt in his life.

He had to break the contact. Step back. Wonder how on earth he was going to deal with what had just happened when his senses were still reeling.

Emma's eyes were closed. He liked it that she'd closed her eyes. And then she sighed happily and smiled. There was no embarrassment in her eyes when she opened them. No expectation that any explanation or apology was needed.

'There you go,' she said softly. 'That's where it came from, I guess. Mistletoe is magical. I'd better finish this and hang it somewhere safe.'

'Aye.' Adam drained the rest of his whisky and took the glass to the sink.

What did she mean by 'safe'? Somewhere he couldn't find it or somewhere he *could*?

He hoped she wanted to put it somewhere he could find it.

There were a lot of berries left on those twigs.

CHAPTER SEVEN

FOR THE FIRST time in her life Emma Sinclair understood why they called it 'falling' in love.

Because she could feel that her balance was teetering. That there was a chasm very nearby that she couldn't afford to fall into. She could get hurt.

Or hurt someone else.

Poppy and Oliver perhaps?

Or Adam?

Her hands stilled in their task of hemming, sinking to end up in the folds of the silky blue dress puddled in her lap, as she stared through the window. It was snowing, she realised with a childish bubble of excitement.

And then she remembered the kiss yet again and the bubble exploded into something decidedly more adult and compelling.

Desire—pure and simple.

Except it wasn't that simple, was it? Oh, she'd noticed how good looking Adam McAllister was in the first moments of meeting him but she'd been a little afraid of him, too, if she was honest. The fierceness of him. The gruffness that came across as anger. The hidden depths that she'd glimpsed on that awful night when he'd ripped down the paper chains and caused the fire. And now she could add the capacity for passion into what this man was keeping hidden because she'd felt it in the touch of his lips.

She'd glimpsed the softer side to him as well, in the love he had for his children and the bond he had with his dogs. Pulling her gaze away from the softly drifting snowflakes, Emma glanced towards the fire. Benji lay on his back like a puppy, his speckled belly exposed, but Bob had his nose on his paws and he was watching Emma. She could swear that the old dog knew exactly what she was thinking and that the liquid gaze was encouraging.

He's worth loving, it seemed to say. *You won't be sorry.*

'But I can't, Bob.' Emma actually spoke aloud. 'I'm only here for a little bit longer.'

Time didn't matter to dogs, though, did it? They took their joy as it appeared, with no questions asked. Even if they were old or sick, they could still be in the moment and experience that joy a hundred per cent.

People could learn a lot from dogs. Especially people who could be facing a terminal illness?

What if she let herself fall for Adam—even if it was only for a blink in time? It wasn't just for the small McAllister family that she'd resolved to make this the best-ever Christmas for, was it?

If it was going to be *her* last Christmas, shouldn't she make it the best ever one for herself, too?

'It's been *such* a long time, Bob,' she whispered.

Such a long time since she had been loved…

Dear Lord, but it was tempting.

Bob's ears were pricked now. He looked like he was asking her a question and Emma found herself smiling at the dog. No—she didn't *have* to disappear right after Christmas, when Catherine McAllister returned, did she? Adam was still going to need a nanny and it wasn't as if she had another job prospect lined up. She didn't need to work at all, in actual fact, because the small inheritance from her mother would be enough for quite some time.

But she couldn't offer Adam anything real. She didn't do that kind of commitment. How could she, when she couldn't offer any guarantee of permanence? When, instead, she could be sentencing someone to share things no one would choose to share.

And he wouldn't want it anyway, would he? The blue of the fabric in her lap seemed to glow more brightly. How could anyone compete with the ghost of the perfect wife and mother? The love of his life that had been tragically ripped away from him and their beloved children?

The recently changed ring tone on her phone was for Christmas and Bob got to his feet as 'Jingle Bells' began. It was getting louder by the time Emma found the phone beneath the shimmery blue fabric.

'It'll be Sharon, I expect,' she said, as Bob gave her hand a helpful nudge.

Except it wasn't.

'*Jack…*' It was such a surprise to hear from him. A shock even, because it pulled her back instantly to somewhere she'd managed to distract herself from completely in the last couple of weeks.

'Hey, Emma. How's it going up there in the wilds of Scotland?'

'It's snowing,' she told him happily. 'And it's just gorgeous. What's it like in London?'

'Cold and grey. No snow. That's why I thought I'd pop up for a visit next week.'

'What?' Emma blinked. The relationship was a complicated mix sometimes and she wasn't sure if he was wearing his 'close friend' or 'oncologist' hat right now. '*Why*?'

'I'm meeting with an oncology guru who happens to be over from the States, tracing his family tree. I must have told you about that international research project we're both involved in. Jenny says I bore everyone with it.' He chuckled, unrepentant. 'Anyway, I said I'd fly up for the day and then I had this idea and got hold of a mate who works in the infirmary in Edinburgh. I pulled a few strings but... how would you feel about having your BMT and maybe getting the results by Christmas?'

'Oh...' Emma had to swallow hard. The unpleasant prospect of having a bone-marrow aspiration done for testing had been off her agenda until she got back to London. 'I'm...not sure how I feel about that, Jack. I...' Oh, help. She could hear the wobble in her voice that threatened tears. 'I was trying to forget about it, you know? To make this Christmas really special, in case...in case...'

'I know.' There was a short silence and then Jack's voice was gentle. 'Things are going to shut down for a while down here, what with Christmas and then New Year. And the baby's not far off making an appearance, which could complicate things a bit for me, but it's entirely your call. It was just an idea.'

Another silence as Emma's mind raced. She would be thinking about it again now, wouldn't she? Distraction would get harder. It could spoil things.

She heard Jack clear his throat. 'How 'bout this for another idea? Get the test done and, if the result comes through in time and it's what we hope it's going to be, I can give it to you as your Christmas present. And we can all really celebrate.'

He was including Sharon in that 'we'. They'd got on famously from the moment they'd first met and had worked closely together to get Emma through the toughest of times.

'And if it isn't?' Emma's voice was so soft she didn't think Jack would hear her but he did.

'Then we'll deal with it. After Christmas.'

Emma closed her eyes. That errant thought that she could perhaps stay in Braeburn longer than originally intended was still lurking in the back of her head and it would be much more convenient to pop over to Edinburgh for the test than go all the way back to London. And the result of that test couldn't possibly be devastating, could it, given that she was feeling so good at the moment? The physical exhaustion that used to ambush her all the time had virtually disappeared so she knew she was getting stronger every day. How amazing would it be to get confirmation of something so wonderful as a Christmas gift?

'Okay...Let me find a pen and paper and I'll take down the details.'

It was proving to be a long day for Adam. Another one where it was difficult to separate his professional and personal lives.

He couldn't blame his patients for making Emma's presence felt in his consulting room or when he was making his house calls, though. No...it was his own disobedient mind.

Or maybe he should blame his body.

He hadn't touched a woman in that way since his wife had died. Hadn't even thought of touching like that, let alone *kissing* someone.

And it wouldn't go away. The memory of how soft her lips had been. How sweet the taste of her had been. The shaft of desire for more that had been sharp enough to be both a physical and emotional pain.

Maybe that was what was making his mouth go a little dry at intervals today and increasing his heart rate until he could feel it thumping against his ribs. Too much adrenaline being produced. And why?

He knew if he looked a little more closely, he would know exactly why.

Fear.

Fear of being inadequate.

What man wouldn't have lost confidence? Especially when avoidance had been the defence method of choice and it was now ingrained as a way of life? His children, his work and his community. Those were the things he could do and do well. Being a husband or even a lover?

That was what he wasn't so sure of any more.

He'd always been good at avoidance, too. Even way back he'd made allowances for Tania's dissatisfaction. She was a city girl, born and bred, so of course she found a small village like Braeburn boring to the point of suffocation.

Emma was a city girl, too, wasn't she? She seemed to love village life but it was just a change for her. A very temporary change. Maybe the novelty would wear off.

Adam drove back to the medical centre that afternoon after visiting a sick baby on a farm that lay on the very outskirts of his practice area. It was starting to snow lightly and the stone walls and hedgerows looked like they were being dusted with icing sugar. The fairy-lights on the village shops were twinkling merrily and the tree in the square couldn't have looked any more perfect.

He could see Old Jock over by the pub with his bagpipes under his arm. Hopefully, he'd go in by the fire and have a wee dram instead of getting too cold, serenading the village. He'd have to chase up those test results when he got back to his office. Something was going on with Jock and while nothing obvious had been noticeable when he'd examined the older man the other day, Adam wasn't happy about it.

He cared deeply about the people of Braeburn. *His*

people. It wasn't just the physical beauty of this place that made it paradise for those who could see it. It was the embrace of a community tight enough to seem like an extended family with both its positive—supportive—side and the more negative—intrusive—one.

Eileen was in position, as always, guarding the reception desk, when he got back to the medical centre.

'Any calls while I've been out?'

'No' yet.' Eileen clicked her tongue. 'There will be, mind... It's snowing.'

'Aye.'

'Someone will fall over and break something, you mark my words.'

Adam smiled and Eileen looked shocked.

'It's no laughin' matter, Dr McAllister.'

'No.'

But the smile still lingered as he went into his office to make some calls. He needed to chase up Old Jock's results and ring to see how the Jessops' premature baby was doing. Still touch and go as far as he knew, but at least the little scrap was hanging in there.

And then he would be able to go home to be with his children and his dogs. And Emma... His home. His family.

It felt like the first time in his adult life that Adam wanted to be at home as much as he wanted to be at work.

Or was that unfair?

The twins had only been babies and then toddlers while Tania had been alive. Even with the help of a nanny it had been exhausting. It was no wonder that she'd demanded to be spoilt in the times he wasn't at work. To be taken out for a candlelit dinner or away to Edinburgh or London for a shopping spree. Away from home. Away from Braeburn. Away from their children...

But he couldn't deny that it had felt so much more *like*

a family since Emma had come into their lives. There was music in the house. A Christmas tree in the living room. Secrets being planned and the excitement of the upcoming Christmas production that was making life crazily busy all of a sudden.

The idea came to him from somewhere out of left field.

Did Emma really love being here as much as she seemed to?

Could she be persuaded to stay *longer*?

It wasn't fear that made his heart rate pick up this time. It was something far more positive but still enough to make him feel oddly nervous. Hope, perhaps?

Amazingly, the snow hadn't been enough to stop the playing of the pipes that Emma was coming to rely on as being a highlight of her new daily routine. It had stopped falling for the moment and the roads were still clear but it was breathtakingly cold and she couldn't sit on the bench because it would be damp even if she swept off the thin white covering.

The village centre was busy. There was a delicious smell coming from the bakery and a cluster of people outside the general store. The women saw her walk past and, instead of pretending not to, one of them nodded in her direction. The acknowledgement came without a smile but it was enough to make Emma grin and wave back. Maybe if she stopped wearing her silly Tibetan hat, she would get a smile next time.

The pipes sounded a little strange today. Had it been harder to warm them up because it was so cold? Sharon would say that some of those notes sounded like a cat being skinned alive and she wouldn't be far wrong.

No wonder the man in the kilt stopped and lowered his instrument to stare at it in dismay.

But…to drop it?

Emma was just registering how wrong the scene in front of her was when she saw the man crumple and fall. Dropping her guitar case, she ran towards him. She'd done a first-aid course before she'd got sick herself. She knew to turn him over and check to see if he was breathing and try to see if he had a pulse.

To start CPR and shout for help.

'Get Dr McAllister,' she heard someone shout. 'Tell him it's Old Jock who needs him.'

'Call an ambulance,' someone else said. 'He looks right poorly…'

It didn't seem like any time at all until the gathering crowd of onlookers parted for Adam's arrival. He was out of breath and carrying his bag in one hand and a large piece of equipment in the other. His ferocious-looking receptionist wasn't far behind either, cradling an oxygen cylinder in her arms.

'You're doing a good job, Emma. Can you keep it up while I get organised?'

'Sure.' Emma ignored the pain from the icy cobbles beneath her knees. She bit her lip and concentrated on where she had her hands—in the middle of the chest—and how hard and fast to push.

Had it been only a matter of weeks ago that expending this much energy would have been impossible? She just had to keep it up. The last thing Adam needed right now was to have someone else collapsing.

'Okay—stop for a moment.' The buttons on the man's waistcoat popped as Adam ripped it open. The buttons on a shirt went the same way but the singlet beneath needed a cut with shears before it would tear. And then Adam attached sticky pads to the bony chest and turned to look at the screen on the equipment he'd brought.

'Move right back, Emma. Make sure you're not touching him. I'm going to give him a shock.'

Emma—and all those watching—got a shock as well, seeing the body jerk in front of them, but she didn't have time to wallow in feeling horrified.

'Start compressions again,' Adam ordered.

'I can help the lassie.' A big man was kneeling beside her. 'I've learned how to do this.'

'Good man, Bryan. Emma—can you hold this, please? And come up by his head. I need a hand to get a tube in so we can breathe for him.'

The next few minutes were a blur. How could Adam stay so calm? He slipped a tube down the man's throat and attached it to a bag that he showed Emma how to squeeze. He put an IV line into an arm and drew up and administered drugs without any discernible shake to his hands.

Emma was shaking like a leaf now from a combination of the horror and the cold.

'Can someone ring and find out how far away the ambulance is?'

'They're sending a helicopter,' someone said moments later. 'It's going to land on the school field. They need people to check that there are no loose objects the snow might be hiding.'

Several people peeled away from the anxious group. 'We'll do that,' a man called. 'And warn the bairns what's going to happen.'

Emma fought off a wave of dizziness. She focused on holding the bag and squeezing it. Counting to ten slowly and then squeezing it again.

'You're doing really well.'

The words were quiet. Only Emma and the big man doing the compressions would have heard it. Bryan didn't look up from his task but Emma did. She met Adam's dark gaze and found encouragement there. Pride even?

She had to swallow an unexpected lump in her throat.

'Do…do we need to send someone to find blankets? It's s-so cold…'

'It's a good thing for Old Jock,' Adam said. 'Sometimes we make patients cold deliberately to protect them from the effects of a cardiac arrest.' He looked away. 'I'll take over in a sec, Bryan. Stand clear, both of you, now. I'm going to try another shock.'

Everyone had to be holding their breath to account for the silence that followed after the warning alarm and then the clunk of the machine delivering its charge. They could hear the beat of the approaching helicopter. And then another sound, much closer. A steady blip, blip, blip that was coming from the machine.

'Is that…?'

'Aye.' Adam caught her gaze again. 'We still need to help him with his breathing but we've got a heartbeat.'

There was triumph in those eyes now. Joy even. A ripple ran through the onlookers that suggested pride in their local doctor. Confirmation that their trust in him was not misplaced.

And then the helicopter crew was there, in their bright overalls and with even more equipment. Old Jock was put onto a stretcher.

'Can you come with us, Doc?'

'Of course.' But Adam turned back to Emma. 'I have no idea when I'll get home. It could be tricky finding transport back from Edinburgh.'

'I could come and get you.'

'What about the children? It'll be too late to be dragging them out.'

'I can take the bairns,' a woman said. 'It's no problem.'

She smiled at Emma. 'I'm Jeannie's mother. Jeannie's Poppy's friend. She'd love to have a sleepover.'

Emma saw the look on Adam's face. He never asked these people for help, did he? She could understand that he might want to protect his fierce independence but these were *his* people. They cared about him just as much as he obviously cared about them.

'Leave it with me,' she told him. 'I'll call you.'

How ironic was it that she was practising the run to the big hospital in Edinburgh, having only made her arrangements with Jack hours before?

Fate seemed to be stepping in again. It had been so easy to arrange care for the children. A very excited Poppy had gone home with Jeannie for the night and Oliver was having his first-ever sleepover at his friend Ben's house.

It made it easy to ask Adam what she needed to ask, after the initial conversation and reassurance that Jock was getting the best treatment possible had faded into silence.

Thank goodness Adam was driving. Emma had used up every ounce of energy she had and she knew she would fall asleep very soon. Maybe it was sheer exhaustion that stopped her feeling hesitant in making her request.

'Would it be all right if I had a day off next week? I've…got a kind of appointment in Edinburgh that I need to go to.'

'Of course you can have a day off. You haven't had one since you came. I keep telling you I can cope at the weekends.'

'The thing is…it's a weekday, not the weekend, and I'd need to stay the night. The…ah…appointment's late so I'd need to wait until the next day to get the train back. It would be fine for the children to stay with their friends again. I…um…checked.'

The sideways look she received was disconcerting. It reminded her of that first time she'd met Adam, when he'd looked at her as if she was the last person he'd want to be looking after his children. The atmosphere in the car suddenly felt like it had on that first day, too, when he'd driven her home and she'd been imagining his wife buried somewhere under the driveway.

It did sound dodgy, didn't it? A late-night appointment? And it was on a day that would make child care a challenge for him and she'd taken a huge liberty in tentatively making arrangements herself. But she couldn't tell him the truth or he might realise he *had* made a mistake in trusting her with his children. That she was sick and... and unreliable.

'It's a...job interview...' she heard herself saying. Unconvincingly? She tried again. 'Music's my first love. That's why I don't take on full-time or permanent jobs. I'm seeing someone about the possibility of a future gig.'

That wasn't so far from the truth, was it? It was just about her whole future and not just a gig.

The silence kept growing. Becoming more and more loaded with every passing second, but Adam was being assaulted by unpleasant emotions.

Had he really thought Emma was incapable of lying? It was *obvious* she was not telling the truth right now. He could hear echoes of Tania.

There's a sale on... It's my favourite designer, darling... It's only for a day...maybe two...

But it wasn't fair not to trust Emma because of the skill with which Tania had manipulated him.

He wanted to trust her. So much.

And it wasn't her fault that it was so hard.

Finally—too late—he managed a grunt in response.

But he couldn't meet her eyes. He had to keep staring at the road ahead of them.

'Do what you need to,' he growled. 'I'll cope.'

Emma woke up as the car jolted over the tree roots on the driveway and, almost instantly, found herself shivering.

It wasn't just the physical cold, although there was enough snow now for her feet to crunch through it as she followed Adam up the steps to the front door.

This was an emotional chill, too.

Adam McAllister had gone back into his shell, hadn't he? Back to being the man who never really smiled and who couldn't bear the celebration of something as joyous as Christmas.

And all because she'd asked for a day off?

No. Emma knew there was more to it than that. Maybe it was the way Adam was avoiding both eye contact and any conversation as they went into the house. Or it could have been the way Bob shot her an almost accusing look before going quietly to his master's side. Most likely, it was catching sight of the mistletoe wreath that Emma had hung in the corner near the coat stand that made it crystal clear.

This was about the kiss.

About *her*.

The desire wasn't one-sided, was it? But Adam didn't know what to do about it because he was still caught in his grief and she'd just made it clear that she couldn't wait to move on—to another *gig*.

For once Adam wasn't rushing into the kitchen where he'd drop his coat over the back of the nearest chair or on the arm of the sofa. He was taking it off slowly and deliberately and clearly intended hanging it on the rack.

Slowly enough for Emma to have another blinding moment of clarity.

She'd thought she had nothing to offer Adam but she had been wrong.

Catherine would applaud the fact that she'd pushed him into allowing Christmas into his house for the sake of the children but…what if she could give him—give *all* of them—more than that?

This man deserved to be loved again.

The children desperately needed a mother, not just a series of nannies.

How perfect would it be if it could be her?

But, if it couldn't, she could still help. She could help him take that first step. They had the house to themselves. Nobody but she and Adam need know.

Maybe the real gift she could give Adam was the permission to be really happy again? To show him what it *could* be like.

She could offer Adam hope. A belief that it was possible. He was an outstanding doctor and father but she could help him get over that huge barrier he'd put around himself as a man.

'Adam?' Slipping out of her own coat, Emma stood beside him at the coat rack. 'I'm sorry… I don't have to go to that appointment in Edinburgh. It's not that I don't want to be here with you and children. It's just that—'

'It doesn't matter. I told you that.'

'But it does,' Emma said softly. 'I don't want to make things difficult. I know I'm not here for very long but I want this to be a special time—one that will make special memories—for all of us…'

Herself included. The whisper in the back of her mind reminded her that this could turn out to be her last Christmas. She had nothing to lose. Adam had everything to gain.

Oh, help…he was standing so very still. His eyes were closed.

When his eyes slowly opened, he wasn't looking down at Emma. He was looking up—at the mistletoe wreath. And then he reached up and picked a whole bunch of those little, waxy white berries.

Finally, he made eye contact and the smouldering depths in those dark eyes stole Emma's breath.

And her heart.

He might be fighting it but he *wanted* her.

Needed her.

Emma had to close her eyes because her own wanting and needing was overwhelming and this had to be Adam's decision. His choice.

She heard his deep groan. And then she felt him move. One arm went around her waist and the other caught the back of her legs. She was scooped up as if she weighed almost nothing and she held on tightly and buried her face against his neck, allowing herself to sink into total trust as Adam carried her upstairs.

To his bed.

She felt so light in his arms. Thin enough to seem fragile as he set her down gently onto her feet when he'd reached his room and pushed the door shut with his foot to keep the dogs out.

To keep the whole world out.

Emma's arms were still around his neck as her feet touched the floor and she must have stayed on tiptoe to reach his lips with her own so easily.

There was nothing fragile about that kiss. He could

feel only the strength of her desire and a need that was as great as his own for the comfort of intimate, human touch.

It had been *so* long. Adam's hands slipped beneath the woollen jumper to feel skin that was like silk. Small, firm breasts that seemed to push themselves into his hands and nipples that were as hard as tiny pebbles.

Touching them with his hands wasn't enough. Not nearly enough. As blissful as it was, kissing Emma, he needed his mouth and his lips to savour other parts of her perfect body.

A tug on her clothing seemed to be enough. Emma dropped her arms and stepped back. Just far enough to grasp her jumper herself and peel it off over her head. And then she began to unbutton her shirt but Adam stilled her hands.

'Let me.'

His fingers fumbled with the tiny buttons and Adam realised, to his horror, that they were shaking. She wasn't watching his hands, though. As he looked up he found she was watching his face. Waiting for a contact that went so much deeper than physical touch. And when he gave it to her, he couldn't look away.

Could he do this? Could he love Emma in the way she deserved to be loved? Without disappointing her?

Emma could feel the tears in her eyes as she felt the way Adam's hands were trembling.

This big, strong man who could save a life and do such intricate manoeuvres with those hands without the slightest tremor couldn't hide his emotions in this moment.

This was huge. So huge that Adam was nervous. It wouldn't last. She knew that as soon as they got over this awkward moment of shedding their clothing and they could touch each other properly, any doubts or nerves on either side would cease to exist.

But in this brief moment of such vulnerability she realised just how much she loved Adam. She wouldn't only be giving him her body tonight. She would be giving him her heart—for as long as he wanted it.

Or as long as fate would allow.

And maybe something of what she was feeling was communicated as they held each other's gaze for such a long, long moment, because she felt that trembling stop. She saw the doubt vanish from Adam's eyes and could see something that seemed to mirror what she was feeling herself. A reflection—or was Adam gifting her *his* heart?

And then she could see—or maybe sense—the moment that desire ignited and there was nothing but the need to be as close as physically possible. There was no further awkwardness. Anything that was going to stop them being skin to skin seemed to be discarded as easily as ice melting in hot sunshine.

Adam flicked back the bed covers and then drew Emma against his body. In a heartbeat they would be lying on that bed together but she loved it that he stopped to gaze at her for a moment longer. To bend his head and give her such a tender kiss that promised he would look after her.

That he intended to make this night unforgettable.

Not that Emma had the slightest doubt that this would be the case but she loved being given the promise. Along with her body and her heart, Adam McAllister had just won her lifelong trust.

CHAPTER EIGHT

THE MAGIC WAS getting stronger.

Emma's gift to Adam had been received so well it seemed that he wanted to unwrap it all over again the following night, and Emma was only too happy to participate, tiptoeing into Adam's room when the children were fast asleep.

How amazing that the same gift could be given in both directions.

And that parts of it could be given to others without them knowing how or why it was happening?

They were being very careful to make sure the children didn't realise what had changed between them but the magic was still happening.

The new connection between Adam and Emma was sending out tendrils that were touching the children. Making them all feel like a family.

Like when naughty Benji had mistaken the old teddy Poppy carried everywhere now, for a dog toy and had grabbed its leg. Poppy had tried to keep hold of it but ended up pulling off the damaged arm and she had been distraught.

'Emma can fix it,' Adam consoled her.

'Daddy can fix it,' Emma said at the same time.

They looked at each other and smiled.

'You're good at sewing,' Adam said. 'I've seen that pretty dress you made Poppy for the play.'

'You're the doctor,' she said solemnly. 'An amputated arm is much more in your line of work.'

'Aye…' Adam nodded thoughtfully but his eyes held a mischievous glint. 'I'll need a scrub nurse, though.'

'I love new jobs.' It was hard not to grin but Poppy was still sobbing.

'We need a clean sheet,' Adam told her, 'so we've got an operating table. Ollie? Can you go and bring my doctor bag, please?'

It was a treat, turning the small disaster into a game that the children were fascinated by. With a clean sheet on the table, Adam pretended to give teddy an anaesthetic with a nebuliser. He'd found masks and gloves for both he and Emma to wear and he seemed more than happy to use up other medical supplies, like the suture kit.

It might have been a game but watching Adam draw the teddy's furry fabric together and make the complicated-looking knots of real sutures impressed Emma as much as it did the children. Their father was doing his important, *real* work at home. For teddy.

'Pay attention, scrub nurse,' Adam growled at one point. 'You have to cut the thread now.'

Emma giggled and, after a startled moment, so did both the children.

Teddy's arm got bandaged when the operation was finished and then he got sent off to Intensive Care in Poppy's bedroom because it was bedtime. Ollie got to carry him because he'd been promoted to orderly.

'I'll bet they'll remember that for the rest of their lives,' Emma told Adam later that night as she lay in his arms yet again. 'The night Daddy operated on teddy.'

'I think I'll remember it,' Adam replied quietly. 'It was special.'

'Magic,' Emma agreed happily.

'Aye...' Adam bent his head to kiss her again. 'Like you...'

The newest member of the Braeburn McAllister clan was born in the new light of the day after teddy's surgery.

Everyone in the village assumed that was why Dr McAllister was looking so happy. He had a bonny new niece and everybody was fine and his mother would head home in a couple of weeks and life would carry on just the same but better.

'They've called the wee lassie Holly—did you hear? Because she's been born sae close to Christmas.'

If anyone wondered why that Miss Sinclair seemed to be just as happy as the rest of the family, even though she was no relation to the new bairn, they just gave each other knowing looks. She was always a happy wee thing, wasn't she? A bit different, mind, with strange clothes and carrying her guitar with her everywhere, but you couldn't say a word against how she looked after those twins and the way she was getting involved with the school's Christmas production and even with the fundraising for the hall committee.

And, oh, my...she *could* sing like a wee angel, couldn't she?

Phone calls and texts and photographs pinged between Scotland and Canada but it was a couple of days before everything came together well enough for a family gathering, courtesy of an online video chat.

Marion and Holly were back home already with Ian— the proud husband and new father—and Catherine was using her tablet. Adam had set up his desktop computer in the living room. With a fire burning merrily in the grate and the lights on the Christmas tree twinkling, it seemed the perfect background for a digital reunion, but Catherine McAllister seemed overwhelmed by the initial visual contact.

'Oh…is that a…a…*Christmas* tree?'

'It's *our* Christmas tree, Gran…' Poppy leaned in close to the computer screen to make sure her grandmother could see her properly. 'Emma helped us paint the balls and we sticked the sweets on the stars and we made paper chains and…and *everything*.'

Catherine probably couldn't see anything except Poppy's nose, Emma thought, but there was no mistaking the pride and joy the small girl was radiating. She could see the screen but she was staying out of range of the camera, sitting on the floor near the fire, flanked by Bob and Benji.

There was no mistaking the voice thickened by tears from the other end of the connection either.

'That's wonderful, darling. It's the most beautiful Christmas tree I've ever seen. Emma's clever, isn't she?'

'Aye.' Adam gently pulled Poppy's head back to allow a wider camera view. 'She's made a dress for Poppy, too. For the school play. I told you that Jemima's going to be in the production, didn't I?'

Laughter came from behind Catherine and the picture on the screen changed angles sharply. They got a view of polished wooden floorboards and then feet and then the picture settled on a young woman sitting in an armchair with a small bundle in her arms. She could be Adam's twin, not just his sister, Emma thought. With that same dark hair and eyes and a smile that was so like Adam's when he was really happy.

She'd seen that smile so often in the last few days.

Everyone had and it was contagious. There was so much laughter in this house now and even people in the village seemed to be smiling more.

'Are you trying to upstage me, Adam? Creating havoc in the village so nobody's got time to talk about my wee Holly? Whose crazy idea was it to take our donkey into the hall?'

'*Emma's*,' the twins chorused.

Oliver pushed past Poppy to take centre stage. 'Aunty Marion—can you come and see our play? I'm going to be Joseph and I get to lead Jemima until we get to the stage and I've got a…a rib that Emma made out of a sheet—'

'Robe,' Adam supplied.

'And I wear a stripy tea towel on my head and Emma's made a special rope thing to hold it on and…'

And Marion was laughing again. 'I can't come this time, pet. I have to be here to look after wee Holly. But *next* year we'll all be back in Braeburn and we'll all come and see the play.'

'But Jemima won't be in it next year.'

And I won't be here, Emma thought. She had to dip her head and swallow hard.

'I think I need to meet this Emma,' Marion declared. 'Where is she?'

'She's here.' Adam turned away from the computer and held out his hand. 'Come over, Emma. Come and meet my sister and our new niece.'

She couldn't not respond to that outstretched hand. To the invitation in those eyes and the smile she was coming to love more and more. With the children standing in front of them, nobody would notice that Adam caught her hand when she got close enough, would they? Or that he laced his fingers through hers and kept holding it as Emma smiled at the screen.

'Hi, Marion. Congratulations. I've seen the pictures of Holly and she's just gorgeous.'

Adam squeezed her hand and it was automatic to look up and return his smile. Hard to look away quickly enough to avoid making it obvious that her relationship with her employer had undergone a radical change recently.

Marion looked away from the screen for a moment, her face a question mark. Was she exchanging a significant look with her mother? But then she was smiling again, possibly even more widely than before.

'I hear you can sing,' she said. 'That you—and the children of Braeburn school—are about to become rich and famous.'

Emma laughed. 'I don't think so. But a local radio station got hold of the story about us making a CD of Christmas carols as a fundraiser. They've organised a bus to take us all into a recording studio and they're going to make it available as a download so lots of people can buy it. With a bit of luck, we'll be able to fix up the hall *and* get a new piano for the school.'

The twins were feeling left out.

'I've got a train, Aunty Marion. It's on the floor by the tree, see?'

'No, I can't see it, pet.'

'I'll get the engine and *show* you.' Oliver wriggled between Adam and Emma and they had to break their handhold.

'And I've got a bear.' Poppy held it up and pressed it against the computer screen. 'Benji pulled him and the arm felled off but Daddy and Emma poperated it and it's all better now.'

'Good heavens…that's *my* old bear,' came Catherine's voice.

'We found it in the attic when we went up to hunt out

the Christmas decorations,' Adam explained. 'You don't mind, do you? Ollie's train was the one I had when I was his age. I'd forgotten it was even there.'

'Of course I don't mind.' Catherine's eyes were suspiciously bright. 'It's wonderful that you found things to use again. Oh…I wish I was there with you. You all look *so* happy.'

If they hadn't noticed anything significant in the glance Adam and Emma had exchanged before, they would surely pick up on something this time as Adam turned to Emma and smiled.

'We are,' he said.

'But what on earth did you do to the bear to fix it?'

'A poperation,' Poppy shouted. 'I *told* you.'

'An *operation*.' Emma was laughing. 'Daddy got a special needle and thread from his doctor's bag and sewed teddy's arm back on.'

'I growled at Benji,' Poppy added. 'And he looked sad.'

'Is Benji going to be in the play, too?' Marion asked.

''Course not.' Oliver was back with the train engine. 'He's a *dog*.'

'Maybe he could pretend to be a sheep?'

'No.' Adam shook his head. 'Don't go putting ideas in their heads, Miri. You're as bad as Emma. We've got more than enough going on right now. I'm helping to shift hay bales into the hall tomorrow. Bryan from the pub is making a manger.'

The connection crackled and the picture pixelated for a moment. By the time it cleared, baby Holly was crying and it was hard to hear conversation.

'We'd better go,' Adam said. 'It's very late for you. We'll try again on Christmas Day, aye? Children—come and blow a kiss to your wee cousin.'

With a chorus of 'Miss you' and 'Love you lots' the call

ended. For a moment the blankness of the screen seemed to dampen the atmosphere in the room.

Emma groaned. 'Oh, no…we forgot to sing the carol for the baby.'

The twins were good at speaking in unison. 'Deck the halls with boughs of *holly*…'

They were also good at looking equally disappointed.

'Never mind. We needed to practise a bit more anyway. We'll be extra-good at it for Christmas Day.'

But Poppy's lip wobbled and Oliver hugged the train engine more tightly.

'It's almost bedtime but why don't we have a quick practice now? Maybe Daddy could record it on his phone and we could *send* it to Gran and Aunty Marion.'

'I'll get your kit-ar,' Poppy offered.

'No.' Oliver glared at her. 'That's *my* job.'

Happiness had been restored yet again, thanks to Emma's way of dealing with problems.

No. Maybe it was being created rather than restored.

That was certainly the case for Adam, he realised much later that night as he held Emma in his arms yet again.

She was asleep but he pressed a gentle kiss to the top of her head and the pressure seemed to bounce back in a shaft that went straight to his chest, where it encased his heart and squeezed it tightly.

Was this what happiness felt like?

But this was something he'd never felt before and he knew there had been times he'd been happy. His childhood had been a happy one. He'd been secure and loved and he'd had friends and he'd loved school and his music lessons. It had been Old Jock who'd taught him to play the bagpipes and he'd been so proud that Christmastime when his pupil had been chosen to be the lone piper for the school production. He'd never said anything to Adam in the years since he'd stopped playing but he knew how happy the old man would be if he confessed that he was ready to pick up his pipes again.

Thank goodness Emma had been there and had known what to do the other day. Jock had been very lucky. He might have still survived his cardiac arrest but it had to be thanks to good-quality CPR that he'd come through without any neurological damage.

Gratitude added another layer to Adam's sense of well-being and his breath came out in a soft sigh.

It wasn't just Jock who was lucky that Emma had come to Braeburn.

His children were as happy as he'd ever seen them. Maybe it was partly due to the festive decorations that seemed to be creeping into every corner of the house. Today's addition had been big tartan bows at intervals all the way up the bannisters on the stairs. Or maybe it wasn't the decorations so much as his giving permission to *have* them?

Had he shut happiness out of the house without intending to? Had it just become a habit because he'd lived with his grief and his guilt for so long?

That he was letting go was thanks to Emma, too. She'd come here with her music and songs and…and her sheer *joie de vivre* and she'd given them all something that could never have been wrapped and put under a Christmas tree.

What was it that was creating this feeling that was almost euphoria?

Part of it was the kind of excitement he remembered from when he'd been a child. On Christmas morning when he would tiptoe downstairs before anyone else was awake to see if the magic had happened and there were mysterious, brightly wrapped parcels under the tree.

Part of it was hope. The kind of hope he'd felt when he'd persuaded Tania to marry him and come to live in his own little patch of the world? He'd thought that he'd never feel that kind of hope again. The one that suggested that he'd found all that he needed to keep him happy for the rest of his life. He'd been wrong that time but the hope had never been this strong, had it? It was time to put it all behind him. Time to take off the wedding ring that symbolised his entrapment in the past?

And Adam knew that part of it was also love. Maybe the biggest part. The kind of love he'd felt when he'd held his newborn babies for the first time. That almost desperate urge to protect them. To hold them and cherish them. For ever. He felt that urge about Emma now and it made him stroke her skin very lightly. Over her shoulder and along her collar bone. She had a tiny scar that interrupted the perfection of her smooth skin. Funny place for a scar— almost exactly where someone would have a central line inserted for a major medical procedure. He'd have to ask her some time how it came to be.

Emma shifted in his arms and made a tiny sound. She would wake soon. Maybe they would make love again. Even the thought of it stirred desire but Adam didn't want her to wake just yet because he knew she wouldn't sleep in his arms again tonight. She would creep back to her own room so that the children wouldn't know she hadn't been there all night.

To protect him—in case they said something at school and then the whole village would know what was going on in the McAllister house?

Maybe it was to protect them—so that they wouldn't get ideas that Emma might be in their lives for ever?

If they asked, he might tell them that he hoped she might

be but hope wasn't something to give lightly. He'd seen it in his mother's face tonight. And his sister's.

In the way they'd looked at each other as if they knew what was going on between him and Emma.

He would have seen it in his own face in the mirror all those years ago, when he'd been getting dressed for his wedding.

Hope was fragile. Like a glass bubble that could shatter all too easily. He hadn't intended ever trying to hold one himself again but it had formed without him really noticing.

And now it was here.

And it was huge.

The days were passing in a blur.

There was so much to do. Emma had never been so busy in her life but she was loving every minute of it. Final rehearsals for the school's Christmas production that would happen on Christmas Eve were in full swing. The junior-school trip to the recording studio had happened yesterday on the last day of school and the CDs were due to arrive today. There had been a picture of them all in the newspaper and already there were apparently orders coming in and people waiting to download the amateur production. Women in the village were not only smiling at Emma, they were *talking* to her. This was the most exciting thing that had happened in Braeburn since…

They never said what else had happened that was so exciting but Emma had to wonder if it had been when their beloved doctor had brought his beautiful young wife home to his village.

Funny how a ghost could cast such a shadow but it wasn't the only shadow Emma was aware of today.

The arrangements were all in place. Poppy was spending the day with Jeannie and Oliver was with Ben. Their mothers would take them to the play practice later and Caitlin had offered to take Poppy to her dance class, where they were also doing a final rehearsal for their upcoming appearance, and Adam would collect her. He would also take Oliver to his music lesson tomorrow morning to prepare for the junior pipers' display. The Christmas Eve school production wasn't just a nativity play from the youngest pupils. It was more like a talent show. A celebration of everything the village children had accomplished for their year.

Nobody seemed to mind that Emma was skipping town for a day and a night. She would be back in time. The knowing looks and veiled comments she'd received had let her know that they thought she was really going to Edinburgh to do some Christmas shopping. The way Mrs McAllister used to. And didn't the bairns deserve something special? Their poor father never had the time to go far afield to create Christmas surprises but Emma was good at surprises, wasn't she?

Oh, yes…the shadows were gathering and, as she sat alone in the train on the way to Edinburgh, they formed a black cloud that threatened a storm.

Had she made a terrible mistake in trying to create a perfect Christmas for the McAllister family? For herself?

She hadn't intended falling in love with Adam but it had happened. And, if this was going to be her last Christmas, how magical was it to feel this happy?

This *loved*.

She hadn't intended to give Adam any more than the reminder of what it was like to let a woman close. To help him step forward from his grief. She hadn't expected him to fall in love with *her*. Not that he'd said anything but she could feel it in every touch. Every kiss. She could see it in his eyes when she turned unexpectedly and found him looking at her.

What if she'd set him up to suffer loss all over again?

And at *Christmas*time?

No. She couldn't afford to let a single bolt of lightning detach itself from that storm cloud. Jack was waiting for her to arrive at the infirmary. She would have the horrible test this afternoon, sleep off the effects of the drugs and then go back to Braeburn and enjoy every moment of this Christmas.

She had to remember to post the CD she had burned last night, too. Not that it would reach Sharon by Christmas Day, of course, but that was okay. The collection of photographs and the song she had written for her best friend would arrive electronically on the right day. The CD was just a back-up. She'd made one for herself as well.

It was snowing again by the time Emma carried her small bag into the brightly lit entrance to the huge hospital. There was a massive Christmas tree in the foyer, covered in silver decorations—like theirs would have been if she and the children hadn't painted all those balls. The girl at the reception desk was wearing a bright badge that had Rudolf the reindeer with a flashing red nose. Even the telephone she picked up to page Jack with was wrapped in tinsel.

And Jack's smile when he saw her looked like Christmas. So warm. Full of hope? His hug was comforting.

'Let's get this over with, Emma. Are you ready?'

Emma could only nod. Her throat felt tight and tears stung the back of her eyes. Hope was like a bubble, wasn't it?

A freshly blown one that caught all the colours of the rainbow and was so pretty that you wanted to catch it and keep it.

But it would only break if you tried.

CHAPTER NINE

THE HUM OF conversation stopped. Even the small girls stopped skipping about and giggling.

'Dr McAllister... What's happened?'

'Nothing's happened. I'm just here to collect Poppy.'

'Where's Emma?'

'She had to go to Edinburgh. She'll be back tomorrow afternoon.'

'Oh...thank goodness for that.' The young mothers shared relieved glances. 'She's not going to miss the performance, then. It wouldn't be the same, would it, without her singing with the children?'

'No.'

The mothers turned their attention to getting their daughters to change their shoes and put coats and hats on before going out into the snow. Having got over the surprise of seeing him at the dance class, nobody seemed to expect Adam to say anything else. People drifted away, leaving him alone with Poppy as he helped her with the laces on her dancing shoes. Because they were so used to giving him the space he'd always demanded by keeping people at a distance? Odd that it felt a little...disappointing?

At least the teacher came to talk to him.

'Did ye get the note, Dr McAllister? About the kilt?'

'Aye…' There had been a note, hadn't there? Weeks ago. Kylie had said something about needing to order a kilt for Poppy for her first dance performance but that had been about the time that his previous nanny had announced her pregnancy and intention of emigrating to Australia and life had suddenly become chaotic. He'd totally forgotten about it.

The teacher gave him a sympathetic smile. 'It's no' essential,' she said. 'I'm sure Poppy's got a skirt she could wear. We can give her a tartan sash.'

'But I want a kilt,' Poppy said. She tugged on her father's sleeve. 'I *love* kilts, Daddy.'

'We'll find you a kilt, pet, I promise.'

How he was going to manage to keep that promise within the next forty-eight hours was beyond Adam at the moment but there were other things to deal with first. Like getting the children home and fed. Looking after the dogs and collecting the eggs from the hens and making sure Jemima had plenty of fresh hay. Poppy took the little donkey a carrot.

'You're going to be in our play,' she said happily. 'You have to be very good and then you'll get more carrots.'

'She *will* have to be very good,' Adam agreed. He couldn't help shaking his head as a wave of bemusement caught him off guard. Were they really going to transport Jemima into the village hall to star in the nativity play?

Extraordinary.

As astonishing as the person who'd made it happen, in fact.

Emma's absence in the house that evening was far more noticeable than Adam had expected. It wasn't just that he had so much more that he needed to do. Everywhere he turned, he could see things that made him think of Emma. The paper chains hanging from the beams in the kitchen.

The Christmas tree in the living room. The children asking for songs instead of a bedtime story.

He did his best but it wasn't the same.

'It's okay,' Oliver said kindly. 'Emma will be back tomorrow.'

It wasn't just the lack of music in the house that made it feel oddly quiet. The atmosphere was different. Emma didn't have to be singing, did she? She only had to be present for there to be a unique energy in the house.

A promise of something good.

Joy, perhaps.

Or love…

To distract himself from what was missing, Adam went online to check out the availability of kilts for small girls. But even that reminded him of Emma. Of the conversation in the kitchen that first weekend she'd been here. When she'd asked him if there was a McAllister tartan and whether he ever wore a kilt.

He'd been terse, hadn't he? Pushed her away, the way he always did when people got too close. It worked so well because they understood why he needed his space. Or they thought they did.

Emma hadn't respected those boundaries, though. She'd pushed until he could see them for what they were. Prison bars keeping him in the past. Hurting his children.

He found a specialist shop and clicked on the Clan Donald tartan. There was a children's section and he found a clan kilt in a new tartan that had been designed in recent years. With a purple background and small gold, red and green stripes, it was far more feminine than the dark colours of the kilt he had hanging in his own wardrobe. It would be perfect for Poppy. It seemed to be in stock in the right size but could they deliver it in time? Adam took note of the phone number. He'd give them a call tomorrow morning after he'd dropped Ollie at his music lesson.

With his hands still hovering over the keyboard, Adam caught the glint that the screen light coaxed from the dull gold band on his finger. It wasn't just the personal barriers he'd erected that were prison bars keeping him in the past, was it?

With a movement familiar enough to be automatic he used his thumb to touch the metal. Did he rub it as a reassuring link to a past he wasn't permitted to forget or was he actually trying to hide it?

On impulse, he closed the fingers of his right hand over the ring and gave it a tug. It didn't budge. He tried twisting it and it moved a little. Enough to make him get up abruptly and startle the dogs, who followed him curiously into the bathroom where he lathered his hands with soap until he could move the ring more freely. It took some effort to get it over his knuckle but—suddenly—it was off.

He was holding the symbol of his past and his failed marriage and the tragedy of losing his wife and… And he had no idea what to do with it now. The thought of taking it up the back of Old Jock's farm and hurling it into the pond was appealing. Just as well it was so late and the pond was frozen over anyway. Back in the library to shut down the computer, Adam dropped the ring into a drawer of his desk.

Walking up the stairs to bed, he was again aware of Emma's absence and this time it came with a yearning ache because he was going to his bed alone. He paused for a moment, in the spot where he'd first heard the haunting notes of that song coming from her room late at night, catching his breath as he realised how much he was missing her.

His left hand was curled, his thumb rubbing the empty

place where the ring had been. There was nothing there to touch. Nothing to hide.

Or should that be no*where* to hide?

It wouldn't be long before someone noticed that he'd taken his ring off. Eileen's sharp eyes didn't miss a thing. There would be talk, of course, but he suspected that the consensus of the village women would be that three years' mourning was more than enough. He had done his duty and upheld the myth that the marriage had been too perfect to move on from and he'd done it for long enough to ensure that the children were protected. They would always have their 'angel' mother but they deserved more than that in their lives. Someone real, who made their lives more joyful.

Would the villagers go further and speculate how much influence Emma's presence had had on his decision?

Probably.

Did he mind?

If he did, he'd get used to it—the way he had got used to carrying the burden of the truth alone. Maybe—hopefully—he'd have to, because he had made more than one decision tonight. He was going to ask Emma to stay in Braeburn longer and he was pretty confident that she would agree. He'd had the strong impression today that she didn't really want to go. She'd seemed reluctant to even go to that job interview in the end. And it was good that she had gone because it gave her options. And if she chose to stay, it would be because she really wanted to.

If she did want to stay, he could start hoping for something more permanent. Not just for the children—he wanted that for himself as well.

The hotel in Edinburgh was a lovely old sandstone building that had been close enough to the hospital to make it the ideal place for Emma to spend the night and sleep off the effects of the drugs she'd been given for her procedure.

Not that she'd slept particularly well. Despite being only two days before Christmas, the hotel was very quiet, which should have been a bonus but it made Emma feel lonely. She missed the sound of children nearby. Even more, she missed being near Adam. So much that it was a physical ache that had nothing to do with the holes that had been bored into her hip bone. She longed for the sound of his voice. The way his presence filled a room. Just a shared look would have been enough—to see the warmth in those gorgeous, dark eyes and the promise that always seemed to be there now.

Oh…help. It was going to be very hard to leave, wasn't it?

At least she could distract herself with some Christmas shopping this morning. She wanted to find something special for Poppy and Oliver. And for Adam. Something that they'd keep for ever and it would remind them of her?

She needed something for Jack as well. He'd gone to a lot of effort to ensure she didn't have the results of this test as a dark cloud hanging over her future for any longer than was absolutely necessary and, as usual, he'd done his best to make the procedure as painless as possible. A bottle of really nice Scotch, perhaps? She could give it to him later because they'd arranged to meet in the hospital café for a coffee before she drove back to Braeburn. Just a quick check, Jack had said—to see that there were no complications from the test. And the results of the blood tests would be back by then, although the examination of her bone marrow would take up to seven days. From past experience, however, Emma knew that the preliminary results could arrive within forty eight hours and, so far, they'd always been an accurate prediction of what lay ahead.

It was a bit painful to walk this morning but a couple of painkillers along with her breakfast and she'd be fine to wander through the lovely boutique shops on the Royal Mile and Grassmarket. A quick coffee with Jack and then she could be on her way, heading back to Braeburn. She wished she could just get on the train and start travelling now. Not that she'd make it back in time for the big dress rehearsal of the play but at least she'd be going in the right direction.

On the way back to the people she had already come to love so deeply.

Caitlin McMurray was coping with at least fifteen over-excited children by the time Adam dropped Poppy and Oliver at the school.

'Och…here's our wee Mary and Joseph.' Caitlin looked relieved. 'Where are our shepherds? Over *here*, Jamie, thank you. No—we're not getting the paints out.' She grinned at Adam. 'Don't you love the silly season?'

Adam smiled back. 'I'm sorry I can't stay to help. I need to get to the clinic and see if anyone needs me.'

Except that he found someone who needed him even before he got as far as the clinic. Joan McClintock, almost buried in her cold-weather clothes, was standing outside the church.

'How are you, Joan?'

'Och…you know, Doctor. I've been better.'

'Still feeling peaky?'

'Aye…'

'You're sounding a bit short o' puff.' Automatically, Adam reached for Joan's hand, negotiating the heavy coat cuff and a woollen glove to find her pulse.

'Aye…I am at that. Must be the cold.'

'Come into the clinic with me. I'd like to check your blood pressure.'

'Och, I didn't want to be a bother, Dr McAllister.'

'It's no bother, Joan.' She was looking pale, Adam thought, and there was something about her that was ringing alarm bells. Made him think of Old Jock, who'd also been a bit 'short o' puff' shortly before he'd collapsed and nearly died.

There were two people in the waiting room but Eileen took one look at her friend's face and made no comment about a disruption to the morning's timetable.

'Och, Joan…you're no' looking right. It's a good thing you're here to see the doctor.'

His elderly patient's blood pressure wasn't concerning and her pulse seemed steady enough but Adam still wasn't happy.

'Is there anything else happening, Joan? You've no' got any chest pain or nausea or anything?'

'Noo… I've just… I don' *feel* right, you know?'

'Aye. I'm going to do a twelve-lead ECG.' He knew it would be a mission to get down to skin and attach all the electrodes but he wasn't going to let that deter him. It was quite possible for someone to be having a heart attack with almost no symptoms—especially a stoic, elderly woman.

Sure enough, the ECG trace showed unmistakeable evidence that Joan was, indeed, in the early stages of a heart attack. She needed to get to a hospital with catheter lab facilities as soon as possible.

'I'm going to send you into hospital,' Adam told her, after carefully explaining what he'd found. 'The sooner you get treatment, the less damage there will be to your heart. I'll get Eileen to call an ambulance.'

'I'm no' going in any ambulance.' Joan was already pulling her clothes back on. 'I'm fine, Doctor.'

'You're not fine, Joan. Here—I want you to chew up these aspirin tablets and wash them down with some water.'

But Joan was too upset to co-operate. Her shortness of breath was increasing and Adam knew that a panic attack was not only imminent but would be the worst thing for her, given that the blood supply to her heart was already compromised.

'All right. No ambulance. I'll talk to Eileen and we'll find someone who can drive you.'

'No...' Joan's face crumpled. 'It's been snowing... it's dangerous... I don't trust *anyone*...to drive me *any-where*...'

Her breath was coming in short gasps now and she had a hand pressed to the centre of her chest. He had to break this cycle before a catastrophe happened—but how?

Adam took hold of Joan's hand with both of his. 'Do you trust *me*, Joan?'

'Oh...aye, Doctor. Of course I do.'

'Would you let *me* drive you to the hospital?'

'But—'

'Wait here. I've going to have a wee word with Eileen and we'll get everything sorted. And then I'm going to pop a wee needle in your hand and give you something to help you relax.' He squeezed her hand. 'It's all going to be all right, Joan. You just need to let me look after you.'

Amazingly, Eileen didn't look remotely outraged at the prospect of having to reschedule the waiting patients and neither of them seemed bothered about the inconvenience. Perhaps the drama of Old Jock's narrow escape was fresh enough to have everyone watching out for each other.

'You just take care of Joan, Doctor.'

'And say hello to Jock while you're in there.'

That was a thought. He could not only check up on Jock

but he could see how Aimee Jessop's baby was doing. He might even be able to pop into the specialty shop and see if he could pick up that kilt for Poppy.

'Oh…' About to head back to get Joan ready for the journey, Adam stopped in his tracks.

'Don't worry,' Eileen said. 'I'll take care of things here. If anyone's looking right poorly, I'll call an ambulance.'

'It's the children,' Adam said. 'They'll be finished their play practice by lunchtime. I'll no' be back in time to collect them.'

'I'll do that,' Eileen said. 'We'll get some lunch and they can come and play here until you get back.'

The suggestion that the children were welcome to come and play in Eileen's closely guarded domain was astonishing but Adam didn't have time to reflect on the fact that it wasn't only in his own home that things seemed to be changing. He needed to look after Joan.

Two hours later, his elderly patient was on her way to the catheter laboratory at the Royal. Adam visited Paediatrics to hear the good news that the Jessop baby was putting on weight and that her mother had been able to hold her, and then he got a surprise in the cardiology ward when he was told that Jock was well enough to go home. They were about to arrange transport.

'He can come back with me,' Adam said. 'I just need a quick coffee and a sandwich and I'll be back to collect him.'

The café at the infirmary was renowned for its good food and great coffee but Adam didn't even get as far as the queue at the counter.

At first, he simply didn't believe what he was seeing. It had to be a symptom of how much space Emma Sinclair was taking up in his head these days that made him see things in other women that reminded him of her.

The petite frame or a tumble of curly hair. Blue eyes or even a song on the radio…

But no. This time it wasn't just a glimpse of something that made him realise how special Emma was and how much he wanted to be with her.

It *was* her.

And she wasn't alone.

She was sitting at a table with a man who was roughly his own age. The way they were leaning towards each other suggested more than simply familiarity and if he'd been prepared to bestow the benefit of doubt, the inclination would have evaporated the instant he noted that they were holding hands. Staring at each other so intently there was no danger of him being noticed.

Not that the inclination to question the evidence had been there in the first place.

Emma had said she was coming to Edinburgh for a job interview and he'd believed her. Trusted her.

Had he really thought she was so completely different from his wife?

Tania had always said she came to Edinburgh to do her Christmas shopping.

He'd trusted her, too.

Were all women like this? No…he knew that wasn't true. So it had to be something to do with *him*. And whatever failing he had, it was accompanied by a blindness he'd never imagined he'd have to face again.

Maybe it was a good thing that he'd had so much practice in turning devastation inwards. Shutting it behind barriers that were impregnable. At least, they had been until Emma had come into his life.

Well… Adam turned on his heel and walked away. He'd just have to do a better job of building them this time, wouldn't he?

CHAPTER TEN

SOMETHING WAS WRONG.

Emma walked into the reception area of the Braeburn medical centre with a smile on her face because she'd been thinking about the first time she'd come through these doors and how different it felt now. Back then, she'd faced the snappy little terrier of a woman whom she'd thought was the children's grandmother and she'd been nervous of the fiercely uncompromising—almost angry—first impression of her potential employer.

Now she knew that Eileen was a loyal receptionist and that, behind the shield, Adam was a passionate and caring man. The most wonderful man she would ever meet in her life.

But her smile vanished as soon as she stepped through the door.

Caitlin had texted her to say that the children would be waiting at the clinic to be collected when she got back and Emma had assumed that Adam was too busy to take them home. Sure enough, the waiting room was packed and Oliver and Poppy were sitting in the corner, but Emma still knew that something was wrong.

There was a basket of toys in the corner but the twins were simply sitting there very quietly, looking as though they were in some kind of trouble.

Nobody else was talking either. Three women, one of whom she recognised as Moira, the Braeburn choir mistress, were intent on their knitting. Another rocked a pram that clearly contained a sleeping infant. Two men were invisible behind open newspapers.

Emma swallowed hard. She smiled at Eileen. 'I've just come to collect the children,' she said.

'Och, aye…' Eileen sniffed. 'We've been expecting you.'

Was that the problem? Was she later than she'd said she'd be? The coffee with Jack had turned into lunch but he'd been so kind and she'd needed someone to talk to. Somehow it made the new joy in her life more real to talk about it but it had the downside of making her fears a lot bigger as well. She'd ended up crying but Jack had held her hand and listened. He'd focused on the good results of the first blood tests that had come through and reminded her of how well they'd predicted results of the bone-marrow tests in the past.

But she'd said she'd be back by three p.m. and it was only a little later than that because it had started snowing again and the train journey had been slow. She'd gone to where the car was parked, too, to hide all her parcels so that the children wouldn't guess she'd been shopping for them.

'How was the rehearsal?' Emma pasted another smile onto her face. 'I'm so sorry I missed it. You'll have to tell me all about it on the way home.'

Oliver was staring at his hands. Poppy's bottom lip wobbled as she looked up at Emma.

'Daddy's cross,' she whispered.

'Is he? Well…he's awfully busy.' Emma glanced around the waiting room. Of course Adam would be annoyed that she hadn't been here to look after his children so he could do his job. That was what she'd been employed for, wasn't it? Except she was more than an employee now, wasn't she?

A prickle ran down Emma's spine. There was more to this than inconvenience. There was something heavy in the air. Something dark. Had somebody died maybe?

The door to the consulting room flew open and someone wrapped in a heavy coat bustled out. There was a short silence and then Adam appeared in their wake.

'*Next*,' he barked.

'That's you, Moira,' Eileen said in a stage whisper.

The choir mistress got hurriedly to her feet, clutching her knitting, but the ball of wool escaped and rolled an impressively long way across the floor. She bent to pick it up but the wool caught on the buckle of her shoe.

'Sorry, Doctor.' She tugged at the wool. A knitting needle came loose and clattered to the floor but Adam wasn't watching the progress of his next patient. His gaze had found Emma standing beside the children.

Suddenly it wasn't amusing to remember the first time she'd been here. Before Adam had known anything about her and had looked at her with a level of suspicion that had suggested she was the last person who might be suitable for looking after his precious children.

That kind of look paled in comparison to the chilly determination with which he was regarding her now. There was no suspicion in this glare. No doubt. No hint of warmth either.

'Take your time, Moira,' he snapped. 'Emma—could I have a word, please? It'll only take a minute.'

The last words were directed at the waiting room in general as Adam turned back to his consulting room. Or perhaps they had been intended to mollify Eileen. If so, it hadn't worked. Moira clicked her tongue and shook her head, the wool snapping as she gave it a harder tug. Eileen's eyes narrowed as she appeared to put two and two together and realise that Emma was somehow responsible for the doctor's bad mood.

This wasn't fair. Okay, she'd been absent for a little over twenty-four hours but it was hardly the crime of the century, was it? It certainly wasn't fair to make the children suffer and she'd never seen the twins look so miserable.

And her painkillers had worn off. A deep ache in her hip made it almost impossible to walk without a limp but somehow she managed it, knowing how many sets of eyes were watching every move she made.

'Shut the door, please,' Adam said, as she went in. 'Have a seat.'

'I'm…okay.' It was better to remain standing. Getting up from a chair might be painful enough to be difficult to hide.

'As you wish.'

He could have been speaking to a total stranger.

No. It was worse than that. He sounded as though he hated her and you couldn't hate someone you didn't know, could you? Emma couldn't stand this a moment longer.

'What's wrong, Adam? What have I done to upset you?'

A soft snort of unamused laughter came from Adam, accompanied by a head shake that emphasised his incredulity.

'I'm sorry if it's been difficult. Was there a problem with the children while I wasn't here or something?'

He was staring at her and, just for a heartbeat, Emma saw the barrier slip. If she'd thought the children looked miserable, it was nothing compared to the pain she saw in that instant in Adam's eyes. He looked…*betrayed*.

'I *know* why you had to go to Edinburgh,' he said.

'What?' Emma could actually feel the blood draining from her face.

'I took a patient through to the infirmary this morning.' Adam's eyes didn't leave hers. His tone was deceptively calm.

Dangerous.

'I *saw* you.'

Oh…dear Lord… He *did* know why she'd been there. He was a doctor who was well known at that hospital. How hard would it have been to get someone to check records and find out what she'd been even so briefly admitted for?

'I…I'm sorry, Adam. I should have told you the truth.'

'Just what the hell did you think you were playing at, Emma? Did you give any thought at all to how this was going to play out down the track? How it might affect the children? *Me*?'

When she *died*? Oh…help. She was going to cry. All she had wanted to do was offer her love.

To be loved in return, for just a blink of time. To make her last Christmas the best one ever.

How selfish had she been?

But the stunning effect of Adam's discovery was wearing off and guilt was getting overtaken by something else. Hurt. How cruel was this to be reminding her that she might not have much time left? To suggest that the effect on the McAllister family was worse than what she might have to face herself?

And why were the children looking so upset?

Emma's inward breath was almost a gasp. 'Have you told Ollie and Poppy?'

'No.' The word was a snap. 'And I don't want to.'

Thank goodness for that. The children must have simply picked up on the atmosphere and then assumed—as children were so good at doing—that it was somehow *their* fault. That was cruel, too, if it wasn't fixed. Emma would fix it as soon as she could.

'What I *do* want,' Adam continued, 'is for you to leave Braeburn. As soon as possible. I realise that it may be too late today but there should be trains running tomorrow. I've booked a room at The Inn for you. That's nice and close to the station.'

'But tomorrow's Christmas Eve.'

'I'm aware of the date.'

'I'm supposed to be helping with the school concert. The…the children's nativity play.'

'You can make some excuse. A family emergency perhaps.'

'And just…leave? Walk out and leave everybody to fill in the gap?'

'We managed before you came, Emma.' Adam was shuffling some papers on his desk now. 'We'll manage after you go.'

He expected her to go now, didn't he? To leave his office and then go home to pack and leave his house. She was being dismissed from her position as a nanny. From her position as his lover. Did he really have no intention of even *talking* about that?

Okay. She could understand why the barriers had gone back up. He knew she had made an offer of something she might not be able to follow through on and he'd seen history repeating itself with a loss in the near future that would have a dreadful effect on the children. And on himself? That was bitter-sweet. He was telling her how much she meant to him even as he pushed her away.

Maybe if it wasn't Christmastime, this wouldn't be happening like this. She'd been the one to force the celebration back into Adam's life and now it must seem like she was about to break his heart in exactly the same way it had been broken three years ago, when he'd lost the love of his life and his children had lost their beloved mother.

This was the first Christmas the children would be really celebrating at home and they were so excited about the play. About being the key characters of Joseph and Mary and—even more—about Jemima being part of the production. It had been her idea to include Jemima. Would that even happen if she wasn't here?

That did it. This might be all her fault but she wasn't going to let everything be ruined.

'No,' she said.

Adam looked up from his papers. 'I beg your pardon?'

'No,' Emma repeated. 'I understand why you want me to go…' Her voice wobbled. She couldn't say anything about how upset she was at him ending what they'd had between them like this because if she went down that track, she'd lose all the courage she knew she needed. 'But I'm not going to leave while I'm needed here. I can find somewhere else to stay but I promised Caitlin I'd be there to help with the singing and the play and…and I promised the children I'd be there.' She lifted her chin and took a steadying breath so that she could sound totally in control. 'I never break my promises.'

Caitlin would put her up for a night or two. Or she could stay at The Inn if that wasn't possible. She'd just have to dream up some reason for her absence to keep Poppy and Oliver as happy as possible.

Adam was looking at his papers again. 'Do what you need to,' he growled. 'I'll cope.'

Where had she heard those words before? Emma wondered, as she managed to find a smile for Oliver and Poppy as she led them out of the clinic.

Oh, yes… That had been exactly what Adam had said when she'd asked for the time off to go to Edinburgh. When she'd lied to him about the job interview.

'Is Daddy still cross?' Poppy asked as Emma clipped the belt over her car seat.

'No, sweetheart. And he was never cross with you.'

'Who was he cross with, then?' Oliver asked.

Me, Emma thought. And she had brought it on herself with her deception. She took another one of those steadying breaths.

'Sometimes grown-ups get cross because there's too much to do and people need things that are hard to give them. Daddy has to help lots of people and sometimes it's hard. Like when Mrs Jessop's baby was so sick.'

'But you help lots of people, too, and *you* don't get cross.'

Emma leaned in to kiss Poppy before she closed the door. In the time it took her to get to the driver's seat, inspiration had struck.

'Miss McMurray has an awful lot to do at the moment to get ready for your concert tomorrow. I know she doesn't get cross very often but I'm going to go and help her to make sure she doesn't. It might get very late so I'll probably stay at her house.'

'But you'll come back, won't you?' Poppy sounded anxious. 'It's only *two* sleeps till Christmas.'

'It *is*.' Emma turned on the car's lights and the windscreen wipers. 'Oh...look at how hard it's snowing. Isn't that pretty?'

Adam's parting words replayed themselves like an echo in Emma's head as she went through what had become such a joyous routine of caring for children and pets and trying to cook. She was getting better at it but it was a bonus to find one of Catherine's casseroles hiding in the freezer when she went to find some frozen peas. It had been wedged behind the turkey.

What had Catherine said about that? Didn't it need to come out of the freezer two days before Christmas so that it had time to thaw? Emma lifted the heavy bird and put it in the scullery tub. Not that she'd be here to cook it and maybe that was for the best. There was no way Adam could avoid celebrating Christmas now, what with all the decorations all over the house and the tree there waiting for the gifts to appear. At least she'd given this little family that much. And Adam probably knew how to cook a turkey.

As he'd said, he'd cope.

The first time he'd said those words had been the turning point, hadn't it? When Emma had decided that the real gift she could give Adam was hope. To show him what it could be like to let someone close. To be really happy again.

Well, it had worked, hadn't it?

Too well.

He'd accepted that gift and given his own in return. He'd shown her what it was like to be truly loved.

And now he knew that it had been false hope that she had offered.

But how could he be so sure? Did he know something that she didn't know? Emma stood there in the scullery, staring at the frozen turkey without seeing it. Had accessing her medical records somehow given him information that Jack had been unwilling to give her so close to Christmas?

A lightning bolt unleashed itself from the dark cloud that was pressing ever closer. If only she hadn't agreed to have the test so soon she could have kept it at bay for just a little longer.

There was no way to push it back now. All she could do was honour the promises she had made and then find somewhere she could gather strength to deal with the storm when it finally broke.

California maybe?

She was gone.

This time, the silence of the house had an almost ominous edge. It wasn't just an overnight absence. Emma was gone from his house and after tomorrow she would be gone from his life as well.

Adam had been late home after going to check that Jock was coping back on the farm and the children were already tucked up in bed and asleep. Emma's bag had been sitting beside her guitar case near the clock and within minutes of his arrival Caitlin McMurray had driven up to collect her. His dinner was keeping warm in the stove, she'd told him. The turkey was thawing in the scullery tub and she'd left some gifts under the Christmas tree and hoped that would be okay. And she'd said that she was sorry...so very sorry...

Too weary to feel hungry, Adam sat on a chair at the kitchen table beneath all those rainbow-coloured paper chains and downed the last shot his whisky bottle had to offer. The emotional roller-coaster of his day had left him drained enough to feel numb.

Or maybe not completely numb. There was pain to be found that had to be coming from the broken shards of that glass bubble of hope. And pain was a close neighbour to anger. Easy to step over the boundary and preferable to direct the anger towards someone else. He'd used this method of defence before but he knew it came with some fine print. It was only a matter of time before the anger turned inwards and became a sense of failure. He hadn't been enough as a husband.

He hadn't even been enough as a lover this time around.

Was he enough as a doctor? Joan McClintock probably thought so by now, as she lay in the cardiology ward of the infirmary, recovering from her angioplasty. And Old Jock definitely did. He'd said as much when Adam had taken the groceries that Eileen had put together and gone up the hill to visit him. He could swear there had been tears in the old man's eyes when Jock had gripped his arm in farewell.

'You and that wee lassie saved my life, son. I might not be up to playing my pipes tomorrow but I'll be back on deck next year, you wait and see.'

The Jessops would be spending a quiet Christmas in the neonatal intensive care unit but it would be a celebration because they'd be able to hold their precious new baby and talk about the day in the not-too-distant future when they'd be able to take her home. She'd need careful monitoring for her first years of life but it would be a joy to be responsible for that.

Yes. Adam could take comfort in knowing that he *was* enough of a doctor for this village. That he was deeply woven into the community fabric and he was needed here.

Was he enough as a father?

With a heavy tread and two unusually subdued dogs, Adam climbed the staircase of his old family home and went to check on his sleeping children. Oliver lay sprawled on his back at an angle that had his head almost touching the wheels of the train engine tucked in the corner beside his pillow. Adam gently moved the toy as he bent to kiss his son.

Poppy was rolled into a ball and her eyes were squeezed tightly shut. She had her Gran's old teddy clutched in her arms.

'Are you awake, sweetheart?' Adam whispered.

She must be dreaming, he decided when he got no

response. He pulled the duvet up to cover her back and kissed the top of her head.

'Sleep tight,' he murmured. 'Love you.'

The hallway outside the children's rooms was quiet and still. The half-open door of the empty guest room further down was eloquent enough to be an accusation. There would be no music coming from that room again. No small, fairy-like woman would emerge with joy in her eyes and laughter just waiting to bubble free. With hands and lips and a body that could make a man feel like…like he was, well, more than enough.

Maybe it would help to shut the door.

Adam wasn't sure why he flicked the light on. Perhaps because it seemed suddenly beyond belief that Emma *had* really gone?

The room was empty, of course. The bed neatly made. A vase that his mother must have put in here before she'd left had a sprig of holly in it—a fragment of the festive bowl that was on the kitchen table downstairs. A tiny bit of the Christmas Emma had been so determined to spread throughout this house.

And there was something else. A glint under the bed that the light was catching. Stooping, Adam found it was a disk. A copy of the recording made with Braeburn school's junior choir? He'd heard all about it but he hadn't actually heard the singing, had he? And it wasn't good enough. With the disk in his hand Adam went back downstairs and into the library to turn on the computer. The fire was only a glow in the grate but the dogs curled up as close as they could on the rug.

He had expected to only hear sound when he pushed play on the menu. The image that filled the screen was a shock. It was Emma and another young woman. The photo must have been taken with a mobile phone. Two happy girls at a party somewhere. Emma looked so much younger. Her hair was a thick mass of curls and her face was different. Plumper. Carefree.

He should have stopped right there—the moment he knew that this was something personal and nothing to do with his children or their carol singing—but the photo was dissolving into the next image in the slide show and the exquisite plucked notes of the guitar were being accompanied by words.

It was the song he'd come to know from the snatches he'd heard late at night as he'd paused at the top of the stairs. A song about memories and friendship. About love. He knew he was seeing something never intended for his eyes when he recognised the man that he'd seen Emma with at the hospital today and he would have stopped it except that the next image was so shocking.

Emma in a hospital bed, completely bald and with her face unnaturally puffy. An IV line snaked beneath the hem of her gown.

Of course. He'd been right in thinking what that tiny scar was about. She'd had a central line inserted as a portal for major drug therapy.

Chemotherapy. That was the only thing that could make someone look like this. And you only got chemotherapy for cancer treatment.

And yet Emma was smiling. Laughing, even? It was so easy to recognise her despite the drastically altered appearance because the image captured that joy that was what Emma was all about.

The stunning effect was still there even as the image dissolved into a new one and it was only then that Adam could register the words of the song's chorus.

*We've shared the sunshine and we've shared the
rain...*
Just by being there, you eased the pain...

He couldn't see the next image. Or the next, because
his vision had blurred. He barely heard the rest of the song
as he bent his head and covered his eyes with his hands.

The longing was too much.

He wanted to be the one to share the good times with
Emma. To be there to hold her in the bad times.

Was she still sick? Was *that* why she'd been at the infirmary?

The longing morphed into a fierce protectiveness. A
need to care for her for as long as possible—even if they
both knew it might not be very long.

Maybe there was another man who was special to her
and there was no future for *him* with Emma, but she might
know that she didn't have much time left and she'd chosen to be *here*. Not with anyone else but with him and his
children. To give herself in every way possible to make
this Christmas special. It was only now that it was dawn-
ing on him how incredibly lucky they'd been.

The children were going to be heartbroken to wake up
on Christmas morning to a house that contained the gifts
but not the person who'd chosen them. The magic she'd
created would be spoilt.

And he'd been the one to send her away. She would be
leaving Braeburn as soon as tomorrow's concert was over.
He'd never have the chance to tell her what she'd given his
children in making Christmas happen. What she'd given
him in that he now knew he was capable of letting go of
the past and that he could find real joy in his life again.

That he could feel hope.

A nudge under his elbow made Adam uncover his eyes. He hadn't noticed the dogs coming to flank his chair and the steady gaze from Bob offered limitless sympathy and something more. Wisdom? He scratched his old dog's ears.

'You're right,' he murmured. 'I can't let that happen, can I?'

CHAPTER ELEVEN

'JANET CALLED WHILE you were in the shower.'

'Oh?' Emma sipped the mug of coffee Caitlin had put in front of her. 'Who's Janet?'

'My brother's girlfriend's aunt. The one who runs the donkey sanctuary.'

'Oh…is there a problem? I thought she was delighted to help with getting Jemima to the concert. Is it the snow?' Emma took a worried glance out of the window. 'It is getting awfully heavy, isn't it?'

Caitlin laughed. 'Don't stress. I'm doing that enough for both of us. No. Aunty Janet's still as keen as mustard. In fact, she's bringing an extra donkey. He's called Dougal.'

'But we don't need *two* donkeys.'

'He's back-up—just in case Jemima doesn't want to co-operate. Apparently Dougal's done this sort of thing before. He's a darling, Janet says, and if Jemima's not used to getting into a float then having another donkey can help. Plus…'

Emma had to smile at Caitlin's expression and the raised forefinger that advertised how important this was. The connection she'd found with this new friend was partly due to how their imaginations were caught by the same things. She had to try and squash the sadness of how much she was going to miss this friendship. Caitlin hadn't asked about how soon she would be leaving Braeburn. She only knew that she was no longer needed as the McAllister nanny.

'Plus what?'

'Well… Dougal's looking for a new home. Janet was a bit worried when she heard that Jemima is an only donkey. She says they get very lonely by themselves and they can get very noisy.'

'Jemima's certainly noisy.' Poppy had said the same thing, hadn't she? That Jemima needed a friend. Another wave of sadness hit as she remembered the time with the children that day. When they'd picked the bunch of holly and made the paper chains. She was so going to miss their laughter and cuddles and the sheer joy of singing together.

'So what I'm saying is that Dougal doesn't necessarily have to go back to the sanctuary. He could be a Christmas gift for the McAllister family.'

'Oh…that's a lovely idea…but…' Emma bit her lip. It wasn't her place to accept, was it? She'd already given things to the McAllisters that were going to have long-term consequences. The thought of the damage she might have done had already formed a horrible knot in her stomach. 'You'll have to ask Adam about that.'

'I'll get Janet to talk to him. She's very persuasive.' With a nod and another smile Caitlin moved on to the next item on the agenda for her busy day. 'I need to talk to Moira about finding another piper to open the concert. Old Jock's always done it but he's not well enough this time. I don't want to offend him by asking someone whose playing he doesn't respect, though.'

Emma grinned. 'Village politics, huh?'

'You're not wrong there.' But Caitlin looked up from her list, shaking her head. 'You know, it usually takes a generation or more before someone becomes part of the heart of a village like this. You've managed to do it in the space of a few weeks.'

'Hardly. I'm still a stranger.' But Emma had to swallow a big lump in her throat. She *felt* like a part of the heart of Braeburn, which was something that could only have happened so fast because it felt like the place she was supposed to be. With the people she was supposed to be with.

'You saved Jock,' Caitlin reminded her. 'You've saved the village hall with the funds that CD's going to raise. Plus...' She held up her finger again. 'You've saved my reputation as the teacher who can pull the end-of-the-year concert together.' She heaved a huge sigh. 'There are still a million things to do, though. There's the backdrop to paint and the hall to decorate and hay to get delivered and I don't know if Bryan's finished making the cradle yet. And I've got to ring Jeannie's mum to make sure they don't forget to bring the baby doll and...'

Emma finished her coffee. This was good. She would be too busy to dwell on what would happen after the concert. 'What can I do to help?'

'Ye canna say no.'

'But, Jock...I haven't touched the pipes in years.' The Velcro of the blood-pressure cuff made a decisive ripping sound as Adam removed it from Old Jock's arm. 'I'd be as rusty as your coronary arteries were before the stents went in.'

'Nonsense, lad.' The old man fixed Adam with a steely glance. 'No laddie I taught ever forgets and you were the best. There's no one else I'd choose to take my place and I told that McMurray lassie from the school that I'd find my own replacement.'

He didn't have time to stand here arguing with Jock. It

had taken time to organise the children this morning and get them to their friends' houses for the day so that he could check on his patients and be available for any emergencies. They'd been so slow, too. Uncooperative. Oliver had kicked his chair more than once and refused to even look for his songbook and Poppy had been in tears and refused to eat any breakfast.

'I want Emma to make my breakfast,' she'd sobbed. 'I *love* Emma.'

He had to try and be home at four p.m. as well for the woman who was coming to collect Jemima in a float. Emma should be there for that, shouldn't she? It had been her crazy idea in the first place. But it was his fault that she wouldn't be there and he had to start fixing his mistake somewhere.

But to wear his kilt... To pick up his beloved pipes that had been gathering dust for three years or more...

Emma would be there.

He wouldn't just be playing for the village and showing them that he was ready to embrace life fully again.

He would be playing for Emma. Showing her the man he really was—the man he wanted to be again. He'd heard so much of her music but she'd never heard his.

Could it be a way to connect again? A chance to talk?

Maybe even a way to persuade her to come back to where she was needed so much?

To come back home?

'All right, then.' The words were the kind of growl everyone was used to from Dr Adam McAllister. 'I'll do it. What song did you have in mind?'

'The usual.' Jock's nod was satisfied. There was even a hint of a smile on the craggy face. '"O Come All Ye Faithful".'

* * *

The stars didn't align well enough for him to make it home by four p.m. and see Jemima loaded into the float, but the donkey was missing so presumably they'd managed without him. At least now he had the time to go and let the dogs out and to collect his bagpipes.

He wasn't the only person who'd been out and about, doing his job, today. A courier had been to the farmhouse and left a special-delivery letter. Unfortunately, he hadn't chosen a good place to leave it and enough snow or sleet had landed to make it very soggy. Soggy enough for the envelope to disintegrate as he picked it up.

It was addressed to Emma, not him, so he had no right to look at its contents.

And he wouldn't have, except that he could see that the stationery was stamped with the logo of the infirmary and he thought that there had to be some mistake and that the letter *should* have been addressed to him.

They were blood-test results. A whole raft of them. With a sticky note stuck to the top one.

Proof. Couldn't be better so far, Em.
Happy Christmas, love, Jack.

Jack. The man in the photograph. The man at the hospital. The 'almost' brother who had become a specialist oncologist and had looked after Emma's mother.

Who was clearly looking after Emma now. His signature was on the test results. This *was* why she'd been at the hospital.

His head was spinning.

He'd known, at some level, how wrong it was to assume

that Emma was deceiving him in the same way Tania had so often.

But why had she looked so stricken when he'd told her he knew why she was there? So *guilty*?

Because she'd been less than forthcoming about the nature of her 'appointment'?

Oh…dear Lord…did she think he was rejecting her because she was sick?

He *had* to talk to her as soon as possible. Never mind thanking her for what she'd done for the children or for him. He had the biggest apology in his life to make.

But he had a duty to do as well. He couldn't break his promise to Jock.

He had to find those pipes. And he had to get dressed for the part. A small part, thank goodness. He'd find a way to talk to Emma as soon as it was over.

The snow had stopped falling over Braeburn village on the night before Christmas. The cobbles of the narrow streets were sleek and dark where they'd been swept clear hours before but the perfect, white snow lay in a soft blanket on rooftops and gardens. It covered the bench where Emma had sat so many times to listen to Jock play his bagpipes and it coated the branches of the huge Christmas tree in the square, which only made the lights seem to twinkle even more brightly.

Not that there was anybody to appreciate the pretty picture. Most of Braeburn's inhabitants seemed to have squeezed themselves somehow into the village hall so that there wasn't even standing room any more.

Peeping through the curtains that were keeping several dozen excited children and just as many adult support crew hidden, Emma still couldn't see Adam anywhere. Surely he wasn't going to miss seeing his children perform? Her frown deepened as she noticed the size of the gap visible in the crowded space that led in a straight line from the entrance to the stage. Would Jemima really cope with carrying Poppy down that narrow aisle?

Aunty Janet didn't seem to think they'd have any problem.

'She's a darling,' she'd informed Emma that afternoon. 'Went onto the float without any trouble at all and then she fell in love with Dougal on the spot. She'll be perfectly happy until it's her turn to perform.'

Which wouldn't be for a little while, although the concert was about to start. The main lights had been dimmed so that only the fairy-lights they'd hung on the walls were twinkling now, lighting up the spruce boughs and holly branches. An expectant silence grew until it felt like the audience was holding its breath, and then Emma heard a familiar sound—somewhere between a honk and a screech—that would have had Sharon putting her fingers in her ears, no doubt. Someone, out in the foyer, was warming up a set of bagpipes. Caitlin hadn't told her who she'd found that could replace Jock without causing offence, but as the first true notes sounded it was obvious that a good choice had been made.

Who knew that bagpipes could play a Christmas carol with such haunting beauty? Coming down the aisle, it was too dark to see the face of the man holding the pipes but he was pure Scot, with the folds of a kilt brushing bare knees and long socks as white as the snow outside. The sight and sound would have been stirring no matter what was being played but the Christmas carol gave it an extra depth that brought tears to Emma's eyes.

This was about Scotland—the place she'd fallen in love with—and about such a special time of year that was all about celebration and family.

And there was a family she'd fallen even more in love with here.

As the lone piper came closer, Emma was sure it was her imagination—or the tears misting her vision—that made her think it was Adam playing the bagpipes. But right in front of the stage he stopped and lowered the pipes before turning to exit from the side door, and there was no mistaking his identity.

He was her gorgeous, gentle Scotsman. The lonely man whose heart she had touched—and then broken again.

She could feel a piece of her own heart being torn off in that moment.

Never again would she love someone as much as she loved this man.

Would it make any difference if she told him about the conversation she'd had with Jack this morning? That the initial results of all her blood tests were so good that he was confident she'd beaten her disease and could look forward to a normal life? He'd known how hard it was for her to believe. He'd said he was sending a copy of the results for her by courier.

It was the Christmas gift she'd wanted above anything else. It should have made her feel ecstatic and yet here she was, watching Adam exit the crowded hall to loud applause, and she was having to fight back tears.

The fear that she had lost something that would have made every moment of the battle she'd had to keep her life more than worthwhile.

Not that there was any time for that dark thought to last more than a heartbeat. The curtains were being drawn back now. Poppy needed a kiss and words of encouragement as she joined the other tiny dancers to start the evening's proceedings.

'You look gorgeous, hon,' Emma whispered. 'I just love

that new kilt that Daddy got for you. He's going to be *so* proud of you.'

She had expected Poppy to be bouncing up and down with excitement and that she would have to say how much she *loved* kilts. Or dancing. Or Christmas. But the little girl seemed uncharacteristically solemn and she clung so tightly to Emma's neck that she had to prise the little arms free as the dance teacher clapped her hands to shoo the troupe of girls into position.

It was Oliver's turn to perform with the other boys on the chanters next but Emma couldn't stop to watch. She had to get Poppy changed into her blue dress and shawl to be Mary amidst the chaos of mothers putting the final touches of moustaches and beards onto the wise men and shepherds and Caitlin trying to be in five places at once as last-minute adjustments were made to the nativity set behind the second curtain. The mothers would take care of Oliver's costume during the next item, which was an older girl reciting a Christmas poem. Emma's job was to go outside and help Janet get Jemima into position and primed for the grand entry.

The icy night air found the gap between Adam's socks and the hem of his kilt and made him shiver as he slipped outside during the applause for his son's performance. Behind him, he could hear Maggie MacEwen being introduced and then the girl's clear voice as she began her recital.

'"'Twas the night before Christmas, when all through the house…not a creature was stirring, not even a mouse…"'

Rounding the side of the village hall, Adam could see where the float was parked. He knew that Emma would have to bring the children and Jemima down this path so that they could make their entrance to the hall.

It still seemed unbelievable that his family's pet donkey was about to star in the traditional nativity play for the village. As extraordinary as the person who'd made it happen?

Yes.

Once she had Oliver and Poppy and Jemima into position at the front entrance of the hall, Adam knew she would take her position on the stage as the curtains were drawn back. With the music from her guitar and her lovely voice, she would lead the junior choir in singing the 'Little Donkey' carol for what would be a breathtaking opening for the traditional play that was the finale of the Christmas concert. Adam couldn't wait to see it.

But he didn't want it to start just yet. Not until he'd had a chance to talk to Emma.

Seeing her slight figure beside the float, holding the lead rope attached to Jemima's halter, made Adam's heart squeeze so tightly it felt like it might burst. She'd won the hearts of so many of those people tucked into the warmth of the old hall beside them, including his own children.

Especially including him.

He hadn't known it was possible to fall in love so fast— and so completely—with someone. Emma had not only won his heart, she would have it for ever, whether she wanted it or not.

She probably didn't want it. Not after the way he'd treated her. But he had to at least tell her how he felt. To explain why he'd reacted the way he had. To take the risk of making himself completely vulnerable in order to fight for the woman he loved so much.

'Emma…'

'Adam…' Emma looked startled but then relieved. 'Can you persuade Jemima to move? Ollie's still getting changed and she won't budge for me.'

Adam took hold of the donkey's halter and made encouraging noises but it was like trying to move a very large rock.

'She's no' going anywhere,' Janet—the woman who'd collected Jemima that afternoon—said. 'No' without Dougal. She's fallen in love.'

'What?' Adam peered inside the float to where he could see the fluffy back end of another donkey. 'There's another donkey?'

'Aye...' Janet's stare seemed intense in the soft light from the hall windows. 'I brought him in case she didn't like the idea of going in the float. But it seems that she's a very lonely donkey. She needs love in her life.'

'Don't we all?' Adam turned to Emma, who was also staring at him with a curious expression. One of hope? Janet had disappeared into the float. 'Emma, I need to talk to you. I—'

'Dougal needs a home.' The donkey had followed her down the ramp. 'Jemima doesn't need to be lonely any more.'

As if to add her opinion, Jemima made a soft, whickering sound and pulled away from Emma to touch her nose to Dougal's. The two donkeys stood there, side by side, their bodies pressed together.

'Do you think you could?' Yes. It was definitely hope in Emma's eyes. 'Adopt Dougal?'

Adam wanted to see her smile. To see the joy he knew would appear, even if it had nothing to do with him.

'Aye... If Jemima's in love then it wouldn't be right to separate them, would it?'

'No...' Emma was smiling. 'And it would make Poppy so happy if Jemima had a friend.' There was more than joy in her eyes. They were soft and full of love. Was it too much to hope that some of that love might include him?

Adam took a deep breath but just as he opened his mouth a figure came swiftly towards them from the street.

'Dr McAllister—thank goodness I've found you. You have to come—quickly. Bryan's fallen off his ladder. He was trying to fix the lights outside The Inn and he's come a cropper. I think he might have killed himself…'

For just a heartbeat longer Adam held Emma's gaze but there was nothing he could say. Not yet. All he could do was to try and communicate that this conversation wasn't finished.

It hadn't even begun, in fact.

He turned away. 'I'm coming,' he said. 'Let me grab my bag.'

It took only a few minutes to get to the scene of the accident. Bryan had, indeed, come a cropper and had probably knocked himself out for a short time. He had a good-sized lump on his head and had a mild concussion, but there didn't seem to be anything seriously amiss. But by the time they'd got him inside to the warmth and Adam had given him a thorough check, repeating his neurological checks at five-minute intervals, and finally decided it wasn't necessary to call an ambulance, at least half an hour had passed.

By the time he got back to the village hall, he knew he had probably missed everything. The entrance of the children, with Poppy riding Jemima, the singing of the children, the whole play perhaps. At least it was being videoed but the twins would be so disappointed that he hadn't been there. He searched for them on the stage where every performer had gathered for a final carol but he couldn't see them.

Emma wasn't there with her guitar either.

And where was Caitlin? Was there a problem backstage?

The children gathered on the stage were getting restless. A hum of conversation began in the audience, too.

It was getting later and a new snowfall could start at any moment. Everybody was ready to go home.

Adam ducked back out the front door and raced around to the side entrance near the stage. He almost knocked someone over who was rushing in the opposite direction.

'Adam... *Oh*...' Emma sounded distraught. 'Have you seen the twins?'

'No. They're not on the stage with the other children.'

'They're not anywhere...' Emma's breath came out in a sob. 'They've *disappeared*...'

Janet and Caitlin weren't far behind Emma. 'The donkeys are gone too. I had them in the float. I was just looking for someone to help me lift the back door.'

'Jemima must have undone the knots.' Emma's voice was shaking. Oliver had told her how clever she was at doing that, hadn't he? 'The children must have gone looking for them...'

Caitlin put her arm around Emma's shoulders but she was looking at Adam. 'They can't have gone far, surely?'

'But it's so dark...' Emma whispered. 'And cold...'

Adam had had plenty of practice in his career of not allowing panic to gain a foothold but this was the hardest test ever.

'It's been snowing,' he said, struggling to keep his tone calm. 'The tracks will be easy to follow. We'll get a group to follow where the donkeys have gone and others to look for what direction the children have gone, just in case they're not together.'

The snow was falling more thickly now. Silent, fluffy, fat flakes that would quickly obliterate any tracks.

They were already running out of time.

'Caitlin—go inside and round up as many people as you can to help us look. Make sure they've got at least one person with a mobile phone in each group. Janet—go with someone who'll help you follow the donkeys' tracks. You'll be the best person to manage them. Emma?'

Her gaze locked with his instantly.

'Come with me.' Her hand joined his outstretched one just as quickly. He held her gaze for a heartbeat longer but he didn't need to say anything.

They both knew they had to find the children. Nothing else mattered.

CHAPTER TWELVE

THE CALL TO action was taken up by every able-bodied adult present in the village hall on that Christmas Eve.

The children were kept in the warmth, guarded by Caitlin and a group of mothers. Braeburn's policeman, Angus, organised everybody else into groups that fanned out from the hall to cover every possible direction the children might have taken.

By the time the groups began moving, Adam and Emma were already in the village square. The lights on the big tree and in the shop windows twinkled as merrily as ever but the square was deserted and Adam's groan of frustration a loud sound in the kind of silence that only came in a snow-covered landscape.

'I thought they'd be here. They could never get enough of coming to see the tree in the last couple of years.'

Having her own hope snatched away had left too much room for fear to fill. Emma's gaze raked the area she knew so well now but there was no sign of any small people and the snow was a smooth carpet. The only footprints to be seen were the ones they were making themselves.

'But it hasn't been like that this year.' Adam seemed to be thinking aloud. 'Because they've got a Christmas tree at home, haven't they?' He raised his voice. '*Ollie*? *Poppy*? Can you hear me? Where *are* you?'

In the distance, they could hear others calling the children's names. Much closer came another shout as a square of light appeared between the windows of the local pub.

'What's going on? Is that you, Doc?'

'Aye, Bryan.' Adam walked towards the inn keeper. 'The twins have wandered off from the hall. We don't know where they are.'

'On a night like this? I'll get my coat and help you look.'

'No. You're supposed to be resting that head of yours. But if you see anything, call Angus. He's in charge of the search parties.'

'I will but I canna understand why the bairns would have done that.' Bryan shook his head as he stepped forward to grip Adam's arm. 'But they'll be all right. They've got an angel looking out for them, haven't they?'

'Aye…' But Adam had already turned away.

Why *had* the children run away? Emma's hand was on Adam's arm the moment Bryan let go.

'They must be looking for you,' she said. 'Maybe they realised you weren't there to see the play.'

'I *wanted* to be there.' The growl reminded Emma of when she'd first met Adam. 'I had no choice…'

'I know that. I'm not blaming you.' Emma squeezed his arm more tightly. 'But where would they go if they wanted to find you? The medical centre?'

'Aye… That's a thought.'

Adam started to move so swiftly that Emma slipped on the cobbles as she tried to keep up. This time it was Adam who caught her arm and then he took hold of her hand again and slowed his pace a little.

Please, be there, Emma prayed silently. *Be sitting on the steps of the clinic, waiting for your daddy.*

But they weren't. The steps were covered by inches of perfect white snow.

'Oh…*no*…' Emma whispered. 'I'm sorry, Adam. We've come the wrong way.'

'It's not your fault. It was a good idea.'

'It *is* my fault. I should have been watching them. It was my job and I didn't do it well enough.' The tear that trickled down felt hot against her frozen skin.

'If it's anybody's fault, it's mine,' Adam said. 'I sent you away. It was my responsibility to look after my children.' He hit his forehead with the palm of his hand. 'I didn't *think*…'

'You're the only doctor this village has. Of course you had to go when you were called to an accident. The children were safely in the hall with dozens of people.'

'I'm no' a good father. Just like I wasn't a good husband.'

'How can you *say* that?' Emma was shocked. 'You're a wonderful father. You love those children to bits, even if you've found it hard to show it sometimes. But everyone understands why. You had a perfect marriage. Everybody knows that your heart was broken when you lost the love of your life.'

'Nobody *knows*…' Adam was looking away from her. Poised to walk in the direction he was looking. To continue their urgent search.

'They do,' Emma insisted. '*I* know, too. And I'm sorry. I've only made things worse but I didn't mean to. I—'

'*She wasn't alone.*' The words were torn out of Adam. He still hadn't turned to meet Emma's gaze. 'When she died in that bed. Tania wasn't alone. She was with her lover. I wasn't enough of a husband for her.'

'*No*…' Shock was laced with anger this time as understanding sank in. As she realised that Adam had been living a lie for so long. To keep such an awful truth to himself to protect his children. Even his own mother didn't know because she'd never have spoken of Tania the way she had that first night if she did.

There was a complete lack of understanding mixed in as well. How could any woman have won the love of this beautiful man and then trampled on it with such devastating effect?

No wonder it was so hard for him to trust again. Or that he'd reacted to her own deception the way he had.

She had to get him to look at her so that he could see the truth. Reaching up, Emma touched his cheek, turning his head so that she could meet his eyes.

'*No*,' she repeated fiercely. '*She* wasn't a good enough wife for *you*.'

She could have come up with any number of reasons why Adam deserved to be truly loved but this wasn't the time and the interruption of Adam's phone ringing made Emma catch her breath. Good news? Had the children been found?

Adam's voice was loud a few moments later. 'What— no sign at all? What about the donkeys?'

He listened again. 'We'll have to go further than the village, then. It's stopped snowing now. If they're moving, they'll start leaving tracks again.'

If they were moving?

Emma couldn't bear to think of why they might not be moving.

Having snapped his phone shut, Adam stood very still and Emma knew he wasn't seeing the street. Or the square at the end where they could still see the flashes of the Christmas tree's lights.

'We need help,' he said slowly. 'A search and rescue team. Dogs.'

'Dogs...' The word was too quiet for Adam to hear. Maybe she hadn't even spoken it aloud but it was enough to trigger a powerful image. An old stone farmhouse at the end of a long drive, with a big kitchen and a fascinating attic. Fireplaces with dancing flames and snoozing dogs on the rugs.

Home.

The image morphed into something that felt like an absolute conviction.

'Adam? I know where they are.'

'Where?'

'They've gone home.'

'Why would they do that? It's miles away. They wouldn't make it. They're just wee bairns…'

'I just know it's the direction they will have taken. Let's get your car and check.'

'But how can you be so sure?'

'It's where I'd want to be,' Emma said softly. 'To be with you.'

For a long, long moment Adam held her gaze. Asking for something. Reassurance that the children would be found safe? Or maybe he was asking if *she* wanted to be with him?

All she could offer was hope.

And a hand to hold.

The house wasn't locked but as soon as they got out of the vehicle Adam knew there was no point in going inside, despite the urgent barking they could hear.

The driveway had been sheltered from a heavy cover of snow by the trees but the tracks were obvious in the headlights as soon as they got close to the house. Messy tracks that were more than just footprints that were marking a path that led towards the orchard and stables.

There was no time to find a torch so Adam used the light from his phone. He offered Emma his hand to guide her through the half-open gate and was still holding it when they got to the door of the stable.

It was a picture he would never forget as long as he lived.

Two donkeys curled up in the thick layer of straw, their noses touching. Between them, protected by the warmth of the fluffy bodies, were the two children. Oliver had one arm around Jemima's neck, his face pillowed on her neck. His other arm was around his sister. Poppy, in her blue dress, still had the baby doll clutched under her arm. Both the children had a healthy, rosy glow to their cheeks and were clearly deeply asleep. An exhausted Joseph and Mary with the baby. It was a nativity scene like no other.

The donkeys were awake. Four huge, dark eyes met the light but neither Jemima nor Dougal disturbed the children by even a twitch.

Adam's first instinct was to gather both children into his arms as if he would never let them go, and he would do that. But first there was something else he had to do. Quietly, he stepped back and made the call to Angus to relay the news that the children were safe and the search could be called off. The inhabitants of Braeburn village could go to their own homes and prepare to celebrate Christmas with their own families.

Emma was still close by and he turned to her as he ended the call. It was time to take the children in to their own beds but catching Emma's gaze stopped Adam again.

'I've been alone for a long time.' His voice caught. 'In a place that I never thought I could share with anyone.'

'I know.' She held his gaze. 'Thank you.'

'What for?'

'Trusting me.' She moved a little closer. 'I understand why you've kept the truth to yourself and that's something that will never go any further. The children—and the people of Braeburn—can always think that the mother of your children is an angel.'

'But you'll know…' Adam could hear the note of wonder in his own voice. 'And that means I'm not alone any more.' He had to swallow hard. 'It's me who should be thanking *you*.'

'There's no need.' It looked like Emma was trying to smile but he could see the way her lips trembled. He suddenly felt a little fragile himself.

'I found your song,' he told her. 'With the photographs. You left it behind yesterday. I'm sorry…I had no idea you were sick.'

'But you saw me at the hospital…'

'I got things wrong…' Adam closed his eyes. 'I saw you with Jack. Holding hands. I didn't know who he was and I thought… I'm sorry. It's no' been easy for me to learn to trust again.'

'But you trusted me tonight. You told me your terrible secret.'

'Aye…I already knew how wrong I'd been. Even before I knew who Jack was.' It was Adam's turn to move closer. Close enough to touch. To cup Emma's face and make sure she knew how much every word meant. 'I've been wrong about a lot of things but there's one thing I can never be wrong about. I love you. I want you to stay. With me. With the children. For as long as we've got.'

He saw a whole range of expressions flicker over the face of this woman he loved. Shock as she probably guessed what he'd thought when he'd seen her with another man. Forgiveness as he admitted his error. The birth of joy as he confessed his love.

And then she smiled.

'It might be a very long time. I haven't got the final

results of my bone-marrow test but so far everything's looking as good as it possibly could.'

'It could never be long enough.' Adam put his arms around Emma and drew her close. His kiss was slow and tender. A promise of what he intended to show her properly, very soon.

'Let's get these bairns safely into their own beds.'

'Aye…' Emma's smile was one of pure joy. 'And then we can get to ours?'

'Aye…'

With their arms still around each other, they went back into the stable.

Poppy stirred as her father lifted her into his arms. 'Daddy…' Her eyes opened and she turned her head. '*Emma*…you're back. You've come home.'

'I have, sweetheart.'

Oliver had woken up, too. 'I told you she wasn't going away for ever,' he told his sister.

'But I saw you leave,' Poppy said. 'I saw you talking to Daddy and you took your kit-ar and…and I was sad.'

'You don't need to be sad any more,' Adam said. 'Emma's not going anywhere.'

'You didn't see our play,' Oliver said. 'We went outside to find you and saw Jemima going home. We tried to catch her and then we got lost.'

'She's got a friend now.' Poppy smiled at Emma. 'She's got Dougal.'

'Dougal likes me,' Oliver said. 'He let me ride him and Poppy rode Jemima and she took us home.'

'I was scared, Daddy.'

'So was I, poppet. So was I.'

'But everything's all right now.' Emma's eyes were bright with tears as she held out her hand to Oliver. 'Let's go inside and get you two into your nice warm beds.'

Poppy was almost asleep again in her father's arms.

'Emma came back,' she murmured. 'I *love* Emma.'

'So do I, pet.' Adam's whisper was loud enough for them all to hear. 'So do I.'

Emma, with Oliver's hand in hers, came close enough to lean against Adam's arm as she returned his tender smile. He could feel the connection of her body against his and he could see a far deeper connection in her eyes. Here they were—the four of them—all connected.

His family. And they were together. And safe. And very, very soon they would celebrate their first Christmas together. A new and wonderful joy misted his vision.

He knew that it would be the first of many, many Christmases.

EPILOGUE

A year later...

No Christmas could ever be as wonderful as this one.

Even the joy of being present for Holly's birth in Canada last year was completely outshone by this day, as far as Catherine McAllister was concerned.

They should have used the table in the big dining room to host a Christmas feast for so many people but the inhabitants of this house had been adamant that they wanted to eat in the kitchen. Like they always did.

Adam was at one end and his gorgeous wife of six months at the other. Darling Emma. Catherine had known as soon as she'd set eyes on the lass that magic was going to happen but she'd never have guessed at quite how much.

At the sides of the table it had been a fair squeeze to fit everybody in. Marion and Ian on one side, with baby Holly in her highchair beside her gran. On the other side was Emma's best friend Sharon, whom they'd all come to love when she'd come over from America to be the bridesmaid for a summer wedding in the Braeburn village church. This time she'd brought her husband Andy as well, and they were flanked by Poppy and Ollie.

There was so much laughter. Like when Adam had been

telling the story of how disastrous last year's Christmas dinner had been.

'Neither of us had any idea what to do with that turkey. It wasn't till after we took it out of the stove that we realised there was a plastic bag inside it.'

Sharon needed a pat on the back so that her amusement didn't choke her. 'I could have told you Emma didn't know how to cook,' she said finally.

'I'm learning,' Emma protested. 'I have the best mother-in-law in the world.'

The real truth was that Catherine was lucky enough to have the most amazing daughter-in-law in the world but she didn't say anything aloud. She just shared a fond glance with Emma and then smiled at how quickly Adam defended her.

'My wife has talents that are far more important than cooking.'

'What's a talent?' Oliver asked.

'It means you're really good at something. Like Emma is with playing her guitar and singing.'

Oliver's nod was solemn. 'Mummy's going to be famous, isn't she?'

'You bet she is, buddy.' Marion had come back from Canada with new expressions. 'I'm not surprised a record company's signed you. That song you wrote for Sharon is just beautiful. No, Holly, don't blow raspberries. Oh…I've got custard all over my new dress.'

Poppy giggled. 'That's really *icky*.'

The delicious sound of the child's laughter and that odd word took Catherine straight back to the day she'd met Emma. To that interview for a position that Adam had clearly intended not to give her. He'd been so closed away back then.

Had he had any idea of how unhappy he'd been?

Things couldn't be more different now. Her son was not only happy again, he was happier than he'd ever been. And Emma looked better than she ever had. It had been such a shock to learn she'd been so sick but she'd just had her twelve-month check a couple of weeks ago and the news had been brilliant. Her doctor had told her she had beaten that dreadful disease and he didn't even want to see her again for at least two years.

No wonder Adam was fair glowing with happiness now. She was loving the grin on Adam's face as he listened to Ian's incredulous query.

'Is it really true that Jemima's pregnant? You're going to have *three* donkeys?'

Adam smiled at Emma as he responded. 'The more the merrier.'

Catherine remembered that smile later as she shooed everyone out of the kitchen to deal with the final clearing up. She put some turkey scraps into the dog bowls, wiped the last crumbs of plum pudding from the table and bent to pick up a scrap of paper left over from the crackers that had been pulled.

Had there been something significant in that shared look and smile? Maybe they were waiting for her to join them before making an announcement? Ducking her head beneath a paper chain that was drooping lower than the others and trying not to get her hopes up, Catherine headed for the door.

In the hallway, she had to smile at the wreath of mistletoe crowning the grandfather clock and the big tartan bows on the banister rails. She could hear a guitar being strummed but obviously not by Emma. The enthusiastic but inexpert performance had to be from Ollie, who would probably be taking his treasured Christmas gift to bed with him. Sure enough, as Catherine entered the living room she saw her grandson sitting at Emma's feet as she showed him where to put his fingers to make a chord.

Adam was right beside her on the couch, with his arm around his beloved wife. Poppy was tucked under his other arm and she was holding her favourite gift as well—fluffy drumsticks that she intended to learn to twirl so that one day she could join a real pipe band. The kind her daddy was playing in once again. The dogs weren't far away either as they lay on the rug in front of the fire.

The other sofa and chairs were taken up with the rest of her family and the special friends who'd been invited to celebrate with them. With the backdrop of the enormous Christmas tree and the screwed-up wrapping paper that Holly seemed to think was her special gift, it all added up to being the picture of a perfect Christmas.

How could life get any better than this?

And then Adam spoke and Catherine realised that life could get even better.

'We have something to tell you all,' he said. 'This summer we're going to have a baby.'

'I *know*,' Poppy squeaked. 'Jemima's baby.'

Adam and Emma exchanged a look that brought a lump to Catherine's throat. Had two people ever been so much in love?

'No, pet.' Adam smiled. 'A real baby. Emma's going to be a mummy.'

The shriek of excitement from Marion and Sharon faded as they all noticed Oliver's frown.

'Emma's already a mummy,' he growled. 'She's *our* mummy.'

Emma leaned down to kiss the small boy. 'I am,' she

agreed. 'But you won't mind having a little brother or sister, will you?'

'No-o-o...' But Oliver hugged his guitar more tightly.

'I won't,' Poppy said firmly. 'I *love* babies.'

* * * * *

CHRISTMAS WITH THE MAVERICK MILLIONAIRE

BY
SCARLET WILSON

MILLS & BOON

Published in Great Britain 2014
by Mills & Boon, an imprint of Harlequin (UK) Limited,
Eton House, 18-24 Paradise Road, Richmond, Surrey, TW9 1SR

© 2014 Scarlet Wilson

ISBN: 978-0-263-90803-9

Printed and bound in Spain
by Blackprint CPI, Barcelona

Dear Reader

Christmas is one of my favourite times of year. My last two Christmas books have been based in my nearest city, Glasgow. This year I decided to go to another Christmas setting—Innsbruck in Austria.

My nurse, Samantha Lewis, is desperate—she needs to work as an agency nurse to pay her mother's nursing home fees. She's used to dealing with children, but her assignment this year is a little unusual—help Mitchell Brody come to terms with being newly diagnosed with diabetes.

Problem 1: Mitchell Brody is an adult.

Problem 2: Mitchell Brody is a rock star—think Michael Hutchence from INXS.

Problem 3: Mitchell Brody has no intention of being 'managed' by anyone.

Problem 4: Being in a house with a gorgeous rock star is more than a little distracting…

Here's to the season of goodwill! I hope you enjoy Sam and Mitchell's story. Please feel free to tell me what you think at www.scarlet-wilson.com. I love to hear from readers!

Scarlet Wilson

Dedication

This book is dedicated to my fellow 'mums', Fiona Bell, Hazel Inch, Wendy Imrie, Deanne McLachlan, Fiona Kennedy, Karen Wallace and, in pastures new, Jeanette Aitken.

Our children are fast on the way to adulthood and it's getting pretty scary. It's great to have friends to share this with. Christmas nights out are never dull!

Praise for
Scarlet Wilson:

'WEST WING TO MATERNITY WING! is a tender, poignant and highly affecting romance that is sure to bring a tear to your eye. With her gift for creating wonderful characters, her ability to handle delicately and compassionately sensitive issues and her talent for writing believable, emotional and spellbinding romance, the talented Scarlet Wilson continues to prove to be a force to be reckoned with in the world of contemporary romantic fiction!'
—*CataRomance*

Recent titles by Scarlet Wilson:

TEMPTED BY HER BOSS
A MOTHER'S SECRET
200 HARLEY STREET: GIRL FROM THE RED CARPET†
HER FIREFIGHTER UNDER THE MISTLETOE
ABOUT THAT NIGHT…**
THE MAVERICK DOCTOR AND MISS PRIM**
AN INESCAPABLE TEMPTATION
HER CHRISTMAS EVE DIAMOND
A BOND BETWEEN STRANGERS*
WEST WING TO MATERNITY WING!

†*200 Harley Street*
*The Most Precious Bundle of All
**Rebels with a Cause

CHAPTER ONE

SAMANTHA LEWIS RAN UP the steps of the agency, pulling her bright pink scarf from her head and scattering a trail of raindrops behind her. The forecast had been clear, but she should have known better in damp London in the middle of December.

As she pushed open the door she was hit by a wave of heat and a rush of noise. No one in the agency seemed to sit down. It was constantly busy, dealing with desperate calls for specialised nursing care over the holiday season. She undid the buttons on her thick grey duffel and tried to find somewhere to perch until she could speak to someone.

It shouldn't be long. She already knew where her assignment would be, and who she'd be looking after—she just needed confirmation. Looking after Daniel Banks—a seven-year-old with cystic fibrosis—was really the perfect job for her. Three weeks' work for the equivalent of six months' worth of her current NHS salary. A match made in heaven.

It was hard work, but Daniel was a gorgeous little boy who needed round-the-clock care. His family clearly adored him, and having an extra pair of hands—expert hands—to watch their little boy over the Christmas period benefited them all.

She caught the eye of Leah, the receptionist, and gave

her a smile. But Leah, who was normally so friendly, looked away quickly and picked up the phone again. Strange.

She watched for a few minutes as a couple of familiar faces appeared, picked up their assignments and headed off back out into the throng of Oxford Street. At least she wasn't alone. Most other nurses she knew wanted to spend time with their families at Christmas.

Then there were the few who were just as desperate as she was. This was the best-paying gig of the year. The last two years she'd lucked out with Daniel's fantastic family. Some of her other colleagues hadn't been so fortunate and had spent the festive period being a cross between a house-maid, a nanny and, in one case, a cook, as well as a nurse.

There was a stiff breeze at her side as another door opened. Trish, the owner, stuck her head out. 'Sam, in here, please.'

She started fastening the buttons on her duffel again. Even though they were inside, the wind whipping around Trish's office was worse than the current gale blowing down Oxford Street. Trish Green was going through the 'change' and her staff knew all about her flushes and had warned everyone not to mention a thing.

'What's up, Trish? Aren't you just going to give me my assignment?'

She closed the office door behind her as Trish gestured to the seat in front of her desk. She couldn't help but notice the troubled look on Trish's face. The happy, shining feeling she'd had while climbing the stairs was starting to leave her.

Trish's face was flushed red as she sat down at the other side, a file clasped in her hand. 'I'm sorry, Sam. I did try to call you.' She hesitated for a second, as if she knew the impact of what she was about to say. 'Daniel Banks was hospitalised last night.'

Sam sat straight up. 'Is he okay? What's wrong with him? Is it a chest infection?'

Chest infections were pretty common for kids with CF and Sam was a specialist, she could give IV antibiotics and extensive physio if required. Trish licked her lips and took a deep breath as she shook her head. 'Nothing so simple. It's pneumonia. He's been ventilated.'

Tears sprang to the corners of her eyes. This was serious. Pneumonia could be deadly to a kid like Daniel. 'No! How is he doing? Have you spoken to his parents? Is there anything we can do?'

Trish sighed. 'Yes, I've spoken to them. They've been warned that all plans will need to be cancelled. They're in it for the long haul.'

Sam rested back in the wobbly chair. Daniel was a lovely little boy, so full of joy, so full of fun, with a body that betrayed his spirit. She couldn't imagine how the family must be feeling.

'Sam?' She looked up.

Trish had worry lines along her brow like deep furrows in the ground. 'I'm sorry, but it means your assignment will be cancelled.'

A chill swept over her body, every tiny little hair standing on end as her breath caught in her chest. It hadn't even entered her brain. Of course, she couldn't work for Daniel's family now. And, of course, she wouldn't be paid.

It was a horrible set of circumstances. Trouble was, her mother's nursing-home fees would still need to be paid at the end of the month. This was why she was here. This was the reason she gave up her holidays every year.

Her chest tightened. She still hadn't released the breath she was holding. She was trying not to let panic consume her. Trying not to say all the words out loud that were currently circulating like a cyclone in her brain. How on earth was she going to pay the fees?

Trish shifted uncomfortably in her chair. 'I had a quick look before you got here, Sam. I don't really have anything similar. I certainly don't have anything that lasts for three weeks and pays the same fee.' She shuffled some papers on her desk. 'I've got a patient requiring terminal care but they're in Ireland, a woman with dementia who needs to be accompanied on a flight to Barbados, and a child with an infectious disease who basically needs to be babysat while the rest of the family go on their Christmas cruise.'

'They're going on holiday without their kid?' She couldn't hide the disgust in her voice. 'What happened to holiday medical insurance and cancelling for another date?'

Trish couldn't look her in the eye. 'The father can't get other holidays, so the rest of the family have to go without the child.'

'That's shocking. Who does something like that?'

Trish shoved the paper under the others on her desk. 'Didn't think that one would be for you.'

The door opened and Leah hesitated in the doorway. 'Eh, Trish? That query earlier—it just came in. It's a definite. Flight's at seven from Gatwick. We need someone now.'

Trish's eyes flickered from side to side, between Leah and Samantha. She bit her lip and took the file from Leah's hand, opening it and sitting it on her desk. For a few moments she scanned the page in front of her.

Sam couldn't stand the silence—it let her hear the thoughts currently circulating in her head. 'Anything I can do?' Was that her voice, sounding so desperate? Had she really just said that out loud?

She needed a job. She needed something that paid her for the next three weeks, otherwise she'd need to go back and plead for extra bank shifts. Would three weeks' overtime pay in the NHS equal what she would get at the agency? Not even close.

Trish fixed her steely gaze on her. She cleared her throat. 'How are you with diabetes, Samantha?'

Sam straightened in the chair. It wasn't easy as every time she moved, the wobbly legs threatened to throw her to the floor. She couldn't help but search her brain desperately. 'I'm fine. I mean, I'm good. No, I'm better than good.'

Yip. Definitely sounding desperate.

Trish's eyebrows had risen, a look of pure disbelief on her face. If this was the difference between getting another job or not, it was time to put on the performance of a lifetime.

Sam took a deep breath. 'Obviously, I know all the basics as a nurse. But my sister is diabetic, diagnosed as a child. I know about hypos, high blood sugars, adjusting insulin doses and all the risks and complications.' It was true. She did know more than the average nurse. Living with someone with diabetes as a child was a whole different ballgame from looking after a patient for a few days in a hospital.

Trish was still studying her carefully. 'How do you feel about working with someone who's just been diagnosed? You'd have to do the entire education package and training with them.'

Sam licked her lips and nodded slowly. The fundamentals of diabetes hadn't changed over the years. She'd watched her sister change monitoring systems and insulin regimes many times. The most important factor was always going to be steady blood-sugar levels. 'I think I can manage that without any problems. What age is the patient?'

Trish was still shuffling papers on her desk. 'Do you have a current passport? And how do you feel about signing a non-disclosure agreement?'

'A what?' Trish still hadn't answered the previous question. Was the patient a baby, or maybe a toddler? Some kids could be diagnosed when they were really young.

Trish was looking a little shifty. She waved a piece of paper from the file. 'A non-disclosure agreement. You'd need to sign it.'

Now she was getting confused. What kind of job was this? 'Why would I need to sign a non-disclosure? That seems a little odd. All nurses are bound by confidentiality anyway.'

'This is different. It's not a kid. It's an adult. And he's a well-known adult.'

Something had just clicked into place in her brain. 'Passport? Is the job not in the UK?'

Trish pushed the file across the desk towards Sam. 'The job is in Innsbruck, a ski resort in the Alps. You'd need to fly there tonight. And this is all the detail I have. I can't tell you any more. You sign the non-disclosure and leave tonight. You don't find out who you're working for until you get there.'

Alarm bells started ringing in her head. 'What do you mean?' She scanned the piece of paper in front of her. It looked as if it had come from some sort of agent. And it was only the basics. An adult male, diagnosed with diabetes less than forty-eight hours ago. Assistance required in helping him learn to manage and deal with his condition over the next three weeks.

Her gaze reached the bottom of the page. The fee. For

three weeks' work. Her eyes were nearly out on sticks. How much??

'Is this safe?' Her voice squeaked.

She was trying to think rational thoughts, even though her brain was moving to rapid calculations of exactly how many months' worth of nursing-home fees that sum would cover.

It was all her own fault. When her mother had had the stroke over two years ago she'd spent the first few months trying to care for her mum herself. When it had become clear that she couldn't care for her mum and work at the same time, she'd changed jobs, swapping from a sister in an ITU, working shifts, to a school nurse with more regular and shorter hours. But the pay cut hadn't helped, particularly when she'd had to pay two mortgages and supplementary day care for her mother. And when the day-care assistants had failed to show for the seventh time and her mum had had an accident at home, she'd finally faced up to the fact that her mother needed to be in a home.

Picking a nursing home that was up to her standards hadn't been easy—and when she'd finally found one, the fees were astronomical. But her mother was happy, and well cared for, hence the reason she needed to work for the agency to supplement her salary.

Trish stood up. 'Of course it's safe, Samantha. I wouldn't send you anywhere you need to worry about. Now, can you be on a flight out of Gatwick at seven tonight?' She held out the non-disclosure agreement again, along with a pen.

Sam hesitated for only a second. How bad could this be? It was probably some aging actor who needed some basic guidance and hand-holding for a few weeks. She'd heard of Innsbruck before—hadn't the Winter Olympics been held there? The money was just too good to turn down. She grabbed the pen and scribbled her signature before she started asking any more questions that might make her change her mind.

She stood up. 'Innsbruck—that's Austria, isn't it?' She wrapped her scarf back around her head, trying to ignore the fact that she and skiing didn't mix. She shot Trish a beaming smile and held out her hand to shake it. 'A ski resort at Christmas? What more could a girl want? This'll be a piece of cake.'

Mitchell Brody felt terrible. He wasn't even going to look in the mirror because then he'd know that he looked terrible too.

The timing couldn't be worse. This was the last thing he needed right now. His tour kicked off in three weeks. He had to be fit and well for that. He needed to be able to perform. He had to get this under control.

The consultant was still shaking his head and frowning. 'You can't sign a discharge against medical advice. I won't allow it.'

Mitchell planted his hands on his hips. 'You can't stop me. Find me someone who can get me through this.'

'I've already put in a call to an agency in London. But it's a difficult time of year, staff are at a premium, and it will be hard to find someone with the skills you'll require.'

He sighed, frustration was building in his chest. 'Just find me someone, anyone, who can do this for me. I can pay. Money isn't a problem.'

The consultant narrowed his gaze. 'You don't understand. This isn't about someone "doing this" for you. You have to do it for yourself. You have to learn to take care of yourself with this condition. This is twenty-four hours a day, for the rest of your life. And it isn't an issue of cost. At this time of year staff come at a premium price. You have no choice but to pay it.'

Mitchell threw up his hands. 'I get it. I just don't have time for it. Not now. I'll learn about it later. I'll take the time then—in six months when this tour is over.'

'No.' The consultant folded his arms across his chest. 'If you don't do as I ask for the next three weeks, I'll notify your tour insurers. You won't be covered.'

For the second time in two days Mitchell was shocked. He wasn't used to people saying no to him. He was used to snapping his fingers and everyone doing exactly as he said. That was the joy of being a world-famous rock star. Once you earned beyond a certain point, people just didn't say no any more.

He could almost feel the blood draining from his body— as if he didn't feel sick enough already. 'You wouldn't do that.' His voice cracked as he spoke. This nightmare was just getting worse and worse. First the weeks of feeling like death warmed over. Then the ill-timed diagnosis of diabetes. Now a threat to his tour.

'I would, you know.' The consultant's chin was set with a determined edge. Mitchell recognised the look because he so frequently wore it himself. 'A sick rock star is no insurer's dream. You need to be healthy and in control to take part in the tour. To be frank, I don't think three weeks of specialist care is going to cut it. Even then, you'll need additional support on your tour. If you can't even adhere to the first set of guidelines I give you, then...' He let his voice tail off.

Mitchell's stomach was churning. It wasn't as if he wasn't rich already. But this tour had been planned for two years. The proceeds were going towards the funding of the children's hospital in this area. He'd supported it for years—but always on the condition that no one knew. The last thing he needed was the press invading the one part of his life that was still private. His funding had kept the children's hospital afloat for the last ten years. But things had changed. The building couldn't be repaired any more, the whole place needed to be rebuilt. And why rebuild anything half-heartedly? The plans had been drawn up and approved for a brand-new state-of-the-art facility. All they needed was the guaranteed cash. That's why he couldn't let them down—no matter how sick he was.

'Fine. I'll do it. Just find me someone.' He walked away in frustration and started stuffing his clothes into a holdall.

The consultant gave him a nod and disappeared down the corridor, coming back five minutes later. 'You're in luck. The agency called, they've found you a nurse. Her qualifications are a little unusual but she's got the experience we need.'

'What does that mean?'

'It means she'll be able to help you manage your condition. I'll send her some written instructions by email.' He glanced at his watch. 'She'll be on a flight out of Gatwick at seven tonight. She'll be here around eleven p.m.' He pointed to the packed bag. 'I'm not happy about discharging you until her plane lands.'

Mitchell shook his head and picked up the case with his injector pen. 'You've taught me how to do the injections. I take ten units tonight before I eat.' Then he pointed to another pen on the bedside table. 'And twenty-six units of that one before I go to bed. I get it. I do. Now, let me go. The nurse will be here in a few hours and I'll be fine until then.'

He could see the hesitation on the guy's face. It had only been two days and he was sick of the sight of this place already. Hospitals weren't much fun, even if you had the money to pay for a private room.

He tried his trademark smile. 'Come on. How much trouble can I get into in a few hours?'

* * *

The plane journey had been a nightmare. The man next
to her had snored and drooled on her shoulder from the
second the plane had taken off until it had landed in Innsbruck. She'd been doing her best to concentrate on the info
she'd downloaded onto her tablet about the latest types of
insulin and pumps. She wasn't sure what kind of regime
her patient would be on but she wanted to have some background knowledge on anything she might face.

Her phone pinged as soon as she hit the tarmac. Great.
An email from the doctor with detailed instructions. She
struggled to grab her case from the revolving carousel and
headed to the exit. She would have time to read the email
on the journey to her hotel.

She scanned the arrivals lounge. Her heart gave a little jump when she saw a card with her name: 'Samantha
Lewis'. It was almost like being a pop star.

She trundled her case over to the guy in the thick parka.
It was late at night and his hat was coated with thick snowflakes. There was something so nice about being in a place
covered with snow at Christmastime. Even if it was bit-
terly cold.

'Samantha Lewis?' He grabbed the handle of her case
as she nodded. 'Is this it? Just one case?'

She grinned. 'Why? How many should I have brought?'

His face broke into a wide smile as he shook his head.
'Last time I picked someone up here she had ten suitcases,
including one for her dog.'

'You can't be serious.'

He nodded. 'No kidding.' He had another look around.
'No skis?'

She shook her head. 'I'm here to work, not to ski.'

The guy's brow wrinkled. 'Hmm. Sorry.' He held out
his hand. 'I'm Dave, Mitchell's sidekick. You name it, I do

it.' He started to walk towards the exit. 'I've got a jacket and hat for you in the car.' His eyes skimmed up and down her body. 'It might be a little big but it's definitely your colour. I know you were called at short notice and we were worried you wouldn't have any gear with you.'

She tilted her head to the side. 'Who is Mitchell? I've not been told who I'm working for yet. And gear for what?'

An icy blast hit them as soon as they walked through the airport doors. Her grey duffel coat was no match for the winter Alpine temperatures. How nice. They'd bought her a coat and hat. She wasn't quite sure whether to be pleased or insulted.

He raised the boot on a huge black four-by-four and pushed her case inside. It was the biggest one she owned but it looked tiny in there. She blinked as she noticed the winter tyres and snow chains. Just how deep was the snow around here? He opened the door for her and she climbed inside. On the seat behind her was a bright blue ski jacket, slightly longer in style so it would cover her bum, alongside a matching pair of salopettes, hat, gloves and flat furlined black boots.

Her fingers brushed the skin of the jacket. It felt expensive. Thickly padded but light to touch.

Dave climbed into the driver's seat and nodded at the gear. 'Told you it was your colour. It matches your eyes.'

She blushed. Her eyes were the one thing that most people commented on. She wasn't sure whether being blonde-haired and blue-eyed was a blessing or a curse.

Dave started the car and pulled out of the parking lot, heading towards the main road. It felt like being in another world. They were surrounded by snow-covered Alps. The lights were glowing in the town in front of them. It looked warm and inviting against the black fir trees and high mountains.

'So, you haven't told me. Who do you work for?'

Dave's eyes flitted sideways for a second to look at her then focused back on the road ahead. 'No one's told you?' There was a knowing smile on his face.

She shrugged. 'Not yet. But I thought I was going to have to sign the non-disclosure in blood.'

'You're lucky you didn't.' She was joking, but he made it sound as if he heard that every other day.

'What's the big secret?' Curiosity was beginning to kill her. She hadn't given it much thought on the plane flight over, she'd been too busy focusing on the diabetes aspects and developing plans for a newly diagnosed adult patient. Plus, she still had that email to read. She glanced at her phone. Her 3G signal had left her. She had no idea what phone signals would be like in the Alps. She would have to ask for wifi access when they reached the hotel.

'Mitchell Brody. He's the big secret. He's just been diagnosed and he starts a world tour in three weeks. The timing couldn't be worse.'

Her mouth fell open and her heart did a little stop-start. So not what she was expecting to hear. 'Mitchell Brody? *The* Mitchell Brody?' Now she understood the need for a non-disclosure agreement. Mitchell Brody, rock star, was pure media fodder. Every time the man blinked it practically made the news. Roguishly handsome, fit body and gorgeous smile. But he was the original bad boy. The papers were full of stories about him waking other guests in hotels by rehearsing at four in the morning. Huge headlines about bust-ups between band members and managers. Wrecked rooms and punch-ups with other stars were everyday news. Whoever was the model of the moment, was usually the woman photographed on his arm. He was worth millions, no, *billions*.

Dave shrugged. 'Is there any other?'

She gulped. The neat plan she'd imagined in her head instantly scrambled. Mitchell Brody wasn't the kind of guy who'd take kindly to planning all his meals and insulin doses. He lived by the seat of his pants. The guy had never played by the rules in his life—chances were, he wasn't about to start now.

She sagged back against her seat as she realised just what she was taking on. 'Wow. I didn't expect it to be him.'

Dave seemed amused. 'Who did you think it would be?'

'Honestly? I had no idea. Maybe some kind of TV soap actor or rich businessman. Mitchell Brody, well, he's just huge.' She looked out of the window at the passing streetlights. The shops were full of Christmas decorations and the buildings lined above were vintage façades of eighteenth-century houses in multicoloured pastel shades of pink, blue, yellow and peach. It was like summer, in the middle of winter. Gorgeous.

The car turned up a mountain. 'What hotel are we staying in? Do you think I'll be able to speak to the chef?'

Dave frowned. 'What makes you think we're staying in a hotel?'

She watched as they started up the mountain range, passing Tirol-styled hotel after hotel. 'Isn't that where everyone stays?'

'Maybe everyone who isn't Mitchell Brody. He's owned a house up here for the last five years.'

'He has?' The snow was glistening around them. The hotels were gorgeous—so picturesque. All set perfectly on the mountainside for easy access to the Innsbruck snow slopes. She shifted a little uncomfortably in her seat. Snow slopes. The signs were everywhere. Why else would anyone buy a house up here? She wrinkled her nose, she couldn't remember any of the press stories being about Mitchell's antics on the snow slopes. Nope, those stories were all about Caribbean retreats and private yachts. She cleared her throat. 'Does Mitchell like to ski, then?'

Dave laughed. 'Does Mitchell like to ski? Do bees flock around honey? Does some seventeen-year-old try and sweet-talk her way past me at every venue we go to?' He shook his head and gestured towards the back seat. 'Why do you think I brought you the ski gear?'

'To stop me from getting cold?' Her voice squeaked as she spoke, as the true horror of the situation started to unload. Her one and only skiing trip as a teenager had resulted in her spending most of her time flat on her back—or face down in the snow. Water had seeped through her jeans and down the sleeves and neck of her jacket. She'd finally hidden back down at the ski centre in front of a roaring fire with a hot chocolate in front of her. When the ski instructor had eventually come looking for her to persuade her back onto the slopes, her answer had been a resounding no.

Even the thought of skiing sent a shiver down her spine, which Dave misinterpreted. 'Better put your jacket on, we'll be there in a minute and it's freezing out there.'

She nodded and wiggled her arms out of her grey duffel and pulled the blue jacket over from the back seat. It was pure and utter luxury, evident from the second she pushed her arms inside. Even though they were still inside the car, the heat enfolded her instantly. She tucked her blonde curls under the matching woolly hat and pulled up the zip. 'It's lovely, Dave. Thanks very much.'

She eyed the salopettes still lying across the back seat. It was a stand-off. No way was she putting those on.

Dave turned the wheel down a long private road. The warm glow at the end gradually came into focus. A beautiful, traditionally styled Tirol chalet. Okay, maybe it was four times the size of all the others she'd seen. But it was gorgeous, right down to the colourful window boxes, upper balcony and black and red paintwork on the outside.

She opened the car door and almost didn't notice the blast of icy air all around her. She was too busy staring at the mountain house. She climbed out and automatically stuck her hands in her pockets. The wind started whistling around her jeans. Maybe salopettes weren't such a bad idea after all.

'This place is huge,' she murmured. 'How many people stay here?'

Dave was pulling her case from the trunk as if it was as light as a feather. 'Just you and Mitchell.'

She sucked in a deep breath. The air was so cold it almost smarted against her throat. So not what she'd expected to hear. 'You don't stay here too?'

Dave laughed. 'Me? No.'

'And he doesn't have any staff?' She was trying not to think the thoughts that were currently circulating in her brain. Alone. In a mountain retreat. With a gorgeous rock star. She could almost hear her friend Carly's voice in her ear, along with the matching action punch in the air. 'Kerching!'

This was really happening.

Wow. Her feet were stuck to the ground. Snow seeped instantly through her flat-heeled leather boots, which had distinctly slippery soles. She should really move, but the whole place looked like a complete ice rink. She wobbled as she turned around and grabbed the fur-lined boots from the car. They had thick treads—obviously designed for places like this. It only took a minute to swap them over.

'Don't believe everything you read in the papers.' Dave strode over towards the entranceway of the house. 'Mitch is really private. He doesn't like people hanging around him. There's no cook. No PA.' He gave a little laugh as if he'd just realised what she'd be up against. 'Yeah, good luck with all this, Samantha.'

She blinked. She was going to be staying in a house *alone* with Mitchell Brody. The hottest guy on the planet. She might even have had a tiny crush on him at some point.

She might have lingered over some picture of him on the internet, showing off a naked torso with a fabulous set of abs, slim-fitting leather trousers and his shaggy, slightly too-long dark hair. The guy made grunge sexy.

She gulped. Her throat had never felt so dry. When was the last time she'd had something to drink? It must have been on the plane a few hours ago. Dave pushed open the door to the house and she stepped inside.

Wow. It was like stepping inside a shoot for a house magazine. The biggest sitting room she'd ever been in, white walls, light wooden floors, with a huge television practically taking up one wall. Sprawling, comfortable sofas and a large wooden dining-room table surrounded by twelve chairs. It screamed space. It yelled money. This place must have cost a fortune.

There was a tinkle of glass breaking off to her right, followed by some colourful language. Dave's brow wrinkled. 'Mitch?'

The headlines started to shoot through her brain. *Please don't let her first meeting be with a drunken rock star.*

She followed Dave as he strode through to the equally large kitchen. It should have been show home material too, but it was in complete disarray. Every door was hanging open, with food scattered everywhere. The door of the biggest refrigerator she'd ever seen was also open and Mitchell Brody was rummaging around inside—a glass of orange juice smashed around his feet. He didn't even seem to have noticed.

She glanced at Dave, whose face showed utter confusion

at the scene around him. Every part of her body started to react. She moved quickly. 'Is this normal, Dave?'

'No, not at all.' He hadn't budged. His feet seemed welded to the floor.

Her instincts kicked into gear. She had no idea what to expect. She knew next to nothing about Mitchell Brody—only what she'd read in the press. But right now he wasn't Mitchell Brody, rock star. He was Mitchell Brody, patient. One who was newly diagnosed with diabetes. 'Is anyone else here?'

Dave shook his head. There was no one she could ask for some background information. Dave had been with her for the last hour, so Mitchell must have been alone. She hadn't even had a chance to read the email from the consultant yet. She strongly suspected his actions were to do with his diabetes but, then again, she might just be about to witness a legendary Mitchell Brody tantrum. No matter what, it was time to act.

She moved over next to him, kicking the glass away from around his feet and touching his back. 'Mitchell, can I help you with something?'

He spun around and she drew in a deep breath in shock. His shirt was hanging open and the top button of his jeans was undone. His face was gaunt, the frame under his shirt thin and the six-pack that adorned teenage walls had vanished, all clinical signs of ketoacidosis. Just how long had it taken them to diagnose him?

'Who are you?' he growled, before ignoring her completely and turning back to the refrigerator and scattering some more food around. An apple flew past her ear, closely followed by a banana, and then a jar of jam, which shattered on the grey tile floor.

The look in his eyes told her everything she needed to know. Mitchell Brody was having a hypoglycaemic attack, his blood sugar so low he would probably pass out in the next few minutes if she didn't get some food into him.

'Move,' he hissed, as he nudged her with his hip. She looked around. She had no idea where anything was in this place. She recognised the belligerent edge to his voice. Her sister had had it frequently as she'd hypoed as a child. That fine line where she hadn't been able to focus or steady her thoughts and had moved into auto-protect mode. It was almost as if the adrenaline fight-or-flight reaction had kicked in and it had been survival of the fittest.

'What does he like to eat?' she asked Dave, as she started searching through the cupboards for something suitable. She needed something to give him a quick blast of sugar in his system.

Dave hesitated. 'Strawberries and apples—he has a smoothie every morning. Or he did, until this happened.'

She reached past Mitchell, who was still fumbling in the refrigerator. 'Get him over to the sofa.' Her words were brisk. She had to act quickly. She grabbed a punnet of strawberries from the fridge and some apples. The blender was sitting on the countertop and she threw the whole lot in and held down the lid while pressing the button. She pulled a carton of yoghurt from the fridge too. It was peach, totally random, but it would have to do. She dumped it in the blender as well and kept pressing. Dave appeared at her side, putting his hands on Mitchell's shoulders and guiding him over to sit down. 'What's going on?'

'His blood sugar is too low. If I can get something into him quickly, he should be fine,' she said over the noise of the blender.

She grabbed a glass from one of the open cupboards and dumped the contents of the blender into it. There were some straws scattered across the countertop and she pushed a couple into the drink. Seconds later she sat down on the sofa next to him.

'Hi, Mitchell, I'm Samantha, your nurse. Can you take a little drink of this for me, please?'

She held the straw up towards his lips and he immediately batted it away with his hands. 'No, leave me alone.' Her stomach was doing flip-flops. Every person was different, but from past experience her sister could also be slightly aggressive while hypoing. Not an ideal scenario. Particularly with a man who had more muscle than she did. Thank goodness Dave was here. Maybe he would respond better to a familiar face?

She held tightly on to the glass and persisted, 'It's your favourite. Just take a sip.'

His eyes had that slightly wild look in them, definitely unfocused as if the world around him wasn't making sense. He hesitated for a second, before finally taking a reluctant sip. After a few moments he sucked a little harder, as if he'd recognised the taste of what he was drinking. He grabbed the glass from her hand and held it close to his chest while he sucked.

It was a slow process, but one that Samantha was familiar with. She was patient, she could wait. Five minutes later the glass was nearly drained. Her hands were itching to find a blood-glucose monitor and check his levels—there had to be one around here somewhere. But she didn't want to leave his side.

Dave was looking pretty uncomfortable. He clearly wasn't used to anything like this and it was obvious she was going to have to give him a few lessons in dealing with diabetes too.

'What do we do now?' he asked.

'Now?' She sat back against the sofa. It was every bit as comfortable as it looked. 'Now, Dave, we wait.'

CHAPTER TWO

THERE WAS AN angel floating around in his vision. An angel with blonde curls, bright blue eyes and a matching jacket. She also had a weird matching hat on her head that made the curls look as if they were suspended in mid-air. Strange. His dreams didn't normally look like this.

The angel kept patting his hand and talking to him quietly. Those weren't the normal actions of a woman this hot in his dreams either. Maybe he was turning over a new leaf?

He smiled to himself. Maybe he could take his dream in another more Mitch-like direction?

There was another voice in the background. It was annoying him. Eating into the little space in his head that was cloudy and comfortable. But something else wasn't comfortable. His back ached. And for some odd reason he felt cold.

His hands touched his bare chest. Why was he half-dressed?

He sat up, trying to unload the fuzzy feeling around him. Ahh. He recognised that voice. The background noise was Dave. He was talking the way he did when he was nervous, too fast, his words all joined up and practically rolling into one.

The blue angel was still misting around. She was talking to him again. 'Hi, there, Mitchell. Are you back with us?' She didn't wait for a reply—just as well really, as his mouth felt a bit thick—as if someone had just punched him and given him a split lip. He stuck his tongue out and licked. No, no blood. But there was definitely something else, something familiar. Strawberries. When had he eaten those?

His brain was starting to function again. Tiny little jigsaw pieces slotting into place to give a bigger picture.

But one thing was still standing out a mile. The unfamiliar.

She touched him again. Only on his arm, but it was enough to make his senses spark. Contrary to public belief, Mitchell Brody didn't like people touching him, pawing at him. It made him feel as if he were for sale. Like a cashmere scarf or leather shoe being stroked in a women's department store. Yuck.

He shrugged her off and sat up. 'Who are you?' He shook his head, it felt like jelly was in his brain.

She smiled. A beaming white, perfect-teeth kind of smile. Who was her dentist?

She held her hand out towards him. 'You've been expecting me. I'm Samantha Lewis, your nurse. The agency sent me to help you manage your diabetes.' The smile disappeared from her face. 'And not a moment too soon. Why did they discharge you from hospital before I got here?'

A frown creased her forehead, ruining the smooth skin and showing little creases around her eyes. He'd liked her better before.

He moved in the chair, turning around to see the mumbling Dave.

'Dave, what's going on here?' His voice sounded a little funny. A little slow. His eyes took in the chaos in the kitchen, which looked as if food had exploded all around it. He stood up and pointed. 'And what on earth happened in my kitchen?'

The last thing he could remember was looking at the clock and wondering when his nurse would arrive. He hadn't even decided what room to put her in.

His shirt was flapping around and he did up a few of the buttons haphazardly. Not that he was embarrassed by his body. The amount of calendars he sold every year put paid to that idea. But it was hardly an ideal meeting with his new nurse. When had she got here?

New nurse. Now his brain was kicking back into gear he was more than a little surprised. He had kind of expected some older matron-type who'd bark orders at him for the next three weeks.

He certainly hadn't expected some cute, slim, blonde-haired, blue-eyed chocolate-box-type cheerleader. In lots of ways he should be pleased.

But he wasn't. Not really. Something wasn't right. Was this what the doctor had warned him about? How sometimes with diabetes you could be unwell?

After tonight's display he needed someone to get his condition under control so he could start on his tour. People were counting on him. Kids were counting on him—not to mention their families. The last thing he needed was some bright-eyed, bushy-tailed young girl hanging around him, distracting him.

She tapped him on the arm. The expression on her face had changed. She wasn't all smiles now. She was deadly serious. 'Mitchell, can you tell me where your blood-glucose meter is? You need to check your levels then we'll have a chat about what just happened.'

She spoke to him as if he was a child. Her tone and stance had changed completely.

So Mitchell did what he always did. He completely

ignored her and walked over to the kitchen, crunching on some broken glass on the tiled floor. 'Who broke a glass?' he yelled, spinning around to accuse Dave and the strange new nurse.

He held his hands out. 'What happened, Dave? Who did it? Who's been in my kitchen?' He didn't like disorder. That's why it was so much easier staying by himself—there was no one else around to make a mess.

Dave was pushing things back into cupboards. He turned around and rested his hands behind him on the countertop, hesitating before he spoke.

'Well, actually, I wasn't here. I went to pick up Samantha at the airport. And when we got back…' His voice tailed off as if he didn't want to finish.

Mitchell could feel his exasperation reach breaking point. He had no idea what was going on in his own home. 'When you got back, what?' He glanced at the clock and blinked, then looked again. The last two hours of his life seemed to have vanished without him knowing where they'd gone.

Dave laid a hand on his shoulder. 'You were raking about the cupboards and the fridge. We weren't quite sure what you were doing.'

It was as if the final piece of the jigsaw puzzle fell into place. Except it didn't slot in quietly, it slammed in, as if banged by a hammer. Realisation dawned on his face and he looked around again. 'I did this?'

Samantha appeared at his side. 'Mitchell, it's time you and I had a talk.'

This time he erupted. 'I don't want to talk! I want to know what the hell happened here!'

But his nurse didn't jump at his outburst. She didn't seem at all surprised. She just folded her arms across her chest as if she were some kind of immovable force. 'From this point onwards you do exactly what I tell you. If I tell you we're going to talk then…' she paused '…we're *going to talk*.' She pointed over towards the sofa. 'So get your butt over there, Mr Brody, and sit down!'

The heat in the kitchen was stifling. Samantha yanked off her goose-down jacket and flung it over a chair. If she kept this on much longer she would be roasted like a chicken. Her face must be scarlet by now.

This was definitely a baptism of fire. She looked at the clock—it was almost midnight and Dave had already told her he didn't stay in the house. 'Dave, why don't you go on home to bed? I'll be fine. I'll need to talk to you in the morning though, it's important you understand how to deal with things.'

Dave gave a grateful nod and disappeared out of the door as if he were being chased by a herd of zombies. All of this was definitely new to him.

Mitchell hadn't moved—probably from the shock of someone talking to him like that. What was she thinking? But she was his nurse. It was her job to take charge. 'Mitchell, your blood-glucose meter, where is it?' He was in shock, she could tell. It looked like he'd just experienced his first full-blown hypoglycaemic attack and was totally confused.

After a few seconds he turned to face her.

Wow. He was just inches from her, and Samantha had just experienced the full Brody effect—those dark brown eyes and perfect teeth. It didn't matter that his face was gaunter than normal and his body leaner. Teenagers all over the world would give their eye-teeth to be in this position. She was trying not to focus on the bare skin on his chest and scattered dark hair beneath the loosely fastened shirt. Trying not to lower her gaze to get another look at his abs.

She was beginning to feel a little hot and bothered again. He hadn't moved. His brown eyes were fixed on hers. Sucking her in and making her forget what she was supposed to be doing. What on earth was he thinking?

Then he blinked.

He pointed over to a blue plastic box nestled behind the sofa. 'It's there.'

The moment was completely lost and Sam mentally kicked herself.

It snapped her back into focus. She was here to do a job. Here to get this man well again. She couldn't stand around, mooning like some teenager. It was embarrassing.

She walked over, picked up the box and gestured to him to sit down again, but he shook his head and moved over towards the huge dining table instead.

As the minutes progressed he was getting more and more back to normal—whatever Mitchell Brody's normal might be. The dining table was more formal than lounging on the sofa. She was kind of annoyed she hadn't thought of it herself. She had to keep this on a professional level.

He slumped down into one of the chairs, his handsome face skewed by a puzzled frown. It wasn't familiar. She'd never seen a picture of him looking so dejected. It made things crystal clear for her. She had to take rock star Mitchell Brody, and what she knew of him, out of this equation.

This was a twenty-nine-year-old guy who'd just been diagnosed with a life-changing disease—and by the look of his body the diagnosis had taken a long time.

She reached out and touched his hand before she spoke. He flinched a little at her touch. 'Mitchell, I'm going to help you with this. Everything will be fine. It's still early days. We've got three weeks to try and help you get a handle on your condition.'

He groaned and shook his head. 'I don't have time for

this right now. I've got a tour starting soon. I need to focus all my energy and attention on that.'

She squeezed his hand but he pulled it away again. He clearly didn't like being touched—she'd have to remember that. It was plain he had a lot on his mind, but she had to bring him back to the immediate future. 'No, Mitchell. You have to focus on *this*. If you don't, there won't be any tour, because you won't be able to perform.'

'I won't?' It was almost as if his stronghold tower was wobbling all around him and about to come crashing down. There was real confusion on his face and it was the first time she'd seen him look a bit vulnerable. Maybe Dave was right, maybe she shouldn't believe what was in the press.

She flipped open the box and pulled out the blood-glucose meter. Although there were numerous kinds on the market, they were all very similar. She handed it to him. 'Let's start at the very beginning.' She gave a little smile. 'A very good place to start. I take it someone at the hospital showed you how to do this?'

He smiled, and opened his meter. 'Yeah, Dragon Lady was very bossy.' His head tilted to the side. 'Shouldn't you be doing this for me? Isn't that why you're here?'

The words were said more curiously than accusingly but it made her realise it was time to be very clear about what her role was.

'This is your condition, Mitchell, not mine. You need to learn how to manage it.' She held out her hands towards the still messy kitchen. 'We can't let things like this happen all the time. You need to learn how to control things. No one else can do it for you.'

She bit her lip. She was praying he wasn't about to have a monster-style, rock-star temper tantrum on her and start ordering her around. It would be so easy to tell him what to eat, check his blood-sugar levels and tell him what insulin to take, but it wasn't safe. He had to learn how to do all that by himself.

Children as young as five were taught how to manage their diabetes. And for all Mitchell was a millionaire rock star, he was still an adult with a condition that needed to be controlled.

She gave a little smile. She had the strangest feeling that Mitchell Brody wouldn't take kindly to being told what to do anyway. She was probably going to have to tiptoe around him.

He zipped open the fabric case and pulled out the meter, slotting a testing strip into place. The meter turned on automatically and she watched as he hesitated just for a second before placing the automatic finger-pricking device over the pad of one of his fingers. Seconds later he put a tiny drop of blood on the testing strip and the machine started its ten-second countdown.

Samantha said nothing. She just watched. He'd obviously paid attention when Dragon Lady had shown him how to use this and he seemed to manage it with no problems. One less thing to worry about.

The machine beeped and she looked at the reading. Four point two. She pointed at the screen. 'Do you know what a normal blood-sugar reading is?'

He nodded and sighed. 'It's supposed to be between four and seven, but mine was much higher than that in hospital.' She wanted to smile. He could obviously remember what he'd been told. Things were beginning to look up.

'It would have been. You'd just been diagnosed with diabetes. It takes a bit of time to regulate things.'

He leaned back in the chair. She could see the release of pent-up muscles, the fatigue that was common after a hypoglycaemic attack, practically hitting him like a wrecking ball. 'So what now, genius?' One eyebrow was raised.

It was too late to do anything but the basics right now and she had to prioritise because it was clear he needed to rest. She stood up and walked over to the kitchen, rummaging around to find some bread and pop it in the toaster that had probably cost more than her car.

'Right now we're going to give you something else to eat. Although your blood sugar is in the normal range, you've probably been running a bit higher than normal for the last few days. It makes you more prone to hypo attacks. The smoothie will have given you a burst of sugar—the last thing we want is for that to fall rapidly in the middle of the night. I'm making you something a bit more substantial to eat.' She glanced in the fridge. 'Cheese or ham on your toast?'

Both eyebrows went up this time. 'You're making me something to eat?'

She wagged her finger at him as the toast popped. 'This is a one-off. My priority is to get you safely through the night. I take it you've still to take your long-acting insulin?'

He scrunched up his face. 'Yeah.'

'Then you can do it after this. We'll talk in the morning about how best to handle things going forward.' She leaned back into the fridge and came back out with cheese in one hand and ham in the other. 'You didn't say which you prefer.'

'Ham, with a little mustard on the side.' She nodded and quickly made up the sandwich. 'We need to talk about food choices tomorrow,' she said, as she sat the plate down in front of him.

He groaned. 'Colour me happy.'

A smile broke across her face. 'Wow. I haven't heard that in years. My grandpa used to say that all the time.'

For a second something changed. The barrier that had been between them from the second she'd got there seemed to disappear. This time his smile reached right up into his weary eyes.

He wasn't the sexy guy whose calendar had adorned the staffroom wall at work. He wasn't the heartthrob who'd played sold-out venues around the world.

He was just Mitchell Brody, the guy she was alone with in a million-pound chalet in the snowy Alps. Right now she was living every girl's dream. Honestly? What nurse did she know who wouldn't kill for this job?

Which was why it made her feel so uncomfortable.

Up close and personal he had the kind of warm brown eyes that could just pull you in and keep you there. The kind that could make you forget everything else around you. And that was pretty much what was happening now.

The meter gave a little beep—reminding them to switch it off—and it jerked her from her daydreams. 'Cup of tea?'

She started boiling the kettle and searched through the cupboards for cups. He was still watching her with those eyes and it was unnerving. His gaze seemed to linger on her behind as she bent down to look in a few cupboards before he finally said, 'Top right for tea, bottom left for cups,' and took another bite of his sandwich. 'To be honest, though, I'd prefer a beer.'

Her brain switched straight into professional mode. 'It's too soon for a beer.' The words came out automatically before she could stop them and she cringed. He was a rock star—of course he'd want a beer. She had to try and push her bossy instincts aside and be realistic and put the patient first.

It was no use telling people who were newly diagnosed what they couldn't or shouldn't do. For most people, it just gave them the urge to rebel or to think their life would

never be the same. And that could be disastrous. She'd
seen exactly how her sister had reacted to things like that.

No. She knew better. This was all about making this
work for the patient. This was his life, not hers. She was
beginning to question her suitability for this job. It would
always be tricky to teach an adult about something they
might consider a new way of life. But to teach someone
like Mitchell Brody? It seemed like an almost impossible task.

She watched as he ran his fingers through his just-too-
long, messy hair. The man didn't know how damn sexy
he was. Then again, with the press and media attention
he got, he probably did. Working with this guy was going
to be more than distracting. Living in the same house as
him? She would have to bolt her door at night and only
hope that she didn't sleepwalk.

As there was no evidence of a teapot she poured the
boiling water into the mugs, squeezing the tea bags out
and adding milk. She put them on the table and took a
deep breath, 'Don't worry. I'll talk you through what to
do with your insulin and testing if you want to have a few
beers.' She paused, choosing her words carefully. 'When
the time is right.'

His hand moved slowly, lifting the mug and taking a
sip. He cringed. 'I like two sugars in my tea.'

She smiled and grabbed her handbag, which had been
abandoned on the table, rummaging around for a few seconds before pulling out a saccharin dispenser and click-
ing two into his cup.

He tried again. This time the grimace was even worse.
'That's disgusting!'

She shrugged. 'You'll adjust. In a few weeks you won't
even notice the difference.'

'Is that a promise?' He held his cup up towards her.

She nodded and clinked her cup on his. This was about to get interesting.

He was still trying to come to terms with the events of the last hour. If anyone had told him a few weeks ago that he'd be sitting in Innsbruck, drinking tea with a hot chick around midnight, he would have laughed in their face.

Drinking tea was not what Mitchell Brody was known for. But the truth was it was actually about all he could face right now.

For the last few weeks leading up to his diagnosis he'd known something had been very wrong. He'd never felt so tired, both physically and mentally. He'd been beginning to question if he was feeling stressed about the tour. Which was why he'd ended up here, his favourite haunt in the world—and the one place the press hadn't figured out he owned yet.

His house in Mauritius was regularly buzzed by helicopters. The townhouse he owned in London practically had the press camped outside the front door, and as for the house in LA. Well, it was a stop on one of the 'houses of the stars' coach tours. Privacy was virtually impossible.

Which was why he loved Innsbruck so much. He'd bought the house ten years ago under his brother's name. Tucked up in the snowy Alps, with direct access to some of the best ski slopes in the world. Who could want to stay anywhere else?

He loved the area. He loved the people. Most of all he loved the staff at the nearby children's hospital. His family had stayed here for just over a year when he'd been six. His father had worked for one of the big pharmaceutical companies that had had business in Austria and the whole family had had to up sticks for a year.

It had been great for two young boys. They'd learned to ski within a few weeks and had never been off the slopes until his brother Shaun's diagnosis. Then they'd spent the rest of the time in and out of St Jude's Children's Hospital.

From the balcony at the front of the chalet he could even see the roof of St Jude's. It was part of the reason he'd jumped at the chance to build here. Although his house was chalet-style, the expansive size almost made a mockery of that description.

He loved it here. He really did. This was his hideaway. There were people here that knew him as Mitch, the boy whose brother had had leukaemia, and had known him for the last twenty or more years. Shaun's recovery had been a long process, and even after they'd moved from Austria his family had continued to holiday here twice a year.

Here, he wasn't Mitchell Brody, rock star. He wasn't the guy with four homes around the world and a dozen fast cars. He wasn't the guy who'd fallen out of one nightclub too many, or had needed to be bailed out of jail the next morning. He was just Mitch, who had to queue in the local bakery for his favourite pastry, like everyone else. And he liked it that way.

He liked somewhere to be normal. He liked to be around people who had no expectation of him—where he was just another guy. Somewhere along the line all that had been lost.

With girls too. He'd been the spotty teenager who'd just wanted his first kiss. The young guy who everyone had laughed at for locking himself in his room all the time to practise his guitar.

But practice made perfect. He was testament to that.

His last album had achieved platinum status in a matter of hours, with women queuing round the block of the hotel he'd been staying in, hoping for a glimpse of him.

It was amazing what a few years of going to the gym, some filling out and a careless approach to haircuts could do.

But that didn't help with the girl sitting across the table from him right now, looking at him with those amazing blue eyes. He'd been so desperate to be discharged from hospital he couldn't have cared less what his nurse looked like. As long as she could get him through the next three weeks, that had been fine by him.

But he hadn't banked on this. He hadn't banked on her.

He squinted at her. 'What did you say your name was?'

She gave her head a little shake and laughed. 'Samantha. Samantha Lewis. I'm your nurse.'

He leaned back in his chair appreciatively. 'Oh, yes, you are.'

Her eyebrows arched and she wagged her finger at him. 'Don't start with me, sunshine. Don't you be giving me that kind of look. I'm here to do a job. That's all. I'm only staying up with you and making you tea so we can check your blood sugar before you go to bed.'

He leaned forward, planting his chin on his hand. 'Let's talk about this job. What *exactly* will you be doing for me?'

He watched her cheeks flush at the way he'd emphasised the word and the way she squirmed in her chair. He liked it. Samantha Lewis was different from the last lot of women he'd been involved with.

Right now, it felt like this diabetes diagnosis was a weight around his neck. Samantha Lewis might lighten the load a little.

'I'll be doing exactly what I should be doing. I'll be helping you monitor your blood-glucose levels, teaching you how to adjust your insulin and how to recognise the early signs of a hypoglycaemic attack. It's important you have good blood-glucose control. It'll help you stay independent and reduce the risk of any complications.'

He groaned. She might not look like Dragon Lady, but she was certainly beginning to sound like her.

'Let's talk about something else.' He leaned across the table towards her. 'Is there a Mr Lewis I should know about?'

Her body gave the slightest backward jerk, as if she was deciding how to answer the question. Then she took another sip of her tea and rolled her eyes at him. Her muscles relaxed a little, as if she was shaking off a little of her tension. 'Not that it's any of your business, but there's no Mr Lewis at present. I'm still interviewing possible contenders.'

Oh. He liked that. But she wasn't finished.

'So, Mitchell Brody—and is that your real name? —should I expect to find the latest female movie star or model hiding in the one of the cupboards in here?'

He grinned. A sparring partner. Samantha Lewis might even be fun. 'Yes, Mitchell Brody is my real name. And, no, there's no females hiding in cupboards, but I reserve the right for that to change.'

Something flitted across her eyes and the soft smile vanished in an instant. 'Are you expecting someone to join you soon?'

What was that? The tiniest spark of jealousy? He pushed the thought from his head in an instant. Ridiculous. She was his nurse. Nothing else. No matter how cute she looked.

'No.' He shook his head and held his hands out. 'To be honest, this place is my sanctuary. I've never brought a female...' he lifted his fingers in the air and made invisible quote marks '...*friend* back here. Dave's the only person you'll find sloping about. Oh, and the local maid service that comes in every day for a tidy up. That reminds me.' He stood up and walked over to the other side of the table where his phone lay.

'What are you doing?'

He scrolled through his messages. 'I got a text earlier and with everything that's happened I forgot to reply.' He looked around the room. 'What do you think? Red and gold? Blues and silver, or purples and pinks? No.' He gave a shudder at that last one.

'Red and gold for what?' She wrinkled her nose up again, it really did define the cute factor in her.

'The colour of the tree and Christmas decorations. The tree will come tomorrow, I just need to tell them what colours I want.' He looked around the sitting room. It really was looking kind of sparse. The tree and other decorations would give it a little warmth to match the fireplace that he'd forgotten to turn on.

'You get someone to bring you a tree and decorate it?'

He nodded. 'Yeah, every year. I just need to tell them what colours I want. What do you think?'

She shifted in her chair. 'Why are you asking me? It's your house, not mine.'

She was being a little frosty with him. He'd liked the version from a few minutes earlier. A sparring partner with some twinkle in her eye.

'Well, you're going to be here over Christmas too. I'd hate to pick something that made you shudder every time you walked in the door. I usually do this at the beginning of December, but with being ill and all I just kind of forgot about it.' He walked over to a big empty space next to the far wall. 'This is where the tree normally goes. They usually put some décor around the fireplace too.'

Her eyes narrowed as she looked around. 'It depends what you want. Red and gold would give some warmth to the place, but blue and silver would probably fit more with your white walls and pale floors.'

He sat down in the chair next to her and gave her a nudge in the ribs. 'Yeah, but which one would you *like*?'

He was teasing her again. Trying to goad that spark back into her eyes.

She gave a little sigh and took the last gulp of her tea. 'I think I'd probably like the red and gold best.' She hesitated. 'But you're missing out. Putting up the Christmas decorations is one of the best parts of Christmas. Getting someone else to do it for you?' She shook her head and glanced at her watch. 'Right, it's time to check your blood sugar again. If it's okay, you can do your night-time injection and go to bed. We'll have a chat about things in the morning.'

Something had just flickered past her eyes. A feeling of regret perhaps? It didn't matter how much he was paying Sam Lewis, she was still missing Christmas with her family to do this job. Maybe he should give that a little more thought?

He raised his eyebrows. 'You're giving me permission to go to bed?' He let out a little laugh. 'Well, that'll be a first.'

Her cheeks flushed again. She was easily embarrassed. It might even be fun having her around for a few weeks. She might make having diabetes seem not so much like a drag.

He sat down and took a minute to retest himself, turning the monitor around to show her the result of eight. She nodded. 'It'll probably go up a little more as you digest your food. That's fine.' She stood up and walked over to the door where her suitcase was. 'Where will I be sleeping?'

Yikes. He hadn't even told her where her room was. Hospitality wasn't his forte. His mother would be furious with him. He moved quickly, grabbing the handle of her case and gesturing for her to follow him. 'Sorry, Samantha. You'll be down here.' He swung open the door to the room. It was at the front of the house and had views all the way down the valley. He heard her intake of breath as she looked out over the snowy landscape and bright orange lights from the streets a mile beneath them.

It gave him a little surge of pleasure that she was obviously impressed. He loved this place and wanted others to love it too. She'd walked over to the large glass doors that led out onto the balcony and pressed her hands against the glass. 'This is gorgeous.' She spun around. 'And the room is huge.'

He pointed to one side of her. 'Your bathroom is in here, and the walk-in closet behind you.'

He pulled open the door to the closet and she automatically walked inside. After a second she threw out her hands and spun around, laughing. 'Mitchell, this closet is bigger than my bedroom back home!'

The sparkle was definitely back in her eyes. And he liked it. 'I'm glad you like it.' He pointed to the wooden sleigh-style bed with the giant mattress. 'Sleep well, because we'll be up early in the morning.'

She looked a little surprised. Did she think he liked to lie in till midday? 'Okay. What time do you want to have breakfast?'

'Six.'

Her eyebrows shot up. 'Six? Why so early?'

This was probably her first time here. He hadn't even asked her if she'd been before. He winked at her. 'Because six is the best time to ski.'

CHAPTER THREE

SHE'D JUST SPENT the best night in the most luxurious bed she'd ever slept in. She couldn't even begin to imagine the thread count on these fabulous sheets but chances were she'd never experience them again. She was half-inclined to try and stuff them in her case as she was leaving.

But the best bit was the morning. She hadn't closed the curtains last night and as the sun had gradually risen over the snow-covered Alps she'd had the most spectacular view. The bedroom balcony looked directly out over the hillside to a blanket of perfect white snow. There was something so nice about lying in bed, all cosseted and cosy, admiring the breathtaking, snow-covered scenery.

No wonder Mitchell loved this place. He'd called it his sanctuary. And as the press were usually clamouring around him for a story she could see why the surrounding peace and quiet was so precious to him. She could quite easily fall in love with it herself.

Everything about this job should be perfect. Everything about this job *could* be perfect—if only she hadn't spent most of last night tossing and turning, fretting about Mitchell's parting comment.

Skiing.

The words sent a horrible shiver down her spine. He'd been joking, right? He had to be. No one had stipulated she had to be able to ski, because that would have been a deal-breaker for her. She couldn't even begin to pretend to be ski-slope-worthy. More importantly, she didn't want to be.

But what about the bright blue ski jacket and matching salopettes? Maybe she should have asked questions as soon as she'd seen them. Maybe she should have asked Dave for more information last night. But there hadn't really been a chance last night.

In the early morning light she peered at her watch. Nearly six. She felt wide-awake now, but she'd probably hit a wall by lunchtime today and need to lie down for an hour. Not ideal when she was supposed to be supervising Mitchell.

Mitchell Brody. She honestly couldn't believe it. She squeezed her eyes shut and resisted the temptation to pinch herself. Her skin was tingling just at the thought of the fact that somewhere in this sprawling house Mitchell Brody could be as partially dressed as she was. Hmm. Or maybe he was in the shower, water streaming over those lean abs...

She wanted to grab her phone and start texting all her friends, but she'd signed that non-disclosure agreement, plus the fact that as a nurse she couldn't talk about her patients.

Chances were she'd finish this job and never be able to tell anyone a thing about it. But no one could stop her imagination...

She'd never been in a situation like this before, itching to talk about something but having to stay quiet. It was weird.

There was a noise outside and her stomach gave a little flip-flop. There was only one other person in this house. He hadn't been kidding. It was almost exactly six and Mitchell Brody was up and around.

'Knock, knock.' The low, sexy voice nearly made her jump a foot in the air. Without waiting for an answer, the door creaked open and Mitchell stuck his head inside. She bolted upright in bed and pulled the covers up underneath her chin. This must be what mild shock felt like; her tongue was currently stuck to the roof of her mouth.

He was smiling, obviously feeling better. He didn't seem to notice her lack of response. 'Hi, there. Gorgeous view, isn't it?' She nodded in agreement. She could hardly disagree. Mitchell was looking bright and sparky and from what she could see was dressed for the slopes. She, on the other hand, was wearing next to nothing.

She was trying not to panic. The easiest thing in the world was to drop back into nurse mode. 'Have you checked your blood sugar this morning? What about breakfast?'

Nurse mode put her on autopilot and before she'd given herself a chance to think about it she threw back the thick duvet cover and bent forward to look for her slippers.

She heard a noise. His sharp intake of breath before she realised what she'd done. Her short red satin slip of a nightie had obviously just given him an eyeful. Her hand darted up to press against her cleavage, trying to keep the garment firmly in place. 'Oh... I, I need to put something else on.'

But what? She'd collapsed on the bed last night with hardly a chance to open her suitcase. Thankfully, her nightie had been on top. But she couldn't even see a glimpse of the underwear she desperately needed right now.

Mitchell had the good grace to look away. But she could see the smile plastered on his face. Yip. He'd definitely got an eyeful. 'There's a dressing gown in the en suite if that will help,' he murmured. 'But don't feel obliged on my account.'

The heat rushed to her cheeks. Six o'clock in the morning and he was starting with his trademark cheek. He was going to have to learn that Samantha Lewis was *not* a morning person.

She walked quickly to the en suite and found the white fluffy robe hanging behind the door. She shrugged it on and tied the belt around her waist, trying not to think if someone else had worn it before her. There. Better. Being covered gave her the confidence boost she needed. Mitchell Brody was usually surrounded by a bunch of skeletal supermodels. She was surprised he hadn't passed out at the sight of some more womanly curves. She was lucky, naturally slim with maybe a tiny trace of cellulite. But absolutely nowhere near a supermodel frame. He didn't need to like it, though, because all that mattered was how she did her job.

She took thirty seconds to brush her teeth and didn't even waste her time looking in the mirror. What was the point? He was still waiting at the doorway as she walked over and put her hands on her hips. 'Now, where were we?'

He shot her a sexy smile. 'You were trying to decide if you should get dressed around me.' The drawl of his voice sent her saliva glands into overload. If her mouth hadn't been firmly closed she would have drooled. She didn't speak. Just gave him what she thought was a haughty stare and raised her eyebrows.

He blinked. 'Blood sugar seven. I've had breakfast and taken my insulin. It's time to hit the slopes before it starts to get busy.' He waggled his finger at her. 'You'll have to get up earlier if you want breakfast here, Sam.'

Her stomach gave an automatic growl. She didn't like to

miss breakfast and it felt like she was being reprimanded on her first day on the job. Cheeky sod.

'What did you eat for breakfast and how much insulin did you take?'

He frowned, his smile disappearing in an instant. 'I told you. My blood sugar is fine.' He glanced at his watch. 'I'm hitting the slopes. You can come if you want to. I'm not sure when I'll be back.'

She felt a wave of panic. There was no way she could hit the slopes next to him, but what if Mitch had a hypo while skiing? That could be disastrous.

'*No.*' It came out like a shout and she cringed inside. 'You're not ready to do anything like that. You need to wait a few more days until your blood-sugar levels are steadier. Then we'll talk about exercise and the effect it has on blood-sugar control, and what you need to do. You were only diagnosed a few days ago. It's far too soon.' Her voice was sounding much more authoritative than she actually felt. Her insides were curling up.

The furrows across his brow deepened, accompanied with a spark of fury in his eyes. 'Look, lady, I don't care what you say. The slopes are perfect and I won't be missing a second. If you want to watch me, come along. If you don't…' he pointed towards the still-warm bed '…feel free to go back to bed.'

He turned on his heel and left, leaving her to scuttle down the corridor after him in her bare feet. 'Mitchell, wait. I wasn't joking. Do you have food with you? Something to eat if you start to hypo on the slopes? Don't you realise how dangerous that could be for the other people around you?'

She was trying desperately to appeal to his sense of justice. Trying to make him slow down for a second. Trying anything to stop him heading for the slopes with her having to follow.

But Mitchell was a man on a mission. There was the briefest hesitation—as if he was giving some consideration to her words—before he clenched his jaw. Everything about him changed, his whole stance tense. The words were controlled but the strain was apparent. 'I'm done with this. See you on the slopes.'

He grabbed something from the countertop then threw open the door, bringing in an icy blast before he disappeared out into the swirls of freshly falling snow. She shouted after him, 'I'll meet you at the mid-station at seven!'

She took a few deep breaths as the skin prickled on her legs. The fluffy dressing gown was no match for the weather outside that currently circulated in chills around her pale skin. She slammed the door quickly, her brain frantic.

Should she throw on her clothes and try and follow him? Had he even heard her? Where on earth had he gone? She didn't even know the way to the ski slopes, let alone anything else.

Her eyes caught sight of what was lying on the counter. A packet of chocolate wafers, with a few missing. She smiled. She breathed the slightest sigh of relief. It might not be ideal, but it was something. He'd grabbed some before he'd left.

She made up her mind. She had the clothes. There were no excuses. She might not be able to ski, but she could be in and around the slopes. There was no way she could sit around here. Right now, she'd no idea if Mitchell intended to ski for an hour or all day.

And his attitude irked her. Mitchell Brody had a lot of learning to do. She flicked the switch on the kettle. The coffee machine looked inviting but she'd no idea how to work it. She'd investigate it later.

The clock on the wall showed six-fifteen. She could shower, dress and have a quick cup of tea before she left. Wherever Mitchell Brody had gone, she could find him.

She was used to dealing with teenager tantrums. A rock star in a bad mood? He would have nothing on those.

Suddenly there was huge boom. The noise was deafening and the glasses in the cupboards around her rattled. What now?

The air was perfect, crisp, clear and icy cold. The snow around him untouched—just waiting for that first winding ski track to mar its complexion. The ski conditions were better than he could've expected. It paid to have people in the know.

For a little extra cash he'd managed to persuade the cable-car operator to start early and he'd been up and down the Hafelekar slope twice. The Nordkette off-piste could be dangerous, with risk of avalanche and warnings posted everywhere stating the falls could be fatal.

But Mitchell knew these slopes like the back of his hand. He enjoyed mornings like this. Most days at this time it was only the die-hard skiers on the slopes. The thunderous detonations that reverberated around the valley in the Nordpark area were the sign that there had been a fresh dump of snow. It was like music to his ears. An early-morning wake-up call that he loved.

Even the exposed walk along the mountain ridge to the Karrine was invigorating at this time of day. From here, the highest point of the mountain, he could ski to the Seegrube mid-station, one third of the way down the mountain, then on down one of the lengthy red runs through the trees back down to the Hungerburg area. It was his idea of heaven. And Samantha was trying to spoil it for him.

Skiing was the best part of the day. He enjoyed the solitude of the slopes. On the ski slopes he could forget about everything. As a child it had been a source of pure enjoyment. As an adult, it had brought back memories of happier times. The last few runs had been different. It had been like transporting himself into another world. One where his head wasn't pickled with thoughts of injections, doses, sugar levels and a whole host of other things he really didn't have the energy to think about right now. Swooshing down the clean white slopes could do that for him— lift the dark pressing cloud from his head and shoulders.

He had no idea where Samantha was. And he couldn't help but feel irritated. He couldn't shake the black mood that was circling around him. What did diabetes have to do with skiing? He hated anything interfering with his skiing. The fact that it was even on his mind as he was flying down the slopes grated. Nearly as much as last night's memory of a pair of bright blue eyes and a curved behind in a pair of denims that hugged in all the right places. And if he even gave a thought to the flash of bare breasts this morning he'd be done for.

This place was his haven. There was an invisibility to being on the slopes. With his hat and ski goggles on it was virtually impossible for anyone to recognise him. That was part of the reason he loved being around here so much. He didn't want anything to affect that. Checking blood sugars on a mountainside? It just didn't seem practical, no matter what his nurse might think.

He'd tried a little gentle flirting with Samantha last night. He hadn't been able to help it. It had been a natural reaction to being around a gorgeous woman. And Samantha Lewis was definitely in the gorgeous category—she was wasted being a nurse.

For a few minutes she'd almost flirted back. He liked it that she had a cheeky side. He'd spent too long around females who had no idea how to laugh at themselves and with those around them.

A bump on the slopes brought his attention back to the here and now. He bent a little lower, curving into the turns on the piste. He could hear the swish of a snowboard close behind him and see another few people at the bottom of the slope. Within the next hour the ski runs would start to get busy. Nordpark was a little unusual, ideal for beginners or extreme skiers, with very little for intermediate ones. He couldn't even guess what stage Samantha was at. But from the expression on her face last night she'd looked shocked at the mere mention of skiing.

She shouldn't be. He'd stipulated in his request for the perfect nurse that he needed someone who was able to accompany him on the slopes.

There she was. In his brain again. Where was this coming from?

He slowed, sweeping to a halt at the bottom of the run. His heart was pounding in his ears, the skin on his cheeks smarting from the cold air. The Seegrube mid-station was a little busier, even though it was still before eight.

The smell of breakfast wafted out to meet him as he stood for a few seconds on the terrace overlooking the valley. Mornings were gorgeous, but it was also beautiful up here in the early evening in the dimming light, with views from the restaurant all over the valley down to Innsbruck. Maybe he would bring her up here later.

And then he spotted it. The bright blue jacket and matching hat emerging from one of the cable cars. He was just about to walk over to one of the red runs and carry on down the slopes, but he could see her head darting around, looking everywhere to see if she could spot him. Where were her skis? He was getting a bad feeling about this. Could they still be in the cable car? This woman was beginning to exasperate him.

He unclipped his boots, and carried his skis and poles over towards her. But Samantha had stopped looking for him. She was too busy staring down the valley at the view. The cable-car building exited onto a terrace with spectacular views, and most people who came off the cable car came to an automatic halt as the sight took their breath away.

He could see the look of awe across her face, almost visible beneath her scowl. There was a little surge of pride in his chest. It seemed important that she like the surrounding area just as much as he did. They were nineteen hundred feet up here and the whole of Innsbruck was laid out beneath them like a miniature toy village. At the bottom of the mountain people moved around like ants, queuing for the cable cars, with some flashes of intermittent colour as skiers and snowboarders wound their way down the slopes.

He put his skis and poles over in a corner and walked up behind her. 'See something you like?'

She jumped and turned around, her nose almost brushing against his ski jacket. She lifted her head and frowned. She didn't look happy at all. 'Where on earth have you been, Mitchell? I told you I'd meet you here. I've been up and down on that cable car twice.' The tone of her voice was like that of a schoolteacher he'd had years ago. He hadn't liked her.

It was amazing how this woman could make him mad within a few seconds.

'Meeting up was your idea, not mine. And I never agreed to anything.'

She folded her arms across her chest. 'Do you know what, Mitchell? You seem to be forgetting that—like it or not—I'm your nurse.' She pointed to her chest. 'You are under *my* care. You might be used to being the boss, but things have changed.'

It was amazing, the talent she had to really rile him and make his blood fizz with pure anger in his veins.

'Who do you think you are? You aren't in charge of me. *I'm* employing you, remember?'

She shook her head. 'You might be footing the bill but until you've got this condition under control, you have to do what I say.'

'I don't have to do anything,' he spat back, making a few people near them turn around.

'Look, buddy, I'm the one that makes the decision about whether you're fit to do your tour or not. And not following my instructions? That isn't going to win you any prizes with me.'

He leaned forward, growling at her, 'I'm not your buddy.' It was the only coherent thing he could say right now. All meaningful arguments and sarcastic comments had sprinted from his brain in a fit of anger.

She sighed and rolled her eyes and he realised how pathetic he must be sounding. This woman made him feel like a naughty teenager. It had been a *long* time since someone had made him feel like that. He almost laughed out loud. No matter how much she was driving him crazy, she had a real spark about her. It was obvious she genuinely didn't care who he was. There was no way she was taking orders from him.

It was refreshing. He'd spent the last few years with everyone around him jumping to do his bidding. It was amazing what money could buy you.

She pointed over her shoulder towards the restaurant.

'I'm sincerely hoping that this snarkiness of yours is a symptom of hypo and not a personality trait. Because if it is...' she lifted her eyebrows '...*buddy*, you and I are about to board a roller-coaster. Now, let's eat, I'm starving. Some of us didn't get to eat breakfast this morning.'

And she didn't wait. She stalked off in front of him and into the canteen.

When was the last time that had happened? He shook his head and followed her, trying not to look at her butt in those jeans.

They walked through the glass doors and he was quickly assaulted by the familiar smell of roasting coffee beans, bacon and sweet pastries. Breakfast at the restaurant catered for all tastes.

He took a deep breath. If he played his cards right, he could get this over and done with in quick time. Then he might actually be able to hit the slopes again, and hopefully shake her off for the afternoon. He had things to do. It was time for the charm offensive—even if he didn't really mean it. He held out his hands and spun around. 'So, Sam, what do you fancy?'

She blushed. Instantly. The colour flooded into her cheeks. It was good for her. Out in the cold her skin had been even paler than before—this way she had colour about her.

The heat in her cheeks was matched by the rush of blood around his body. He'd been joking, of course he had. But, from the looks it, the thought of Mitchell as anything other than a patient had at least crossed her mind. That was good enough for him.

She hesitated. 'We really should sit somewhere and check your blood sugar. That's why I'm here. To make sure you don't run into any problems on the mountain.' Was she saying this out loud for his benefit or for hers?

'And how do you expect to do that in those?' He pointed at her flat rubber-soled boots, before looking around again. 'Where are your skis anyway?'

'Let's do this first.' She grabbed a tray and headed along the short line in the restaurant and he followed reluctantly. His stomach gave a growl. He was feeling hungry again, even though he'd had breakfast this morning. Then he remembered something else. The look on her face last night when he'd mentioned skiing. He'd assumed she just hadn't welcomed the early start. But now it was adding up to something else entirely.

There could be an opportunity to take Ms Bossy Boots down a peg or two. This could actually be fun.

Just then a group of boisterous boarders came flooding through the glass doors. It was obvious they were on the adrenaline high of just having finished a run. There were no manners, no decorum, it was almost like a bull stampede. Three of them jostled and knocked into Sam, all of them talking at the tops of their voices and not even noticing what they'd done.

She teetered then toppled, her face heading directly for the floor.

'Hey! Watch out!' He made a grab for Sam's arm, catching her just before she made contact with the floor. 'What do you think you're doing? You ignorant little gits.' He stood Sam back on her feet and turned to the nearest guy, who had an indignant look on his face, and gave him a shove that sent him flying into his pack of friends. 'How do you like it?'

He could feel the blood pumping through him, his temper flaring easily and his fingers clenching into fists. 'Who's next?'

The guys looked at one another, obviously contemplating whether to take him up on his offer or not. But Sam positioned herself between them all.

'Mitchell, stop it. I'm fine. Don't cause a scene.'

He was barely listening, still focused on the group of guys. 'I don't care about causing a scene. I care about people treating you as if you're not even there.'

One of the guys straightened himself and for a second it looked as if he was going to take Mitchell up on his offer. Instead, he offered a mumbled apology to Sam for knocking her over and moved away.

Just as quickly as the flare-up had started, it was snuffed out. Sam was still standing in front of him, eyes wide and slightly horrified.

He swallowed. Should he be embarrassed? Because he wasn't, not at all.

'Where were we?' He was starting to feel a little calmer.

'Breakfast,' she muttered, picking up her tray and pushing it along the line.

He picked up some wholegrain bread and put it in the nearby toaster, grabbing a handful of low-fat spread. He watched as she hesitated over the cheese and ham then selected a croissant with some butter and jam. They reached the part where the local barista was standing. *'Sacher melange.'* He nodded.

'What's that?' Sam asked as she pulled her woolly hat from her head, releasing her curls. Pretty as a picture. She was obviously calming down a little with him now. Trying to get things back onto an even keel.

'It's hot black coffee, foamed milk, topped with whipped cream. Want some?'

She sighed. 'We really need to talk about your dietary choices, Mr Brody.' She raised her eyebrows. 'And a few other things.'

'Forget it. The wholemeal toast cancels everything else

out.' He folded his arms. 'And you don't get to advise on anything other than the diabetes.'

'Is that the way you work?'

'That's exactly the way I work.' He took his steaming cup from the server. '*Danke schoen*. What do you want?'

'I want a patient who'll take responsibility for his disease and be a grown-up about it.' The words were like a sucker punch. Just when he thought they might start being civil to each other she was reminding him exactly why she was there. He almost bit his lip to stop himself saying exactly what he wanted. 'Hey.' He shrugged. 'Don't hold back.'

She had no idea the impact all this was having on him.

When he'd started to feel unwell, all he'd been able to focus on had been the fatigue and weight loss. He'd convinced himself that he was going to be diagnosed with the same condition his brother had as a child—acute lymphoblastic leukaemia. He'd ignored the raging thirst and crazy appetite. He'd ignored the fact he didn't have obvious bruising. He'd only focused on the familiar. And it had filled him with fear and dread.

It had also stopped him from visiting the doctor until very late.

Diabetes should have been a diagnosis that filled him with relief. But for some strange reason it just didn't.

The thought that this disease—this…condition—had caused him to lose part of his evening was more than a little disturbing. His brain had been on overdrive in the early hours while he'd imagined other potential situations and their outcomes if something like that happened again.

He was no angel. The press he'd had was testament to that. But whatever he'd done in the past—and all the related consequences—had been outcomes of his actions. Things he'd *chosen* to do. Sure, on occasion there might have been a little alcohol or bad temper involved, but that didn't matter. He'd still been able to make a decision.

Last night had been nothing like that. Last night was a few fuzzy memories then a big black gaping hole. The thought of not being in control was playing nearly as much havoc with his senses as being around his new nurse.

She was talking about being a grown-up. Right now he wanted to play nursery games. Right now he wanted to stick his head in the sand and pretend he was an ostrich.

He had responsibilities she knew nothing about.

He glanced sideways. A small smile had started to creep across her face. She'd obviously realised he was ignoring her barbed comment.

Her stomach rumbled loudly and she laughed, squinting up at the menu on the wall written in German. She shrugged. 'Well, it's all double Dutch to me. I'll have the hot chocolate, thanks.'

She really was cute when she smiled. He was trying to see a way forward. Maybe he should try and win her around with his charm? The thought started to play around in his brain. He smiled, his eyebrows raised. 'With whipped cream?'

'Is there any other way?'

He grinned. 'Why, Ms Lewis, I think we need to discuss your dietary choices too.' He decided to move in for the kill. 'Have you ever been to Innsbruck before?'

'I've never been to Austria before. What kind of things are there to see around here?' She waved her hand around and laughed. 'Apart from the obvious.'

'There's loads to do around here. There's a zoo at the foot of the mountain. Did you see it? It's the highest zoo in Europe. And Christmas is really the best time of year to be here. There's a gorgeous Christmas tree in front of the Golden Roof, with a Christmas market in the surrounding square.' He couldn't hide the affection in his voice for the place that he loved. It was a whole lot easier to talk about this place than anything else.

She turned to face him again. 'A golden roof? On a house?'

'I'll take you there later. I'll explain then.'

She looked down through the glass and pointed at the houses on the edges of the city. 'I love the coloured houses. They look like sweeties. And I love the style of all the buildings. It's so atmospheric here.' She looked over in the other direction and pointed at the tall, distant silver and blue glass structure. 'And what's that? It's like something from the space age. It's like being in two different time zones here.'

'Ah, that's Bergisel, the ski jump. It was built in 2002. There are lots of ski and snowboarding competitions held there.' He gave her a wink. 'They've even got a panoramic restaurant too.' He glanced over his shoulder. 'But I prefer this one.'

There it was again. That little flicker of something. He just didn't know what.

She wasn't girlfriend material. She was his nurse. He just couldn't quite equate this girl with a twinkle in her eye to the Dragon Lady in the hospital. It was hard for him to put people into boxes—that they should be just one thing.

She was watching a snowboarder moving more quickly than a speeding car, weaving his way down the mountain with skill and expertise. But she was frowning. He could almost picture her brain computing all the possible injuries. There was no love for the sport on her face.

'Do you board?' he asked.

'Not in this lifetime,' she muttered, and gave a little shudder. She hadn't even realised she'd answered.

His smile grew wider. He'd bet if he put Samantha

Lewis on a snowboard or pair of skis she'd spend most of her time face-planting in the snow. It wasn't an ideal situation, but for the moment he was inclined to go with the flow. It could be fun.

He settled the bill while they waited for her order then carried the tray over to a nearby table that looked out over the spectacular view. 'There's a terrace outside. It's still a little cold right now, but around lunchtime lots of people will be sitting out there, eating their sandwiches.'

Someone walked past with a huge pile of pastries and chocolate cake on their tray. Samantha shook her head, shuddered and squeezed her eyes closed. 'It's eight in the morning. How can they eat those?'

The smell of hot chocolate was drifting all around her and as she bent over the steam tickled her nose. She pulled out the monitor from her pocket and put it on the table.

'Check your blood glucose before you start eating.'

He stared at it on the table between them—like a stand-off. It only took one deep breath to make up his mind. One sharp inhalation of the crisp new snow and the fresh smell of the pine and larch trees surrounding the area made him realise he wanted this over and done with.

'Bossy boots.'

'Says the man who had a monster-sized temper tantrum first thing this morning, and then again here.' She leaned back in her chair. 'Don't push me, Mitchell. Last time I saw one of those I was dealing with a three-year-old.'

He gave her a wry smile. 'Who won?'

'You have to ask?'

'I guess not.'

Yip. The rock star was going to be a monster-sized problem. And in a way it annoyed the life out of her. She hadn't been joking when she'd called him on his temper tantrum.

How come it seemed okay to tell kids when behaviour was inappropriate but not adults? Particularly adults who were paying your giant wage.

A wave of emotions started simmering to the surface. She'd phoned her mum before she'd come up the mountain this morning. She'd sounded great—so happy with the nursing-home staff and the care she was receiving. It was just the reminder she needed as to why she was doing this.

The home before had been awful. The staff hadn't been bad, there just hadn't been enough of them, meaning the standard of care had been low. Hell would freeze over before she let her mother go back there.

As for Mitch? She probably wasn't handling him as well as she could, but at least for now he was doing as he was told.

It took him less than thirty seconds to check his blood sugar. Five. His stomach grumbled again. 'I'd planned on going back down the piste and finishing that run. I would have come back for something to eat then.'

She pulled her gloves off and reached across the table, her hand touching his. It surprised her how warm his skin was. 'You need to eat. Any lower than that and you would start to hypo again. Skiing obviously burns off a lot of energy. Finishing the run and then getting food might have been too late.' She let her words hang in the air as he buttered his toast and started eating.

His eyes were fixed on something on the horizon now and she could tell he was in a bad mood. But that was too bad. Mitchell needed her there. He needed constant reminders that he couldn't just forget about his diabetes. There was no reason that he couldn't continue to ski. He would just have to make sure he had things under control.

His gloves and hat were sitting on the chair next to him, his hair sticking up in every direction but the right one. There was something vaguely familiar about all this. 'Don't you advertise hair products?' she said as she took a sip of the hot chocolate. Hmm. 'Ooh, this is fantastic. It definitely hits the spot.'

He ran his fingers through his mussed-up hair. 'Yip, and I have about a million dollars' worth of products in my garage in LA. Here? I have nothing. Haven't you heard grunge is in?'

She laughed. His eyes met hers again. There was something else there. A flicker of something she hadn't seen before. Worry. Stress. Or maybe the distracted look was just how he was before he started to hypo.

She pushed his coffee towards him. 'Drink this and finish your toast.' And to her surprise, he did. The coffee seemed to settle him. The cream and milk, along with the wholemeal toast, would help bring his blood-glucose levels up in a steady manner. She spread the jam and butter on her croissant and consumed it along with her hot chocolate. 'If I do this every day, I'll put on twenty pounds,' she sighed.

His brown eyes fixed on hers. A little twinkle appeared. 'Don't worry, Samantha. You'll work off all those calories again with your skiing.'

It was the way he'd said it. The tone and intonation of his voice. It was almost as if he was taunting her. Almost as if he knew.

'I didn't bring skis,' she said quickly. 'No one mentioned anything about skiing when I took the job.'

'Even though it was a condition for my nurse?'

'Really? Yikes.'

He reached over and gave her hand a squeeze. 'Well, don't worry. I'll hire you a set up here. That's no problem at all. Now, which piste would you like to go down first? You've never been here before, and there isn't much for intermediate skiers. Would you like me to shadow you down?' He leaned forward. 'Look at it out there. All that perfect powder. Think about the feel of the air rushing past those curls of yours.' He reached over and brushed his hand to the side of them.

The rat bag. He definitely knew.

She fixed him with a hard stare as she took another sip of her hot chocolate then held up the glass towards him and used her best sarcastic tone. 'You know, you're spoiling this for me.'

'How's that?'

'You know I can't ski. Why don't you just give it up?'

'You can't ski?' She couldn't help but laugh at the mock horror on his face. 'But everyone can ski, Samantha.'

She rolled her eyes. 'Maybe if you have a billionaire chalet in a ski resort. The rest of us chumps just go on a very bad ski trip with the school and vow never to put on a pair of skis again.' She leaned forward to emphasise her last word. 'Ever.'

'Come on, Samantha, it's fun. I'll get someone to teach you. Think of the feel of the wind in your hair and the air rushing past your cheeks. Come to think of it, have you got sunscreen and lip balm on?'

She shook her head. He reached into the inside pocket of his jacket and tossed her a small tube. 'Total sunblock. Put it all over your face, your ears and the back of your neck. You're almost as white as the snow, you'll burn in an instant.'

She examined it in her hands, her nose wrinkled. 'See? That's what's wrong here. I shouldn't need to think about this kind of stuff. All I should be worrying about is if you're going to fall off this mountain or not.' She raised her hands. 'While there's no denying the view is spectacular, why couldn't you have had a hideaway on some mysterious Caribbean island? I know how to swim. I know how to sunbathe. I might even have agreed to go jet-skiing with you. And there I would have known to wear sunscreen when I was out at seven in the morning.'

He took a sip of his coffee and shook his head. 'How did you get this job, Samantha?'

For a second she felt offended. 'What do you mean?'

'I mean, I deliberately specified that I needed someone who could ski and not only that but they could extreme ski and accompany me on the slopes.'

'You did?' She was shocked. Not once had Trish mentioned the skiing part. But then again she'd been desperate to find someone—anyone—to take the job. And she had been desperate for the money.

He nodded solemnly. 'I did.' He was teasing her again.

'Well, I hate to break it to you, Mitchell, but extreme skiing, diabetic nurse specialists, on a few hours' notice, over Christmas and New Year—well, they seem to be in short supply. After all, I had to fight off at least a thousand others to get here.' She started laughing at him. 'Do you really think you can buy whatever you want?'

'Face it, Sam. Everything's for sale—and everybody. Tell me, why exactly are you working over Christmas and New Year? Don't you have a regular job? Isn't there anyone you want to spend Christmas and New Year with?' he countered. Smart guy. Nosey too.

She could easily take umbrage at those words. 'I do have a regular job. One that I changed just recently and it means I get Christmas and New Year off. I worked last year at this time, and at Easter. Agency work at this time of year pays well.' She stopped there. No need to say any more. He knew exactly how much he was paying for her services. She was annoyed by his comment that everybody was for sale but didn't really feel in a position to argue with him about it, given the circumstances.

But he wasn't about to stop. 'So, is money an issue for you, Sam?'

She bristled at his words. Cheeky git. 'Is money an issue for you, Mitchell?'

His eyes immediately fixed on the horizon. 'You just never know,' he murmured.

She shifted in her chair. Her comeback had been more than a little tetchy. She hadn't really meant to sound like that. After all, this job was going to save her money problems for the next six months. And she wasn't too sure about his response. Surely the last thing a man like Mitchell Brody would have was money problems.

She shrugged. Time to cover her foot-in-mouth disease. 'I don't know what the big deal is about having a nurse that can ski. As long as I'm around the slopes and can keep an eye on you it shouldn't be a problem. I quite liked the ride up in the cable car. I'm happy to keep doing that.'

'But what if I have a hypo attack while I'm skiing?'

She took a deep breath. 'You'll check your blood sugar before you start. If it's low, you'll eat something and wait until it comes back up before you get going. Face it, Mitchell, whether you like it or not, you're going to have to meet me at regular intervals.'

He baulked then groaned and she raised her eyebrows, trying not to feel insulted. 'The medical science isn't there to change this right now. Don't fight me on this. For once in your life be sensible.'

His expression changed. The cheeky glint in his eyes was back. 'You think I'm not sensible?'

She looked out over the snow at the busying slopes as she stirred the contents of her mug. 'I'm just saying that I'm not the one who got caught on a rooftop in New York, in the middle of a snowstorm, naked.'

He went to interrupt but she lifted her hand. 'And I'm

not the one who decided the best way to pick a new car was to buy one in every colour.'

He sat back. 'Oh, yeah, that.' He shrugged his shoulders. 'The first one…I'm not admitting to. The second? Well, maybe…but not *every* colour. I definitely didn't get the yellow.'

'The yellow? Why not? I would have thought that matched your sunny personality?'

He threw back his head and laughed. 'Oh, snarky Samantha. I like it. Can I see more, please?'

She stood up. 'There's lot's more where that comes from. Now, come on. I take it you want to ski down? I can catch the cable car back down and meet you there. I can do this all day.'

He shook his head. 'Actually, I planned on finishing after my third run. I come early so I can ski before the slopes get busy. I have other things to do.'

'Like what?' She was feeling hopeful. Maybe they would go into Innsbruck and see a little of the city.

Something flickered across his eyes. It looked like he was about to say something then the shutters slammed down and he stood up.

'Look, Sam, I've done what you asked. I'll finish my ski run and meet you once more at the bottom of the mountain. After that—that's it. I don't need to tell you every minute of my day. You work for me, remember?'

He picked up his hat and gloves and stalked away, leaving Sam stunned.

What on earth had just happened there?

CHAPTER FOUR

FOR THE FOURTH day in a row, Mitchell failed to meet her when he should have.

She was ready to erupt. It was like dealing with a child, not an adult, and she was getting sick to death of it.

She'd never met a rock star before, but she'd worked with enough kids to understand when someone wasn't taking things seriously. When someone was running scared.

She stepped out of the cable car. It was five o'clock in the evening. For the fourth day in a row, Mitch had skied the slopes in the morning and disappeared without a backward glance in the afternoon. It was driving her crazy.

Had he really no respect for her and the job she was doing?

She wandered around the Seegrube station, trying to spot his red jacket. She'd almost given up hope when she heard his laugh. His deep, hearty laugh.

She rounded the corner to the terrace. She really hadn't expected to find him here, but as time had marched on she hadn't really known where else to look.

And there he was. Not a blooming care in the world. Laughing and drinking with a group of guys she'd never seen before.

She blinked. Drinking. Drinking *beer*.

The red mist started to descend around her. She'd reached her limit with this guy.

She walked straight through the middle of the drinking buddies. 'Mitch?'

A silence fell over the group, quickly followed by a snigger then a low whistle.

Samantha ignored them all. 'You were supposed to meet me back at the house at four.'

Four days in a row. Four days in a row she'd sat and stared at four walls in his luxury chalet while he'd been who-knew-where. It made her mad. It made her seethe.

She might have agreed to work over Christmas but that didn't mean she didn't miss her family—didn't miss her mum. At least for the last two years she'd always felt useful. She'd been kept busy with Daniel and his family and that had stopped her missing her mum too much. But this? This wasn't working for her at all. Her patience had finally run out. It didn't matter how much she needed the money right now, being treated like crap and having her professional advice ignored was the last straw.

He looked more than a little stunned. Embarrassed by her. 'Give it a rest, Samantha,' he murmured, trying to appear casual.

'Snarky girlfriend,' came the murmur behind her.

She tilted her chin. 'No, Mitchell. I won't give it a rest. We had a meeting. That's the fourth day in a row you've blown me off. It's about time you started to take this seriously.' She pointed at the bottle in his hand. 'Beer, Mitchell? Really?' She paused, conscious of the audience around them. She glared at him. 'You and I need to talk. Now.'

Mitch felt the blood rush into his cheeks. He wasn't embarrassed—well, yes, actually, he was. But the rush of blood was due to the fury building in his chest.

He stood up and grabbed hold of Samantha's wrist and

pulled her behind him. He could hear the yelps and cat calls from the snowboarding guys. The shouts of 'Being whipped' and 'Under the thumb'.

He walked quickly, rounding the corner away from the crowds, away from the bustle of people exiting the cable cars, and pulled her up next to him.

'Don't you ever do that to me again!'

She didn't even flinch. 'Likewise.'

'What's that supposed to mean?' All he wanted was a bit of peace. A bit of privacy. These few weeks were supposed to be his holiday. His chance to kick back and relax before the tour. If he wanted to have a beer with a few friends, then that's exactly what he would do. And he certainly didn't need Samantha Lewis's permission for that.

'I'm sick of this. It's about time you started to take this seriously. I can't help you get your diabetes under control if you don't follow my instructions. These first few weeks are vital. This is the time we need to iron out any problems.'

She was serious. Her pretty face was marred by a frown. And she had a weary look in her eyes. But he was too angry to care.

'Right now my only problem is you.'

'Then I'll say it again. Likewise. This isn't working for me, Mitch. I'm ready to pack up and go home and spend Christmas with my mum. Why waste my time here? Why waste my time on you? You don't deserve it. You don't care. So why should I?' She looked him up and down. 'I'm not here because I like you, Mitch. I'm not here because I'm a fan. I'm here because I'm paid to be.'

He got it that she was mad. He just didn't expect her to slam dunk him like that. Nothing like getting to the point.

'Who are you to tell me I don't care? Of course I care. I care about my tour. I need to be well to go on tour. That's why you're here, Sam. To make sure I'm fit enough to do the tour. But I don't need to report in to you every second of the day. I'm entitled to a private life of my own. And I certainly don't need you to babysit me.'

She sighed and shook her head. 'Actually, you do. That's exactly what I'm being paid for right now.' She folded her arms and stared off into the distance. 'That's it, Mitch. I can't say you're fit for your tour. I don't think you're taking this seriously at all. It would compromise my professional competency if I said you were fit when you clearly aren't.'

She looked him squarely in the eye. 'I won't do it. You might want to put your health at risk, but the nurse in me won't allow that to happen. You won't tell me where you're going or what you're doing. I can't help you monitor your levels or plan your meals or insulin doses. I'm not prepared to keep banging my head against a brick wall.' She lifted her hands. 'You just don't get it. I don't actually *care* what you're doing or who you're doing it with. I just need to know. I need you to work with me. I need *you* to care.'

The penny dropped like a hammer to the head. She thought he was sneaking away every afternoon for some secret rendezvous with a lady. He tried not to smile as he imagined how she thought he was expending his energy.

And as much as he hated to admit it, she had him. He needed her. He needed her to sign him off as fit for this tour.

He let out a sigh of exasperation. He hated everything about this. He had never explained himself to anyone. Starting now, at this stage in his life, was unthinkable.

'I'm done, Brody. Book me on the next flight home.' Her voice was subdued, almost whispered. She was staring out over the landscape with those killer blue eyes and a resigned look on her face. He'd pushed her too far.

Samantha wasn't like every other employee. He couldn't push her around like he had others.

Something inside him cracked.

If she told the insurers he wasn't adhering to his treatment plan, his whole tour would go up in smoke. A wave of panic started to wash over him. He hadn't really believed it was a possibility. For some strange reason, he'd just assumed she wouldn't do that.

Obviously not. It was a harsh reality check.

It was time to try and salvage what he could—to stop her leaving on the next available plane.

He took a deep breath. 'Sam, I'm going to tell you something that hardly anyone on this planet knows.'

Her brow furrowed. She recognised the sincerity in his voice, and since it was something she hadn't heard much, she obviously took it seriously. 'Okay,' she said slowly.

He put his hands on her shoulders and spun her round to look out over the view below. 'See that building with the green roof, off to the left?'

She squinted as the sun was in her eyes. 'Yeah, I think so. The one that sits by itself? What is that?'

'It's the children's hospital. That's where I spend most of my afternoons.'

He heard her sharp intake of breath. She spun back round, concern written all over her face. 'What haven't you been telling me? You have a sick kid? A relative?' Her voice trembled as she spoke. 'Why do you spend so much time at the children's hospital, Mitch?'

It was time to put everything out there. He had to stop her leaving. 'Because that's where I spent most of my childhood.'

CHAPTER FIVE

IT WAS LIKE being home. This was one of the few places on the planet that Mitchell Brody felt entirely relaxed, entirely himself.

As soon as they crossed the threshold of the children's hospital it was like being in another world. The temperature was different, the mood was different—even the lighting was different. Lots of these kids were pale to the point of almost being blue and the warm-coloured lighting seemed to lessen the severity of their appearance. Making them look not quite so unwell.

More importantly, around Christmastime the staff always bent over backwards to make the whole place something special. There was a huge Christmas tree at the entrance, another at the end of the corridor, and another in the kids' playroom, each decorated in a different colour. A whole variety of kids' paintings showing Santa and reindeers and multicoloured presents decorated the walls. Even the kids who were in isolation—at risk of any kind of infection—had fibreoptic trees outside their windows, so the changing lights would be reflected back inside their rooms.

He gave a quick hug to the nurse in charge. 'Lisa, this is my friend Samantha Lewis. She's here to visit with me today.'

Lisa's smile reached from one ear to the other. She was always glad to see him. There were never any airs or graces here. The truth was if he tried to order someone around here he'd get a swift kick to the butt. And he liked it. It was exactly how it should be.

Lisa gave Samantha an interested nod. He'd never brought anyone with him before, apart from Dave, of course. But he was careful not to introduce Samantha as a nurse. He didn't want to give anything away. He particularly didn't want to alert any of the staff at the children's hospital to his health issues. No way. He didn't want them to think that anything would get in the way of him funding the new build.

Lisa checked some notes. 'Okay, Rooms 4 and 5 are out of bounds.' It was the quickest glance that spoke volumes. The children in those rooms must be at the end of their lives. The muscles in his chest tightened. He'd been there. There had been a few times that they'd thought his brother might not make it. But they'd all been lucky. He was still here.

But lots of other families didn't get the miracle that they had. Even though cancer was better diagnosed and treatments were better targeted some kids were just too sick to get better. And this children's hospital didn't just look after children with cancer. It looked after children with a whole range of conditions that could be terminal. No child and their family would ever be turned away from St Jude's Children's Hospital.

'No problem. Is there anywhere you want me to spend time?'

She smiled and gave him a nod. 'You know there is. Luke Reynolds in Room 3 would love a visit. Brian Flannigan, the teenager in Room 14 would love to play guitar with you, and Lindsay Davenport, the twelve-year-old in

Room 17, wants some Hollywood gossip.' She raised her eyebrows. 'She particularly wants to know if Reid Kerr from your band is secretly dating a supermodel.'

'Aha.' He couldn't help but smile. The kids here were great. Most of them were constantly surrounded by friends and family, but sometimes it helped to have another face in the mix.

Lisa turned to Samantha. 'How are you with babies?'

Her eyes widened and she looked a little shocked. To be honest, he was breathing a huge sigh of relief that she'd actually agreed to stay at all. He should have warned her that it was all hands on deck in here. But she was a nurse, he was sure she could cope.

'I deal mostly with teenagers...' she nodded her head slowly '...but I'm sure I can help out with a baby. What can I do for you?' She was already unzipping her jacket, ready to get to work.

'We've got a young mum whose four-year-old has leukaemia. She's got a new baby too, who has a real dose of colic.' She smiled sympathetically. 'It might be a bit sore on your ears, but would you mind giving mum some respite so she can spend time with her son?'

Samantha nodded her head and pushed up her sleeves. 'No problem. I can pace the floors with a colicky baby. Which room?'

Lisa pointed down the corridor. 'Room 8. Mum will know I've sent you. There's a quiet room at the bottom of the corridor that no one else is using. It's got some music and nice lighting, and some rocking chairs. You could try in there if you like.'

Sam put her arm on Mitch's arm. 'Okay, I'll see you in a little while. Come and find me if you need me.'

She was being serious. She'd obviously picked up on the fact he hadn't mentioned who she was but was still trying to make sure he understood why she was doing this. He was still a little worried she hadn't made up her mind about staying yet.

She walked down the corridor and he couldn't help but admire her curves in her figure-hugging jeans. Lisa followed his gaze and folded her arms across her chest. 'Well, Mitchell, who is that?'

There was amusement in her voice and a gleam in her eyes. He met her grin head on. 'I have no idea what you mean.'

Lisa had worked here for three years. She was fantastic with the kids, mainly because she was good at reading people. And she was using all her professional skills on him right now. 'I like her,' she said approvingly. 'She didn't hesitate to help. I'm just surprised to finally meet one of your friends.' She gave him a knowing nod and emphasised the final word.

'It's not like that,' he said quickly. Too quickly. Because it just made her grin even wider.

She copied Sam's movements and tapped his arm as she walked past. 'Not yet it's not. But give it time...'

She grabbed an apron, gloves and mask and walked off to one of the other rooms. Darn it. She could read him too well. It was almost as if she could see all the pictures that were being conjured up in his mind. And one thing was for sure—they definitely couldn't be shared.

He pushed all thoughts from his mind. He loved this place but, for the first time, being here made him feel a little uncomfortable. Maybe it was the unspoken looks in all the staff's eyes. The expectation that he was about to make things so much better for them.

And he would. No matter how sick he was, or what else was going on in his life. He couldn't let anything get in the way of this tour and the money he would earn for the children's hospital. Never mind what Samantha Lewis's cute behind looked like in those jeans. She was only interested in his blood-sugar levels. Not his hormone levels.

He checked the board again and made his way towards Luke Reynolds's room. The little guy had an insatiable urge to play board games. He was only six but Risk was his favourite and he was ruthless. A few weeks ago he'd been in isolation because his blood count had been so low. It was good that he was finally picking up a little.

Spending some time with Luke was a sure-fire guarantee that he could put everything else out of his mind. His tour. His disease. His nurse.

Samantha's ears were ringing. Ninety minutes. That's how long little Rose had screamed for, drawing her legs up in pain from the colic. It was no wonder her mum needed a break to spend time with her already exhausted four-year-old.

Sam had done everything she could think of—rocking, massaging, walking. But colic was hit or miss. Sometimes you just had to hold the little one and offer some comfort.

Finally Rose was exhausted and snuggled against Sam's pink woolly jumper. Was that a snore? She was in the rocking chair now; soothing music was playing in the background and there were interchanging coloured lights in the corners of the room. Any more of this and she would fall asleep herself.

She checked her watch. It really was time to find Mitchell and ask him to check his blood-glucose level again. It should be fine. They'd had lunch together before they'd got here and he'd eaten sensibly. She was just worried that his exercise from earlier could cause his glucose levels to dip a little later in the day.

Moving as silently as possible, she put Rose into her

pram and walked her down the corridor towards her brother's room. She gave her mother a signal through the glass and left the pram outside.

She wasn't sure what room Mitchell would be in but strolled slowly along the corridor to see if she could hear his voice.

But it wasn't his voice that she heard. It was the sounds of a reverberating guitar filtering through the door. Lisa gave her a smile as she hurried past, nodding her head in the direction of the room. 'Soundproofed. Just as well!'

Samantha's hand hesitated at the door handle. Should she go in, or should she wait?

She was curious about Mitchell in this environment. He seemed to have left the rock persona at the door. This was all about the kids and there was something so nice about seeing that.

Lots of things about him were surprising her. With the exception of Dave and the cleaning service, he wasn't surrounded by 'people' doing his bidding. He didn't have an entourage. She hadn't even heard him mention his manager.

The house was gorgeous, and the furniture and equipment were miles out of her price range. But his stubborn streak and lack of acceptance of his condition were still a major headache. If he didn't start following the rules, this could all end in disaster.

Truth was, the most disturbing thing about Mitch was being at close quarters with him. The photo shoots and calendars didn't do the man justice. He had a way of looking at you that made you feel you were the only person in the room. On some occasions she had been, but the rest of the times?

It made her feel like a fool. It made her feel unfocused and unprofessional. She was here to do a job. That was all.

In a few weeks' time she would be back in rainy London, working in a school in Brixton again.

The revelation about the hospital had been a bolt out of the blue. She'd never heard a word in the press about any of this. But he had been quite clear that no one knew he helped out here—and it was to stay that way.

She turned the handle on the door. The noise almost blasted her backwards and she quickly stepped inside and closed the door behind her.

Neither male had noticed her, because both of them were on the bed, playing some kind of electric guitars and shaking their heads like mad rockers.

She recognised the tune—of course she did. It had been number one in numerous countries around the world for weeks.

But watching this kid, this teenager, rocking out with Mitch was something else entirely. Mitch might have been sick, but he looked a whole lot healthier than this young boy with no hair left on his head and skin so pale it was almost translucent. What was magnificent—what really pulled at her heartstrings—was the absolute energy and commitment the young boy had to the task at hand. He was having the time of his life.

The music built to a crescendo. The speed of their hands on the strings increasing, followed by a scream from each as they leapt off the bed towards her. They'd obviously done this before.

Before the last echoes of notes had even left the room they were high-fiving each other and laughing loudly.

'Fabulous, Brian, you get better every time.'

The young boy's eyes sparkled at the praise from his idol and Mitchell looked genuinely happy to be there. This wasn't a rock star doing something to help his image. No one even knew that he came here. It surprised her that one of the kids or their relatives hadn't spilled the beans to the press. But maybe his obvious pleasure at being here motivated them all to keep quiet. This place was a haven, very much like Mitchell's home.

If the press knew about his involvement the quiet and sanctity of this place would be destroyed in a heartbeat.

'I don't know why I'm getting better, my teacher's old enough to be my dad!' Brian's teenage bravado was coming through, but the look on his face and his trembling lips told Samantha that he was barely containing himself beneath the surface. Her nursing instincts kicked in straight away and she walked over then put her arm around his shoulders.

'Well, old teacher or not, that was the first time I've heard you and I thought you were fabulous.' She gave him a conspiratorial wink. 'In fact, I think you might even have been better than your teacher. You look tired after that. How about we find you something to drink and some cakes? I'm sure they'll have some around here.'

Mitchell gave her a little nod and she steered Brian out of the room and down the corridor to the TV room, where one of the staff was just setting out sodas and cookies. Once she was sure he was settled she went back to find Mitchell.

He was sitting at the nursing station with his feet on the desk, sprawled out across a chair, breathing heavily. It wasn't just Brian who was tired.

She pulled up a chair next to him as he opened one eye and looked at her. 'Did you bring me a cake, too?'

She shook her head. 'If you behave and check your blood sugar, I'll hunt you down a coffee and an apple.'

It was almost as if an unheard clock struck somewhere but doors started opening around them and kids and their parents all started filtering down to the TV room, where more food was being set out.

Mitch saw her curious expression and shrugged. 'Some of the kids can't eat around dinnertime. They like to have a constant supply of food around this place, and while most of it is healthy, they are pretty lenient with the kids.' He pulled his feet from the desk and leaned forward, resting his elbows on his knees. His voice had lowered, 'Sometimes, if they're midway through chemo, they just can't face regular food. At that point the staff will give them anything that they can stomach to get some calories in them. I once had to go out at midnight to try and track down a particular kind of candy bar.'

She smiled. There was no one around them now. It was just the two of them, alone.

She sat forward too, her hair cascading around her shoulders.

'Brian's got the same kind of leukaemia that my brother Shaun had—acute lymphoblastic leukaemia. That's why I spent a lot of time here as a kid.'

Her eyes widened and her stomach flipped over but he waved his hand. 'Don't ask. Not now. I'll tell you later.'

Of course. Things were starting to make sense. She'd wondered why he spent time here. Only someone who had firsthand experience would have such a good relationship with the staff. She just hadn't expected this. It was like a bolt from the blue.

But Mitch was focused again. He kept talking. 'Brian's not been so lucky. Even though it was caught early, his leukaemia's been really aggressive. Some days I come to visit and he can't even lift his head from the pillow. Days like this are good days.'

Her head was spinning but as he said the final words with a big sigh it made her realise he was still a little more out of breath than he cared to admit. The onset of his diabetes had implications for his health. With the skiing this morning, followed by more this afternoon, his body wasn't quite ready for all the physical exercise, but somehow she knew that asking Mitchell Brody to slow down would be pointless.

And a little part of her didn't want to. She didn't want to hide the person that Mitchell was, and would continue to be. Even though he was probably in recovery mode, it was important that she help him mould his diabetes to his life—within reason, of course. He had to be able to live normally and function on his own.

She looked up. Their heads were so close they could be touching, but Mitchell had his eyes closed. It could be fatigue, or it could be the emotion of what he'd just shared.

She couldn't think of him as a patient right now. Every instinct in her body wanted to comfort him and she did the most natural thing in the world for her. She reached out and touched him.

His hand was warm and soft, and as her palm brushed over the back of his hand he flipped it over and intertwined his fingers with hers. There were no sweaty palms here. There was just a whole host of tingles shooting straight up her arm.

He closed his fingers a little more. Locking their hands together. His eyes were still closed and his breathing was slowing. She was mesmerised by the rise and fall of his chest.

Suddenly his eyes opened, darker brown than ever, and fixed on her face. He leaned forward a little more and she felt her breath hitch in her throat. He rested his forehead against hers.

What am I doing? her brain was screaming in her ears. But she couldn't move—she couldn't pull her hand away from his. She didn't want to break this moment. No matter how many messages reverberated around her brain.

They stayed like that for more than a minute. Then his head lifted slightly and his eyelashes brushed against her forehead, before he dropped a gentle kiss on her head. His other hand came up and rested at the back of her hair. 'Thank you for coming with me today, Samantha.'

Words were stuck in her throat. Anything that came out right now would make her sound like a blundering idiot. This was crazy, but it felt special. She didn't feel like a teenage fan girl any more. She certainly didn't feel like his nurse. She felt something else entirely.

She stared down at their still intertwined hands. It was so much easier than looking up—if she did, they'd be nose to nose and she didn't even want to guess what could happen next.

She sucked a breath to steady her nerves and licked her, oh, so dry lips. 'Any time, Mitchell.' Her voice sounded so much steadier than she actually felt. She pulled back a little. There. That was better. Now she could look at him.

'I've liked it here today.' Her words were almost whispered. 'I've liked you here today.' Saying them out loud made her feel very vulnerable. 'I feel as if I understand you a little better now.' Was she saying that to quantify what she'd just said before? Her insides were instantly cringing, wishing she could pull those words back.

This time when he smiled at her it wasn't with his trademark rock-star smile. It wasn't the kind of confident smile he used, knowing he was one of the sexiest guys on the planet. This smile was totally different and it reached right up into his dark eyes.

He held her gaze. Her lungs were going to explode. *Please look away so I can breathe soon.* 'Me too,' he finally said, as he untangled his hand from her hair and stood up.

It was over. That little minute was gone. But he hadn't let go of her hand and he gave it a little tug. 'Let's go and join in the cake party.'

All her good intentions about healthy eating shot out of the window. 'Sure,' she said, as she wiped her other hand on her jeans and allowed him to lead her down the corridor towards the TV room.

What on earth was she doing?

CHAPTER SIX

MITCH STARED OUT at his view of the perfect snow. Today it wasn't perfect. Today it was blighted by little blue and red figures dotted around on the landscape in amongst the trees. On any other day he might have gone out and shouted that they were on private property. But right now he just didn't have the energy. Plus the fact he didn't seem to have a sensible thought in his head right now.

They'd come back from the children's hospital a few hours ago, the palm of his hand still burning from where he'd tangled it in her hair and held her hand. He wasn't quite sure what had happened between them.

Had anything really happened? He just knew he'd been inches away from devouring those perfect pink lips. For a few moments at the nurses' station they'd felt like the only two people in the world. Samantha hadn't been looking at him like his nurse. She hadn't been looking at him like some love-struck fan either. She'd been looking at him as if she finally got him. Finally got the kind of person that he was and what was important to him.

It was a connection. He just didn't know what to do about it.

Part of him felt that it was his fault. He'd never taken anyone to the children's hospital before. That part of his life was totally private. So why had he felt the urge to share it with Sam? He didn't understand himself.

Maybe it was because she'd held him to ransom this afternoon. She'd told him she was ready to quit and walk away.

He'd sat down an hour ago in his recliner chair to stare out at his private view. And that had been the last thing he remembered. This lack of energy and total physical exhaustion was driving him nuts. He'd always been the kind of guy who could be up early and stay awake easily to the small hours. He'd kind of assumed once he'd got a diagnosis and started his insulin that everything would just return to normal. But it was official. This diabetes was kicking his butt. Maybe it was interfering with his brain too?

He also had the biggest range of Christmas decorations in the world to put up. After Sam's remarks about missing out, he'd asked the company just to deliver the decorations and planned that he and Sam could put them up together. He wasn't quite sure why he'd done that—and he hadn't even told Sam yet. It would have been so much easier to let someone else do it, but Sam had seemed sad that day.

There was a quiet knock at the door. 'Mitchell, are you okay in there?' She peeked around the door and he pushed the recliner upright with a bang.

'Yeah, yeah. I'm fine.'

'Good. We need to talk.' She walked across the room and perched at the end of his sleigh-style bed. He gulped. Boy, oh, boy. He was trying not to admire her curves in the figure-hugging jeans or the way the blonde curls bobbed as she strode across the room. He was especially trying not to think about pushing her backwards onto that bed.

'We need to try something new. A little different.'

Wow. Where was this conversation about to go? He was all ears.

She reached her hand up and started twiddling with her ear. 'We need to let you hypo in a controlled environment. We need to see what warning signs you have and if you can recognise them.'

'What?' He was standing now. Apart from the fact it was so not what he was expecting to hear, he didn't like the sound of this at all. 'Are you crazy? You've seen me hypo once—why do you need to see it again?'

She stood up and took a step closer. It seemed that their earlier interaction made her not so conscious of keeping him at arm's length. 'This isn't about what I've seen, Mitch. This is about you. It's all about you. And it's not crazy.' She folded her arms across her chest. 'A teenager or child who was newly diagnosed with insulin-dependent diabetes would never be allowed to go home until they'd hypoed in a controlled environment, preferably with both their parents there to recognise the signs and symptoms. It's part of the learning process about the condition.'

He wrinkled his nose. 'Well, I don't like the sound of it.' He waved his arm towards the window. 'Look at it out there. The sun's just about to go down. I was thinking we could go down into Innsbruck and have dinner somewhere. Doesn't that sound much more like a plan?'

He saw it. That fleeting moment of temptation that raced through her eyes. But she kept her resolve, stepping forward and touching the seam of his shirt at the front of his chest. Was this a persuasive tactic? Because he could tell her right now it would work.

'It does sound like a plan. But I'm in charge of planning, Mitch, not you. So we're going to do things my way. We'll do the hypo first, and if you feel up to it, we'll eat dinner later.'

He liked the way her voice had a little stern edge to it.

He liked it even better that her eyes didn't look quite so distant as before.

'I'm not sure I want to do this. I lost two hours of my life last time around.' The words were out before he had a chance to think about them. And he cringed. They made him sound weak. It was so not what he was.

But Samantha nodded her head slowly. 'I get that, Mitch, I do. I hate the feeling of not being in control. But this is important. This will ultimately let you be more in control. It will give you the chance to realise if something is going wrong and take corrective steps to stop you getting worse. Last time around wasn't a good example.' She hesitated for a second. 'Do you want to ask Dave to be here? It's important that he can recognise signs too.'

Mitch shook his head. 'No. Absolutely not. Dave can't handle this kind of stuff. If this is going to happen, it's just you…' he met her gaze '…and me.'

'You and me.' She repeated the phrase, holding his gaze for a few seconds, then seemed to snap back into work mode. She moved towards the door. 'Let's do it.'

Words he so wanted to hear her say. Just not about this.

They were in the large sitting room. He'd checked his blood sugar and taken a small shot of insulin. It was a fast-acting insulin that should start to take effect within ten minutes. But every patient was different. It could be up to thirty minutes. She would just need to wait it out with him.

'So, what do we do now?' He'd adopted his rock-star drawl. It was sexy as hell. But it wasn't the real Mitch. She knew that now.

She put her feet up on the table. Determined not to fall for any of his lines. She gestured towards the TV. It took up practically the whole wall. 'We could watch a movie or a TV show.' She shrugged. 'Listen to some music. Read a book.'

'You're being sarcastic now.'

She smiled. 'Am I? You just don't look like a book reader to me.'

He turned towards her more, hitching one leg up on the sofa and letting his arm fall behind her shoulders. 'And are you?'

She nodded. 'It's my secret addiction. Before my mum got sick I read a book a day.'

His body straightened up. 'Your mum is sick?'

She shouldn't have said that out loud. She was here to do a job. Not give away information about her family. She bit her lip. 'She had a stroke.'

'Is she better?' His words came out straight away and brought a lump to her throat.

She wasn't really sure how to answer. 'Well, yes and no. She's somewhere now that can take care of her.'

His brow wrinkled. 'Like a nursing home?'

Tears formed in her eyes. Why? She'd made her peace with this. She had. She'd spent weeks finding the best home for her mum and securing her a place there. But every now and then the overwhelming guilt that she hadn't managed to do the job herself chipped away at her.

'Is that why you're doing this job?' For reasons she couldn't explain, she just couldn't speak right now. So she nodded, and prayed that one of those tears wouldn't sneak down her face.

He reached over and grabbed her hand, encapsulating it in his own and squeezing it tightly. 'Being away at Christmas must be tough.'

She tried to paste a smile on her face as she blinked back those pesky tears. 'It's fine.' She shrugged her shoulders. Darn it. Now her voice had gone all wobbly. 'The holidays are always the best time of year to earn extra money. Lots of people don't want to work them.'

He was looking at her again. The top few buttons on his white shirt were undone and a few hairs curling up towards her. Her gaze was fixed there, even though she was willing herself to pull it away. He was still holding her hand. Still sending a little buzz up her veins. It was nice. It was more than nice. It was making her heart drum against her chest and beat out of sync.

He didn't let go.

'Why do you need to earn extra money, Sam?'

She flinched. It was too personal. No matter what he'd revealed to her today. She bit her lip. 'Doesn't everyone need a little extra money now and then?'

It seemed an innocuous answer but something flitted across his face. A look of distaste? She was trying to forget about her threat to quit today. She'd meant it. She would have walked away if he hadn't started to bend a little. But it would have caused her endless financial problems that she could really do without.

She pulled her mind back to the job. Back to monitoring Mitchell Brody for signs of his hypoglycaemic attack.

'How are you feeling?'

'Fine.' His answer was as quick as a flash, and he was wearing that sexy grin on his face again. 'Want to do something a little bit different?'

'What does that mean?' Her heart was giving the strangest flutter.

He walked over to a cupboard and pulled out the biggest stack of cardboard boxes—all brand new. 'You make a start on these, and I'll go and get the main event.' He walked over to the front door and pulled it open.

She glanced at the boxes and followed him to the door. What on earth was he doing? She watched as he opened the door to the nearby garages and started to wrestle the biggest tree she'd ever seen out through the garage doors. It was obviously much more awkward than he'd expected—the top part of the tree kept catching on the brickwork.

'Careful,' she shouted as she ran out to help, grabbing any part of the prickly branches she could get her hands on. It took careful manoeuvring. The heavy base had Mitch red in the face, with the veins nearly popping in his neck. Thankfully it was only a few steps back to the doorway. 'How long has this been in the garage?' she asked, as she tripped down the steps towards the lounge.

'Four days,' he muttered through gritted teeth. 'There!' With a huge grunt he wrestled the tree upright and into place next to the fireplace, before collapsing with laughter onto the rug below.

She sagged down on to the rug beside him. 'I thought you were getting some company to decorate for you.'

'So did I. But *somebody* told me I'd be missing out if I did that.'

She gave a little smile. Mitchell had actually listened to her. There was hope after all. She pushed herself upwards and slammed the front door to stop the icy blast coming into the house. She lifted the corner of one of the boxes and smiled, pulling out a ready-made red, green and gold garland for the fireplace. 'Do we actually have any real decorating to do?'

He gave her his lazy smile. 'I'm starting simple. Those ones we just hang up. But one of the boxes has the tree lights and the tree decorations. We have to do those ourselves.'

She couldn't help but grin. There was something so nice about that. She lifted down the next cardboard box and opened it. It was full of Christmas lights, gold stars and red berries. She lifted them out and started to try and untangle them. Mitch stared at her. 'What are you doing? Can't we just put them on?'

She shook her head and handed him the plug. 'No. You've got to be methodical about it. Haven't you ever decorated a tree before? We need to check the lights are working first.'

He hesitated for a second. 'We didn't really do trees in our house. We spent most of the time at the hospital. There wasn't much point putting a tree up in the house.'

Her heart gave a little squeeze. It was time to ask the question that had been floating around her head. 'So, what's the story with the children's hospital? You said they looked after your brother?' She hesitated as she realised she'd never asked about the outcome for his brother. Mitch hadn't referred to him in the past tense, had he? Her insides started to cringe.

But Mitch just replied in a matter-of-fact tone. 'Shaun was sick for a few years. He had chemotherapy and radiotherapy but eventually needed a bone-marrow transplant. He was cured after that, and he's never had any relapses.'

He flicked the switch on the lights and they flickered on, a warm glow of gold twinkling stars and deep red berries. Sam gave a little gasp. 'Oh, these are great. Just leave them on while we put them up.' Should she ask the next question? This was the first time Mitch had really been open about his family. 'Who was the donor for the bone-marrow transplant, your mum or dad?'

He shook his head. 'Nope. It was me.'

She felt shocked. Of course she'd heard of sibling donations, but surely he'd been too young? She was starting to wind the lights around the branches. 'Come and help, I need an extra set of arms.' But instead of positioning himself at the other side of the tree, Mitch came around behind her, putting his arms around her back to catch the drooping coils of light. 'What age were you?' She tried to calculate in her head. 'You wouldn't even have been a teenager.'

He nodded, dropped the lights again and tugged at his jeans, pulling them down a little, revealing the upper part of his buttock and hip joint, 'I don't even have a scar,' he announced. Then gave her a wink. 'No war wounds to show the girls.'

He was trying to make light of it. But Samantha knew better than that. She knew exactly how painful it would have been for a young boy to donate bone marrow to his brother—he'd probably spent the best part of a week in bed.

Her professional head was spinning. This had been twenty years ago. She knew exactly how things operated now—how they endeavoured to protect children—but had they been the same then? 'Did you understand what you were doing? Did you want to do it?'

He leaned towards her, picking up the coils of lights again and letting her inhale his woody aftershave. 'Of course I did. Shaun is my brother. I would do anything for him.' His eyes flickered with the recognition of what she meant. 'No one coerced me. No one made me do it.'

'And how is Shaun now?' They were moving slowly around the tree together, stringing the lights as they went. She was curious. He'd said his brother was well, but it wasn't Shaun that was here, visiting a children's hospital full of sick kids every afternoon. It was Mitchell. Why did he feel such strong ties?

He reached up to place the last string of lights near the top of the tree, his chest brushing against her shoulders. It should be too close for comfort. But it wasn't really feeling like that.

She stepped away, trying to keep her head in focus. She picked up the next box full of gorgeous red and gold baubles and blown-glass ornaments. 'These are beautiful, Mitchell. I've never seen decorations like this before.' They were mesmerising, and probably cost more than she earned in a month. Her mother would love these.

'It seems like you should have the honours of decorating your first official Christmas tree.' She started to pass them up to him one at a time.

'Don't you want to do it?' He looked confused. 'I thought that's what you wanted.'

'So did I,' she said quietly. 'But it's reminding me of how much I miss my mum.'

He paused, hanging the first few from the branches. She was lost for a second. Seeing the decorations like this was bringing a whole host of forgotten memories to mind. She could almost smell the cinnamon-scented candles her mum had used. He seemed to know to give her a little space, but she was conscious that the way he looked at her was changing. Her hands worked like clockwork, handing him one decoration after another, until the box was empty and the room was filled with lights glistening and reflecting on the glass ornaments.

The mood in the room had changed. He moved, coming closer like a prowling lion stalking its prey. He pulled her upwards from the rug and guided her over to the sofa, his hand plunking down on one side of her hip, the other reaching across her shoulders. Mitchell Brody was right next to her, the sides of their upper bodies and thighs touching. Way, way past invading her personal space.

'My brother Shaun lives in the States. He's married with two kids. Two unexpected bonuses.'

'What do you mean?' There were tiny little freckles just across the bridge of his nose.

'He'd been warned that his radiotherapy and chemotherapy could affect his fertility later in life.' He smiled. 'It seems he lucked out.'

Something clicked in her brain as he licked his lips and looked at her appreciatively once again. No one could predict what someone's hypo symptoms would be. Trembling, shaking hands were common. Some people became really quiet and withdrawn. Her sister had a slight aggressive streak. Mitch? It was beginning to look as if he had a flirtatious streak. Maybe low blood sugar meant that some of his normal defensive walls were slipping. This could be dangerous. She was trying not to read anything into this. She was trying to keep things normal.

'So, shouldn't it be Shaun who wants to pay it forward to the hospital, instead of you?'

He gave a lazy smile and shook his head slowly. 'You should get it, Sam. You're a nurse. St Jude's changed everything for our family. If we'd lost Shaun…things would never have been the same. We would have been damaged. We would have been lost. They patched us up when we were falling apart. You don't forget that. Not ever.'

The Christmas decorations sent a red and gold glow around the room, bathing them both in the warm light. His face was inches from hers. And a very handsome face it was too. His scraggy hair was falling towards her and she resisted the urge to reach up and touch it. Any minute now she'd talk him into checking his blood-sugar level.

Mitchell sighed and shook his head. 'You've no idea, Sam. None at all. One minute everything's fine in your world and the next…' he lifted his fingers and blew on them '…everything is just scattered in the wind.'

She swallowed. It brought back a whole host of memories. Blowing dandelion seeds in the wind had been something she'd loved to do as a child with her mother. She could almost see them floating around as they stood there.

He wasn't finished. It was as if the walls had come down on the normally guarded Mitchell Brody. 'I didn't know what to do. I heard words. I'll never forget one of the doctors telling my parents to prepare for the worst and that Shaun could be terminal. They think kids don't understand words like that. But when you're six—in a place like that—you learn very quickly what those words can mean. I was so, so scared. I remember the rage. It was like a red mist descending all around me. Uncontrollable rage.' He gave a little smile. 'And I wasn't that kind of kid at all. I ended up running out of the hospital and kicking a wall so hard I broke the bones in my foot. One of the nurses had to come and help me.'

'Oh, Mitch.' She reached over and touched his arm. 'That's awful.'

He couldn't look at her. She could see the sheen in his eyes. 'Back then Shaun was my world. We lived in each other's pockets. I mean, he's good now, he's healthy. We've both grown up and he's married with kids. I've got a totally different lifestyle from him. But the connection, and the memories from so long ago, they just never leave you. St Jude's gave us the lifeline we needed as a family. It feels like my duty to do that for other families.'

He held out his arms. 'I mean, look at me. The amount of money I get paid for playing guitar and singing? It's ridiculous. I'm the first person to admit that. But that's why it's so important that I keep doing something good with the money. Shaun doesn't earn anything like what I do. If the shoe were on the other foot, this is what he'd do with his money too.'

Sam was just listening, being as quiet as possible to let him speak. Her fingers were brushing the hairs on his arm. She whispered, 'I do get it, Mitch. I do. I might not have a sick brother or sister but I get that feeling of helplessness.

I get that feeling of being out of control. I mean—I'm a nurse. I'm supposed to take care of people. I'm supposed to make people better.

'But I couldn't do that for my mum. I wanted to—I really did. But—' her voice cracked a little '—it's so hard. It's so different, taking care of your mum. I think I'm a good nurse, I do. But looking after someone else's loved ones is so different from looking after your own. I felt so guilty I could barely function. Any time she was sore, any time she was hungry or thirsty, I felt as if I wasn't doing a good enough job.'

He frowned. 'I don't believe that, Sam. You'd do a great job with your mum. But it's impossible for anyone to be there twenty-four hours a day. How could you support her if you couldn't work?'

She pressed her hand against her heart. 'Maybe so, but it didn't feel like that in here. I always felt as if I could do better.' He pulled her closer and shifted a little. The weight of his body against hers made her slide a little down the sofa.

She was acutely aware of the heat of his body. It seemed to reach through the thin cotton of his shirt and wrap itself around her. She tried to adjust her position, but there was nowhere to go.

This didn't feel wrong—even though it should. He'd just shared something with her, and she with him.

He dipped his head, brushing his nose against hers. She caught her breath in her throat.

'So, Samantha. How did I manage this?'

Less than an inch. His lips were less than an inch from hers. She could feel his warm breath tickling her skin. It was delicious. It was playing with her mind. Making her lose focus.

'How did you manage what?' Her voice came out as a squeak. The lights on the tree started to flicker on their automatic timer. The natural light around them had been fading as they'd talked and the red and gold glow was practically the only light in the room. It made her think of old Christmas movies. And how did they all end?

The laughter lines reached up to his eyes, crinkling the skin around them in a warm, sexy manner. 'Manage to get the hottest nurse on the planet.'

It was definitely time to move. It was definitely time to take steps. Were his eyes a little glazed over, a little unfocused?

She would love to think that Mitchell had her pinned to the sofa because he thought she was the sexiest woman in the world. She would love to think that she was a star in her own personal Christmas movie where the little shop girl got swept off her feet by the millionaire businessman who'd never noticed her before, to the sound of some Christmas carol.

But every nurse sense told her this was no movie. This was an interesting case of hypo symptoms. Trust her to get the one patient in the world to get horny when he hypoed. This could get him in all sorts of trouble in later life.

She licked her lips and he growled. 'Oh, don't do that. It drives me crazy,' he taunted her, brushing his left cheek against her right. 'Have you any idea how good you look in these jeans?' This time he changed direction, dipping his head to the other side to brush alternate cheeks together. Her heart was racing in her chest. But part of her brain was still functioning. Was this all pre-programmed in him? Were these the moves he normally used around women? Because, truthfully, they were good. They were working.

His hair tickled the side of her face as his mouth approached her ear. She couldn't move. She just couldn't. Now his shoulders were pinning hers to the sofa. But she didn't feel scared, she didn't feel threatened. Mitch wasn't like that. He whispered in her ear, his voice a sultry growl, 'Have you any idea how much I've wanted to get my hands on you in those jeans?'

She cleared her throat. It was time to break out of the fantasy. It was time to be a nurse. No matter what the flickering Christmas lights were telling her.

But Mitch had other ideas. His lips trailed around her ear, dancing slowly across her face until they reached her own lips. Her natural instinct was to lick them again, moisten them as his mouth closed over hers.

It was only for a few seconds. But that was all it took. All it took to tip her world upside down and *kersplat* on the floor like an upturned trifle. Because, hypo or not, Mitch Brody was the *best* kisser she'd ever encountered in her life.

He didn't just kiss. He adored. He swept you away on a puffy pink cloud, kissing as if his life depended on it, and if he parted from you he would surely die.

She could almost hear the carol singers breaking into song around her and the movie credits starting to roll.

Enough.

She was losing her mind. All rationality, every sensible thought she'd ever had shot out the window as soon as his lips touched hers. His hair was tickling her face.

She pulled back, her head being about the only part of her body she could move.

'Mitch. Stop it. Get off me. Let me up.' She tried to bat his hair away but he laughed.

'Haven't you heard? Grunge is in.'

There it was again. The slightly glazed expression. His brow wrinkled and she arched her shoulders towards him to try and push him away a little. Only it didn't work. All it served to do was push her breasts up against the hard planes of his chest and bring the little twinkle that had vanished from his eyes for a few seconds rushing back like a freight train.

His mouth closed in on the pale, sensitive skin at the bottom of her neck. The one spot on her body that was guaranteed to turn her legs into a pool of mush. Just as well she was lying down.

At least this way she could move her hand a little. Dangerous waves of sensation were sweeping along her spine, nerves dancing with glee at a long-awaited touch.

How long had it been? Nearly two years? She'd been so busy with her mum these last few years that men had been the last thing on her mind. Maybe that was it. Maybe that's why her brain was on a murky spin cycle right now. Her body was finally revelling in the sensation of being touched again. And while selfish parts of her would like this to continue, professional parts of her were on complete alert.

She squeezed her hand between their chests and pushed him back. 'Stop, Mitch. Stop now.'

Her push had a little more force than she'd anticipated and he landed straight backwards onto the floor.

'Ouch!' The fall to the floor seemed to bring a little focus back into his eyes. The Christmas tree was directly behind him, the blinking lights sending his silhouette dancing across the wall. It was almost like being at one of his concerts.

She jumped from the sofa and knelt down next to him. 'Sorry. Are you okay?'

His gaze narrowed and he scowled at her. She stood up and held out her hand. 'It's time to check your blood-glucose level. How are you feeling?'

He ignored her hand and stood up with a little stagger. 'Fine,' he grunted.

She put her hands on both his shoulders. 'No. I want

you to really think about it. Do you feel shaky? Sick? Hot? Any of the above?'

He shook his head. 'Just a bit, well…strange.'

'Good.' She led him over to the table and sat down in a chair next to him, pushing the meter towards him. She flicked the overhead light, sending bright white spilling across the room. He flinched. There. Much more appropriate. It would stop the Christmas movie tunes from circulating around her head.

He didn't speak. Just opened the meter, pulled a stick from the tub and loaded it. She breathed a sigh of relief. He still had enough of his faculties to know what he should be doing. His hands were trembling slightly as he used the finger-pricking device to draw a little blood. The tiny spot of blood seemed to be magically pulled from his finger into the stick as he touched it. It was amazing how little blood was actually needed. They both watched the ten-second countdown.

Four point zero. She stood up. 'It's official, Mitch. You're having a hypo.'

He glared. Again. 'Between four and seven is normal,' he grumbled. He was getting snappier, more argumentative. Good to know. It seemed he started at the amorous stage and moved from there.

'Between four and seven is normal for people who have been controlling their diabetes for a few months. I've told you this before. Your levels have been running higher these past few weeks, and it will take a little time for them to settle down. For you, right now, you hypo around four.'

His hands were definitely starting to shake a little more and sweat was forming on his brow. It was important that he recognise these signs. She sat down next to him and pulled over the supplies she already had ready. 'Look at your hands, Mitch. They're shaking.' She lifted his hand to his brow. 'And you're sweating. Do you feel it?'

'Of course I feel it. It's running down my back,' he snapped.

She ignored the snappiness. 'Good. These are things you need to take notice of for the future. Here...' She reached into the supply kit. 'There are some glucose tablets or a sugar drink in here. You need to take something to bring your level up quickly. What will it be?'

'I hate that stuff.' He pointed at the bright orange liquid in the bottle. 'I'll never drink it.'

'Try one of these, then.' She pushed the glucose tablets at him and he ripped open the packet and put one in his mouth.

It lasted around two seconds.

'Yuck.' He spat it into his hands. 'That's disgusting, powdery. I'm not eating that.'

He walked over to the kitchen and flung it in the trash can. She followed close behind. Under normal circumstances Mitch would never do something like that. But he was the same as most diabetics, all walls of reserve came tumbling down once the hypo started.

'What do you want, then?' She started looking through the cupboards. Her first idea had bombed. It wasn't practical to start making a smoothie like the last time—that had been a one-off situation. She needed to find something more accessible than that. Something Mitch could carry around with him that would act quickly.

'Chocolate.'

She blinked. He hadn't eaten any chocolate around her in the last few days. But if that's what he said he would eat, then that's what he would get.

She found some chocolate bars in a tin in one of the

cupboards. She skidded one across the worktop towards him. 'This will have to do. Eat it now.'

He barely acknowledged her and it was worrying. His blood sugar would be dropping lower. Thankfully, Mitch wasn't the kind of diabetic to refuse to eat when it was obvious he was hypoing. They could be the absolute worst.

He ripped open the chocolate bar and ate it in two bites. All her instincts wanted to do everything for him. But this was about him learning, not her. She'd already learned everything she needed to about his symptoms. Now it was about teaching him what to do next. The chocolate bar was enough to bring his level up. It was time to be patient and give it a chance to work. Ten minutes should be enough. Then he'd need to make himself something a little more substantial. She'd already figured out that would probably be toast for Mitch. But he wouldn't always have her—or anyone—around when he hypoed. So he had to do these things for himself.

'I'm going to sleep,' he announced, walking over to the sofa he'd just had her pinned to and throwing himself down. Fatigue. Another late-onset symptom. Something else to remember.

She glanced at her watch and followed him over to the sofa. Not ideal, but she was here to watch over him. She'd wait ten minutes then give him a shake. If Mitch were on his own, this could be dangerous. Particularly if he didn't recognise the signs of hypo and didn't eat but instead just tried to sleep. She glanced at the timer of her watch again. Nine minutes to go.

But it didn't take that long. After seven minutes his eyes opened and he sat up and ran his fingers through his dishevelled hair. His forehead wrinkled and recognition crowded his eyes. 'Oh, no.'

She smiled. 'Oh, yes. Time to check your level again.'

He sighed and stood up. 'This is becoming a bit of a drag.' She followed him over to the dining table and watched while he checked his blood glucose, turning the monitor around to let her see. Seven.

'What now?' He rubbed his eyes. 'I feel as if I've done ten rounds in a boxing ring. I really could hit the sack.'

She nodded. 'It's not uncommon after a hypo to feel tired. What you have to do now is have something more substantial to eat. Something with more complex carbo-hydrates that will break down more slowly.'

He shook his head as if the weight of the world was on his shoulders. 'Toast.' He said it simply and moved to-wards the kitchen. His actions were mechanical. Putting bread in the toaster and finding butter in the refrigerator.

Then he halted, as if something had just lit a candle in his mind. His words came out slowly, deliberately, as if he was thinking about every one. 'I don't think dinner in Inns-bruck is a good idea tonight. I'm not really feeling up to it.'

She stepped forward quickly. 'That's fine. No prob-lem. Feel free to rest.' Her stomach had started doing flip-flops. He wasn't looking at her. He was deliberately looking away. Had he remembered what had happened between them? Remembered the kiss? Oh, no. Mitchell Brody wasn't embarrassed. He wasn't the kind of guy who would ever be embarrassed. But he might well be the kind of guy who felt guilty about his actions and regretted them.

Now, that would be humiliating.

She headed towards the door. She could check on him later. Do her nursing duties and forget about the whole thing. But Mitch wasn't finished. He put down the plate and knife in his hand and turned to face her.

'I get it. I get why you made me do this.' His sigh could fill the whole room. 'But I don't like it. I don't like not being completely in control. I don't like the fact that something like this could happen and I wouldn't be able to act to stop it.'

She moved closer, her fears forgotten. This was her job. This was why she was here. To educate, to reassure. It was time she learned to keep her mind on the job. 'But now you can. You got a little shaky, a little sweaty. You start to feel confused—unfocused. Now you know what you're looking for, it might make things a bit easier if it happens again.' She held up the meter and picked a chocolate bar out of the tin. 'You just need to make sure you have these on you at all times.'

'But what if I don't? What if I'm halfway up or down a slope and have none of those things?' His voice was different now, more vulnerable, and she could tell he was struggling with this.

She stayed firm. She pointed at the things again. 'It's simple. You don't ever leave home without them. You have to take charge of this, Mitchell. This is your body. This condition is manageable. You just need to keep on top of it.'

The words conjured up another kind of picture in her brain and from the rueful smile that danced across his face it was clear it had sparked a memory in him too.

His voice dropped. 'Shaky and sweaty weren't the only symptoms, were they Sam?'

She couldn't answer. It just didn't seem appropriate. She had wondered if he'd even remember. It wasn't exactly the most tactful thing for her to bring up.

'We can talk about this in the morning,' she said swiftly as she moved back to the doorway, her cheeks beginning to burn. She could still feel his breath on her cheek, the touch of his lips on hers, the brush of his chest against hers.

'Sam.' His voice sent a shiver down her spine. It was the way he'd said her name. As if it was honey on his tongue. As if he was caressing every part of her. 'I might hate everything about this, but I don't regret kissing you. Not for a single second.'

She didn't stop. She kept walking. Straight down the dark hall and into her bedroom, closing the door behind her before her legs turned to jelly.

What on earth had she got herself into?

CHAPTER SEVEN

Two days later Sam was still tiptoeing around Mitchell. They'd fallen into an easy routine. She didn't seem to have any problem getting up early and joining him on the slopes. Even though she categorically refused to set foot on the snow, she was happy to wait for him at the Seegrube mid-station.

It was even more of a relief that she had no qualms about going back to St Jude's every afternoon with him. Some of the kids even knew her by name already.

His phone beeped and he pulled it from his back pocket. *Can you call me?* It was Lisa. Their relationship was purely professional. She must be texting about one of the kids.

He pressed the dial button straight away. 'Lisa, what's up?'

'Thanks for calling, Mitchell. It's Brian. He became really sick last night. His dad had just flown out for emergency business in Dubai.'

'What happened?'

'You know he's been up and down. He spiked a fever really quickly. He's under emergency care and they've put him on the bone-marrow transplant list.'

Every hair prickled at the back of his neck. A deterioration like this could be deadly. He couldn't bear the thought that the young guy he'd played guitar with had become so sick so quickly.

'Is there a donor?'

There was a sigh at the end of the phone. 'Neither Brian's dad or mum is a good enough match. Nor is his brother. He's going to have to go on the general list.'

'Can I see him?'

'That's why I phoned you. Brian's dad has barely touched down in Dubai and is scrambling to get a flight back. His mum has flu and is holed up in the parents' room.'

Everything fell into place for Mitchell. 'And you've put Brian in isolation because his blood count is so low?'

'Yeah. He's isolated. We can't let his mum in. If Brian caught flu right now...' Her voice tailed off. She didn't need to say any more. Mitchell understood completely.

'I'll be there in fifteen minutes.' He hesitated. Should he take Samantha with him? But his brain was so fixated on getting there that he only gave it a few seconds' thought before he scribbled her a note and let the door slam behind him.

Half an hour later he was masked, gloved and gowned. Barrier nursing. More like space-age nursing. Luckily Brian was old enough not to be scared. Or so he thought. It was sometimes hard to remember that thirteen was still really a child.

Lisa was hovering around him. 'You're definitely not sick? There's nothing wrong with you?' Her eyes were scanning up and down his body. He could tell there were a million things going through her head right now—all of them about Brian's safety.

'Just say what you mean, Lisa.' He wanted to get in there. He didn't want to stand around a doorway.

'It's just...you've lost so much weight in the last few

weeks. I know you say you're fine, but…well, it's not normal. Is there something you're not telling me?'

It didn't matter that he didn't want any of hospital staff to know what was wrong with him. It didn't matter that he didn't want any of them to think the tour was in jeopardy. He wasn't important right now. Brian was. And Lisa was asking all the questions an experienced nurse should.

'I've been diagnosed with diabetes in the last few weeks. That's why the rapid weight loss. Sam assures me it will go back on.'

The jigsaw pieces of recognition fell into place. He lifted his hand. 'Swear to me that you won't breathe a word.' He glanced through the glass. 'I've only told you so you won't worry about me being in with Brian.'

She gave a brief nod of her head. 'Now I know why Samantha's here. She told me she was a nurse.'

He put his hand on the door. 'Okay to go in now?'

She nodded, but she was still mumbling. 'Pity. I thought for once you might have found a decent girlfriend.'

He paused. 'What do you mean?'

She gave the slightest shake of her head. 'You know, one that doesn't care about fame and headlines.' She gestured with her head towards the room. 'Someone who knows what's important in this life. Someone with a heart.' She turned on her heel and walked down the corridor, leaving his brain whirling.

Was that what people really thought? That anyone who dated him only did it for the fame? It was more than an insult, it was a crushing blow. Mitch had always thought his looks and charm were the hit with the ladies. Most of the women he dated might not earn the same as he did, but they could certainly afford the life of luxury.

He thought back over the last few. Misty Kennedy had

been fun for about ten minutes, but vain beyond all belief. She didn't eat. Full stop. And he didn't like it.

Carrie Beaulaux had been nice—if a little shallow. Truth was they just hadn't really had much to say to each other.

As for Lightning Adams, she was the true definition of a diva. Demanding and a control freak who seemed to have the press photographers at her beck and call. But the day that she'd spoken horribly to Dave, that had been her ticket out of there. He'd deposited her, her free designer wardrobe and her ten-thousand-dollar face cream on the sidewalk outside his LA home, just as a 'houses of the stars' coach tour was passing by. It might have made the headlines.

He watched Lisa round the corner at the end of the corridor. He liked her. He respected her opinion and the job she did. But it was the first time she'd ever made a straight mention of his rock-star persona. Much to his relief, she'd always totally ignored that. But her comment about Samantha bothered him.

Someone who knew what was important in this life. Someone with a heart.

It prickled every sense in his body. Was that why he was feeling the overwhelming pull towards her? At first he'd thought it was just his normal male hormones. Then he'd suspected a weird case of Stockholm syndrome. But maybe it was time to get to the bottom of this.

Maybe it was time to ask himself why a cute blonde with startling blue eyes was all he could think about these days. Was she the most gorgeous woman on the planet, with the best body? Maybe not in the world's eyes. But she was certainly looking good from his. He definitely wanted to know what lay underneath the array of cute jumpers and blue jeans.

But now wasn't the time. Now he had to concentrate

on a thirteen-year-old boy who needed someone to hold his hand.

This young guy had reached a crisis point without his family support system around him. He'd be terrified. And Mitch understood. He just had to let Brian know that he did. There was no time to consider pretty nurses and blonde curls.

He pushed open the door and went inside. Brian's colour was so pale he was practically fading into the white sheets. He had an IV in place and his arm was littered with angry purple bruises.

He was so tired he barely lifted his head from the pillow. But the corners of his lips turned upwards. He recognised Mitch, even though he was hidden beneath a gown, cap, mask and gloves.

Mitch's heart gave a little surge. 'Hey, mate,' he said, sitting in the chair next to Brian and lifting his gloved hand to clasp the boy's.

This was why he did this. This was why he was determined to complete the tour. Nothing could get in the way of this.

Not even a beautiful nurse.

Sam's anger had only lasted about twenty seconds. Once she'd realised Mitchell hadn't just dived off to the slopes without her she dressed as quickly as she could. Her nurse brain was ticking. She grabbed extra supplies just in case in his rush to reach the hospital he'd forgotten his insulin and testing equipment.

The snow was much heavier today, the car tyres barely coping on the ten-minute drive. She wasn't used to this. Dave had assured her that driving wouldn't be a problem, but shouldn't she have those snow things on her tyres?

Lisa was panicking. Two of her staff were out with

norovirus and the two replacements she'd tried to call were unavailable. She took one glance at Samantha and gestured her over. 'Mitch told me about the diabetes, so I know why you're here. But what do you know about cystic fibrosis?'

Sam blinked. 'Eh, quite a lot, actually. That was the job I was supposed to be doing before I took the job with Mitch. I was supposed to be a specialist for a little boy with the disease.'

'So you've dealt with it before?' Lisa wasn't wasting any time.

She nodded. 'Yeah.'

'What about oxygen regimes and doing chest physio?'

She was beginning to sense where this was going. 'I'm fine with all that. Do you need some help, Lisa?'

Lisa turned the computer around and pulled up the web page for the UK national nursing body. 'Are you registered as Samantha Lewis?'

She smiled and bent over her, typing in her name and bringing up her registration status. 'That's me. Paediatric nurse and registered general nurse.'

Lisa turned to face her, desperation in her eyes. 'I wouldn't ask but…'

'What do you need?'

'Could you special a seven-year-old boy with cystic fibrosis for the next few hours until I can find someone else?'

Samantha nodded. 'I'm happy if you give me some background on the little boy.' She glanced down the corridor. 'I should check first. Is Mitchell okay?' Her fingers were jiggling the insulin pen in her pocket.

Lisa smiled. 'I put some food in the room earlier for them both. Everything should be fine.' She reached over and touched Sam's arm. 'You're good for him, you know.'

She was surprised. 'I am?'

'Take it from someone who's watched from the sidelines all these years. I was pretty shocked when he told me about his diabetes diagnosis. He might not give it away to the press, but Mitchell Brody is a control freak. I don't envy the job you have.' She gave her a wink. 'But I think you've got it covered.'

She waved her arm along the corridor. 'Now, come with me so I can find you some scrubs for the next few hours and give you a rundown on our patient. And, Samantha—' her grey eyes were serious '—I can't thank you enough for this.'

She felt a little flush of pleasure. She'd been looking forward to working this Christmas with the little boy she knew with CF. It was a real, hands-on nursing job. Sometimes she missed that. School nursing was great, very diverse with lots of social issues as well as health ones. But sometimes she missed doing the actual physical care.

It only took five minutes to change into a pair of pink scrubs and flat shoes. Lisa briefed her on the patient and she had a quick read over his notes. Rudy Jones had a lung infection, which was exacerbating his condition. The thick, sticky mucus in his lungs was making it difficult for him to breathe and his oxygen saturation was low.

'Hi, there, Rudy.' She walked into his room with gloves and mask in place. It was important not to introduce Rudy to any further germs. His defences were already low and his medication chart showed he was on two different types of antibiotics and some steroids. The bronchodilator that was currently running was causing little clouds around them.

She sat down next to the bed and spent the next ten minutes talking to him. He was frail, with an oxygen monitor attached to one finger. It was clear he was underweight— as a lot of the children with CF were because they couldn't digest certain nutrients in food.

It was easy to see how much strain his body was under. All the accessory muscles around his chest were working overtime. It was important to try and relieve some of the pressure on his lungs by loosening some of the mucus. Physiotherapy was a daily part of a CF child's life. Sometimes it could be fun, but sometimes it could be exhausting and difficult. Samantha was lucky. She'd had specialist training when she'd been a sister in ICU, so it meant she knew exactly how to help.

'Rudy, have you got a device to help with your physio?'

He nodded and pointed to the top of the locker. There was a 'flutter'—a handheld device shaped like an asthma inhaler—that delivered vibration to the airways of the lungs, making it easier to cough out mucus.

'Okay, we're going to start the active cycle of breathing techniques. Are you ready?'

He nodded and they moved the pillows on the bed to make him more comfortable.

She positioned her hands carefully to complement his breathing cycle of deep breaths, 'huffing' and coughing. She worked with him, vibrating certain sections of his chest with his huffing and coughing to try and loosen the mucus in his lungs and let him cough it up. It was a slow, painstaking process, with her monitoring Rudy throughout. He managed to expectorate quite a bit of mucus with the help of his 'flutter' device.

By the end he was exhausted—just as she'd expected he'd be. But his breathing was a little easier and his oxygen saturation had climbed a few digits. She wondered how Mitch was doing with Brian. Being with a kid like that would stir up a lot of memories for him. Here's hoping he wouldn't forget about his diabetes in the process.

His dedication here was much bigger than she'd expected. He showed real commitment to this place. And it was clear it was genuine.

When other stars were involved in places like these they usually had the paparazzi positioned on the doorstep or a camera crew filming their 'charitable' work.

Mitch was nothing like that. He was here because he wanted to be.

He was here because he cared. And it made her like him all the more.

She smiled at Rudy. Time to get the little guy to eat and increase his calorie intake. 'Okay, Rudy, what's it to be? Custard or chocolate pudding?'

Today had been the best day yet.

She'd managed to help a child when she'd needed to, and she finally felt as if she knew Mitchell a little better.

He wasn't the playboy rock star the media portrayed at all. He was sensitive, stubborn beyond all belief and had a serious, unwavering commitment to this hospital and its patients. She actually wondered if it was a little to his detriment. Was there something she didn't know? Obviously, there was.

Mitchell had been so focused on young Brian today he'd pushed everything else aside. She hadn't ignored her responsibility to him. And it was clear Lisa was wise beyond all measure. Any time she'd enquired about what was going on in the barrier nursing room, Lisa could tell her about food intake, blood sugars and insulin doses. It was clear, now she knew what was going on, that she understood completely. If Sam hadn't been happy that Mitchell was stable, she couldn't have helped with Rudy. Lisa had clearly been giving him 'prompts' as she'd dealt with Brian, in order to keep both her desperately needed assistants in place.

It wasn't as if she couldn't see into the room. She could. Young Brian had deteriorated quickly since yesterday, his colour and skin tone frightening. But she could see Mitchell—even if he didn't notice her. He was engrossed in talking quietly to Brian, entertaining him, being supportive.

One week ago she wouldn't have believed this. She would have searched around for the secret camera crew that must be filming Mitchell Brody doing his superstar 'good deeds'. But nothing could be further than the truth.

A regular nurse for Rudy had shown up around thirty minutes ago, just when she'd finished all the physio and then spent an hour trying to encourage him to eat. But she didn't mind. She loved working with kids. It made her feel useful. It made her feel worthwhile. This job with Mitch was the strangest she'd ever had. It didn't help that he was blurring a lot of lines for her.

He gave her a nod through the glass. It jolted her. She'd thought she might as well have been invisible. She held up the little sign she'd made, letting them know when Brian's dad's flight would land. There was no point in her going into the room and potentially exposing Brian to more bugs. The fewer people in his room the better.

Mitchell gave her a thumbs-up and wrote her a reply.

Dinner tonight in Innsbruck. 8 p.m.

She tried to ignore the flutter in her chest or the way her stomach just flipped over. He'd promised to take her out for dinner and show her around the city. Now that he knew when Brian's dad was arriving, it was clear he meant to see it through.

She tried to appear casual, giving the slightest nod and wave before strolling back down the corridor. What on earth would she wear? She didn't have any dressy clothes with her. She hadn't thought she would need any.

Lisa caught her puzzled look. 'What's wrong?'

'What do you wear to dinner in Innsbruck? It's minus four outside and I have no idea what to wear.'

'Something with an elastic waistband,' was the instant response.

Samantha smiled. Now, that did sound good. She hadn't had a chance to eat in the city yet. Most of the food in Mitch's house was very traditional. It would be nice to sample some of the local delicacies.

Lisa touched her hand. 'And definitely *always* leave room for pudding in Austria.' Her eyes ran up and down Samantha's frame. 'You know, I might have something I can lend you. We look around the same size.'

'You do? That would be great.'

Things were looking up. She didn't have any doubt that whatever Lisa had it would be perfect. Probably a hundred times better than anything she could have brought from home. She looked out of the window at the view of the city beneath them. The sun was beginning to set, sending a warm glow over the snow-topped roofs and coloured houses. The white-tipped mountain peaks seemed to blush pink at sunset. The lights in the houses underneath twinkled. It looked magical, as if anything could happen down there. The question was, did she want it to?

It was like having two mother hens pecking at him now. Mitch almost regretted telling Lisa about his diabetes as she'd clucked around him all day about eating, testing and injecting. And he really didn't like thinking of Samantha as a mother hen, because he had a whole host of other ways he could think about her...

It had been a whole week and he hadn't even taken her

to the city yet. What an appalling host. His mother would be enraged. She'd brought her children up to have much better manners than that.

Tonight he would be the perfect host. Tonight he would show her the wonders of Innsbruck, all while trying to keep his hands to himself.

He left his black shirt untucked with the first two buttons undone. Mitchell Brody didn't dress up. He'd thought about taking her to one of the many local gourmet restaurants, before finally deciding to take her to one of his favourite Alpine inns. She'd never seen the Christmas market before and he wanted her to have time to wander around without being tied to a dinner reservation.

He glanced at his watch. It was only seven-thirty, but hopefully she would be ready early and they could head down the mountain. Now that Brian's dad had arrived, he felt as if he could finally relax.

It happened every time. Every time one of the kids he'd bonded with got sick, he couldn't get them out of his mind. The pale skin, the bruising, the lack of energy and appetite. Just like his brother.

It didn't matter that his brother lived a healthy life now. While they'd been there as children they'd seen other friends become sick and slip away. That reality was still there now, and he couldn't let that affect his work with the hospital. In fact, it made it much more important. Every family should feel supported, no matter what the outcome for their child. His tour money would allow that to continue in an environment more appropriate than they had now.

He'd been surprised to see that Lisa had persuaded Samantha to help out one of the sick kids. Lisa was wildly protective of her charges and the fact she'd relied on Sam, even for a few hours, was a big deal.

There was still that tiny doubt at the back of his mind—

mainly stemming from the comment that Lisa had made. Samantha was clearly here to do a job. She'd already told him she needed the money. There was nothing hidden, nothing untoward. But was Samantha like the rest of the women Lisa had alluded to? If Samantha wasn't his nurse, would she only be interested in him because of his money?

He couldn't imagine for a minute that she was a fan or interested in the media. She hadn't made a single comment like that. But money could be a big draw for people. Maybe he'd made a fool of himself by kissing her the other night. She hadn't objected, though, and now it was eating away at him. Samantha seemed spunky enough to tell him not to make assumptions about her. He was cringing at the thought that he might have pushed himself on her unwillingly. Now he was beginning to doubt himself. Was the underlying attraction between them really there? Had it truly been there with any of his past relationships? Or had he just been too blind to see that women weren't actually interested in him, only his money?

It was the first time in his life he'd ever had thoughts like this. And he certainly didn't like the way they were playing on his mind.

Tonight would solve that. Tonight would let him forget about all that. Tonight would be about showing her around a city that he loved. It would be about introducing her to the local customs and traditions he'd known since he was a child. He ran his fingers through his hair one last time.

The smell hit her as soon as she stepped from the black four-by-four. 'Oh, wow, what's that?' She sniffed the air hungrily. The whole area around her smelt good enough to eat.

Mitchell grinned as he got out of the car. They'd been lucky to get parked as the streets were crowded around them. He moved out of the way of some locals and walked around next to her. 'That is the smell of Tyrolean fritters, mixed in with the smell of gingerbread and punch.' He held out his arm. 'Welcome to the Christmas market.'

She wrinkled her nose but couldn't stop smiling. 'Okay, you've got me. What's a Tyrolean fritter? And should I really be eating anything like that?'

'A Tyrolean fritter is the best thing in the world, especially if it comes with lingonberry jam.'

She shook her head as she pushed her gloves on her hands. 'I don't even know what a lingonberry is.'

He steered her through the crowds, past the floodlit white Imperial Palace set against the background of the Alps and the luminescent St Jacob's Cathedral swathed in a multitude of coloured lights. They almost took her breath away.

'Can we go inside the cathedral?'

He nodded. 'It won't be open right now, but we can come back during the day. Would you like to see around it?'

'Absolutely. I love buildings like this.'

As they walked through the streets the sounds of Christmas carols echoed around them. It seemed like the whole of Innsbruck was in the Christmas mood. The entrances to every door were covered in garlands of evergreen boughs and red velvet bows. Christmas-tree lights glittered in the windows all around them.

The Christmas market in the old town was magical. Stars and fairy-lights were strung across the streets. Figures from well-loved fairy-tales gazed down from the windows of the old town houses.

The smell of hot spiced wine surrounded them and they stopped at a large copper cauldron. Mitchell handed over some money and brought back two steaming cups. Just a sip was enough to catch in her throat and send a warm feeling down to the tips of her frozen toes.

'What's this called?'

He smiled. 'Glühwein. Any more than a cup will give you a major headache in the morning.' There were other stands all around them and the air was filled with a whole host of tantalising and unusual aromas. Even in the space of a few paces she could smell everything from doughnuts to roasted chestnuts, chocolate and candied apples and garlic bread. He stopped in front of the next stand with some shiny brown pretzels and stuffed fritters, carefully placing his virtually untouched glühwein to the side.

Four teenagers with bright pink candy floss wandered past them while they waited in the queue. Mitchell gestured towards one of the stuffed fritters, dusted it with sugar and wrapped it in a napkin before holding it out towards her. 'I don't want to spoil your appetite before dinner, but you've got to try this.'

He was holding the wrapped fritter with both hands and she could smell the warm jam inside. She eyed the dusted sugar around it, 'Please, don't tell me this is one of your addictions?'

He laughed. 'Fortunately, no. But everyone who comes to Innsbruck at Christmas should definitely taste one of these. Think of it as one of the unwritten rules.'

She bent forward and took a bite. It only took the briefest seconds for the taste explosion in her mouth. The fritter wasn't heavy, as she'd feared. It was light and crispy, but the jam inside was much hotter than the mildly warm fritter. 'Ow-w-w!' she yelped, closing her mouth in shock, then opening it again quickly in the hope the cold night air would help with the jam burning her tongue. She panted, blowing out clouds of hot air into the icy night.

Mitchell was laughing, watching the steam rise from the fritter in his hand. 'Sorry, I should have warned you.'

It took a few seconds before she could speak, then she felt a drip of the still boiling jam slide down her chin. She took a deep breath and swallowed as quickly as she could, desperate to try and regain what was left of her dignity.

But Mitchell stepped forward, pulling his hand from his glove and catching the sliding drop with his finger. He did it so gently, so delicately that for a moment she felt as if she were in some expensive beauty parlour. He was so close, blocking out some of the coloured lights around them, leaving him bathed in a beautiful glow. His eyes were darker than ever and his frosty breath mingled with hers. He held up his finger, which was coated in rich red jam. 'Want to finish this?' he whispered, as he lifted the edge of the paper napkin and wiped it down her chin.

Her tongue darted out automatically, licking her lips and picking up the last delicious vestiges of jam. She shook her head.

She was finding it difficult to say anything. The close-ness wasn't disturbing. It was tantalising. Just above his head was a string of white star lights. If this were a movie there would be electric sparks shooting off in the background.

'Good,' he said huskily as he put the finger in his mouth and sucked off the jam.

Oh, no. She couldn't start thinking thoughts like these. They were in the middle of a street, surrounded by hoards of other tourists and locals.

Street entertainers were playing cow bells and accordions, other locals were yodelling and doing traditional dancing, causing anyone nearby to start tapping their feet automatically. They walked towards another square, bustling and full of people with an enormous Christmas tree at one end, but it was the glistening above it that took her breath away. Golden glittering tiles on the roof of a three-storey-high balcony overlooking the plaza.

Samantha spun around. 'You mentioned this, didn't you? Wow, it's spectacular. It's not real gold, is it?'

The lights around the roof made the reflections from the roof glitter wildly. More coloured lights that were strung across the plaza bobbed in the wind. It made the reflections even more magical, blue, red, pink and green.

'They're gold-plated copper tiles. There's more than two thousand of them. It was built by some archduke in the fifteenth century.' He glanced towards her, his smile reaching from ear to ear, and his arm settled around her back. 'It's always more spectacular to see it first at night. Especially with all the Christmas decorations around.'

He was right. She could hardly draw her eyes away. All around them the flashes of cameras popped, sending even more reflections out into the night. She could stand here and watch this all night. Never mind the warm arm around her waist, resting on her hip bone and pulling her close enough to make her feel that she should actually be there.

It was like being in the middle of a Christmas card. All around them were wonderful sights, sounds and smells. The Tyrolean folk seemed larger than life, friendly and welcoming with singers and musicians in all corners of the marketplace. Any minute now some fairy-tale king was going to appear on the balcony above. Out of the corner of her eye something flashed white. Was this one of the proverbial unicorns?

No. It was beautiful white horses, being led around the square with young children on their backs, part of another parade.

Mitch walked her backwards towards the façade of one the shops. She turned to peer through the window. It was full of candy canes and carved wooden objects, more traditional items that just made her smile even more. Up in the chalet in the mountains she'd had no idea about the world of Tyrolean traditions down here. She would have to persuade him to bring her back down here tomorrow so she could do some serious shopping.

'Come on.' He slipped his hand into hers. 'The inn will be busy. If we hang around too long we'll never get a table.' He pulled her through a labyrinth of alleyways until they reached the door of a white and black painted inn.

He pushed it open and she was immediately surrounded by warmth. She pulled the zipper on her blue ski jacket. The inn was crowded, but it didn't seem to be full of tourists, from the language around her, this inn was full of locals.

Lisa had chosen well. Her black sequined tunic over black leggings and boots was pretty, without being over the top. Sam was twinkling almost as much as the Christmas lights, and from the way Mitch was looking at her, he seemed to appreciate it.

They took a table next to the flickering fire. She glanced at the menu in front of her and shrugged. 'Well, I don't have a clue. I'm sorry to say I can't read a word of German.'

Mitch pulled off his jacket and hat, leaving his hair mussed around his head. 'Would you like me to order for you?' He hadn't even looked at the menu.

She looked around. 'Do you eat in here regularly?'

He winked. 'That would be telling too many secrets.' He leaned back in his chair. 'I suggest some of the local cuisine. If I promise to bring you back another day to sample the cakes and desserts, will you trust me to order you dinner?'

She put her elbow on the table and rested her head on her hand, letting her eyes drift into the corner of the room.

'Will I trust you? Now, there's an interesting question...' She let her voice tail off.

The waiter appeared at their table, filling their glasses with water and nodding at the requests made by Mitchell.

She waited until he'd left then narrowed her gaze, 'Go on, then. Surprise me. What have you ordered?'

'All my favourites—fresh Bergkäse, Tyrolean gröstl and Plattin.'

She rolled her eyes as her stomach rumbled. 'Now, tell me what that is in a language my stomach understands.'

He laughed. 'Mountain cheese, roast meat and potato pancakes.' He pointed to her rumbling stomach. 'Believe me, you'll love it.'

There was a clink of glass as the waiter delivered a soda for Mitch and a glass of white wine for her. She raised her glass. 'Are you sticking to the diet soda?'

He nodded in response. 'I've only drunk diet soda...' he let out a sigh '...and I'm planning on giving alcohol a miss until I get this diabetes thing under control.'

She smiled, a little surprised. It was so nice to hear him say that. It was the first time he'd actually made a comment that made her think he was willing to do some work himself.

She took a sip of her wine. It was good, light and fresh, just what she liked. She sucked in a deep breath. Mitch had intrigued her today. There was more to him than met the eye—and she definitely wanted to dig a little deeper. Her head was trying to reason with her curiosity. If she knew him better, she could help him tailor his diabetes to suit his lifestyle. But that wasn't really why she wanted to know more about Mitch...

'So, Mitch. It's just you and me. I watched you today at the hospital. I can tell how much you care about these kids. But wouldn't you like to stay here a bit longer? Give yourself time to get more in control?'

She was trying to tug at his heartstrings. The thing she knew was important to him. Maybe it was a bit manipulative. But if it worked…

She kept going. 'Why are you so focused on this tour? Wouldn't it be simpler just to delay the whole thing until you were in better health?'

He shook his head. 'You make it sound so easy. It's anything but.'

She held up her hands. 'But why? You're Mitchell Brody. You've got the world at your feet. Don't you just click your fingers and everyone comes running?'

He let out a short burst of laughter. 'I wish!' He raised his eyebrows. 'You certainly don't.' He let the words hang there as he ran his fingers through his hair and rested his elbows on the table. 'This tour has taken two years to plan. Two years to iron out with my management and band members.'

She was trying not to smile at his first comment, but she was still confused. 'What did you have to iron out?'

He hesitated. 'Things are a bit different about this tour. It's not as straightforward as it seems.'

'Why?' She wasn't going to let it go. She wanted to understand if something about this was putting him under more pressure. It was an important factor in controlling his diabetes.

He couldn't seem to look her in the eye. 'My share of the tour proceeds and a certain percentage of the profits are tied up somewhere else. I mean, the guys aren't getting what they normally would on a tour.'

'Why?' She couldn't stop asking the question. The guy was a billionaire, did he have some kind of crazy debts?

An uncomfortable prickle went down her spine. How well did she know Mitchell Brody really?

This time he did meet her gaze. Uncompromising. 'Because I asked them to.'

It was the way he said it. The sincerity behind his brown eyes. Every hair at the back of her neck stood on end as if a cool breeze had just blown past.

She could tell he wasn't going to say any more. His tone had more or less let her know the conversation was over. But it only succeeded in making her more curious than ever.

'What do you need the money for?' Her voice came out as a whisper, almost lost in the background noise and chat. There were deep furrows across his brow.

He didn't have time to answer before the plates were put down in front of them. It only took a few seconds for the wonderful aroma to engulf her. It wasn't the only thing to engulf her. A wash of relief was sweeping over her too. She'd asked a question she wasn't sure she wanted an answer to.

The frown on his forehead made it clear he wasn't happy with her comments. Mitch leaned forward and murmured what each dish contained. He picked up his knife and fork and started eating quietly. The silence was painful.

Things had been so much fun earlier, so festive, so flirty. She certainly knew how to create an atmosphere.

Panic started to flow through her veins. What if he decided to sack her? She needed the income for her mum.

This job was playing havoc with her senses. One minute she was threatening to quit and walk away, the next she was feeling panicked about getting sacked.

The truth was this should all be about the money—and her responsibility to care for her patient. But, slowly and surely, this complicated man was starting to get under her skin.

The rational part of her brain started to kick in. She'd merely asked a few questions. Sure, she was curious about the personal stakes, but the initial questions had been based around his condition. That was fine. That wasn't a sackable offence.

She took a mouthful of food then sucked in a deep breath. It was time to take a different tack. 'What about practising, I mean, rehearsals for your tour? Shouldn't you be doing that now? Your tour starts in two weeks. Isn't this the time to be running about like crazy, doing all those sound-check things?'

The corners of his mouth turned up and his shoulders relaxed a little at her lack of showbiz knowledge. 'We've done all the rehearsing. We did it in advance as we all wanted to take some holiday time over Christmas and New Year. It was during the rehearsals that I became unwell.' He ran his fingers through his hair again. 'I just thought I was working too hard—becoming too focused on what we had to do.'

Pressure. Stress. Those were the words that jumped into her head. Always risk factors for diabetes. Was the tour putting him under undue stress? Because that could affect his diabetic control too.

She was a little surprised. 'But these are your songs. You know them back to front. I would have thought the rehearsals would have come easy to you.'

He smiled. 'Just because I can play the guitar and sing the song doesn't make it easy. There are hundreds of things that can affect a performance. Every arena is different and because of the amplification and the way it can affect the sound, we have to take all of that into consideration. We're constantly tweaking for every venue we'll play at.'

'But what about your health? Isn't that important to you, Mitch?'

The frown fell back into place. 'My health is the least of my concerns right now. I just need to be able to stay on my feet and complete this tour.'

The words made her feel uncomfortable. Her nursing instincts were firing shots across her brain. 'You're not making this easy. If I don't think you're fit I'll have to say that. I've got to be confident that you can keep your blood sugar under control.' She bit her lip, 'The truth is, Mitchell, I've seen you skiing and we've worked out how much carbohydrate you burn while doing that. We can tailor what you eat and how much insulin you take for that activity. But a two- or three-hour concert? I wouldn't even know where to start.'

She reached across the table and touched his hand. The pads of her fingers tingled as soon as she came into contact with his warm flesh. 'I'm worried, Mitch. The last thing I want is for you to have a hypo attack in front of thousands of fans. That would be a nightmare. Truth is, the timing of all this is really difficult. The first few weeks of diabetes should be about seeing how to work things around your normal routine. Once that is sorted, then we can look at how a performance affects your blood sugar and plan for that.' She gave her head a little shake. 'I hate to say it, but I really think the best thing you can do is cancel.'

'What?' His voice echoed around the room, and several heads turned in their direction. Sam felt herself sink into her chair.

He realised immediately what he'd done and lowered his voice, leaning across the table towards her, eyes blazing. 'I wasn't kidding when I said this had taken two years to plan, Samantha. You think I can just cancel and set this up for a few months down the line? Not a chance. These venues, these arenas are booked out nearly eighteen months in advance. The timetabling for the band is done even further ahead than that. We have commitments to record a new album. Frank, the drummer, needs surgery—even that's had to be fitted into our timetable. Cancelling this tour would be a disaster.' He paused. 'And not just for us.'

He was deadly serious and her brain was scrambling to decide how to handle this. No matter what she'd seen at the hospital today, Mitchell Brody was used to getting his own way. Like it or not, she was going to have to try and work in a way that fitted around his demands.

He was staring off into space again, lost in his own thoughts. She'd have to give this some consideration. She needed him to work with her, not against her.

His eyes locked on hers. She could almost see the shutters falling into place. If she couldn't turn this around it wasn't only dinner that was going to be a bust.

'We'll need to do some rehearsals. I'll need to see you perform for the whole length of the concert. And not just once. We need to do it a few days in a row to see if the overall build-up affects how much insulin you'll need. This is complicated, Mitch, I can't just make up these calculations in my head. We need to base it on real life.' She was bending. She knew she was bending. But she was still allowing for her professional judgement to say no.

His brown eyes fixed on hers. 'Fine.'

Just like that. No argument. No ranting. Each concession was taking a little less time. A little less effort.

Then it happened. He gave a little shudder, as if he was shaking off the black cloud around his shoulders. She saw him inhale deeply and his gaze softened and he tried to smile.

He leaned towards her. 'So, Samantha. What about you? How do you feel about being away for Christmas?'

Wow. What a turnaround. She felt a little uneasy. But it was probably best just to go with the flow.

She looked around the room with its evergreen garlands and red bows, the shimmering tree in the corner of the room. There didn't seem to be a single part of this city that didn't scream Christmas at you. The Austrians did Christmas like no others.

It did give her little pangs. It took her back to years gone by when she and her sister hadn't slept at night with excitement. Their mum had loved Christmas, their whole house full of brightly coloured tinsel. Nothing could beat that feeling of waking up on Christmas morning to see a stuffed-full Christmas stocking at the bottom of their beds. Even as an adult she missed that. No matter how silly it seemed.

She took a deep breath. The words were hard to say. 'My life has changed. This is how it's got to be. I know that my mum is somewhere she's being looked after. I have complete faith in them—and that's a big thing for me. Trusting someone else with my mum's care is hard. But I have to do this. Christmas is the most profitable time of year for agency nursing. The last few years I've been with a family, caring for a little boy with CF.'

'Like Rudy at the hospital?'

'Exactly. They were great. They made me feel like part of the family. His mum and dad really wanted to do everything for him, but they had two other kids to consider too. It made a huge difference for them to have an extra pair of hands they could count on. It meant the whole family could enjoy Christmas with no pressure. I enjoyed doing that for them.'

It was true.

'Yeah, but Christmas at a price.' His voice dripped with cynicism.

She shifted uncomfortably in her seat. 'Don't say that. I know what you mean. And, yes, his family could afford it. But the whole job, it just didn't feel like a job. It felt like being part of the family. And at this time of year that's important.'

He took another forkful of the stew and lifted his eyebrows. 'So what happened this year?'

'The little boy—Daniel—he was sick. He's in hospital.' A cool chill washed over her skin. She hadn't phoned Trish to see how he was and she should have. She'd been so wrapped up in Mitchell this last week that she just hadn't got around to it. What was wrong with her? She never forgot things like that.

Mitch nodded slowly. 'So Daniel's loss was my gain. That's why you were available to do this job.'

Her eyes met his. Was he being sceptical? Or just matter-of-fact? She wasn't entirely sure. It was almost as if he was trying to weigh things up in his mind, and for some strange reason she felt as though he was finding her wanting.

It was the oddest feeling. And this was nothing to do with her nursing skills. This was about her, and her methods. Her, as a person. Her goals. Her values.

She'd never felt like this before. Never been so much on the spot. But the bottom line was, yes, she was here for the money.

Would she really leave her mum at Christmas for any other reason?

Her Christmas agency shifts were the only reason she'd managed to keep her head above water these last few years. This way she paid her mortgage, paid her mother's mortgage and paid the nursing-home fees. They'd tried selling her mother's house to help with finances. But the market was dead right now and homes just weren't selling, and, the idea of selling her mum's house didn't sit well with her anyway.

This was the answer. This was the thing that she could manage to do.

So why did it suddenly feel so wrong?

The food in front of her had lost its appetising aroma. Her stomach was still empty but churning. She couldn't even force a sip of her wine.

With a simple few sentences he'd made her mind spin. This was all because she'd crossed a line. Without even meaning to, she'd mixed business with pleasure.

Sometimes it felt as if he was looking at her, *really* looking at her with something special in his eyes. More than just a friend. More than just a colleague. As for the kiss?

Who was she kidding? Half the females in the world probably wanted to be kissed by Mitchell Brody, and she was a fool if she thought she'd managed that through anything but default.

Sure, there was sometimes a twinkle in his eye when he talked to her. On occasion it did feel like he was flirting with her. But maybe that was just Mitch? Maybe she'd misread everything. Including the fact he'd murmured he didn't think it had been a mistake.

Her warped brain was letting her imagination run wild and she'd actually believed that Mitchell Brody could be interested in her.

It was time for a reality check.

Then something else struck her. If this tour was really so important to Mitchell, could there be a chance that he was playing her?

Trying to get her to say that he was fit to do something he might actually not be? Now, that worried her all the more.

That compromised her professional integrity. Something she really didn't want to happen.

This night had started out so perfectly, with so much promise.

But the course of one conversation just seemed to have killed it, and all the friendly tones, stone dead.

So much for the festive spirit.

CHAPTER EIGHT

WHAT WAS WRONG with him?

Samantha had spent the last few days tiptoeing around him. And no wonder. He was acting like a bear with a sore head.

Every day she met him halfway up the slopes, their coffee drunk in silence as she watched him check his blood-sugar level and administer insulin.

Afternoons were spent avoiding each other at the children's hospital. She still seemed happy to go there—in fact, it was the only part of the day she seemed to enjoy. She'd developed an even better rapport with Lisa, the rest of the staff and the kids, which made him seem even more unreasonable.

But he just couldn't get things out of his head.

And it was all his own fault anyway.

For the first time in his life money was keeping him awake at night.

Samantha was here because she wanted to get paid. She had no loyalty to him, or interest in him personally.

After she'd spoken about the other family she normally spent Christmas with—for a price, of course—he'd felt a lousy second choice. Something else that he wasn't used to.

First there had been the comments from Lisa about finally picking 'a good one', then there had been the implication that Sam was desperate for money. Almost as desperate as he was.

But it was worse that that. Much worse.

Because her lips, her skin, her curls were haunting his dreams. It was like having an impossibly ripe peach sitting in front of him that he couldn't touch. Even though he tried to forget about her, he couldn't.

Samantha Lewis had burrowed her way under his skin.

He was trying to stay focused. He was trying to think of a way to make sure he could keep on top of the diabetes long enough to get through this tour. Once he was at the end of the tour he could take as much time as possible to look after himself.

The worst thing was he wasn't in control. No matter what it looked like from the outside. He was trying his best, he really was. But last night he'd woken up shaking, with the bed drenched in sweat.

Thankfully, Sam had already warned him about nighttime hypos and there had been an easily accessible bar of chocolate next to the bed. He hadn't even waited to check his blood-sugar level. And, yes, he knew it was wrong. But he'd been gripped by an unholy terror. Usually, he was in his house alone. What if he hadn't woken up? What if he'd slept right through? Would he have been dead in the morning?

He couldn't face going through in the middle of the night and waking her up to tell her, because if he did, he might see her in that short satin nightdress again and start to imagine unthinkable things. He'd just slammed the chocolate down his throat and waited until he'd eventually stopped shaking. Then he'd stumbled through to the kitchen and made himself some toast. It was becoming his staple go-to food.

By the time he'd eventually got around to checking his

blood sugar it had come up to six. He could only imagine what it had been before. And that scared him. That *really* scared him. The whole out-of-his-control element was unbearable.

But he just didn't feel he could talk to her about it. Would she understand? Would she care?

This whole thing had him tied up in knots.

But one thing did make sense. Whether she was only here for the money or not, she'd told him that they needed to assess how his time on stage affected his diabetes. At some point he was going to have to do a mock gig—probably more than one. Three hours of full-on stage performance, checking his blood sugar before, during and after.

The thought of it made him cringe. Why had this happened to him? The very last thing he wanted to do was collapse on stage in front of thousands of fans and be unable to perform. He could only imagine what the press would speculate about then.

That hypo last night was really playing on his mind. It had been his first experience of dealing with a hypo himself. Granted, Sam had only been down the corridor and had disaster struck she would have checked on him in the morning and intervened. But he couldn't rely on that. He didn't *want* to rely on that.

He wanted to be able to look after himself. He didn't want to be second-guessing himself every minute of the day—or minute of the night.

How on earth was he going to get through a tour if he didn't have things under control?

He sighed, leaning forward and running his fingers through his hair. He had to find a way through this.

He sat upright. Money. Maybe if he offered her enough money she would stay for the tour. It was four months, but she could travel with him, stay in luxury hotels and make sure his diabetes stayed on track.

But no. She had a permanent job back home. This was her holiday time. And it was unlikely she'd want to give up her permanent job and travel the world for four months when her mum was in a nursing home back in England.

He let out a long stream of air from his lungs. What else was there? He could always find another nurse. But that thought appeared like a big black smoking cloud. Another nurse wouldn't have Sam's blue eyes, cute curls or even cuter bum.

She'd said that money was her motivating factor and he believed her. But he'd also heard how she'd spoken about her mum. Somehow he knew he could offer Samantha a big wad of cash and she still wouldn't want to be separated from her mum for too long.

Then there was the other stuff. The crossing-the-line, *I kissed her and wanted to do a whole lot more* kind of stuff. He groaned. What was wrong with him?

Mitchell Brody. See a girl, like her, ask her out. That's the way he'd always been. And for the most part it had served him well.

But this time was more than odd. For a start, he was sharing a house with said girl. He wasn't seeing her at gigs or occasional parties. For another, he wasn't entirely sure he was reading things correctly. They'd kissed. They'd flirted. They'd said things to annoy each other. So why was this different from any other time?

The diabetes was like a floating elephant in the room. He wasn't sure he could handle this on his own. In fact, he was quite sure that in these early stages he couldn't.

But he didn't want Sam here because of his diabetes. He wanted her here for *him*.

Ugh. His brain wasn't helping. Nothing made sense to him any more.

He walked over to the window and looked out at his precious mountains. It was only a few days until Christmas. Maybe he'd been harsh the other night? She must be missing her family. And maybe he'd taken her comment too personally about how special Christmas was with the other family. Of course Christmas was special for kids. That's exactly the way it should be.

Something pricked in his brain, sending a smile across his face. That's it. That's what he'd do. He already had plans at the hospital for Christmas. But maybe if he could make her see that Christmas was special here too, she might just start to come round. She might *want* to be around him, rather than feel obliged to be.

He couldn't rationalise why that was important to him. He just knew it was.

She hadn't seen the outdoor ice skating rink yet in Innsbruck. That's where he'd take her tonight. She'd already been impressed by the Christmas market, golden roof and cathedral. It was time to show her what the rest of Innsbruck had to offer. That's what he'd do.

Enough of the awkward silences. It didn't matter that they'd mainly been his fault. He needed Sam onside badly. And if charm was the way to do it, then Mitchell Brody could certainly oblige. Charm was easy. Charm was slick. He could do that.

He would play nice. He would do everything she wanted. Then, when the time was right, he'd suggest to her that she might want to work with him a little longer.

Of course he would pay her. He would never let her be out of pocket. But it was more important that she *wanted* to do it rather than *had* to do it. The money should be a nice bonus, not the deciding factor.

He could even offer to fly her home every other week to see her mum.

He made a quick call. Done. A large hangar booked for between Christmas and New Year to practise his set for the tour. That would give them a guide to how much energy he used during a performance. Hopefully it would be enough to tailor his food intake and insulin. It was so important that Sam said he was fit to continue the tour. Anything else would be a disaster.

In the meantime, he would do everything possible to keep her sweet. It wasn't as if that would be a struggle. Samantha was a honey. If he could just get her to leave her nurse's hat at the door, she could be a whole lot more.

There. Much better. He started to pull some clothes from the cupboard. It was time for him to pick himself up and start putting his plans into effect.

His gaze swept across the distant roof of St Jude's. He was doing this for the right reasons. Of course he was.

So why did he still have an uncomfortable feeling churning in his stomach?

She was living the dream. And ultimately it was her nightmare.

She was the invisible presence in his home. It was like being a ghost. Or, even worse, an unnoticed servant, which, in fact, she was.

He probably wouldn't even acknowledge her if she ran screaming through the house naked. The thought had crossed her mind.

What on earth was wrong with him?

She may have asked him a few difficult questions, and made a few suggestions he didn't like. But that didn't mean he could completely ignore her.

She was here to do a job—and she couldn't do it if he wouldn't communicate with her.

But it was more than that. Even if she didn't want to acknowledge it.

It annoyed her—embarrassed her even—that she still felt a little starstruck around him. She shouldn't, of course she shouldn't.

She was dealing with Mitchell Brody, patient, not Mitchell Brody, rock star. She'd already learned that most of the assumptions and gossip about him in the press was just a smokescreen.

But what really annoyed her was the kiss.

The way it had made her skin tingle. The way it had conjured up a whole host of fantasies in her mind about how it could have continued. And how it had ruined practically every night's sleep since.

There were moments she spent with Mitch when she felt they really connected. When she felt he might actually be interested in her, Samantha Lewis. She wasn't just the convenient female presence in the house. She wasn't just the hired help.

And it was those little moments, those knowing smiles and locked gazes that made her stomach flip flop.

She kept telling herself this was crazy. Her mixed-up head was reading things that weren't really there at all. It had been one kiss. Just one completely perfect kiss.

But right now it felt like in fifty years she would still remember it. Still remember the feel of his skin against hers, the brush of his hair tickling her cheeks, the intensity of the look in his eyes. How many other women had lived out their fantasies in the Mitchell Brody experience?

She shook her head. No. She didn't even want to think about that.

That was horrid. That was painful. That was…

'Sam?'

He was standing in the doorway, dressed in a black leather jacket, jeans and boots. She scrambled to sit up on the bed, pushing away the pillow she'd been lying against and pulling up the wide-necked T-shirt that had fallen down one shoulder.

'Do you want to go to the hospital?'

It seemed the safest assumption. He certainly didn't seem to want to spend any time around her.

He shook his head and walked into the room. The indignant part in her chest wanted him to ask her permission to enter her room. The self-conscious part was running her tongue across her teeth and trying to remember if she'd actually put any make-up on today.

How did he make a pair of jeans look so sexy?

He sat down on the edge of her bed and looked at her red-painted toenails. 'I think our differences in opinion might have affected my manners the other night.'

You don't say. Was he about to make an apology? Because he just didn't seem the type.

This was probably the time to bite her tongue and stay quiet. But that had never been in Sam's nature. 'I'm your nurse, Mitch. You don't have to like what I say, but that won't stop me saying it.'

'Yeah, you're my nurse.' He stared out of the window towards the perfect white snow. If he mentioned he wanted to go skiing she might pick up her nearest shoe and throw it at him. Climbing up a freezing mountain was *so* not what she wanted to do right now.

His hand reached over and touched her foot. Her first instinct was to flinch and pull it away, but he was holding on, not tightly, just enough to keep it in place. 'It's Christmas in a few days, Sam. I feel as if I haven't been very hospitable. You asked me to take you down to Innsbruck shopping—I haven't even done that.' He shook his head and let out a laugh. 'Have you any idea how much trouble I'd be in with my mother and Granny Kirk if they knew?'

She smiled. She couldn't help it. 'You make it sound as if you do what your mum and gran tell you.'

He rested his elbow on the bed, his chin near her knee. 'Disobeying Granny Kirk could result in a fate worse than death. No one, but no one ever argued with that woman. As for my mother, she has the best disapproving stare in the world. Award-winning. She's also the master of the tut.'

'The tut?'

He nodded, his face deadly solemn. 'Oh, yeah.' He made the noise with his tongue and shook his head along with it. 'That tut is actually about five hundred disapproving words all rolled into one.'

He smiled at her. Really smiled. She was being white-washed with his teeth. His whole face could light up with that smile. How many other women in the world would love to be on a bed with a smiling Mitchell Brody at their feet?

The thing was she didn't really care about any other women. She just cared about herself.

Oh, for a pair of stiletto heels, a perfect fake tan, a de-signer figure-hugging dress and sultry red lips. Wasn't that the kind of woman he was used to? Darn it. She'd forgot-ten the thirty-two double-Ds.

Nope. She was Samantha Lewis. Unruly blonde hair. A bit of tinted moisturiser if she was lucky and some cherry lip balm. Her current jeans were from the supermarket, along with her push-up bra.

But Mitchell didn't look as if he cared. He was crawl-ing up the bed towards her.

'What do you say you let me be the host with the most?'

'Most what?' Her voice came out in an embarrassing squeak. Her brain was in places it shouldn't be. But then again, she was on a bed with Mitchell Brody, so maybe her current fantasies weren't as far-fetched as she suspected.

He reached the top of the bed. Planting one hand on either side of her, positioning himself directly above her. She was having flashbacks to that night on the sofa. It was all she could do not to let out an involuntary moan.

The beaming grin was still in place, and that twinkle in his eye she'd spied on a few occasions was definitely back. The guy was playing with her.

And, what was worse, she kind of liked it.

Their faces were inches apart. His hair fell forward, tickling her cheekbones, his warm breath making her skin tingle. He knew. He knew exactly what he was doing.

Those deep brown eyes were drawing her in, taking down her defences like a swirling whirlpool with no chance of escape. And she didn't want to.

He bent closer. She held her breath. For a second she was sure he was going to kiss her. Just like he had the last time. Her body was craving his touch. All she wanted was to feel his lips on hers.

But instead he whispered in her ear, 'The guy with the most beautiful girl in the world.'

It would be so easy. So easy to believe that and drink in every word.

But the truth was the words fell a little flat. Because she knew—the whole world knew—the kind of girl Mitchell Brody usually had on his arm.

But the thing was, he was looking at her as if she *were* the most beautiful girl in the world. She could almost believe it.

His lips brushed against the tip of her ear as his face appeared back in front of hers. 'How about some fun?'

She could feel herself pull back against the comfortable mattress, her eyes widening. This was beginning to feel like some crazy daydream. Maybe while she'd been lying on the bed she'd actually fallen asleep. In a few moments she would wake up and realise it had all been a dream.

But the warm breath on her skin wasn't a dream. Neither was the persistent smile in front of her eyes.

'Let's go back into Innsbruck. I haven't shown you around much. I know you hate skiing, but what about ice skating? There's a rink right in the middle of one of the markets, we could go there. And shopping? Would you like to get some things for Christmas? I haven't got you a present so how about you choose something?'

Definitely a dream. He was making it sound like she was about to get free rein on a credit card. She moved her foot, pressing her toes hard against his outer leg. Nope. He was still there.

She could smell him. She could smell the leather of his jacket. His aftershave was drifting around them, mixing with the smell of his shampoo. 'What do you think?'

This time his stubble scraped the edge of her nose. This was no dream.

She blinked, trying to decide what to say, trying to decide how to act. He was practically on top of her but she still felt as if she was misreading signals all over the place. If he'd wanted to kiss her, he could have. But he hadn't. It was almost as if he was wanting her to take the lead.

Should she?

She pressed her lips together, feeling the lip balm between them. Her tongue slipped out, an automatic reaction to what was going on in her brain.

His eyes caught the flicker of her tongue and she felt his body stiffen above hers. Then more, a natural male reaction started to take place. She couldn't help it, her smile was reaching from ear to ear. 'Is this how you ask all the girls to come and play with you, Mitch?' she quipped.

He threw back his head and laughed, flipping over and landing on his back next to her on the bed. There was no point trying to hide what had just happened. The evidence was there.

He turned his face towards her, both of them lying on the comfortable pillows. 'You're making this difficult, Sam.' He shifted again, leaning his head on his hand. 'What do you say?' The twinkle was getting sparkier by the second. 'Do you want to play with me or not?'

How to answer. The air was rich with innuendo. She could either fully embrace it or kill it stone dead. And nothing about this was straightforward. Her senses were on overload. Her hormones could currently light up the Christmas-tree lights for the whole of Innsbruck.

She wanted to tease him. She wanted to play him at his own game. She didn't care about the models or his past gorgeous girlfriends. What she cared about was that right now Mitchell Brody was interested in her.

She turned on her side to face him, lifting her finger to the little gap in his shirt where she could see a few curling hairs. She laid her finger on his skin. 'Well, that would depend.' She was smiling. She could see his reactions to her one solitary touch.

'Depend on what?' he growled.

She kept her voice low, almost a whisper. 'Depend on how things progressed.' Had she really just said that out loud? It almost sounded as if she was propositioning him.

This time it was he who licked his lips. She liked the effect she was having on him—the direct effect on his erogenous zones. It made her feel in control. It made her feel important.

'Well, what do you want to happen, Sam?' He was holding his breath. He was waiting to see what she might say.

The million-dollar question, and all the power was in her hands.

How brave was she? She moved her lips closer to his and whispered.

'Let's find out.'

CHAPTER NINE

THANK GOODNESS FOR interruptions. Dave rang the bell a few moments later and they both jumped apart. She could barely breathe and her heart was thudding in her chest.

Mitchell pulled himself together first as she straightened her clothes. When he padded back to the room a few minutes later it was with a rueful expression on his face. 'That was Dave. Dropping off some groceries.'

She'd already collected herself and pulled on a jumper and some boots. She gave him a bright smile. 'Ice skating, then?'

He rolled his eyes and nodded, picking up his discarded leather jacket from the floor. 'Ice skating it is.'

Being around Samantha was a pleasure. The diabetes stuff wasn't even annoying him as much any more. She didn't need to prompt him. When they sat down for coffee he pulled out his meter and checked his level, she glanced at the screen and said nothing, letting him adjust his insulin dose himself, taking into account what he was about to eat.

If he'd been doing something wrong she would tell him. Sam was no shrinking violet. But this way he felt more in control. She didn't feel so much like his nurse, more like the girlfriend he was beginning to imagine her being. If Dave hadn't interrupted them…

The ice rink was busy, full of stumbling families and the occasional pro weaving their way through the falling bodies. He finished fastening the skates he'd just hired. Years ago he'd fancied himself as a speed skater for about ten minutes. He could skate. But the type of blades on these hire skates were different from what he was used to.

He watched as Sam finished fastening hers and stood up. She didn't hesitate, just stepped out onto the ice and skated straight to the middle, stopping herself by spinning around. 'Come on, slowcoach!' she yelled.

Mitch didn't need to be told twice. He crossed the ice in a few seconds and circled his hands around her waist. His stop wasn't quite as elegant as hers, but he managed to stay upright.

'Is there something you haven't been telling me, Samantha Lewis?' he murmured as their noses touched.

She pushed backwards, skating a little away from him before pushing off and twirling round a few times with her hands in the air. 'I can't imagine what you mean,' she said wickedly.

He slid forward, grabbing her around the waist again and pulling her tightly against him. 'So what were you? The ice-skating princess? The champion twirler?'

'All of the above. I might have done figure skating for a few years.'

'How many years exactly?'

She started skating backwards, lifting up her foot behind her, above her head and catching the bottom of her blade with her hand and spinning around.

'What on earth is that called?'

'A Biellmann spin.' She winked. 'It requires great flexibility.' She was teasing him again. And it made his heart thud a little quicker in his chest.

Sure, he'd been physically attracted to his partners in

the past but Sam was different. It wasn't *just* physical attraction, and that's pretty much what it had been for the rest of his conquests. That, and publicity material.

Everything about that went against his principles, but when he'd started in this business and the band had been trying to make a name for themselves he'd more or less done whatever the management team had advised. If that had meant dating one pretty actress or model after another he'd decided it wasn't too big a strain.

But over the last few years he'd grown frustrated. He didn't want to be on display. There were parts of his life he wanted to keep quiet—including his work with the children's hospital. He didn't want to play games any more.

Sam was different. The only agenda she had was money. But it wasn't as ruthless as that. She had good motivation for what she was doing. It was obvious she struggled with the fact her mother was in a home. If this was the way she had to supplement her income to ensure her mum stayed in the best place possible, he really couldn't fault her for that.

But could he trust her?

Would Sam sacrifice other things for money?

Years ago, one of Mitch's old school friends had sold a story to the press about his brother's illness. Up until that point no one had known. It had blazed across the headlines for a few days then, thankfully, disappeared. There wasn't much interest in a brother who'd survived and made a good recovery.

But Mitchell hadn't forgotten the betrayal. It had been a hard lesson. Desperation for money could put people in a situation where consequences seemed unimportant.

He couldn't afford that to happen. He couldn't afford St Jude's and its patients to be subjected to unending press interest and speculation. The sanctuary of the specialist hospital would be ruined for the kids and their families who relied on it.

But could he trust Sam with his secret? Everything about her said yes. Her attitude, her unwavering sense of right and wrong.

His initial plan to win her round by charm and casual flirtation was sitting really uncomfortably with him now. There wasn't any question that he'd do anything to keep this tour on track, but using Sam just seemed so wrong.

He liked her. He more than liked her—that was the problem. But he couldn't allow his growing feelings for her to cloud his judgement. If he let his heart rule his head it could be disastrous. What if she didn't feel as strongly about him? What if she was starstruck by the whole idea of being around someone in the media? He hoped not. He really hoped not. But the trouble was, he just didn't know.

He couldn't take the chance and he hated it that he had these little doubts about Sam. But he'd only known her just over a week. It wasn't enough time to really get to know someone well. All his instincts told him she was a good person.

He'd already had comments from Lisa. Dave seemed to like her too. People he respected and trusted.

He tried to shake it off. This was his problem, not hers. This all came down to the fact that she'd been honest and told him she was only here for the money. He couldn't judge Sam because of the betrayal of another friend years ago.

She might have only been here for the money originally, but what about now?

She was still pressing up close to his chest, the two pairs of skates making small movements on the ice. She smiled up at him, her blue eyes and blonde curls peeking out from under the bright blue hat.

Her cheeks were flushed from the exertion of her skating, or maybe from something else. He could stay here all day with his arms tightly around her waist, but the ice rink was busy with kids and families. He interlocked their fingers. 'Go on, then, take me a few times around the rink.'

He was laughing at her, knowing he could match her pace for pace. But it was nice to let her take the lead as she pulled him forward, weaving expertly between the skating and stumbling bodies until eventually they ended up at the exit again.

'So what did you think?' he asked as she unlaced her boots. She ran her finger along the blade. 'Well, they're definitely not what I'm used to—these skates are blunter than a wooden spoon.'

He shook his head as he picked them up to return them to the hire booth. 'Okay, you missed out on dessert last time we were here. Fancy some good Austrian coffee and cake?'

She nodded enthusiastically and he grabbed her hand, weaving through the winding streets towards his favourite café. She stopped at a few windows, gazing in at some of the items on display. 'Want to go inside?'

She shook her head and they drifted forward. Her footsteps slowed outside one of the designer women's clothes shops. He was conscious of the fact he'd offered to buy her something but she didn't seem to want to take him up on the offer. Her eyes had fixed on a gorgeous red dress in the window. He rested his chin on her shoulder. 'I think you would look spectacular in that.'

She started out of the daze she'd been in and shrugged her shoulders. 'It's not like I would have anywhere to wear something like that. It's much too elegant—too impractical.' She stomped her boots on the ground, knocking snow from them. 'I'll stick with the boots and jacket you already supplied. That's more than enough.'

Her eyes drifted towards the shop next door, where display cases of exquisite jewellery were on show, all made by the master craftsman inside. It was difficult to know what had caught her attention. The window was jammed full of gold and silver jewellery, along with glittering coloured gemstones. He smiled. His last lady friend would have fixated on the massive pink solitaire diamond at the front of the display. But Samantha's gaze was nowhere near there.

She shot him a smile and tugged at his hand. 'Okay, enough window-gazing. Let's find this coffee shop. I'm starved.'

He couldn't stop his eyes lingering on the window as he walked past. What was it that had caught her attention?

He pushed open the door of his favourite coffee house. The smell of rich coffee, steamed milk and succulent cakes surrounded them instantly. Samantha pulled off her gloves and rubbed her hands together, her eyes sparkling. 'I love it already.'

She went to sit down at one of the tables but he caught her elbow and guided her over to the huge glass cabinet with all the cakes on display. 'Have a look first and see what you like.'

Her eyes widened at the huge array of cakes and desserts. She shook her head at the small signs in front of each of the delicious-looking cakes. 'You're going to have to tell me what they all are. I don't have a clue where to start. We could be here all day.'

He nodded and pointed towards the cabinet. 'We'll start with the most traditional.' He gestured towards a rich chocolate cake. 'That's Sachertorte, a chocolate cake with apricot jam filling, probably the most famous—you'd usually eat it with whipped cream. Among the cakes with the longest tradition is the Linzer Torte. The one next to it is caramel-flavoured Dobostorte, the cream-coloured cake is Esterhazy Torte—it's really a Hungarian cake, buttercream spiced with vanilla sandwiched between layers of almond meringue.' She smiled as he continued down the cabinet.

'There are also the traditional pastries with fresh fruit and cream, and then there's Punschkrapfen. You might like that—it's a classic Austrian pastry, a cake filled with cake crumbs, nougat chocolate, apricot jam and then soaked with rum.'

She folded her arms across her chest. 'You seem to know a lot about cakes. Should I be concerned?'

He laughed. 'I've pretty much sampled everything in that cabinet at least a dozen times. But you've got to remember I've been coming here since I was six. I'm a cake connoisseur.' He gave her a wink. 'But my true downfall is the coffee in here. It doesn't matter what you pick, there isn't a bad one.'

She hummed and hawed around the cabinet before finally throwing caution to the wind and choosing the traditional chocolate Sachertorte with whipped cream. Mitchell was much better behaved, choosing a light pastry with fresh fruit and some low-fat cream. He ordered coffee for them both and it was only a few moments before the frothed milk concoctions appeared before them.

The sun was just beginning to dip outside and the Christmas lights were coming on all around them. He watched as she tasted the delicious chocolate cake and let out a little sigh. 'Oh, I can tell why you keep this a secret. It's gorgeous.'

He sipped his coffee. She was licking cream from her lips and it was playing havoc with his senses.

He glanced at his watch. He still wanted to visit the hospital again, but he'd had an email from his manager letting him know the insurance company was looking for a report on his diabetes. There was only one person they could ask for that report. Sam.

'Have you checked your emails today?' His insides turned over as he said the words. She was still concentrating on the cake, licking some chocolate from her spoon.

She shook her head. 'Nope. Should I have?'

He was about to do something wrong. Every cell in his body told him not to try and manipulate her, but his protective instincts towards the hospital just couldn't be smothered. Now he knew what being caught between a rock and a hard place was actually like.

He slid his hand across the table and intertwined his fingers with hers. 'I think you'll get asked about me soon.'

'Asked what?' Furrows appeared along her brow.

He tried to appear casual, but the handholding kind of negated that. 'About how I'm doing—if I'm fit enough to do the tour.'

'Oh.' The fork she had poised in her other hand was gently laid on the table. Her eyes focused on her coffee and she lifted it up for another sip. It was obvious she was trying to think of what to say.

All her reservations were practically on display. She hadn't pulled her hand away, but he knew she was currently questioning his motivation. Was he interested in her or the tour?

Both. He wanted to say the words out loud. But didn't want to see a glimmer of hurt in her eyes.

She tried to paste a smile on her face. It pained him. With Sam, he was used to the smile lighting up her eyes, but this time it wasn't there.

'Well, I guess it's time for me to see you rehearse.'

'What do you mean?'

She shrugged. 'We've already spoken about this. Keeping your diabetes under control in everyday life is different from performing on stage. I need to see you rehearse. I need to see how much energy you use up and the effect on your blood-sugar levels. That way, we can tailor what you eat and how much insulin you take before you do a show.'

Everything she said made sense. He knew that it did. But it didn't stop his stomach from churning. That little element of not being in control. He wanted to wave all this off and just say he would be fine.

He'd be even happier if Samantha thought that too. But it was quite clear she didn't.

She bit her bottom lip. He could tell she wouldn't be moved on this. She wouldn't compromise her professional integrity no matter how much he flirted with her or tried to keep her onside.

He tightened his grip on her fingers, giving them a little squeeze. 'And if we practise and everything's fine, you'll tell the insurance company?'

She pulled her fingers out of his grasp. Her voice was steady. 'If everything is fine, I'll say so. But if I have concerns, I'll also let them know. I'm not going to lie for you, Mitch.' There was the tiniest waver in her voice. As if she was struggling with being put in this position.

That was his fault. If Samantha was just his nurse, she wouldn't struggle with this at all. She'd be professional through and through. But he'd crossed the line, he'd kissed her, and that had messed with both of their emotions. Including the ones that were currently building in his chest.

'I don't expect you to lie for me.' The words came out angrier than he'd meant them to. But the truth was he *did* want her to lie for him. He wanted her to assure the insurance company that there was nothing to worry about and the tour was safe.

There was no question about his ability to perform.

The only question was whether he'd make it to the end of each night.

'How many rehearsals?'

'It would be best if we could do at least three nights in a row. Could that work?'

He sat back in his chair and took a deep breath. 'There's an old aircraft hangar near here. It's what we've used before for rehearsals.' He shook his head. 'The rest of the band are home for their holidays. I can't ask them to come back. But there's no reason we can't do the full rehearsal in the hangar.' He shrugged. 'I can play the guitar and sing as normal.' He gave her a little smile. 'There just won't be any screaming fans around us.'

She nodded slowly. 'What time do you normally do a gig?'

'Around nine o'clock at night. Why? Is it important?'

'Very. We need to do your rehearsal at the same time of day you'll actually be performing. On a performance day you'll burn up calories and carbohydrate at a different rate, at different times. After the performance we'll need to monitor your blood sugar late that night and the next morning. We don't want you to go home and hypo.'

He could feel a flicker of irritation. Why did things have to be so regimented? Sometimes after a gig he liked to party, sometimes he liked to chill out with the rest of the band and have a few beers. Sometimes his adrenaline was buzzing so hard it was hours before he could sleep. Would her strict inventory allow for that?

He sighed. Loudly. Frustration was just bubbling under the surface.

He was staring out of the window, watching as the garlands across the street flickered into a burst of colourful lights, one after the other.

He was conscious of her staring at him, running her fingers through her blonde curls and then lowering her head.

'You can be as mad as you like, Mitchell.' She'd started eating her chocolate cake again as if it was the most natural thing in the world. 'It doesn't change the fact that you're diabetic and I am your nurse.' She sipped at her rich coffee, smiling as it slid down her throat. 'You forget. I'm used to teenage tantrums.' She bit into a rich blob of cake and cream and raised her eyebrows. 'A rock-star temper tantrum is nothing to me.' A smile crept across her face as she shrugged. 'I can wait it out.'

She folded her arms across her chest and sat back in her chair.

He couldn't help the way the feelings of pleasure started to creep across his skin. Being in Sam's company was almost certainly becoming addictive. She could dissipate his frustration and anger in only a few words. No one else had ever been able to do that for him.

He grinned as she licked the last remnants of chocolate from the spoon. 'You're just trying to drive me crazy, aren't you?'

She raised her eyebrows suggestively as she took her last lick. 'I've no idea what you're talking about, Mitch.'

Sure she did. Because every time their flirtation went down that road she got that crazy little twinkle in her eye. If he could bottle and sell it, he could easily fund the hospital from now to eternity.

'You could have timed things a little better.'

She wrinkled her nose. 'What do you mean?'

He held out his arms. 'Look around you. We're in the middle of the festive season here. In three days' time it's Christmas Eve. Do you think I'll be able to book the hangar at nine o'clock on Christmas Eve? Who is going to want to work then?'

She shrugged. 'Who else do we need Mitch? Can't you flick an electrical switch to turn the power on? It's not like we have anything else to do.' As she said the words she looked up at him through lowered lids. 'It doesn't need to be anyone else but us.'

Oh, he could think of a whole host of other things to do. Rockets were currently firing through his veins. Mitchell Brody was known for being cool. But that was the last thing he was feeling right now.

He leaned over the table towards her, catching a waft of her perfume. 'You're right. It doesn't need to be anyone else but us.'

Her eyes locked with his. There it was. The unspoken implication. Made by both of them. He didn't have a single doubt they were on the same wavelength. There was no way he was reading this wrong.

He stood up and held out his hand towards her. 'Come on. We'll have a look around the rest of the shops before we head home.' She nodded and pushed her arms into her jacket. 'We won't have time tomorrow,' he added.

And there it was. Her sexy little smile appearing on her face once again. She put her hand in his. 'Sure, let's window-shop a little more.' She moved ahead of him, giving him his favourite view of her backside in figure-hugging jeans. She glanced over her shoulder at him as they approached the door. 'There are some things I just don't want to miss.'

CHAPTER TEN

Two nights. Two nights in a dark aircraft hangar with thudding music and ice cold air.

Only the air around them didn't seem that cold. The temperature between them was positively rising.

Watching Mitchell Brody thrash about the stage, singing his heart out, was igniting a whole new fire inside her.

There was something so primal about it. To all intents and purposes, when Mitch was on the stage he was as exposed as he'd ever be.

They'd fallen into an easy routine. He skied in the morning, they visited the hospital in the afternoon, had dinner together, then headed to rehearsals.

Only it wasn't so easy.

He'd hypoed a few times in the last two days, all because of the amount of energy he'd been expending. She'd reduced his insulin doses carefully, but each hypo had been another opportunity for amorous Mitchell to appear. They'd headed off the hypos quickly. He was recognising the symptoms as easily as she was. But the flirtations between them were making her internal temperature soar.

It all seemed to heading somewhere, she just wasn't quite sure where.

* * *

It had seemed like such a good idea at the time. Yesterday afternoon she'd felt bold. She'd felt flirtatious. But the whole of today her stomach had been doing flip-flops.

Mitch was as cool as ever, cooking them a late breakfast then spending the time he always did down at the hospital. Christmas Eve in the hospital was magical. Even the sickest kids were excited.

Lisa was a blur, moving up and down the corridor at top speed. Mitch grabbed her arm on the way past. 'How's the list?'

She broke into a radiant smile and nodded her head. 'Come this way.'

She opened a door to a nearby cupboard. It was packed to the seams with brightly wrapped presents all with the children's names attached. 'The list is perfect. The delivery came right on schedule. With the amount of electronic gadgets you've just bought I think this place is going to spontaneously combust.' She was excited. It was clear—her eyes were sparkling and her hands never stopped moving.

'So, what's the plan? Same as last year?' He glanced towards Samantha.

'What did you do last year?'

Lisa laughed. 'Oh, Mitch doesn't only buy the presents. He likes to play Santa Claus too. He comes back at midnight, dresses up and puts the presents in each kid's room.'

'Really?' She couldn't believe it. Her brain was spinning. How far away was the hangar? Would he be able to rehearse and be back here on time? More importantly, would he be fit enough to do it?

'Do some of the kids wake up?'

Lisa nodded and gave a little sigh. 'Some of our kids are so sick that they're up most of the night. Catching sight of Santa Claus is a real boost for them.'

Mitch nodded. 'Except for last year, of course.' He exchanged a glance with Lisa.

Sam could tell from the expressions on their faces that they'd been caught. 'What happened?'

Lisa shook her head. 'Oh, genius here got caught by the three-year-old brother of one of our kids with leukaemia.'

Mitch rolled his eyes. 'Boy, did I. That little guy could talk for *hours*. He gave me a whole new list of toys that he wanted and Lisa and I were scrabbling about at three a.m., trying to find other presents for him.'

Samantha started laughing. 'And did you?'

Lisa nodded. 'Thankfully, we buy spares. We buy enough presents for the kids here, and their brothers and sisters. Some families spend their whole Christmas in hospital so we don't want anyone to miss out. We always think we've got things under control by having a list for every child. Then…we get Mr Three-in-the-Morning who wants things he's never mentioned before.'

Samantha was watching Mitch's face. 'Pressure was on then, Santa. The little guy met you in person. Can you imagine the bad press you would have got if you'd given him the wrong gifts?'

Mitch turned to Lisa. 'Is he here this year? Tell me if he is you'll sedate him with something.'

Lisa started laughing. 'No, Riley isn't here this year. His brother is currently in remission.'

Mitch's face broke into a wide smile. 'Oh, wow. That's great news.' It was just the way he said the words. The absolute genuineness in them. The way his shoulders sagged in pure relief. He was truly grateful that the little kid had turned a corner, because he knew how much that meant to the family.

Something curled up from deep inside her as she studied the small lines on his face around his eyes and mouth, and the intensity of his sincere brown eyes. As her eyes lowered to his mouth a little shiver shot up her spine, along with a sinking realisation.

Everything about Mitch Brody just cried out to her. From his masculine frustration at dealing with a new condition to his undivided devotion to this children's hospital and all its residents. This wasn't the guy she'd had a teenage crush on.

This was becoming a whole lot more.

Her breath caught in her throat. The thought panicked her. This was ridiculous. Okay, Mitchell Brody may have flirted with her, held her hand and kissed her. But there was no way he would even consider her in that way.

No, the woman Mitchell Brody would truly want would be a super-gorgeous, super-slim model or actress. She'd be a celebrity in her own right and they could be paid millions for their wedding pictures in some flash magazine.

Mitchell Brody wouldn't ever be interested in a girl like her. Why would he be, when he had so many other options?

She could feel tears prickling at the backs of her eyes. This was no one's fault but hers. She'd allowed herself to be drawn in by his sexy smile and charm. Who knew how many other women had had the same treatment from Mitch? This was probably just the norm for him, but her own sensibilities and emotions were reading things that probably weren't there. Maybe other women liked casual flings and flirtations, but that wasn't her. Being street smart wasn't really an aspect of her life. Oh, she could be street smart at work as a nurse, but as a regular human being?

'Sam, is something wrong?'

Lisa had walked back down the corridor and Mitch

was standing right in front of her, his arms resting on her shoulders, his brown eyes studying her face. She blinked back the tears quickly. 'No. Of course not.' She shook her head, trying to convince herself as much as him.

He tilted his head to the side. He was still looking at her, obviously unconvinced by her answer. But thankfully he let it go, reaching down and taking her hand. 'Then let's go. We've got some planning to do, and it might be better if we chill out for an hour or so before we hit the rehearsals.' He spoke quietly. 'It's going to be a late night. I hope you're up for that on Christmas Eve.' The words were whispered in her ear, giving a sense of intimacy and sending electric pulses along her nerves.

This isn't what you imagine it to be. She tried to quell the thoughts running around her brain. This was about doing her job. This was about making Christmas special for these kids. This wasn't about her. It never would be.

'I'm fine with that,' she said quickly. 'It'll be nice to come back here later.' Her eyes swept up and down the corridor, taking in all the decorations and twinkling lights. The atmosphere around here was charged already. These kids, and their families, were *so* ready for Christmas. No matter what other crazy thoughts were going on in her head, she felt honoured to be a part of this.

It didn't matter that he was still holding her hand and the tingles were reaching up across her chest. She squeezed her eyes closed for a second as he led her down the corridor. But her attempt at a reality check did nothing for her body responses. They were all still completely tuned in to the radio station that was Mitchell Brody.

She let out a sigh. One more week. She could do this for one more week. Then she'd have enough money to pay her mum's nursing home fees for a whole year and she could get back to reality. Back to her school nursing job and her small flat that she'd always loved.

So, why all of a sudden, did it seem like not nearly enough?

Dave pulled the black SUV up outside the hangar. 'Wow, I knew it was an aircraft hangar, but I didn't expect it to be so—so big.'

Mitch smiled and he climbed out of the car and automatically reached for Sam's hand. He couldn't help himself. Every time he was near her he just wanted to touch her—even if it was only for the briefest of seconds.

He opened the door to the hangar and switched on the electrical supply. The lights flickered, taking a few seconds to spring to life and show the true expanse around them. There was a stage at the other end, stretching from one side to the other.

Sam walked ahead, her freezing breath clearly visible in the air around them. She rubbed her arms up and down the sides of her bright blue jacket. 'Third night in a row and this place doesn't get any warmer. Brrr.'

He walked over and flung an arm around her shoulders. 'What did you expect? Balmy heating in the middle of the winter?'

She rested her head on his shoulder. 'Why do you have to practise somewhere so big?' Her voice was quiet, as if she was sad about something.

'Acoustics,' he said quickly. The place really was impersonal. And if he was honest, that really wasn't what he'd wanted for tonight. Things were changing between them—he wasn't sure how much longer he could keep his hands to himself.

He turned quickly and nodded to Dave, who was waiting at the door. 'Can you come back for us just after eleven and take us to the hospital?'

Dave gave a quick nod and wave and disappeared back outside the door. It only took a few seconds before they heard the engine of the SUV start up and he disappeared into the night.

Mitchell didn't hesitate. He crossed the hangar in long strides. He almost felt her bristle as he pulled away. But the temptation to pull her around into his arms and not concentrate on the job at hand was just too high.

This was it. This was the night he had to prove himself fit and well. If she gave a good report to the insurers the tour could go ahead with no problems. He'd worry about himself later. Right now, all he could let himself worry about was the kids in that hospital.

The air around him was practically dripping with ice. At a normal performance, by the time the band arrived, the sweat was in the air all around them. Temperatures in the venues usually went through the roof because of the number of bodies packed in tightly.

Would changing temperatures have any effect on his blood sugar? He had no idea.

He flung his jacket to the side and walked across the stage, grabbing his guitar and switching it on. The feedback in the open area let a loud squeal reverberate around the metal building.

Samantha looked so alone, standing in the middle of the concrete floor. The cold air made his skin prickle, but it wouldn't last long. As soon as he started playing and singing he would heat up.

He dug into the back pocket of his jeans and pulled out his monitor. He still hated it, but he had the routine of checking his blood-sugar level down to a fine art. The whole process could be completed in under twenty seconds. He'd done everything she'd suggested. Eaten a little more carbohydrate and reduced his insulin dose by a few units to see how much energy he used up during a performance. His big worry was not recognising signs of a hypo attack.

Tonight would be easier. This was his third rehearsal. He'd be looking for it every second. He wouldn't be distracted by the rest of the band and thousands of screaming fans. He wouldn't be carried away by the atmosphere and the electricity in the air.

Tonight was a solo performance for one.

On second thoughts, that might actually be worse.

He tucked the monitor back into his pocket and put his guitar strap over his shoulder, stepping up to the microphone. Rock music wasn't normally used as a serenade to women, but that's what it felt like right now.

He plucked the first notes on his guitar. It was time to get started.

Samantha was mesmerised. She couldn't help it.

After the first few minutes she forgot she was the only person in the room. For at least ten minutes it felt as if she was in a time warp. The kind you dreamed about as a teenager where your idol was singing only to you.

But this was no dream. This was reality. And no one could put a price on this.

The lights changed automatically with the music, going up and down depending on the tempo, and at certain points in the music sending strobes across the stage.

Mitchell was lost in the music, his body swaying as his fingers strummed out every tune and he belted out the lyrics into the microphone. He was singing as if there was a whole crowd in this room—not just her. He moved across the stage, rocking it out, jumping on speakers at high points in the songs and only slowing down when he sang the band's only rock ballad.

Every hair on her neck stood on edge, because at that point he was singing only to her.

Every time she closed her eyes she found herself swaying along to the music, murmuring the lyrics quietly.

After the first hour Mitchell stopped for a few seconds at the side of the stage. He picked up a container of milk and waved it at her, drinking most of it in under a minute. 'It's not the same as a beer,' he muttered into his microphone.

'Give it a few concerts,' she shouted back. 'When word gets out you'll be offered a million-pound contract to advertise milk!'

He looked up from the microphone. 'Will you drink it with me?' His gaze was heavy, his voice low, and even though the words echoed around the hangar it seemed like the most intimate, most loaded question in the world.

He didn't wait for an answer, just continued straight into his next set, strumming the guitar strings and moving on to the next song. 'Maybe,' she whispered under her breath. Could she really last another week around Mitch Brody?

'Sam? Sam, come up here.' His voice echoed around the hangar, yanking her out of her daydream. Her feet were frozen to the spot. Oh, no. This was the part that always made the headlines. The part where Mitch Brody pulled a fan from the crowd and serenaded her.

Except there wasn't a crowd here. There was only her. It was obvious Mitch was taking this rehearsal seriously. She shook her head. 'No, Mitch.'

'Yes, Sam.' She could see his smile reaching from ear to ear. He held out his hand towards her. It was so enticing. She could feel the pull—even from this far away. She could feel his warmth reaching out towards her across the frozen hangar.

Her feet started to move forward. She didn't want to go up on stage. That just wasn't her style and Mitch seemed to sense that, because as she neared the stage he started plucking at the strings of his guitar and singing one of the band's most popular slow songs. A million brides and grooms across the world must have danced to this.

But right now there was only him. And her.

Her throat was dry. She knew this was a performance, but it didn't feel like it. It felt like something much more personal. Something entirely for her.

He was reaching out to her again. The rock star under the spotlight. Every word was sending shivers down her spine and the blood racing around her body. Every tiny little hair was standing on end. All for her. Right up until the last note, the last string had been plucked and the last echo had faded around the hangar. Mesmerising.

Sweat was dripping from Mitch's hair, his face was flushed and skin glistening. She waited for a full minute before she walked over towards the front of the stage.

She was close enough to see his rapid breathing. Close enough to see his dilated pupils. Her brain switched into gear. Was this just the effects of the performance? Or was this the start of a hypo?

The selfish part of her wanted to think that she could have that effect on him. The professional part of her tried to be rational.

She bit her lip and stayed silent. It was important that Mitch recognise any symptoms himself. This had to form part of her assessment—whether she liked it or not.

What she really wanted to do was switch into nurse mode and go up and order him to test his blood sugar immediately. But that wasn't right for him, and that wasn't right for her.

So she waited.

After a few minutes he jumped down from the stage and walked over to her. His hair was tangled and damp, and she was sure she could practically smell the pheromones.

'What did you think?' His face was inches away from hers. All of a sudden he wasn't the distant teenage crush on stage, he was a living, breathing six-foot-four-inch man of sculpted muscle, sinfully dark eyes and perfect teeth right in front of her.

This was it. The final scene in the movie, when the hero swept the heroine into an embrace. She was holding her breath. Waiting for him to do something.

His head tilted to the side and his gaze narrowed. 'Didn't you like it?'

Her brain sprang back into life. 'I did. I-it was good. It was g-great,' she stammered.

'Great?' The look on his face was anything but. She'd said the wrong thing. Of course she had. He was an artist—a performer. He revelled in his job and he wanted everyone to love it as much as he did.

There was a noise behind him as the door slammed open and a huge blast of icy wind swept around them.

'Ready, folks?' Dave shouted.

The disappointment in Mitch's eyes shone brighter than any spotlight. 'Yeah, we're ready,' he said, as he stalked back to the stage and picked up his leather jacket. 'Let's go.'

This time he walked straight past her towards the open door.

Her heart lurched in her chest. *It was spectacular. I loved it* echoed around her head. The words she'd been afraid to say out loud. Afraid she would reveal exactly how she felt around him. This was so much harder than she'd anticipated. So much harder than she'd expected. Being a fan and admiring someone from afar was *so* different from admitting to yourself that you felt so much more. And it was so much harder when you knew there was no point.

She sighed and turned around. Next year she'd think twice. If she couldn't work with Daniel's family—the little boy with CF—then she'd have to reassess her finances. Maybe it was time to change jobs again? She had to think of a way to stop being so financially dependent on this extra work.

Not when this was the price.

Mitchell felt as if a black fog was hanging around his head. Was his ego really that big? Just because Samantha hadn't fawned over his performance?

The snow-covered roads were passing swiftly outside. He needed to pull himself out of this mire. Christmas Eve was usually his favourite time of year. Sneaking around the hospital and putting the presents out for the kids was always special. There was always some pale-faced little person who was awake and wanted to open their present in front of Santa. He couldn't hide the joy that gave him. Seeing the little eyes widen at the gift of their dreams and knowing that he'd given just a little happiness to a child who might not have a lot of time left on this earth.

The thoughts strengthened his resolve. He couldn't let anything get in the way of this. He would do anything to make sure he continued to provide for these kids.

Anything at all.

The car pulled up to a halt outside the hospital. It was eleven-thirty. Hardly time to get ready at all. Thankfully Lisa was waiting, the costume, beard, shoes and Santa sack already laid out. She put her fingers to her lips and led them into the staff changing room. 'Shhh, we have a few still awake. And it looks like you're going to have to come back and refill your sack at least five times. I've put the presents in for the kids in Rooms 4, 5 and 6 first. They are furthest away.'

Mitch nodded and stripped off his clothes without a second thought. 'Give me five minutes, Lisa. I need to shower.'

She slipped out of the room into the darkened corridor, leaving Sam and him alone. The silence was deafening. He took out his monitor and spent twenty seconds checking his level. It was on the way down so he'd need to eat something soon, but it wasn't urgent.

Sam was bent over the Christmas parcels, organising the next load for the sack. He flicked the switch on the shower, filling the room with steam.

It was almost as if she was waiting to say something to him. Trying to work things out in her head. But Mitch wasn't feeling rational—he wasn't feeling patient. For some reason the pent-up frustration and anger from earlier was returning. He had a million fans around the world. Why did the opinion of Samantha Lewis, his nurse, matter so much? Three weeks ago he hadn't even known her. He would have walked past her in the street without a second glance.

Well, maybe that wasn't quite true. There was no way he wouldn't have noticed those big blue eyes and jeans-covered curves.

He just couldn't work out why what she thought mattered so much. This wasn't about the diabetes any more. Granted, he still wanted her to give her blessing for the tour. But how she looked at him, what she said to him, how she felt about him seemed to matter so much more.

She was still hovering around. So he did what any self-respecting guy would. He dropped his boxers on the floor and stepped into the shower, giving her a view of his naked backside.

Some girls would have paid money for that. Samantha Lewis wouldn't.

Mitch had never been shy about his body. After a few weeks of looking a little puny, his muscle tone and weight was starting to return. In another few weeks—just in time to start the tour—he should look normal again.

He heard her choke a little outside. Was it the steam? Or was it something else?

When he emerged from the shower a few minutes later she'd made a sharp exit into the corridor. He was disappointed. But what had he expected to happen here, in a staff changing room?

He pulled on the costume, fixed the beard to his face and lifted the sack. It was like a rush of pure endorphins. Playing Santa for these kids was the best job in the world.

Sam was waiting at the door, shifting on her feet continuously. 'Do you want me to sit down somewhere and wait for you?'

Of course. Part of him wanted to say yes. He loved doing this. But the reluctance he thought he might feel wasn't there. He kind of wanted Sam to play a part in this too. He was sure she would find it every bit as magical as he did.

He shook his head and gestured for her to follow him along the corridor. It was dark, lit only by the multicoloured lights and white stars that were wound around the windows and strung across the ceiling.

The bells that were stitched into the sleeves of his coat jangled gently as he moved down the corridor. Sam let out a nervous laugh. 'I love it,' she whispered. 'It's almost as if they can hear the reindeers and sleigh landing on the roof.'

He raised his eyebrows. 'Watch out. There's a thought. I should have made you dress up as a reindeer.'

The nerves and anxiety previously obvious on her face were gone. Now all he could see was the softness of her eyes. The jingling continued as he reached the first room. Lukas Wagner was fast asleep. He was recovering from emergency cardiac valve surgery and his colour had improved rapidly in the last few days. Mitchell moved quietly, slotting the gift-wrapped tablet and games machine into the carefully positioned stocking at the bottom of the bed. Sam added various little extras from the bag she carried, mainly nuts, fruit and chocolate, and they both crept back out.

Anna Gruber, in the next room, was also sleeping. She'd wished for a pink tablet and crying baby doll. Her sleepy mother gave them both a wave from where she was dozing in the recliner chair, whispering her thanks as they left.

It was Brian Flannigan's room next. The teenager had made some progress towards recovering from his recent dip in health. His wasn't a small electronic parcel. His was a full-scale guitar. Sam smiled as Mitchell pulled it from the sack and ran his fingers over the gold paper.

'Do you think the wrapping is a bit of a giveaway?'

He smiled. 'You try wrapping one of these things. It's no easy task.' He pushed open the door and Brian's eyes flickered open immediately.

He blinked again, taking a few seconds to recognise the thinly disguised Santa Claus. 'Mitch,' he croaked, as he tried to push himself up in the bed.

'Hey, buddy.' It was so nice to see him with a little more colour about his face. He was still thin and pale, but he was obviously managing to eat a little better.

'Am I supposed to pretend to be sleeping when Santa Claus appears?'

Mitch sat down next to the bed. 'You can do whatever you like. I'm just glad to see you're looking better and that you're out of isolation for a while.'

Brian nodded. 'I've responded well to the antibodies they've given me. But I'm still on the bone-marrow transplant list.' He didn't sound nearly as breathless as he had before. He gave a weak smile. 'They told me today that there's a possible match. In the next few days I could be a new guy.' There was such hope in his voice—the possibility of an end to all this sickness—that Mitch wanted to reach over and hug him, but instead he squeezed his hand. 'That's the best news you could give me.'

Brian nodded towards the present. 'Santa's brought me a guitar.' He glanced around the room. 'Is it midnight yet? Can I open it?'

'Absolutely.' He was trying not to let tears form in his eyes. He knew what this little guy had ahead. A bone-marrow transplant could be the gift of life, just like it had been for his brother. If the match was confirmed, sample collected and things went well, Brian Flannigan could be walking out of here to a whole new way of life.

Testing for the next few years would be inevitable. But after that? No more avoiding every single friend with a sniffle or sore stomach. No more worrying about sports and activities he couldn't take part in. Mitchell couldn't help but smile and say a silent prayer that Brian would be as lucky as his brother had been.

Brian ripped at the gold paper, tearing it off in a few quick strips. His eyes grew as wide as saucers. 'Oh wow! A Fender.' He hugged the black guitar towards his chest. 'It's the best thing I've ever seen. Is it mine? Really?'

Mitch nodded. 'Really. Once this bone-marrow transplant is done, I expect to hear that you're practising all the time.'

For the first time in a long time Brian's cheeks actually looked flushed. 'Oh, I will. I promise. This is the best Christmas *ever*!'

Mitch stood up, giving him a tap on the shoulder. 'I'll see you some time in the next few days, buddy. Meanwhile, Santa has other presents to deliver.'

As he left the room Brian was already starting to strum the guitar strings as he lay in bed. Samantha was waiting by the door, the expression on her face matching entirely how he felt. She placed her hand over her chest. 'Oh, Mitch, I thought I was going to cry. That's such great news for him. I hope it works out.'

'So do I.' He'd whispered the words. A whole host of memories was flooding around him, reinforcing just how important all this was.

Sam walked over and laid her hands on his chest. 'I get why you do this, Mitch. I really do. I just wish the world could know you like I do.' She wound her hands around his neck and stood up on tiptoe.

He responded immediately, his whole body in tune with hers. Nothing and no one could get between them now. Their lips made contact, hers soft and sweet with a taste of warm orange. The girl had more lip balms than he had guitars. His hands went automatically to her hips, pulling her towards him. Everything about this felt so right. She was the girl who was meant to fill his arms. He'd never felt this way about anyone before. No one else had ever come close.

This wasn't meaningless press-associated passion. This was heartfelt and true. And the more he kissed her, the more he resented the barriers in his way—they were in a corridor in the children's hospital, and all items of clothing had to stay exactly where they were. Imagine the scandal if a partially dressed Santa Claus was found in a compromising position!

No. It was the other kind of barriers. The emotional ones that made him feel as if he'd had to build a fortress about himself. His diabetes. His tour. His responsibilities. And the ugly, black fact that he'd been quite willing to try and charm her, to manipulate her to keep his tour on track.

He didn't want her to go. The thought of Sam getting on a plane to go home when her contract was up made him want to pull her even closer. He didn't want to let her go.

His natural instincts were to deepen the kiss, to slide his hands underneath her short jumper and feel the softness of her skin. But even he knew that was for later—not here, and not now.

Instead, he pulled back gently, a smile reaching from ear to ear. 'What do you say we deliver these presents as quickly as possible?' His sleeve tinkled as he moved it. 'My reindeer are getting impatient on the roof.'

She blinked, her pupils wide in the dim lights, and smiled back at him. 'I think this could be a busy night for Santa, he'd better not waste any time.'

And he didn't. He refilled his sack four times as he supplied presents to every room, pausing only to speak to a little girl, Anneline, who wanted to know if he could bring his reindeer into her room. She was more than happy when he suggested she open one of her presents instead, and wrapped her arms around a blonde-haired doll as she went back to sleep.

Mitchell's legs were working nearly as quickly as his brain. No time for Santa-suit removal. He grabbed Samantha's hand once he'd delivered the last present, tossed the Santa sack and beard back in the staffroom and grabbed their jackets. 'Let's go.'

The car was outside, waiting for them. Dave had already

been sent home and Mitch let her take the lead. She jumped in, and he drove the car back up the mountain towards his house.

The air in the car was thick was tension. Instead of laughing and joking, neither one of them said a word, willing the miles to speed past on the dark road. It was late but he didn't feel tired. It would probably be best to have something to eat when he reached the house, but if Sam had other priorities...how could he argue?

The car finally skidded to a halt outside the house and both them were out of the car in a matter of seconds. The only lights on in the house were the twinkling red and gold ones lighting up the Christmas tree and the sparkling gold stars strung along the walls. Could there be a more perfect setting?

He slammed the door behind him with one hand and reached for Sam with the other, pressing her against the wall. Her leg hitched against his hip and her arms wound around his neck. 'Where were we?' he murmured, as he unzipped her padded blue jacket and threw it to the floor.

Her lips touched his neck. 'I think we were right about here,' she whispered, as the brush of her skin against his sent his senses alight. He shrugged off his leather jacket, quickly followed by the top half of the Santa costume. Now was the time to get rid of layers—the quicker the better.

He moved her around, keeping her in his arms and walking her backwards towards the sofa. One arm twitched. Just a little, but enough to distract him from the overwhelming surge of hormones. He kept walking, pushing her gently onto the sofa and positioning himself above her.

There it was again. Just as he moved his hand to re-distribute his weight, a little tremor. He paused above her neck. Her eyes were half-closed, her lips just begging him to touch them. His body was reacting just the way it should—and just the way it shouldn't.

He tried to ignore it. Tried to ignore the nagging voices in his head. But it was the oddest feeling. Almost fight or flight. Survival instinct. He pulled back, changing his position from lying above her to sitting on the sofa by her feet.

'Mitch? What's wrong?'

He wanted to scream in frustration. He'd known earlier that his blood-sugar level had been on its way down. He should have found something to eat then.

She sat upright, tugging at her displaced jumper, obviously wondering what on earth she'd done wrong. He pushed himself to his feet, shifting his trousers to a more accommodating position and heading for the kitchen. 'I'm sorry. Give me five minutes.'

Was this it? Was this how things were going to be for the rest of his life? Was his sex life going to be ruled by his blood-sugar levels? His fingers tightened into a fist, his nails burning into the palms of his hands.

He yanked open the nearest cupboard door, grabbed a couple of chocolate biscuits and ate quickly. He could feel sweat breaking out on his body and the tremble of his hands was getting worse. The rest of the biscuits were slammed off the nearest wall.

His monitor was in the back pocket of his jeans. With growing frustration he sat down at the table and started to go through the motions. He waited for the beep and, sure enough, his blood-sugar level was low. Lower than when he'd checked earlier, but not as low as when they'd deliberately made him hypo.

He ran his fingers through his hair. He could feel his heart thudding in his chest. How long would this take? How long until he started to feel the effects of the chocolate getting into his bloodstream?

There was a movement out of the corner of his eye. Sam. Standing in the doorway with her hands folded across her chest. He couldn't read the expression on her face. Couldn't read it at all.

Eventually she walked over and sat down next to him, spinning his monitor round and pressing the button to see the last result.

'Why didn't you tell me, Mitch?' Her voice was quiet, but she was closer now, and it was clear from the look in her eyes that she felt hurt.

He felt a wave of panic. His mouth started to run away with him. 'I should have eaten earlier—but I felt fine. I checked my level and meant to eat before we left the hospital. You told me I had to be able to recognise the signs of a hypo and act myself. Well, that's what I did. Even though I wanted to be doing something else entirely.' He couldn't help the implication in his voice.

He could see her suck in a deep breath. 'What have you eaten?'

'Biscuits. I've had two biscuits. I'll be fine in a minute. Just give me a minute. Don't judge me on this. You can't do anything that will affect the tour. I'll be fine on tour. This was our first real practice. I'll know now to eat when I come off stage, whether I want to or not.'

He started to shake his head. 'This tour is far too important. Far too important to let this diabetes get in the way of. Don't say anything about this, Sam. You won't, will you? Because I recognised the signs. I did what I was supposed to do.'

She moved her hand across the table as if she were about to touch him, then pulled it back. '*You're* too important, Mitch. Not the tour. I get that you recognised the signs. But I still think it's too early. I still think there's a danger you might be distracted by other things and not recognise the signs in time. Tonight it was only you and me. What happens when it's twenty thousand fans shouting for an encore? What will you do then?'

He shrugged. 'I'll eat something and play it.'

'It's not that simple, Mitch. You know it isn't.' She stood up. 'This is my fault. I've crossed a line with you that I shouldn't have. I'm supposed to be your nurse. I'm supposed to be looking after you—not kissing you!' She flung her arms up in frustration and started shaking her head.

'I can't do this any more, Mitch. This isn't working. And I definitely have reservations about saying you're fit for a tour that starts in ten days.'

'What? You've got to be joking.' Now the panic was truly setting in. 'You've *got* to say I'm fit for this tour. Everything depends on it. Those kids depend on it. If I don't do this tour, they don't get their new hospital. I don't care what happens to me, I care about what happens to them. No one else can fund the place the way I can. I *need* this money. I *need* this tour.'

He started to pace. Irrational thoughts were spinning around his head. What did she mean—she couldn't do this any more? Surely she didn't mean him and her? Because that was the one thing that was right in all this.

Her face was pale and her eyes wide. 'What are you talking about? St Jude's? The money is for the hospital? That's why you're so desperate to do this tour?'

She started shaking her head again. 'Why on earth wouldn't you tell me? Is that why you can't rearrange the tour? You wouldn't be able to give them money?' She frowned. 'How much money are we talking about here?'

But he wasn't listening. He was focusing on her frown and shaking head. All he could think about was that she might actually say no. More importantly, he couldn't stop his obvious hesitation.

'I wasn't sure. I didn't know if I could trust you. I don't tell anyone about the hospital. *Anyone.* The press would have a field day if they knew I was involved.'

Her eyes were wide with disbelief. 'You're paying to rebuild the whole hospital? Can't they get money from somewhere else?'

He shook his head. 'They've tried, time and time again. I can't let this place disappear. This place was the difference between my brother living and dying. The difference between my family unravelling at the seams and staying strong and happy.'

'So why didn't you just say?' She was shouting now, obviously exasperated by all this. 'You don't trust me? What have I ever done, or said, that made you think you couldn't trust me? Why would I tell anyone about this?'

He ran his fingers through his hair. It was like a permanent fog had settled around his brain. 'It isn't you, Sam. But I've been down this road before. I've been sold out by a friend. I couldn't take the risk. Not with St Jude's. It's just too important. Too special.'

'And I'm not?' The words hung in the air between them. He was so confused. All he could think about was trying to protect the hospital.

'What will it take, Samantha? How much? Just tell me and I'll give it to you. I know you need money for your mum's nursing-home care—how much do you need?'

Her head shot up. 'What?' The frown deepened, accompanied by a look of fury as she stepped right up to him with her hands on her hips. *'What?'*

Where had those words come from? His brain was still in that slight hypo state. The one where there were no safeguards, no reservations on what he said. He felt as if he were a few seconds behind everything. What had she just said? *And I'm not?*

'You're trying to buy me off? You honestly think I would do something like that?'

She didn't hesitate for a second, just spun on her heel and grabbed for her bag. As she walked past she swept her jacket from the floor.

'Sam…' He was still panicking. Now for a whole host of other reasons. She was special. More special than anyone he'd ever met. He just hadn't had a chance to tell her yet. And as soon as this fog lifted from his head, he would.

She turned back and marched up to his face, putting her finger inches from his nose. 'Don't you dare. Don't you dare say another word. I'll send an email. I'll let you do your damn tour. But I'll recommend you have another diabetic nurse with you every step of the way. If they're happy to take that risk, that's up to them. But don't you dare put this on me.'

She grabbed the car keys from the table and stamped across the room, leaving the door wide open and an icy blast circulating around him.

His focus was starting to return. The sugar burst was finally making him come to his senses. Oh, no. What had he done?

He stood up, his legs still a little shaky, and walked to the door.

But it was too late. Tyres squealed as she disappeared into the night.

She couldn't think straight. She was so angry. It was her own fault—his too. But she'd been delusional to think there was ever a chance of anything happening between them when the guy obviously didn't trust her.

The tears started rolling down her cheeks. What on earth was she going to do? It was after midnight on Christmas Eve. She was in Austria. She didn't have any friends here. There wasn't exactly anywhere else for her to go.

The road signs loomed before her. Airport. Yes. Where else could she go? There would still be flights, and the one thing she was sure of was that she had her passport in her bag.

She turned the wheel and put her foot on the accelerator. It was time to get away from here. It was time to get away from Mitchell Brody.

It was time to get on with her life.

CHAPTER ELEVEN

'THIS HAD BETTER be good, Mitch, it's three o'clock on Christmas morning.' Mitch bristled at Dave's words. He hated having to do this.

'I need a lift. In fact, I just need the car.'

'You've got a car.'

'I don't. Samantha took it when she left.'

'She left? Where has she gone?'

'I don't know.' He sagged against the wall and listened to the monster-size groan at the end of the phone.

'You idiot. What have you done? She was the best thing that's happened to you in years.'

He tried to swallow the huge lump in his throat. Dave was one of the only people on this planet who would speak to him like this. But it was exactly what he needed. 'I know.' He struggled to get the words out. A thought flickered into his brain. 'She hasn't appeared at your place, has she?'

'Not yet she hasn't. And I doubt she would. If you've upset her I'm probably the last person she wants to see.'

'But where on earth could she be?' He was sounding desperate and he knew it. 'She liked the skating rink—maybe there? Or the Christmas tree in the square?'

'Are you nuts? Have you any idea what the temperature is out there? This is the worst night of the year to try and find somewhere to go. Everywhere is closed for Christmas.'

He squeezed his eyes closed. 'You're right.' Worry was beginning to wash over him. She was out there. Alone. And it was his fault.

'Where would you go in a foreign country after a fight with a fool of a man?' Dave clearly wasn't going to forgive him for this. 'Did she take anything with her?'

'Just her bag.'

'So she has the car and her handbag, which might contain her passport?'

His eyes opened. 'Do you think she's headed to the airport? But she doesn't have her suitcase, she doesn't have her clothes.'

Dave sighed. 'I think we can safely assume she's not caring about any of that right now. Give me ten minutes. I'll pick you up. And, Mitch?'

'Yeah?'

'We're not done talking about this.' He hung up the phone.

Mitch almost smiled. Dave was going to blast him all the way to the airport and back. But he didn't care. He just hoped she was there. He just hoped she was safe.

His eyes fell on the little blue-wrapped box next to the phone. The present he'd bought her. The one he'd spent nearly an hour deliberating over. He'd wanted to give it to her tonight once they were back from St Jude's, but he'd forgotten all about it.

He turned the little box over in his hands.

Would she like it?

Would she talk to him again? Would she even agree to *see* him again?

He had no idea.

But one thing was crystal-clear.

He was willing to spend the rest of his life trying to find out.

* * *

The short-stay car park was the most expensive at the airport. But Samantha was determined not to think about it. Once she was back in the UK, she'd phone Dave and let him know where to pick up the car.

She hurried across the concourse in the airport, her footsteps echoing all around her. The place was virtually deserted with only minimal staff in place. There was a tired-faced woman behind the desk of the most popular UK airline. 'Do you have any flights back to the UK?'

The woman nodded and smiled wearily. 'There's one taking off at six a.m.' She glanced at the clock. 'You can buy a ticket for the next fifteen minutes. After that, there isn't another flight until five p.m.'

'I'll take it.' She pulled her passport and credit card from her bag, trying not to recoil visibly as the woman said the price out loud.

It only took a few minutes to process the payment and print out her paperwork. Samantha smiled thankfully and turned to look across the airport.

It was almost as if all her energy suddenly started to leave her body. She'd been running on pure adrenaline, and there just wasn't any left. Her shoulders sagged and her legs started to shake. She walked to the nearest seat and sat down for a few minutes, trying to pull herself together.

It was easier to lean forward, her head almost between her knees. But she couldn't get comfortable, the thick, bright blue jacket limiting her movements. In a last spurt of frustration she tugged the jacket off. The airport was warm so there was no need for it in there, and even though she'd loved the jacket, it was another reminder of Mitch. She emptied the pockets and stuffed it in the trash can next to her.

It would be cold when she got back to the UK, but she'd

worry about it then. For now she didn't need anything else to remind her of how much she'd screwed up here.

She didn't want to wear something that he'd bought her. The very fact that she'd allowed him to buy her anything now stung like a scorpion. If she could possibly have refused her salary for the last few weeks, she would have. But any day now she'd need to make another payment to her mother's nursing home. This wasn't just about her. Like Mitchell, she had responsibilities.

That thought made her breath catch in her throat. His financial responsibilities were every bit as important to him as hers were to her. She could understand that, she could. There was nothing she wouldn't do in order to keep her mother in the best place possible.

'You really don't want the jacket?'

The bland words sent a shard through her heart. She couldn't help but sit bolt upright. She was almost afraid to turn around, afraid of where the next steps would take her. Because the last few had been difficult enough.

But she didn't need to. Mitchell walked around in front of her, kneeling down until their faces were on a level. He tugged at the sleeve of the jacket still sticking out of the trash can. 'It's a pity, you know, it really is your colour.'

'I don't want it to be.'

'But haven't you noticed? Sometimes things are just naturally matched together, even when you fight against it? And even when you don't completely understand why?'

He wasn't talking about a jacket any more.

It was just him and her. He was looking at her with those deep brown eyes. There was no sexy, charming smile. There was no cheeky twinkle. All she could see was complete sincerity.

She squeezed her eyes shut, willing the tears that had automatically formed not to spill down her cheeks. It was easier not to look at him. 'You didn't trust me, Mitchell. You thought I might sell you out for money. You thought I would betray the staff and those kids at the hospital for money.' She pressed her hand to her chest and this time she did open her eyes. 'That's the kind of person you believe me to be.'

He shook his head fiercely. 'No. No, I don't. I'm just so used to protecting that place, so used to counting on one hand the number of people that I can actually trust, that I was on autopilot.'

'You were on autopilot?' She couldn't hide the scorn in her voice. 'And did that apply to everything we did together—autopilot?'

He didn't hesitate in his response. 'Absolutely not. Definitely not.' He reached out to touch her but she pulled her hand away as if he'd given her an electric shock.

She couldn't deal with the sensation of how her body reacted to his on top of everything else.

'Can't you tell that everything between us was special—was meant to be?' This time he didn't let her shy away. His hand reached out and cupped her cheek.

'I didn't know that this diabetes would be the best thing that could happen to me. I didn't know that it would bring me you.'

Her heart was thudding in her chest. She wanted to believe all this, she wanted to respond. But too many other things were getting in the way. What if this was all just an elaborate plan to continue with the tour?

She shook her head. She couldn't meet his eyes. She didn't want to be sucked in by the pleading look in his deep eyes.

'You can't play me, Mitch. I won't be part of your façade. I've told you. I'll send the email saying you can do the tour—as long as you have supervision. And I don't care who that is, as long as it's not me.' She waved her hands. 'I can bet there will be a million specialist nurses who can't wait to help you out. I can even give you a recommendation or two.'

'Is that what it will take?'

The short answer pulled her back into the present. 'What do you mean?'

He stood up, grabbing her arms and pulling her towards him, his face inches from hers. She didn't even have the opportunity to move as he put a hand on either hip and held her firmly in place.

'Is that what it will take? Hiring someone else to be my nurse, to get you to come back? Because I'll do it. I'll do anything you want. I would much rather that *you* were my nurse.' He tilted his head to the side. 'You have a certain way with you.'

She couldn't focus. 'Why, why would you want me to come back?'

He shifted his hand from her hip and pressed it on her chest. 'Because I can't think without you. I can't sleep without you. I can't breathe without you. And none of it is to do with a medical condition. I need you, Samantha. There is no me without you.'

'You can't mean that.'

'I can. I know how I feel. I want that moment back, Sam. That moment in the hangar when it was just you and me. You were looking up at me on the stage as if I were the only man in the world. I want that. I want that for a lifetime.' He moved his hand to his chest. 'I know how I feel in here. Tell me you don't feel that way too. Tell me right now, and I'll let you get on that plane back to England. I'll pay your fees and never see you again.' His voice was getting desperate as his emotions were overcoming him.

She felt her legs start to tremble again. The one thing

she didn't want. The one thing she could never want. Never to see Mitchell Brody again. Never hear his voice, never feel the touch of his skin next to hers. It was almost unbearable.

A tear rolled down her cheek. 'I don't know, Mitch. I just don't know.' She was shaking her head again. 'I'm so angry at you for not trusting me. I don't know how to get past that.'

He nodded. 'I know. It's like my brain doesn't function properly when I'm having a hypo. It feels as if all bets are off. My mouth says all the things that ever flit through my brain—even just for a second. You know, the thousands of things that you would never actually say out loud. I can't control it, Sam. I really can't.' He reached up and stroked her hair. 'Just know that it's not how I really feel. It's not what I really think. I love you, Sam. I don't want you to go anywhere. In fact, whatever you want, just name it. I'll do anything for you, Sam Lewis.'

She bit her lip. She had experienced this before. She had seen the quietest kids in the world have a hypoglycaemic attack and become completely unrecognisable—say and do things she would never have expected. Mitch wasn't so unusual. He'd been desperate. He was trying to save the place that had helped give him his brother back.

He reached into his pocket. 'If you'd waited another five minutes, my head would have been back in place and I could have told you all this then. I also could have given you this.' He held out the little blue box.

'What is it?' Her hands were trembling as she pulled at the little ribbon on top of the box. She lifted the lid. There, sitting on the pale blue velvet, was a thick silver bracelet and beautiful silver charm in the shape of a pair of skates. Along the blades glittered clear white stones—she could only guess they were diamonds.

It was the charm she'd spotted in the window of the shop in Innsbruck. Only the charm had been customised. Another few bright blue stones glittered next to the catch on the bracelet. It was truly beautiful.

She was struck by how thoughtful the gift was. Mitchell Brody was wealthy enough to buy the biggest diamond necklace or ring in the world. But it would be meaningless to her.

This wasn't. This was something that they'd shared together. Something he'd valued enough to make special for her.

He pointed to the blue stones. 'They match your eyes. Just the perfect colour.'

She smiled. 'It's beautiful, Mitch. I love it. Thank you.'

He looked scared to smile in return. 'What does that mean? What does that mean for us? Will you stay?'

She shook her head and spoke quietly. 'I'm not going to stay, Mitch.' She wound her hands around his neck. 'I'm going to go home to see my mum.'

His face fell. She'd never seen him look so wounded, so dejected. So she pressed her lips close to his ear. 'But I'm kind of hoping you'll come with me. I'm hoping you'll decide to spend the few days between now and your tour coming home with me to meet my mum.' She laughed. 'I can't possibly consider dating someone my mum hasn't met yet.' She got serious again. 'I want that moment back too, Mitch. You and me. For a lifetime. I want to hear you sing like that to me every night for the rest of my life.'

She could feel the tension dissipate throughout his body, the relief flood through his veins. He turned his face to press his lips next to hers. 'I think I can do that.' He slid his hands down her sides. 'And dating? Is that what we're going to be doing? Because I'm versatile with my singing,' he whispered in her ear. 'I can even do it naked.'

She raised herself up on tiptoe. 'Well, we've got to start somewhere,' she said with a twinkle in her eye, 'but let me keep that naked singing as a definite possibility.' And she kissed him, over and over again.

EPILOGUE

PRESS RELEASE:

After disappearing for a few months after his spectacular worldwide tour Mitchell Brody seems to have been making good use of his time.

He's just announced that he's married twenty-nine-year-old Samantha Lewis, who was originally acting as his nurse after his surprise diagnosis with diabetes last year. Mitchell, who is now an ambassador for diabetes worldwide, also announced the arrival of his son, Jude Shaun Brody, who was born last night weighing seven pounds three ounces.

He and his family ask for some privacy at this time to enjoy married life and their new arrival.

* * * * *

MILLS & BOON®

Want to get more from Mills & Boon?

Here's what's available to you if you join the
exclusive **Mills & Boon eBook Club** today:

✦ *Convenience – choose your books each month*
✦ *Exclusive – receive your books a month before
  anywhere else*
✦ *Flexibility – change your subscription at any time*
✦ *Variety – gain access to eBook-only series*
✦ *Value – subscriptions from just £1.99 a month*

So visit **www.millsandboon.co.uk/esubs** today
to be a part of this exclusive eBook Club!